pc

Lucky's Lady

LOVESWEPT®

DOUBLEDAY

New York   London   Toronto   Sydney   Auckland

Lucky's Lady

Tami Hoag

LOVESWEPT®
PUBLISHED BY DOUBLEDAY
a division of Bantam Doubleday Dell Publishing Group, Inc.
666 Fifth Avenue, New York, New York 10103

DOUBLEDAY and the portrayal of an anchor with a dolphin
and the word LOVESWEPT and the portrayal of the wave device
are trademarks of Doubleday, a division of
Bantam Doubleday Dell Publishing Group, Inc.
All of the characters in this book are fictitious,
and any resemblance to actual persons, living or
dead, is purely coincidental.

Library of Congress Cataloging-in-Publication Data
Hoag, Tami.
Lucky's lady / Tami Hoag. — 1st ed.
p.   cm.
"Loveswept."
I. Title.
PS3558.0333L83   1992
813'.54—dc20   91-22865
                                    CIP

ISBN 0-385-42289-X
Copyright © 1992 by Tami Hoag
All Rights Reserved
Printed in the United States of America
February 1992

1   3   5   7   9   10   8   6   4   2

First Edition

"Le coeur a ses raisons que la raison ne connaît point."
The heart has its reasons that reason knows nothing of.

— FRENCH PROVERB

Lucky's Lady

Chapter One

"You want to do what, *chère?*"

Serena Sheridan took a deep breath and tried again. "I need to hire a guide to take me into the swamp."

Old Lawrence Gauthier laughed as if at the punch line of some grand joke. His voice rang out through the shop, drowning out the Cajun music coming from the radio on the cluttered shelf behind him as well as the noises of the all-star professional wrestling emanating from the black and white television that sat on the counter. Lawrence sat on a stool behind the counter, his slender legs crossed at the knees, slouching in a posture reminiscent of an egret on a perch—thin shoulders hunched, head low between them. His face was narrow with a prominent nose and eyes like jet beads. His skin was tanned dark and lined like old leather.

His laughter ended in a fit of coughing. He reached for his cigarette makings and shook his head. "What for you wanna do dat, *chère?* You goin' after dem crawfish, you?" He laughed again, trying to shake his head and lick the edge of his cigarette paper at the same time.

Serena smoothed her hands down the front of the immaculate oyster-colored linen blazer she wore over a matching pencil-slim skirt. She supposed she hardly looked dressed to walk into such a place, much less make the request she had. "No, I'm not interested in fishing."

She looked around the store, hoping to spot someone else who might be able to help her. It was the middle of the day and Lawrence appeared to be the only person tending the dingy, dimly lit sporting goods store, though some banging noises were coming from behind him, from a room Serena knew to be an even dingier workshop where men fussed with their boats, drank beer, swapped outrageous tales, and passed girlie magazines around.

She knew because she had once snuck in there as a girl. A headstrong child, she had taken exception to being denied the chance to go in with her grandfather and had stowed away inside his bass boat under a canvas tarp. Her vocabulary had gained a number of choice words that day that their housekeeper had later attempted to wash out of her mouth with soap.

"I need to find my grandfather, Mr. Gauthier," she said. "Apparently he's gone out to his fish camp. I need someone to take me to him."

Lawrence looked at her, narrowing his eyes. Finally he shook a gnarled finger at her. "Hey, you dat Sheridan girl what left to be a doctor, no?"

"Yes."

"Yeah, yeah! *Mais yeah!*" He chuckled, tickled with his powers of recollection. "You lookin' for Big Giff."

"Yes, but I need someone to take me. I need a guide."

He shook his head, still smiling at her as if she were a dear but infinitely dimwitted child. "*Non, chérie,* all what fishin' guides we got 'round here is gone busy now till Monday. Lotta sports coming down to fish these days. 'Sides, ain't nobody crazy 'nough go out to Giff's. Go out there, get their head shot off, them!"

He sucked on his little cigarette, holding it between thumb and forefinger in an unconsciously European fashion. Half of it was gone before he exhaled. He reached out with his free hand and patted Serena's cheek. "Ah, *ma jolie fille,* ain't nobody crazy 'nough to go out to Big Giff's."

As he said it, a loud bang sounded in the shop behind him, followed by a virulent French oath. Lawrence went still with his hand halfway to a tin ashtray on the counter, an unholy light coming into his eyes, a little smile tugging at a corner of his mouth. "Well, mebbe there's somebody. Jes' how bad you wanna go, *chère?*"

Serena swallowed the knot of apprehension in her throat, clasping her hands together in front of her like a schoolgirl. Now was not the time for a faint heart. "It's imperative. I have to go."

He bent his head a little to one side and gave a Gallic shrug, then shouted over his shoulder. "Étienne! *Viens ici!*"

What Serena had braced herself for she wasn't sure, but it certainly wasn't the man who filled the doorway. The impact of his sudden presence had the same effect as being hit with the shock wave of an explosion, jolting her chest with a hollow thud and literally making her knees go weak—a phenomenon she had heretofore not believed in.

Her first impression was of raw power. Broad shoulders, bulging biceps. His chest, bare and gleaming with a sheen of sweat, was massive, wide, and thick, slabs of hard muscle beneath taut, tanned skin. The strong V of his torso narrowed to a slender waist, a stomach corrugated with muscle and dusted with black hair that disappeared beneath the low-riding waistband of faded green fatigue pants. Serena was certain she could live to be a hundred and never find a more prime example of the male animal.

She raised her eyes to his face and felt a strange shiver pass over her from head to toe, making her scalp tighten and her fingers tingle. He stared at her from under sleepy lids with large, unblinking amber eyes, eyes like a panther's. His brow was heavy and straight, his nose bold and slightly aquiline. His mouth did the most damage to her nervous system, however. It was wide, with lips so masterfully carved, so incredibly sensuous they would have looked perfect on a high-priced call girl. The effect of that mouth on a face so masculine—all lean planes and hard angles and five-o'clock shadow—was blatantly sexual.

He regarded her with a subtle disdain that suggested he didn't much care for women other than to bed them—something he appeared to be capable of doing on a more than regular basis. Pulling a cigarette from behind his ear, he planted it in the corner of his mouth, lit it, and said something to Lawrence Gauthier in rapid Cajun French, a patois no Parisian could begin to understand. The dialect had nearly been eradicated by the Louisiana school system decades before. And although it was making a comeback of sorts due to the latest craze for all things Cajun, it was still not widely spoken. This man spoke it as if it were his primary language.

Having grown up in Louisiana's French Triangle, Serena had

picked up the odd word and phrase, but he spoke too quickly for her to understand anything more than the implication. That was clear enough by Gauthier's reaction—another laughing and coughing fit and a slap on the shoulder for his barbarian friend.

Serena felt her cheeks heat with embarrassment as the man sauntered to the end of the counter and leaned a hip against it, all the while assessing her blatantly with those lazy amber eyes. She could feel his gaze like a tangible caress, drifting insolently over her breasts, the curve of her waist, the flare of her hip, the long length of her legs. She had never imagined it possible to feel so naked while dressed in a business suit.

He took a leisurely drag on his cigarette, exhaled, and delivered another line to keep Gauthier in stitches. Serena gave him her coolest glare, defending herself with hauteur. "Excuse me, but I was raised to believe it is extremely rude to carry on conversations not all those around you can understand."

One black brow sketched upward sardonically and the corner of that remarkable mouth curled ever so slightly. He looked like her idea of the devil on steroids. When he spoke to her his tone was a low, throaty purr that stroked her senses like velvet. "I told him you don' look like you're sellin' it or givin' it away," he said, the words rolling out of his mouth with an accent as rich as Cajun gumbo. "So what could I possibly want with you? I have no interest in *américaine ladies.*"

He drawled the last word with stinging contempt. Serena tugged at the lapels of her blazer, straightening the uniform of her station. Her chin went up another notch above the prim collar of her fuchsia silk blouse. "I can assure you I have no *interest* in you either."

He pushed himself away from the counter and moved toward her with the arrogant grace of a born athlete. Serena stubbornly stood her ground as he stepped near enough for her to feel the heat of his big body. Her heart fluttered in her throat as he stared down at her and raised a hand to smooth it back over her hair.

"That's not what your eyes are tellin' me, *chère catin.*"

Serena dragged in a ragged breath and held it, feeling as if she were going to explode from sheer fury. She slapped his hand away and took a step back from him. "I didn't come here to be insulted or manhandled. I came here to hire a guide, Mister—"

"Doucet," he supplied. "Étienne Doucet. Folks call me Lucky."

Serena vaguely remembered a Lucky Doucet from high school. He'd been several classes ahead of her, an athlete, a loner with a reputation as a bad boy. The girls whose main interest in school had been guys had swooned at the mere mention of his name. Serena's interests had lain elsewhere.

She looked at him now and thought whatever reputation he had sown back then he had certainly cultivated since. He looked like the incarnation of the word *trouble.* She had to be half mad to even consider hiring him. But then she thought of Gifford. She had to see him, had to do what she could to find out what had made him leave Chanson du Terre, had to do her best to try to convince him to come home. As tough as Gifford Sheridan liked to pretend he was, he was still a seventy-eight-year-old man with a heart condition.

"I'm Serena Sheridan," she said in her most businesslike tone.

Lucky Doucet blinked at her. A muscle tensed, then loosened in his jaw. "I know who you are," he said, an oddly defensive note in his voice. Serena dismissed it as unimportant.

"I came here to hire a guide, Mr. Doucet. Gifford Sheridan is my grandfather. I need someone to take me out to his cabin. Mr. Gauthier has informed me that all the more reputable guides are booked up for the weekend, which apparently leaves you. Are you interested in the job or not?"

Lucky moved back to lean negligently against the counter again. Behind him, Lawrence had switched off his wrestling program in favor of live entertainment. In the background Iry LeJeune sang "La Jolie Blonde" in crackling French over the radio. *The pretty blonde.* How apropos. He took a deep pull on his cigarette, sucking the smoke into the very corners of his lungs, as if it might purge the feelings shaking loose and stirring inside him.

When he had stepped from the back room and seen her he had felt as if he'd taken a vicious blow to the solar plexus. *Shelby.* The shock had dredged up memories and emotions like mud and dead vines churning up from the bayou in the wake of an outboard motor—pain, hate, fear all swirling furiously inside him. The pain and hate were old companions. The fear was for the control he felt slipping, sliding through his grasp like a wet rope. The feelings assaulted him still, even though he told himself this wasn't the woman from his past, but her sister, someone he had never had any contact with. Nor did he want to. They were twins, after all, maybe not perfectly identical, but cut from the same cloth.

He stared at the woman before him, trying to set all personal feelings aside to concentrate on only the physical aspects of her. It

5

shouldn't have been difficult to do; she was beautiful. From the immaculate state of her honey-colored hair in its smooth French twist to the tips of her beige pumps, she radiated class. There wasn't anything about her that shouldn't have been carved in alabaster and put in a museum. His gaze roamed over her face, an angel's face, with its delicate bone structure and liquid dark eyes—eyes that were presently flashing fire at him—and desire twisted inside him.

He swore, throwing his cigarette to the battered wood floor and grinding it out with the toe of his boot. Without looking, he reached behind the counter and pulled out a bottle of Jack Daniel's, helping himself to a generous swig. Lawrence said nothing, but frowned and glanced away, tilting his head in silent reproof. Resenting the twinge of guilt pinching him somewhere in the vicinity of where his conscience had once resided, Lucky put the bottle back.

Damn. He damned Gifford Sheridan for having granddaughters that looked like heaven on earth. He damned women in general and himself in particular. If he had a lick of sense he would send Miss Serena packing. He would go about his own business and let the Sheridans do what they would.

That was the kind of life he had chosen to live, solitary, and yet other lives kept drifting into his. He didn't want to be touched. He didn't need the trouble he knew was brewing on the Sheridan plantation, Chanson du Terre, didn't need the reminder of past pain. But Giff had dragged him into it to a certain extent already and there was too much riding on the situation for him to decline playing so slight a role in the drama.

He cursed himself for caring. He had thought himself beyond it, thought the capacity to care had been burned out of him by the acidic quality of his experiences. But it was still there, which meant he had to find the strength to deal with it. God help him.

Serena gave him one last scathing glare and turned on her slim, expensive heel, heading for the street entrance of the store. Lucky swore under his breath and went after her, catching her by the arm.

"Where you goin', sugar? I never said I wouldn't take you."

She looked pointedly at the big dirty hand circling her upper arm, then turned that defiant gaze up to his face. "Maybe I won't take you, Mr. Doucet."

"The way I see it, you don't have much of a choice. Ain't nobody else gonna take you out to Giff's." He laughed without humor. "Ain't nobody else crazy enough."

6

"But you are?"

He smiled like a crocodile and leaned down toward her until his mouth hovered only a few inches above the sweet temptation of her lips. "That's right," he whispered. "I'm over the edge. I might do anything. Ask anyone 'round this town here. They'll all tell you the same thing—*Il n'a pas rien il va pas faire.* There's nothing he won't do. That Lucky Doucet, he's one bad crazy son, him."

"Well, I'm a psychologist," she said with a saccharine-sweet smile. "So we ought to get along just peachy, shouldn't we?"

He let go of her arm as if she had just told him she had leprosy. The expression of smug male arrogance abruptly disappeared, and his face became blank and unreadable. He turned and strode for a side door that stood open and led directly onto a dock.

Serena stood a moment, trying to gather some strength, her gaze on Lucky Doucet's broad bare back as he walked away. Her limbs felt like jelly and her stomach was quivering inside. She could feel old Lawrence staring at her, but she didn't move. She'd never had such a . . . primal reaction to a man. She was a sophisticated, educated woman, a woman who prided herself on her ability to maintain control in every situation. But that foundation of control was trembling in the wake of Lucky Doucet, and she didn't like it. He was rude and arrogant and . . . The other words that came to mind were far too flattering. What difference did it make what he looked like? He was a Neanderthal.

He was also her only hope of reaching Giff. And she had to reach him. Someone had to find out what was going on. Shelby claimed she hadn't a clue as to why Gifford had suddenly deserted the plantation in favor of living out in the swamp. It might have been nothing more than a matter of Giff getting fed up with having Shelby and her family underfoot while their new house was under construction, but it might have been something more. It wasn't like him to leave during a busy time of year, simply turning the reins of the sugarcane plantation over to his manager.

Shelby had peevishly suggested Gifford was getting senile. Serena couldn't imagine her grandfather as anything other than sharp as a tack, but then, she hadn't actually seen him in a while. Her practice in Charleston kept her too busy for many visits home. She had been looking forward to this one, looking forward to simply enjoying her ancestral home in all its springtime glory. Then Shelby had greeted her at the door with news of Gifford's defection to the swamp.

He'd been out there two weeks. Two weeks with no word, and Shelby had done nothing about it except complain.

"What did you expect me to do?" she had asked. "Go out there after him? I have two children to raise and a real estate business to manage and a husband, and I'm the chairperson of the Junior League drive for canned goods for the starving peasants of Guatemala. I have responsibilities, Serena! I can't just jump in a boat and go out there! Not that he would ever listen to a word I have to say anyway. And you can't expect Mason to go out there. You know how beastly Gifford is to him. I'm just at my wit's end trying to deal with him. You're the psychologist. You go out there and talk some sense into that hard head of his."

Go out there. Into the swamp. Serena's blood had run cold at the suggestion. It ran cold now at the thought. But she was just angry enough and stubborn enough to get past her fear for the moment. She had stormed from the house to go in search of a guide without even bothering to change her clothes. She wouldn't allow herself to dwell on her fear. She had to see her grandfather and there was only one way to do that. She had to go out into the one place she thought of as hell on earth, and the only man available to take her had just walked away.

Serena rushed after Lucky Doucet, struggling to hurry in her narrow skirt and shoes that had not been intended for walking on rough planking. The midday sun was blinding as she stepped out onto the dock. The stench of dirty water and gasoline hung in the thick, still air. Lucky stood at the open door to the workshop.

"We haven't discussed your fee," Serena said, ignoring the possibility that he had changed his mind about taking her. She struggled for an even breath as she faced his chest. Even up close he looked as if he were cast in bronze rather than flesh and bone.

He looked down his nose at her with an expression that suggested she had just insulted his mother. "I have no need of your money," he said contemptuously.

Serena rolled her eyes and lifted her hands in a gesture of exasperated surrender. "Pardon me for thinking you might like an honest wage for an honest job. How bourgeois of me."

He ignored her, bending to pick up a heavy cardboard box full of oily black motor parts. He lifted it as though it weighed no more than a kitten and set it on a workbench to sort through it. His attitude was one of dismissal and irritating in the extreme.

"Why are you making this so difficult?" Serena asked.

He turned his head and gave her a nasty, sardonic smile. "Because I'm a difficult kind of guy. I thought you might have figured that out by now. You're an intelligent woman."

"Frankly, I'm amazed you would credit a woman with having a brain. You strike me as the sort of man who sees women as being useful for only one purpose."

"I said you were intelligent, not useful. I won't know how useful you are until I have you naked beneath me."

Heat flared through Serena like a flash fire. She attributed it to anger. Certainly it had nothing to do with the sudden image of lying tangled in the sheets with this barbarian. She crossed her arms in front of her defensively and made a show of looking all around them before returning her belligerent gaze to Lucky. "Pardon me, I was just checking to see if I had somehow been transported back into the Stone Age. Are you proposing to hit me over the head with a dinosaur bone and drag me back to your cave, Conan?"

He raised a warning finger, his brows drawing together ominously over glittering eyes. "You got a mouth on you, *chère.*"

He shuffled toward her, backing her up against the door frame. Serena managed to swallow her first gasp, but couldn't help the second one as his spread thighs brushed the outsides of hers. He braced his forearms on the wood above her head and leaned down close. His breath was warm against her cheek and scented with the smoky taint of tobacco and whiskey.

"I have *never* forced a woman," Lucky said, his voice low and soft, the molten gold of his eyes burning into Serena's. "I never have to."

He stared at her mouth with rapt fascination. It was rosy and soft-looking and he wanted badly to taste it, but he denied himself the luxury. She was a spoiled society bitch and he wanted nothing to do with her. He'd been burned badly enough to know better. *Dieu,* he'd learned his first lesson at the hands of her twin! To get that close again was to give in entirely to the demons of insanity.

Still, desire ribboned through him, as warm as a fever in his blood. The subtle, expensive scent of her perfume lured him closer. He dropped his head down near the curve of her shoulder and battled the urge to nuzzle the tender spot just below her ear and above the prim stand-up collar of her dark pink blouse. He could feel his sex growing warm and heavy.

"I'm hiring you as a guide," she said through her teeth, her voice trembling with rage or desire or both. "Not for stud service."

Lucky mentally thanked her for breaking the spell. He stepped back, cocking one hip and hooking a thumb in the waistband of his pants. He gave her a devilish grin. "Why not, angel? I'd give you the ride of your life."

She glared at him in utter disgust and walked away to stand at the edge of the dock, her slender back rigid. He had no doubt irreparably offended her ladylike sensibilities, he thought. Fine. That was exactly what he wanted. The more emotional distance he put between himself and a woman like Serena Sheridan, the better. His mother would have peeled the hide off him for talking that way to a woman, but this was more than just a matter of manners, it was a matter of survival.

He scooped up the box of motor parts and started down the pier with it, calling over his shoulder as he went. "So, you comin', *chère,* or what? I don't have all day."

Serena turned and stared in disbelief as he headed down the worn dock. She noticed for the first time that his hair was nearly as long as hers, tied in a short queue at the back of his thick neck with a length of leather boot lace. A pirate. That was what he reminded her of—in looks *and* attitude.

"You're leaving *now?*" she said, once again rushing to catch up with him.

He didn't answer her. It was perfectly obvious he meant to leave. Serena cursed Lucky Doucet and spike heels in the same breath as she picked up her pace. Talk about your grade-A bastards, this guy took the prize. And she wanted to be the one to personally pin the medal on him, preferably directly onto that bare boilerplate chest of his. If they were in Charleston, never in a million years would she have put up with being treated the way he was treating her. She had too much sense and self-respect to fall for that tame-the-rogue-male syndrome, no matter how overwhelmingly sexy the rogue happened to be. But they weren't in Charleston. They were in South Louisiana, at the edge of the Atchafalaya Swamp, some of the wildest, most remote swampland in the United States. And Lucky Doucet wasn't some button-down executive or construction worker she could bring to heel with a cool look. He was a breed unto himself and only marginally more civilized than the bayou country around them.

Abruptly, the heel of one of her pumps caught between planks in the dock and gave way, nearly pitching Serena headfirst off the pier and into the oily water. She swore aloud as she stumbled awkwardly, hampered by the narrow skirt around her knees, just managing to catch her balance before it was too late.

Lucky stopped and turned toward her with a look of mock affront. "Why, Miz Serena, such language! What will the ladies at the Junior League think?"

She narrowed her eyes and snarled at him as she hopped on her ruined shoe and pulled the other one off. The instant she put her foot down, she ran a sliver into it, but she refused to cry out or even acknowledge the pain. She limped up to Lucky, struggling to maintain some semblance of dignity.

"I'm not prepared to leave just now, Mr. Doucet," she said primly. "I was thinking more along the lines of tomorrow morning."

He shrugged without the least show of concern. A brilliant white grin split his features. "Well, that's too bad, sugar, 'cause if you're leavin' with me, you're leavin' now."

Chapter Two

It was a no-win situation. If she stood her ground, she lost her ride. If she gave in, it was another blow to her pride and another peg up for Mr. Macho's overinflated ego. Serena took a slow, deep breath of air that was as dense as steam and tasted metallic and bitter. Maintaining as much of her dignity as she could, she lifted her slim nose and gave Lucky a long, cool look.

His eyes flashed as gold as doubloons behind ridiculously long paintbrush lashes. One corner of his lush mouth curled like the end of a cat's tail. "What'sa matter, *chère?* You'd rather give orders than take them? Well, I'm not your hired boy. You want a ride, then you climb in the boat. You wanna boss somebody around, you can take a hike."

Serena was certain she could actually feel her temper start to boil the blood in her veins. She clenched her jaw and fought a valiant battle to keep the lid on when all she wanted to do was tell Lucky Doucet to take a long walk off a short pier. Despite her name, her apparent serenity was little more than a shield, a defense mechanism, protective camouflage. All her life she'd had to struggle with strong doses of Sheridan temper and stubbornness. Now she wrestled one into submission with the other. The man was doing his best to make her angry, so she stubbornly refused to lose her temper.

"You are a remarkably obnoxious man, Mr. Doucet," she observed in the calmest of voices, as if she were commenting on nothing more interesting than the weather.

"I always try to excel."

"How admirable."

"So are you comin'?" He set his box down on the dock and sat beside it, dangling his long legs off the pier.

"I'll need to stop by Chanson du Terre for a few things. You wouldn't have any objection to that, would you?"

He gave her a flat look.

Serena motioned impatiently to the suit she was wearing. "You don't really expect me to travel out into the swamp dressed this way, do you?"

He scowled and grumbled as he lowered himself into his boat. *"Non.* Come on, then. I been here too long already. Just look at the trouble I got myself into, havin' to haul you around."

Serena moved to the edge of the dock and looked down. It was then that the full folly of what she was about to do hit her. Lucky's boat was no more than twelve feet in length, slender as a pea pod, and it looked about as stable as a floating leaf. Sitting in it would put her no more than an arm's length from the black water of the bayou.

Fear rose up in her throat and wedged there like tennis ball. What was the matter with her? Had she completely lost her mind? She was about to put her life in the hands of a man she wouldn't sit next to on a bus and trust him to take her into the deep swamp in a boat that looked about as seaworthy as her broken shoe.

The swamp. Where anything could happen. Where people could get lost and never be found.

A chill raced over her flesh, settling into her arms and legs in trembling pools. She clenched her jaw and held her breath, forgetting every relaxation technique she taught her own patients. It had been too long since she'd been assaulted by this fear. The strength of it took her by surprise. It swelled and shook her, crowding at the back of her throat like a scream demanding release.

Lucky stood in the pirogue, watching her, annoyed by her daw-dling. Then the color drained out of her face and his annoyance was replaced by something he refused to name. Serena Sheridan had come across as a lady who could handle herself in most situations. She had stood up to him better than most men did. Now she looked like a piece of porcelain about to crack from some fierce internal pressure. Something deep inside him responded to that, commiserated with it.

He ground his teeth, resenting the feeling and giving in to it at the same time. As hardened as he liked to think he was, he couldn't just stand there and watch her fall apart. He told himself it was because he didn't want to have to deal with a woman in hysterics. Besides, he had already decided the safest thing for him was to keep her half mad at him all the time. A man stayed wary of a snake poised to strike; it was the ones that appeared to be docile and dozing in the sun that were dangerous.

"You don' like my boat, *chère?*" he drawled, an unmistakable note of challenge in his voice.

"A—um—" Serena pulled herself out of her trance with difficulty, trying to focus not on her memory but on the boat and the man standing in it leaning indolently against a long push-pole. "It's not exactly what I had in mind. Don't you have something a little . . . bigger?"

"Like a yacht?" he asked sarcastically. "This ain't Saks Fifth Avenue, sugar. I don't have a selection for you to try on for size. Now, are you gonna get on down here or do I get to spend the rest of the day lookin' up your skirt?"

A welcome surge of reckless anger warmed the chill that had shaken Serena from within. She narrowed her eyes as she pressed her knees together demurely and pulled her slim skirt tightly around them. Clutching her purse and shoe in one hand, she lowered herself awkwardly to the rough planks of the dock, dropping her legs over the edge and grimacing as she felt her pantyhose run all the way down the back of one leg.

She looked down at the pirogue bobbing gently on the oily water and a second wave of apprehension rose up to her tonsils. She hadn't gone out on the bayou in a boat of any kind in fifteen years. She doubted she would have felt safe on the *Queen Elizabeth II*, let alone this simple shell of cypress planking. Still, why couldn't he at least have had a nice big bass boat with a motor on it? Nobody used pirogues anymore . . . except Lucky Doucet.

"My pirogue is all the boat I need," Lucky said as he reached up for her. "What'd you think—that I'd go around in a cabin cruiser on the off chance I might have to give some belle a ride somewhere she hadn't oughta be going in the first place?"

14

Serena flashed him a glare. "No. I was just hoping against hope that you weren't as uncivilized as you appear to be."

He laughed as his big hands closed around her slender waist. Serena's eyes went wide with surprise as his thumbs slid upward and brushed the undersides of her breasts, sending sparks shooting through her. She gave a little squeal of protest as he lifted her down into the boat. The pirogue rocked beneath his spread feet and she sacrificed pride for panic, dropping her shoe and purse and grabbing on to Lucky's biceps for support.

For an instant she clung to him as if he were the only thing keeping her from falling into the gaping jaws of hell, and in that instant the hard masculine contours of his body branded hers. Every line and plane of muscle etched itself into her memory, never to be forgotten. Her breasts pressed against his upper rib cage, her belly arched into his groin as his big hands splayed across the small of her back, holding her close. His thighs were as solid as oak trees against hers. A shiver of primitive awareness shimmied down her back she looked up at him.

He flashed her a smile that would have given the devil goose bumps. "Oh, I'm every bit as uncivilized as I look." His voice dropped to that throaty purr that set all her nerve endings humming like tuning forks. "You gonna try to do somethin' 'bout that, *chère?* You gonna try to domesticate me?"

The suggestion elicited an involuntary trill of excitement inside her. It was like a starburst of sensation deep in her belly, and Serena cursed it for the foolishness she knew it was. Any woman who took on the task of domesticating Lucky Doucet was just asking for trouble. Still, she couldn't seem to quell the feeling as she looked up at him, at his hard, beard-shadowed jaw and that decadent mouth. She steeled herself against it, pushing herself back from him. He let her put an inch of space between them, but only after letting her know he could have held her there all day if he'd been of a mind to.

"Domesticate you?" Serena said derisively, arching a delicate brow. "Couldn't I just have you neutered?"

"No need." He gave her a little push that landed her on the plank seat of the pirogue with an unceremonious thump, and turned to get his box of motor parts. "I wouldn't touch you with a ten-foot pole, *lady.*"

"That's the first good news I've had today," Serena grumbled, ignoring the twinge of disappointment that nipped her feminine ego.

15

Ignoring, too, the obvious comparison to be made between Lucky Doucet and a ten-foot pole.

She fanned herself with her hand, feeling suddenly flushed, and watched as Lucky lifted his box off the dock, back muscles bunching and sliding beneath his taut, dark skin. He settled the box in the bow of the boat, then moved gracefully toward the stern, stepping over the jig and over the seat, carelessly rocking the tippy pirogue.

Serena's fingers wrapped around the edge of the seat like C clamps, and her gaze drifted longingly down the pier to a shiny aluminum boat. It seemed huge and luxurious compared to the homemade pirogue. A fat man wearing a black New Orleans Saints cap and a plaid shirt with the sleeves cut off sat at the back of it, jerking the rope on the outboard motor.

"You might think about joining the twentieth century sometime soon," Serena said, shooting Lucky a sweet smile. "People use motors nowadays."

Lucky stared at the gas and oil bleeding into the water from the outboard as the fat man yanked on the rope. He frowned, brows pulling low over his eyes as he took up his push-pole. "Not me."

He poled the pirogue away from the dock and let the nose turn south.

Serena jerked around, looking up at him over her shoulder with alarm. "This isn't the way to Chanson du Terre or Gifford's fish camp. Just where do you think you're taking me, Mr. Doucet?"

Lucky scowled at her, but lifted his gaze quickly to avoid the sight of her breasts straining against the fine silk of her blouse. "I got other things to do besides haul your pretty face up and down the bayou."

It was apparently all the answer he was going to give her. He had set his face in an expression that declared the subject closed, and Serena decided not to push her luck. After all, he wasn't running a taxi service. She had no claim on his time. Considering his attitude, it was a wonder he had agreed to take her at all.

She faced forward and tried to concentrate on the scenery instead of the sinuous feel of the boat sliding through the dark water. They were at the south edge of town, and the only buildings along the banks of the bayou were the occasional bait shop and a couple of dilapidated tar-paper shacks on stilts with boathouses made of rusting corrugated metal.

A spindly-legged blue heron stood among the cattails near the bank, watching them pass. Serena focused on it as if it were the subject of a painting, its graceful form set against a backdrop of orange-blossomed trumpet creeper and clusters of dark green ferns. Rising in the background, hackberry trees reached their arms up to a china-blue sky and live oak dripped their tattered banners of dusty gray Spanish moss.

Their destination eventually became clear as Lucky poled toward the bank and a wharf hung with barnacle-encrusted tires to buffer its edge. The structure that rose up on stilts some distance behind it was as big as a barn, an unremarkable clapboard building with peeling white paint and a sign hanging above the gallery that spelled out MOSQUITO MOUTON'S in two-foot-high red letters. Rusted tin signs advertising various brands of beer were nailed all along the side of the building above a long row of screened windows. Even though it was only the middle of the day, cars were parked on the crushed-shell lot and Zydeco music drifted out through the double screen doors in swells of sound accented by occasional shouts and laughter.

"A *bar?*" Serena questioned imperiously. She looked up at Lucky, incredulous, as he brought the boat alongside the dock. "This is where you had stop to delay us? A *bar?*"

"I've got some business here," he said. "It won't take long. You wait in the boat."

"Wait in the—?" She broke off, watching in disbelief as he hauled himself onto the dock and headed for the bar without looking back. "Swell."

God only knew what his business was or how long it would take. In the meantime she could sit and rot in his stupid boat. The sun beat down on her, its heat magnified by the humidity. She could feel her linen suit wilting over her frame like an abused orchid. Not that it was going to be salvageable after today anyway, she thought, grimacing at the greasy handprint on the sleeve of her jacket.

She cursed her temper for getting her into this. If she hadn't let Shelby goad her into rushing right out to find a guide . . . If she hadn't let old feelings of inadequacy push her . . . If she had taken the time to think the situation through in a calm and rational manner, as she would have back in Charleston . . .

This was what coming home could do to a person. She had an established persona back in Charleston, an image she had fashioned for herself among acquaintances she had chosen. But this was home, and the minute she came back here, she became Gifford Sheridan's granddaughter, Shelby Sheridan's twin, the former captain of the high school debate team; old feelings and old patterns of behavior resurrected themselves like ghosts, peeling away the veneer of adulthood like a pecan husk.

It was part of the reason she stayed away. She liked who she was in Charleston—a professional woman in control of her life. Here she never felt in control. The very atmosphere wrested control away from her and left her feeling unsettled and uncertain.

This place, Mosquito Mouton's, was a perfect example. It was the most notorious place in the parish. She had been raised to believe it was frequented by hooligans and white trash, and no decent girl would come within shouting distance of it. Sitting in Lucky Doucet's pirogue, she had to quell the urge to look around for anyone who might recognize her. She felt as if she were a teenager cutting class for the first time.

Crossing her arms in front of her, she heaved a sigh, closed her eyes, and thought of her cool, pretty apartment back in Charleston. It was done in soft colors and feminine patterns and had a view of the water. There was a garden in the courtyard, and it was a long, long way from the swamp and Lucky Doucet.

The instant the screen door banged shut behind him, heads turned in Lucky's direction.

The place was about half full and would be bursting at the seams by sundown. Mouton's was the hub of trouble. There was gambling in the back and girls who might do anything for a few bucks or just for the hell of it. From here a man could find his way to a dogfight or a fistfight or a whorehouse or any number of dens of iniquity that were no longer supposed to exist in the civilized South.

It was the hangout of poachers and men whose backgrounds were filled with more shadows than the swamp. And even among them, Lucky Doucet stood out as a remarkably dangerous sort of man. The men sized him up warily, the women covetously, but no one approached him.

The bartender, a portly man with a dense, close-cropped salt-and-pepper beard, groaned and rolled his eyes like a man in pain. He brought up the rag he was wiping the bar with and patted it against his double chins like an old matron trying to ward off a fainting spell.

"Jesus, Lucky, I don' want no trouble in here," he wailed, waddling toward Lucky's end of the bar. His little sausage fingers knotted together around the towel in a gesture of supplication. "I just barely got the place patched up from the las' time."

Lucky shrugged expansively, blinking innocence. "Trouble? Me cause you trouble, Skeeter? Hell, I just came in for a drink. Give me a shot and a Jax long-neck."

Muttering prayers, Skeeter moved to do his bidding, sweat beading on his bald spot like water on a bowling ball.

Lucky's gaze homed in on Pou Perret, a little muskrat with a pockmarked face and a thin, droopy mustache. He was sitting at the far end of the bar, deep in conversation with a local cockfight referee. Picking up his beer bottle by the neck, Lucky sauntered down to the end of the bar and tapped the referee on the shoulder. "Hey, pal, I think I hear your mother callin'."

The man took one look at Lucky and vacated his seat, shooting Perret a nervous glance as he moved away into the smokier regions of the bar. Sipping his beer, Lucky eased himself onto the stool and hooked the heels of his boots over the chrome rung.

"How's tricks, Pou? Where's Willis? In the back cheatin' at *bourré?* You out here keepin' watch or somethin', little weasel?"

Perret scowled at him and shrunk away to the far side of his stool like a dog afraid of getting kicked. He muttered an obscene suggestion half under his breath.

"That's anatomically impossible, *mon ami,*" Lucky said, taking another sip of his beer. "See the things you might have learned if you'd stayed in school past the sixth grade? All this time you've probably been wearin' yourself out trying to do that very thing you suggested to me." He chuckled at Perret's comically offended expression as he helped himself to a pack of cigarettes lying on the bar. He lit one up and took a leisurely drag. Exhaling a stream of smoke, he shrugged and grinned shrewdly. " 'Course, mebbe Willis, he helps you out with that, eh?"

Perret narrowed his droopy eyes to slits. "You bastard."

Lucky's expression went dangerously still. His smile didn't waver, but it took on a quality that would have made even fools reconsider the wisdom of getting this close to him. "You say that in front of my *maman,* I'll cut your tongue out, *cher,*" he said in a silky voice. "My folks are respectable people, you know."

"Yeah," Perret admitted grudgingly, bobbing his head down between his bony shoulders like a vulture. He scratched his chest through his dirty black T-shirt, sniffed, and took another stab at belligerence. "How'd they ever end up with the like of you?"

Lucky's eyes gleamed in the dim light as he looked straight into

Perret's ferret face. "I'm a changeling, don'tcha know. Straight up from hell."

Perret shifted uneasily on his seat, superstition shining in his dark eyes like a fever. He lifted a hand to the dime he wore on a string around his neck. He snatched his cigarettes out of Lucky's reach and shook one out for himself, sliding a glance at Lucky out the corner of his eye. "What you want, Doucet?"

Lucky took his time answering. He stood and shoved the barstool out of his way so he could lean lazily against the bar. He set his cigarette in an ashtray and took another long swallow of his beer before turning to look at Perret again.

"You been sniffin' 'round the wrong part of the swamp this last couple of weeks, louse," he said quietly. "Me, I think it might be better for your health if you go raidin' elsewhere."

Perret made a face and shrugged off the warning. "It's a free country. You don' own the swamp, Doucet."

Lucky arched a brow. "No? Well, I own this knife, don't I?" he said, sliding the hunting knife from its sheath. He grabbed a fistful of Perret's T-shirt and leaned over until Perret nearly fell off his stool. The wide blade gleamed just inches from the man's nose. "And I can cut you up into 'gator bait with it, can't I?"

Conversations around them died abruptly. On the other side of the bar, Skeeter Mouton whimpered and crossed himself, sending up a prayer for the survival of his establishment. Clifton Chenier's accordion sang out from the speakers of the jukebox, sounding as raucous and out of place as a reggae band in church.

"Come on, Lucky, don' go cuttin' him up in here," Skeeter pleaded. "I won' never get all the blood out the floor!"

Perret turned gray and swallowed as if he were choking on a rock, his dark eyes darting from Lucky's face to the knife and back.

There was a commotion at the back of the room as a door burst open and a group of men emerged, their expressions ranging from avid interest to livid anger. At the front of the pack was Mean Gene Willis. Willis had been a roughneck down in the Gulf and a convict in the Angola penitentiary. He was a good-sized man with fists as big as country hams and a face like a side of beef. He made a beeline for Lucky with murder in his eyes.

Lucky let go of Perret, snatched up his untouched whiskey, and flung it into Willis's face. The big man howled and lunged blindly for Lucky, who met his advance with a boot to Willis's beer gut. Perret took advantage of the distraction to grab Lucky's beer bottle and break it on the edge of the bar. As he swung it in an arch for Lucky's head, a gun went off. Women screamed. Someone kicked out the plug on the jukebox. There was an instant of deafening silence, then a man's voice rang out.

"That's enough! Y'all stop it or I swear I'll shoot somebody and call it in the line of duty."

Perret dropped his broken bottle and slinked away like the rat he was. Willis lay groaning on the floor, holding his stomach.

Lucky stepped back casually and sheathed his knife, his gaze drifting over the uniformed agent who had hurried out of the back-room card game with Willis. He had gone to school with Perry Davis and had disliked him since kindergarten. Davis was a man of fair, baby-faced looks and an annoying air of self-importance that was only more grating in adulthood, considering the fact that he was lousy at his job.

Lucky picked up his cigarette from the ashtray on the bar and took a slow pull on it. "Is this the kind of thing they were referring to when they named it the Department of *Wildlife* and Fisheries, Agent Davis? You playing *bourré* in a roadhouse?"

Davis gave him a cold look. "What I'm doing here is none of your business, Doucet."

"No? A respectable employee of the government gamblin' on tax-payer's time? That's none of my business?"

"What do you care? I doubt you pay taxes and you sure as hell aren't respectable."

Lucky chuckled. "That's right, *cher,* I'm not. You'd do well to remember that."

"Are you threatening me, Doucet?"

"Who, me? I don't make threats." His gaze took on the cold, hard look of polished brass, and his voice dropped a notch. "I don't have to."

A muscle worked nervously in Davis's jaw. "I'm not afraid of you, Lucky."

Lucky smiled. "Well then, I guess it's not true what folks say about you, is it? You're every bit as dumb as you look."

Davis's pale complexion turned blotchy red, but he said nothing. He holstered his gun and turned away to shoo the bar's patrons back to whatever they had been doing before the ruckus.

Willis struggled to his feet. Doubled over with an arm across his belly, he glared at Lucky. "I'll get you, you coonass son of a bitch. You wait 'n' see."

Lucky dropped his cigarette and ground it out on the floor with his boot. "Yeah, I'll be losin' sleep over that, I will," he drawled sardonically. "Stay out of my swamp, Willis."

He turned toward the door to make his exit and his heart jolted hard in his chest. Serena Sheridan was standing right in front of him with her little calfskin purse clutched to her chest, her eyes wide and her pretty mouth hanging open in shock. In her prim suit and slicked-back hairdo, she looked like a schoolmarm who'd just gotten her first eyeful of a naked man.

Lucky swore under his breath. He didn't need any of this. He would have been just as happy never to have to tangle with the likes of Gene Willis and Pou Perret. He sure as hell had never asked to baby-sit Serena Sheridan. This all came back to the other lives that kept insisting on crossing paths with his, and it was damned annoying.

He took Serena by the arm and ushered her toward the door. "You've got a real knack for showing up in places you hadn't oughta be, don't you?"

Serena looked up at him but said nothing. She suddenly felt way out of her depth. Anyone with half a brain would have spotted Lucky Doucet for a tough customer, but she hadn't quite realized just how tough, just how dangerous he might be. Somehow, the fact that he knew her grandfather had diluted that sense of danger, but what she'd just witnessed had brought it all into sharp focus.

He was a poacher, a thief. He was a man who threatened people with knives and thumbed his nose at authority. He had practically laughed in the face of the game warden. God only knew what other laws he might break without compunction.

"Serena? Serena Sheridan?" Perry Davis stepped in front of them with a questioning look that clearly said he couldn't have been more surprised to see her there on the arm of a gargoyle. "Is this man bothering you?"

Serena's gaze darted from him to Lucky. This was her chance. This was the part in the movie where everyone yelled at the screen for the heroine to cut and run. But she couldn't seem to find her voice, and then the opportunity was lost.

"Take off, Davis," Lucky said on a growl. "The lady is with me."

Davis looked anything but convinced, but when Serena made no move to object, he shrugged and turned away.

"You know that guy?" Lucky asked, steering her toward the door again.

"He's a friend of the family."

Lucky sniffed. "You gotta choose a better class of friends, sugar."

Serena almost burst out laughing. She shook her head and marveled at the whole scene. What the hell was she doing here? Why wasn't she taking the opportunity to get away from him? She looked at him with something like amazement, trying to see some sign, some sterling quality shining through all the rough machismo.

"I thought I told you to wait in the boat," he grumbled irritably, dodging her gaze.

"I *was* waiting in the boat until a truckload of roughnecks pulled up. Then it became a matter of the lesser of evils. I decided the riffraff in here was probably safer than the riffraff out there."

"And now you're not so sure?"

He opened the door for her and she stepped out onto the gallery to a chorus of wolf whistles and crude come-on lines. Closing her eyes, she sighed a long-suffering sigh and rubbed her temples. This just wasn't her day.

The screen door banged behind her and the harassment ceased abruptly as Lucky walked up beside her and put an arm around her waist. It was a possessive gesture, a protective one, not anything sexually threatening. In fact, it was almost comforting. Serena looked up at him, surprised. He was scowling at the oil-rig workers assembled on the wide porch.

"Don' they teach you respect for ladies where you boys come from?" he asked in that silky-soft tone that raised the hair on the back of Serena's neck.

No one said anything. The men who worked the oil rigs were a rough breed. They wouldn't back down from a fight, but they didn't appear ready to pick one either. They were probably exhibiting better judgment than she was, Serena thought. Perhaps they had met Lucky and his friend Mr. Knife before. They were probably all sitting there wondering what she was doing with the most dangerous man in South Louisiana.

She lifted her chin a notch and drew together the tattered remains of her composure as Lucky guided her down the steps and across the parking lot.

"I'd like to go home now, if you don't mind," she said. "I can see you're a busy man, Mr. Doucet. I can make other arrangements to get to Gifford's tomorrow."

Lucky stopped and jammed his hands at the waistband of his pants. He looked out at the bayou, squinting into the afternoon sun, and exhaled a long breath through his teeth.

This was stupid. He wanted to be rid of her, didn't he? He wanted her to think the worst of him, didn't he? He should have been happy that she was ready to give up, but he wasn't. *Dieu,* what a masochist he was! Why should he care that a woman like Serena Sheridan looked at him with wary contempt? The feeling was reciprocated a hundred and ten percent. He couldn't look at her without feeling . . .

What?

Hot. But that was just an instinctive response. He was a highly sexed man; of course he wanted her. Any man with feeling below the waist would want her. She was beautiful in the cool, ethereal way of a goddess. Of course it drove him wild. Of course he wanted to pull the pins from her hair and run his fingers through the masses of honey-colored silk. Of course he wanted to bury himself between those long, sleek legs. Of course he wanted to stroke and kiss those high, proud breasts. But he knew too well that what lay under those pretty breasts of hers could be pure evil.

Anger. That was what he really felt, he told himself. Anger. Resentment. She was her sister's twin. She was Shelby with a doctorate in psychology—*Dieu,* what a nightmare!

She was also Giff Sheridan's granddaughter. And he had made Giff a promise. The reminder made him sigh again and mutter an oath in French.

"Look," he said quietly. "I don' know what all you saw or heard in there, but it's got nothin' to do with takin' you out to Giff's. I promise you'll get there in one piece. I'm not gonna feed you to the 'gators or sell you to white slavers or anything like that. Giff's a friend of mine."

Serena watched him closely, amazed. There was a flush on his high, hard cheekbones. He shuffled his boots on the crushed shell of the parking lot and refused to look at her. He actually looked contrite and embarrassed and . . . well, cute.

Lord, what was the matter with her, thinking he was cute? Puppies were cute. Boy scouts were cute. Lucky Doucet was a grown tiger. He probably had boy scouts for lunch and ate puppies for dessert and picked his teeth with prim blond psychologists who saw redeeming qualities where there were none. She shouldn't be thinking any kind thoughts about him. She should be afraid of him . . . but she wasn't.

She was obviously losing her grip on sanity. It was this place, this wild, primal place. The air was ripe with scents that invaded the brain. What common sense she had left told her not to trust this man any farther than she could throw a horse, but she couldn't bring herself to walk away from him.

"I'm amazed," she said at last.

"What?" He gave her a narrow look. "That I wouldn't sell you to white slavers?"

A corner of her mouth lifted in a wry smile as she started toward the dock. "That you have a friend."

Chapter Three

Chanson du Terre. If she lived to be a hundred, Serena knew she would never tire of seeing it. It gave her a feeling of security and tradition. Sheridans had lived there since winning it in a card game in 1789. She may not have chosen to live there herself, but it was her heritage.

The house stood at the end of an *allée* of moss-draped live oak, the broad crowns of which knitted together to form a high bower above the drive. The house was an old Creole chateau, a combination of French Provincial and West Indies in style, with a sloping roof and broad galleries surrounding it on both the upper and lower levels.

At first glance the house looked the same as it always had to Serena —graceful, welcoming, impressive without being ostentatious. Then she blinked away the golden glow of her memory and saw it exactly as it was, as if seeing it for the first time ever.

The roof was in a state of disrepair, due to heavy spring rains. Shingles were missing and a bright blue tarp had been thrown over a portion near the west dormer. The columns of the upper gallery needed paint and some of the balusters were missing from the handrail, giving the house the appearance of having a wide gap-toothed grin. The brick of the ground floor and the wooden siding of the upper story were still painted yellow, but the color had faded with age to the shade of old parchment instead of the butter-yellow of her memory.

Memory was flattering, Serena reflected; reality was like seeing a beloved relative who had passed from middle age to old age between visits.

She made her way across the broad lawn at a hurried, half-lame walk, her shoes and purse cradled against her. A screen door on the upper level of the house swung wide open and her niece and nephew burst out like racehorses from the starting gate. Six-year-old Lacey ran shrieking down the wide steps, a blur of blond ringlets and pink frills, with eight-year-old John Mason right behind her, a bullfrog clutched between his hands and a maniacal grin on his face.

"John Mason, leave your sister alone!" Shelby Sheridan-Talbot shouted, bustling out onto the gallery.

She was a fraction of an inch shorter than Serena with a softer, slightly rounder figure. Her brown eyes were a bit more exotic in shape, and her mouth seemed perpetually set in a petulant frown. Beyond those slight differences they appeared very much the same physically. Shelby looked ready to address the chamber of commerce in a bright yellow suit with a fitted jacket that flared out at the hips in the current style intended to denote femininity. The emerald silk blouse beneath the jacket sported a flamboyant candy-box bow at the throat. Serena felt like a bag lady in comparison.

"Oh, my Lord, Serena!" Shelby exclaimed dramatically. She pressed perfectly manicured hands to her cheeks, displaying a diamond ring big enough to choke a cat and a large square-cut topaz. "What on earth has happened to you? You look like you've been mugged or run over by a truck or both."

"Gee, thanks," Serena trudged up the steps, uncharitably wishing that she had been born an only child. Shelby's temperament was as capricious as the weather—sunny one second and stormy the next. She tended to be silly and frivolous. Her constant theatrics were tiring in the extreme, and she had a way of saying things that was at once innocent and cuttingly shrewd and that made it exhausting to endure a conversation with her.

Serena frowned at her as she limped onto the gallery and Shelby inched back, making a moue of distaste, careful not to brush up against her.

"I'm not having a great day here, Shelby, and I don't have time to go over the gory details with you," Serena said. "I've got to change and get going. Can you please arrange to have someone pick up my car in town? I left it down by Gauthier's."

Shelby's expression quickly clouded over from feigned concern to childish annoyance. "Of course, Serena. I have nothing better to do than run errands for you. My stars, you come home looking like something the cat dragged in, worrying me to a frazzle, and the first thing out of your mouth is an order. Isn't that just like you."

Serena limped past her sister. She seriously doubted Shelby had given a single thought to her absence from the house. Shelby's most pressing concerns in life were her children, her wardrobe, and her prominence in community affairs—which she entered not with an eye to civic duty but social status. She was as pretty and shallow as a lily pond in a Japanese garden.

Serena stepped into the house and made her way down the hall, regretting the fact that she didn't have time to take in the ambience of the home she'd grown up in. Aside from one major renovation in the early 1800s and modifications since then to install plumbing and electricity, it had remained largely unchanged over its long history. It was a treasure trove filled with heirlooms and antiques that would make a museum curator's mouth water. But there was no time to appreciate the cypress-paneled walls painted a mellow gold or the faded Turkish rugs that spilled jewel-tone colors across the old wood floor. She went directly toward her old bedroom, where earlier in the day she had done nothing more than deposit her suitcases before storming off in a stubborn huff to find a guide.

"Going, did you say?" Shelby questioned suddenly, as if Serena's words had only just managed to penetrate through her sense of indignation. She rushed to catch up, plucking at the sleeve of Serena's rumpled jacket like a child trying to catch its mother's attention. "Going where?"

"To see Gifford."

"You can't go now!" Shelby whined in dramatic alarm, following Serena into her room. She positioned herself well within her sister's range of vision and put on her most distressed expression, wringing her hands for added effect. "You simply can't go now! Why, you only just arrived! We haven't had a chance to chat or anything! I haven't had a chance to tell you a thing about our new house or about how well the children are doing in school or how I may very well be named Businesswoman of the Year by the chamber of commerce. You simply can't go now!"

Serena ignored the dictate and began undressing, tossing her ruined clothes into a pile on the floor. She frowned at the suitcase on the bed, knowing there was nothing in it suitable for a swamp. She might have grown up dogging Gifford's heels around the cane fields, but the woman she had become in Charleston had no call to wear jeans or rubber knee-boots.

"And Odille is making a leg of lamb for supper," Shelby went on. She moved around the room in quick, nervous motions, flitting from place to place like a butterfly, lighting only long enough to straighten a lace doily or fuss with the arrangement of cut flowers in the china pitcher on the carved cherry dresser. "You can't know the battle I had to wage to get her to do it. Honestly, that woman is as churlish as the day is long. She has defied me at every turn since Mason and I moved in. And she frightens the children, you know. They think she's some kind of a witch. I don't doubt but what she told them she'd put a spell on them. She's just that way. I don't understand why Gifford keeps her on."

"He enjoys fighting with her, I imagine," Serena said, smiling as she thought of the cantankerous Odille facing off with the equally cantankerous Gifford.

Odille Fontenot was as homely and hardworking as a mule, a tall rack of bones with the hide of a much smaller person stretched tautly over them. Her skin was as black as pitch, her eyes a fierce shade of turquoise that burned as bright as gas jets with the force of her personality. She was dour and superstitious and full of sass. She had taken over as housekeeper after Serena and Shelby had gone and Mae, the woman who had helped raise them, had retired. Odille was probably well into her sixties by now, but no one could tell by looking at her and no one dared ask.

Serena opened her suitcase and pulled out a pair of white crop-legged cotton slacks and a knit top with wide red and white stripes. A quick glance in the beveled mirror above the dresser confirmed her suspicions that her hair was coming down, but there was no time to fuss with it.

"Besides," she said, her voice muffled as she pulled her top on over her head, "Odille's brother is Gifford's best friend."

Shelby abruptly stopped rearranging knickknacks on the dresser and looked sharply at her sister's reflection in the mirror. "Did you say you're going *after* Gifford? You're going out into the swamp?"

Serena zipped her slacks, meeting Shelby's gaze evenly. "Isn't that what you told me to do?" she said with deceptive calm.

Shelby's cheeks flushed beneath her perfect makeup, and she glanced away, suddenly uncomfortable. "I guess I didn't think you'd really do it. I mean, for heaven's sake, Serena, *you* going out into the swamp!"

"What did you think I'd do, Shelby? Nothing? Did you think I'd just ignore the problem?"

Shelby turned and faced her then, her mood changing yet again. "Ignore it the way I have, you mean?" She narrowed her eyes and pinched her mouth into a sour knot. "Well, I'm sorry, Serena, if I don't live up to your standards, but I have many other responsibilities. If Gifford wants to go live in the middle of some godforsaken, snake-infested swamp, I can't just drop everything and go after him."

"Well, you won't have to," Serena said tiredly. "Because I'm going."

"Yes." Shelby flitted to the French doors that opened onto the gallery. She drew a length of sheer drape through her fingers, then twirled away, tossing her head. "Won't Giff be tickled to see how you've overcome your fears."

Serena gave her twin a long, level look brimming with anger and hurt, but she made no comment. She refused to. She had never once discussed with Shelby her fear of the swamp or how she had acquired it. The topic had tacitly been declared off-limits years earlier, a dangerous no-man's land that Shelby danced along the edge of when she was feeling spiteful.

Serena wasn't even certain her sister realized how potentially volatile the subject was. It wasn't that Shelby was stupid; it was just that she magnified the importance of things that pertained directly to herself and tended to minimize all else.

Stepping into a pair of red canvas espadrilles, Serena snapped her suitcase shut with a decisive click. She had no time to analyze her sister's psyche even if she had wanted to. She had a boat to catch.

"I'm leaving now," she said softly, still struggling to control her temper. "I don't know when I'll be back. Knowing Gifford, this could take a day or two."

She slung the strap of her carryall over her shoulder and hefted the suitcase off the bed. Without so much as glancing in Shelby's direction, she left the room and headed for the front door.

"Serena, wait!" Shelby called, her voice ringing with contrition as she hurried down the hall.

"I can't wait. Lucky gave me ten minutes and I have no doubt he'll leave without me just to prove his point if I'm not there on time."

"Lucky?" Shelby's step faltered as she repeated the name. "Lucky who?"

"Lucky Doucet," Serena said, bumping the screen door open with her hip. "He's taking me out to Giff's."

Shelby's face fell and paled dramatically, but Serena wasn't looking.

"Good heavens, Serena," she said breathlessly, scurrying out onto the gallery. "You can't go off with him. Do you have any idea what people say about him?"

"I can well imagine."

"Mercy," Shelby fretted, patting her bosom with one hand and fanning herself with the other, as if she might swoon like a belle of old. "I don't know how his poor mother can hold her head up in public. And she's just the dearest woman you'd ever care to meet. The whole family is perfectly nice with college degrees and I don't know what all, but that—that—Lucky . . . Good heavens, he's nothing but trouble. He's been living like an animal out in the swamp ever since he got out of the army. Folks say he's half crazy."

"They may be right," Serena conceded, remembering Lucky's own words to that effect. "But he was the only person I could find to take me."

"Well, I don't think you should go with him. Who knows what he might do or say?"

Serena sighed heavily. "Shelby, one of us *has* to go talk to Gifford. You're not willing and Lucky Doucet is the only person able to take me."

Shelby pouted, plumping her lower lip out and batting her lashes. "Well, I just don't think you should, that's all."

"Your protest has been duly noted. Now, I'm off. Give my apologies to Odille."

"Be careful."

Serena paused on the last step at her sister's hesitant admonishment. It was one of the rare shows of concern from her twin that always made her do a double take. Shelby was for the most part completely self-absorbed. She could be silly and frivolous, petty and downright cruel on occasion. Then every once in a while she would suddenly come forth with a small slice of affection, concern, love, offering it like a jewel. The gestures were both touching and unsettling.

"I will be," Serena said quietly.

She crossed the lawn at a hobbling half run once again, suitcase banging against her leg, foot throbbing from the sliver she had yet to remove. She set her sights on the landing and worked unsuccessfully to force Shelby from her mind.

All their lives people had remarked to them how special, how close they must feel being twins, what a unique bond they must share. Serena had always taken the comments with sardonic amusement. She and Shelby had never been close. Aside from their looks, they were as different as summer and winter. By Shelby's decree, they had been rivals from birth. Shelby had always seemed to resent Serena for being born at the same time, as if Serena had done so purposely to steal Shelby's glory. In her attempts to avoid rivalry, Serena had drifted further away from her sister, cultivating separate interests and separate dreams, creating an even wider gap between them.

Serena had always regretted the fact that they weren't close. Being the twin of a virtual stranger seemed much lonelier than being an only child. But they were too different, existing on separate planes that never quite seemed to intersect. They shared no telepathy. Sometimes it was almost as if they didn't even speak the same language. The only thing that seemed to bind them was blood and heritage and Chanson du Terre.

The elements of their relationship were complex. As a psychologist, Serena might have found it fascinating—had it been someone else's relationship, had she been able to look at it with cool objectivity. But she was too close to the subject; there were too many painful memories binding all the facets together like vines, and she was too afraid of what she might find if she ever did tear all the clinging creepers away, afraid the core might be as shriveled and dead as a sapling that had been smothered by the growth around it. And then what would happen? She would have to let go of the hope she still harbored in a corner of her heart. It was easier for them both to simply leave it alone.

As she neared the landing, her niece and nephew came running from the bank, screaming as if the devil were chasing them. They ran past her without slowing down, flying toward the safety of the house and their mother. Lucky stood on the dock smoking a cigarette, one hip cocked and a nasty smile tugging at a corner of his mouth. Serena scowled at him.

32

"Can't you go ten minutes without terrorizing someone?"

"Your ten minutes were up five minutes ago. You're just lucky I didn't leave without you."

"That's a matter of opinion," she grumbled. "What did you say to them? You ought to be ashamed, trying to give little children nightmares."

Lucky rolled his eyes and tossed the butt of his cigarette into the bayou. "Those two *are* nightmares."

"I wouldn't say that within Shelby's earshot if I were you."

"There are far worse things I could say to that one," he said, almost under his breath.

Serena gave him a curious look. His expression had gone cold and closed. He had slammed a door shut, but she felt compelled to push at it anyway. "You know my sister?" she asked. It seemed as unlikely as . . . as herself going into the swamp with him.

Lucky didn't answer. His relationship with Shelby Sheridan had never been shared with anyone, not brother or stranger or priest. He certainly had no intention of sharing the story with Shelby's twin. It had happened in another lifetime, in another place. He preferred to leave the wound scarred over, if not healed. There was no way on earth he was going to tear it open for this woman. In addition to the sin of being Shelby's sister, she was a psychologist. The last thing he needed was some college girl digging around in his psyche.

He turned his attention to the luggage she carried and the stylish outfit she wore. "Where do you think we're goin', *chère?* Club Med?"

Serena gave him one of her haughty ice-princess looks. "For your information, Mr. Doucet, my wardrobe doesn't hold an extensive collection of army fatigues and waders. You may find this hard to believe, but I don't particularly care to spend my free time in the swamp."

"Oh, I don't find that hard to believe a-tall. I'm sure you're far too busy givin' dinner parties and goin' to concerts to even think of a place such as the swamp."

"Why should I think of it? It doesn't require anything from me. It simply is."

Not for long. Not if your sister has anything to say about it. The thoughts passed instantly through Lucky's head, but he didn't speak them aloud. He was as involved as he intended to get, ferrying Serena out to Gifford's cabin and doing the odd reconnaissance job. It wasn't up to him to save the swamp. It couldn't be. *Dieu,* he had his hands full just trying to save himself.

What would be the point in arguing with Serena anyway? She was a slick, sophisticated city dweller who obviously had no affinity for the area she had grown up in. What would she care if Tristar Chemicals furthered the ruination of a delicate ecosystem man had been bent on destroying for years? For all he knew she was well aware of the situation and was going out to Giff's only to badger him into selling his land. She was her sister's twin, after all. How could he expect anything better of her than deceit and treachery?

He looked at her now in her prissy little designer sportswear outfit. She was a woman born to money, used to fine things. It stood to reason she would want more. That was the way of women of her class —see to the comfort and luxury of number one and to hell with the rest of the world. She wouldn't listen to him. He was just a means to an end . . . again.

"Get in the boat," he said with a growl, his temper rising like a tide inside him.

She took another step toward him, her chin lifting to a stubborn angle. "You know, Mr. Doucet, we would get along a whole lot better if you would stop bossing me around."

Lucky all but closed the gap between them, leaning over her, trying to intimidate her with his size and the aura of his temper. "I don't want to get along with you. Is that clear enough, *Miz* Sheridan?"

"Like crystal."

She tilted her head back to meet his furious gaze, refusing to back away from him. Lucky's breath caught in his throat. *Bon Dieu,* she was beautiful! It didn't seem to matter to his eyes that she was everything he needed to stay away from. It didn't matter to his hormones that she represented more trouble than he could afford to handle. For an instant, as he leaned close and the scent of her perfume lured him closer still, desire flared hot and bright inside him and burned away all common sense.

His gaze drifted over the elegant line of her cheek and jaw, the perfect angel's-wing curve of her brows, the delicate pink bow of her mouth. He wanted nothing more at that instant than to kiss her, to taste those lips, to trace his fingertips over cheek and jaw and brush back the errant tendrils of golden hair that had escaped the bonds of style. He wanted to kiss her, taste her, plunge his tongue into her mouth. It was crazy.

Crazy.

A shudder went through him and he tore his gaze from her. He turned away from her abruptly, jerking her suitcase from her grasp and climbing down into the pirogue with it. He settled the bag on the flat floor of the boat, up in the bow with the rest of his cargo, and moved back toward the stern, taking up the push-pole. His hands were shaking.

Sweet heaven, he thought, gripping the pole and looking away as Serena eased herself into the boat; the sooner he got her to Gifford's, the better. He didn't need this kind of torment in his life. All he wanted was to be left in peace.

Peace, a derisive voice sneered inside his head, what was that? A dream. Something he was continually longing for that seemed forever beyond his reach. Something Serena Sheridan seemed to hold effortlessly, he thought, taking in the air of calm she wore like a queen's cloak as she settled herself primly on the seat of his pirogue. He couldn't help but envy her that. But if she were a cold, unfeeling bitch like her sister, why wouldn't she feel peace? Nothing would penetrate her armor of selfishness. She would be safe from caring and pain.

He heaved a sigh as he poled the boat away from the dock and steered it around, pointing the bow upstream, away from civilization and toward his home, his heartland—the cypress swamp of Bayou Noir. He focused on the wilderness that had been his salvation, never turning his head to catch the bright flash of yellow on the gallery of Chanson du Terre.

Chapter Four

The first thing that always struck Serena about the swamp was the vastness of it. What land there was in this part of the state was criss-crossed by a labyrinth of waterways, some so wide they appeared bent on swallowing up everything in their path, some so narrow they were hardly more than a series of puddles cutting through the dense over-hanging growth of willow and moss-draped hardwood trees. As far as the eye could see there was nothing but water and woods twisted together in combat with one another—water eating away at land, land rising up where water had been.

It was a place where one could literally spend days wandering the bayous, trying to reach a point only a few miles away. It was a place where trails twisted and turned, cut back and looped around until the traveler had no concept of direction. A place where shadows distorted the perception of time.

The area was inhabited by few people. Those who still made their living in the swamp generally preferred the comfort and convenience of civilization, buzzing into the wilderness in their aluminum boats only to return at the end of the day, leaving the bayous to such native inhabitants as snakes and alligators . . . and Lucky Doucet.

The waterway they were on branched off again and again like cracks in a windshield. It seemed to Serena that Lucky turned at random, steering the pirogue east, then west, then turning south again, then north. They weren't thirty minutes away from Chanson du Terre and already she was hopelessly lost, her fear robbing her of the ability to remember the route. She sat on the hard bench with her back straight, arms at her sides, fingers curling around the edge of the seat, bracing herself as if for a fierce blow.

"What'sa matter, darlin'? You afraid the boat's gonna sink?" Lucky punctuated the question by shifting his weight to set the pirogue rocking.

Serena felt the meager contents of her stomach rise up the back of her throat. She swallowed hard, concentrating on keeping her fear contained inside a shell of outer calm. *Don't let him know you're afraid. Don't let him know you're afraid.*

"O-of course not," she stammered.

Lucky sniffed, offended. "The only way this pirogue is gettin' water in it is if it rains. I built it myself. This one, she rides the dew."

"Is that what you do for a living? You build pirogues?" Serena asked, looking at the paraphernalia in the front of the boat. There was an assortment of gunny sacks and red onion bags, wire and mesh crawfish nets, a bundle of mosquito netting. Fisherman's gear. She thought of the knife he carried and corrected herself. Poacher's gear.

"Non," he said shortly.

"What do you do?" she asked, twisting around to squint up at him. He looked like a giant looming over her. She wondered if he would take the opportunity to lie to her or try to shock her by telling the truth. He did neither.

"I do as I please."

Serena arched a brow. "Does that pay well these days?"

Lucky tilted his head and looked away, giving her his profile. *"Pas de bêtises,"* he muttered. "Sometimes it doesn't pay at all."

He thrust the pole down into the muddy bottom and pushed. The boat shot ahead, nosing the edge of a floating platform of water hyacinth, delicate-looking lavender flowers shimmering above dense masses of green leaves. They turned again and the bayou grew narrower and darker. The pirogue skimmed the inky surface like a skater on ice, cutting across a sheet of green duckweed as they aimed for a narrow arbor of willow trees with streamers overhanging the water from either bank.

Serena took a slow, deep breath before they entered the tunnel of growth. Her throat constricted at the sudden absence of light. Her skin crawled as the willow wisps brushed against her like serpents' tongues.

When the boat emerged on the other side of the bower, they had an extra passenger. A thick black snake lay like a coil of discarded electrical cord on the floor of the pirogue near the toes of Serena's red shoes. Serena tried to scream, but couldn't. She bolted back on the seat, pulling her feet up and rocking the pirogue violently as she scrambled to escape, reacting on sheer instinct. She might have flung herself out of the boat if Lucky hadn't caught her.

He banded her to him with one brawny arm, bending her over backward as he reached down to snatch up the snake and fling it into the water.

"Just a little rat snake," he said derisively as he released her.

Weak-kneed, Serena wilted down out of his embrace. A shudder passed through her as she watched the snake swim for shore, nose above the water, body undulating like a ribbon in a breeze. She didn't care if it was made of rubber and came from Woolworth's. It was a snake. Still, she didn't like the idea of this man knowing her fears, so she forced herself to recover quickly. Control was her best defense.

"Pardon me for overreacting," she said primly.

Lucky scowled down at the back of her head. Wasn't there anything that could put a permanent wrinkle in that serene demeanor of hers? She'd come unglued at the sight of the snake, but that fast she was Miss Calm-and-Cool again, apologizing as if she had burped at the dinner table. He felt ready to explode from pulling her against him for that brief second; she sat there looking unmoved.

An irrational burst of anger shook him. How could she look so unaffected? How could he want her so much? How could he stand there looking at her, wanting her, knowing what she'd done—

What her *sister* had done . . .

Everything inside him went still as he realized what he was doing—substituting Serena for Shelby, letting an old hatred bubble up like rancid air that had been trapped in the bottom of a pond. After all these years it could still emerge, just as acrid as ever.

"*C'est ein affaire à pus finir,*" he muttered, shaking his head in an effort to clear it.

38

"I beg your pardon?" Serena asked, turning a questioning look up at him.

"I said, you'd better get used to seeing snakes if you think you're gonna stay out here, sugar. There are fifteen species of nonvenomous and six venomous—coral snakes, cottonmouths as long as whips, copperheads as thick as a man's wrist."

Serena squeezed her eyes shut, as if that would somehow keep her from hearing him. Her mind took advantage of the blank screen to throw up one of her most terrible memories—muddy water swirling toward her, three dark, slender shapes writhing at the base of her perch, black heads shaped like arrows and mouths that flashed pinkish-white as they opened and came toward her . . .

What the hell had possessed her to come out here? She hated this place. It terrified her the way nothing else could. It shattered her sense of control. She looked around at the ghostly gray trunks of the huge cypress trees, the impenetrable growth beyond them, all of it shrouded in sinister shadows and hung with a tattered bunting of dirty-looking moss. It was a place of nightmares.

Tears stung Serena's eyes. She wanted to cling to her façade of calm, but she could feel her grip on it slipping. It inched away as if through sweaty hands that struggled frantically to hang on. To this point she had run on stubbornness and steam, but her anger and her singlemindedness had suddenly seemed to desert her, leaving only her fear.

Think, Serena. Think about something, anything.

This boat is too damned small.

"Hand me that canteen."

Her heart jolted at the sound of Lucky's voice. She snapped back to reality, glad for the distraction. She picked up the canteen and handed it back to him, giving him a wry look as she turned to sit sideways.

"Please, Miss Sheridan?" she said sweetly. "Thank you, Miss Sheridan. You're most welcome, Mr. Doucet."

Lucky rolled his eyes. He unscrewed the top on the canteen and took a long drink, the muscles of his throat working rhythmically as he swallowed.

"What is that you're drinking?" Serena asked, trying to drag her eyes away from the thick column of his neck.

He wiped his mouth with the back of his hand. "Water," he lied.

Serena's gaze flicked to the canteen. Unconsciously, she drew the tip of her tongue across her bottom lip and swallowed.

Heat seared through Lucky's veins.

He thrust the canteen toward her in an ungracious offer, angry with himself for caring at all about her comfort and angrier still for not being able to control his body's response to her.

She took the canteen and sniffed dubiously at the opening.

"This isn't water, it's liquor," she said, making a face.

Lucky scowled at her. "It has water in it."

Serena gave a little snort of disbelief. "You drink it like water, which probably accounts for your foul temperament."

"I like my temperament just fine," he said on a growl.

"Well, you're a minority of one, from what I've seen." She sniffed again at the canteen and grimaced.

"Are you gonna take a drink or are you afraid you might catch something drinking out of the same can as the likes of me?" Lucky asked sarcastically.

Serena narrowed her eyes at him and took a swig from the canteen, partly to prove him wrong and partly to bolster her flagging courage. The professional in her frowned on the latter reason. There wasn't anything healthy about rationalizing alcohol consumption. But she ignored the disapproving inner voice. She wasn't a professional out here; she was scared. The kind of fear that she was experiencing was terrible. She would have done just about anything to escape it. If nothing else, this experience was giving her a renewed sympathy for her patients who suffered from phobias.

As she had suspected, the brew in the canteen was nothing that had ever graced the shelves of a liquor store. It was homemade stuff so potent there probably wasn't a proof percentage high enough to categorize it. It was the kind of stuff that could double as paint thinner or battery acid in a pinch. Liquid fire seared a path down her throat and sizzled as it hit her belly, spreading warmth through her. As if she wasn't already warm enough from looking up at her guide, she thought, cursing her hormones.

Perhaps this physical attraction to him was some kind of temporary insanity, she reasoned. Perhaps Lucky Doucet with his mile-wide shoulders, his panther's eyes, and courtesan's mouth was the thing her mind wanted to focus on instead of the swamp. That was the only reason that made any sense. Aside from his looks, his list of faults was endless. He was rude, crude, chauvinistic, overbearing, arrogant, had a violent temper, and he drank. No sensible, self-respecting woman would entertain a single thought about getting involved with him on any level.

Her gaze drifted once again over his physique. Well, maybe there was *one* level . . . but of course she wasn't interested in that. She didn't involve herself in affairs that were strictly sexual. In fact, she hadn't involved herself in an affair of any kind for what suddenly seemed like ages.

She kept busy with her practice and her volunteer work at a mental health clinic in one of Charleston's poorest areas. She had friends and a nice social life, but no serious romantic entanglements. She'd been married once to a fellow psychologist, but the marriage had fizzled for lack of interest on both their parts. It had been based on friendship, mutual interests, convenience. Noticeably absent had been the kind of intense physical magnetism that often acts as an adhesive to hold the other parts of a relationship together. They had drifted apart and divorced amicably four years after taking their vows.

Since the divorce, Serena had dated sparingly, casually, never finding a man who motivated her to anything more than that. She had decided that perhaps she simply wasn't a sexual creature. She hadn't inspired that much passion in her husband, nor had he excited her to the kind of mind-numbing ecstasy she'd heard about from other women. She had decided she simply wasn't made to react that way to a man. It probably had something to do with her need for emotional control. Looking up at Lucky Doucet, she decided she may have to rethink the issue.

"Like what you see, sugar?" he drawled lazily, staring down at her with those unblinking amber eyes.

"Not particularly." She thrust his canteen back at him in an effort to keep him from noticing the telltale blush that warmed her cheeks.

"Liar."

It was a statement of fact more than an accusation. He took the canteen, deliberately brushing his fingertips over hers. Serena jerked her hand back, winning her an amused chuckle.

Serena lifted her chin a defiant notch. "You have an amazingly high opinion of your own appeal, Mr. Doucet."

"Oh, no, *chère,* I just call 'em like I see 'em."

"Then I suggest you make an appointment with an optometrist at the earliest possible date. A good pair of glasses could save untold scores of women the unpleasantness of your company."

Their gazes locked and warred—hers cool, his burning with intensity. She congratulated herself on defusing a potentially disastrous sexual situation. He congratulated himself on goading her temper. Both went on staring. The air around them thickened with electricity.

On the eastern bank of the bayou an alligator roused itself from a nap, plowed through a lush tangle of ferns and coffee-weed stems, and slid down into the water.

Serena jumped, jerking around to stare wide-eyed at the creature. The alligator was lying in the shallows among a stand of cattails, just a few feet away from the pirogue, its long, corrugated head breaking the surface of the murky water as it stared back at her.

Lucky gave a bark of laughter. *"Mais non, mon ange,* that 'gator's not gonna get you. Unless I throw you overboard, which I have half a mind to do."

"I don't doubt it—that you have half a mind, that is," Serena grumbled, snatching the canteen away from him to take another swig of false courage.

And just how much of a mind do you have, Serena, antagonizing this man? Good Lord, he was a poacher and a bootlegger and who knew what else. He gave her a nasty smile, reminding her enough of the nearby alligator to give her chills.

"No wonder Gifford's holed up out here," he said, taking up the push-pole again and sending them forward with the strong flexing of his biceps. "I don't see how a man could stand to be stuck in a house with two just like you."

Serena kept one eye on the alligator and both hands firmly clamped to the edge of the seat. "For your information, my sister and I are nothing alike."

"I know what your sister is like."

The cold dislike in his statement made her glance over her shoulder at him. "How? I can't imagine the two of you run in the same social circles."

Lucky said nothing. That mental door slammed closed again. Serena thought she could almost hear it bang shut. He looked past her, as if she had ceased to exist, his face a stony mask. His silence left her free to draw her own conclusions.

Perhaps Shelby had made some kind of public statement against poachers or places like Mosquito Mouton's. It would be like Shelby to get on a soapbox and publicly antagonize people she thought of as unsavory. Her views would be met with widespread approval among the upstanding members of the community, something that would

42

appeal enormously to her ego. Shelby had always required a great deal of attention and praise, and had been willing to go to whatever length she needed to to get those things. It wouldn't have been beyond her to pick on a man as dangerous as Lucky Doucet. She would have considered the potential for self-aggrandizement long before giving a thought to the potential for trouble.

Serena wondered if her sister had any idea she'd made an enemy of a man who carried a hunting knife the size of a scimitar.

They moved on up the bayou, the silence of the swamp as heavy and oppressive as the heat. The denser the vegetation became, the more overwhelming the stillness. It played on Serena's nerves, tightening them so that something as innocent as the "quock" of heron set them humming.

The deeper they penetrated into the wilderness, the less it looked like man had ever intruded upon it. The most conspicuous sign of human habitation Serena saw was the occasional slip of colored plastic ribbon tied to a branch to mark the location of a crawfish trap.

Lucky pulled up beside one of these—a red ribbon tied to the branch of a willow sapling—and set about emptying the dip net set in the shallow water beneath it. The thin mesh was brimming with red crawfish. He raided four nets along the same bank, emptying their contents into the onion sacks he had stored in the bow of the pirogue, going about his task as if Serena were nothing more than an annoying piece of cargo he had to step around. She watched him with interest, not daring to ask if the traps he was harvesting were his.

"Are we nearly there?" she asked as Lucky once again began to pole the pirogue north, then east.

"Nearly. You'll know when we're just about onto Gifford's."

"I doubt it. It's been years since I've been out here."

"You'll know," he said assuredly.

"How?"

"By the gunshots."

Serena made a face. "That's ridiculous. Old Lawrence said something about people getting shot at too. I know my grandfather can be cantankerous, but shooting at people? That's absurd. Why would he shoot at people?"

"To scare them off."

"And why would he want to scare people off?"

"So they'll leave him alone."

Serena shook her head impatiently. "I don't understand any of this.

43

In the first place, it's not like Giff to desert the plantation for so long a time, not even during crawfish season."

"He's got his reasons," Lucky said enigmatically.

Serena gave him a long, searching look. She didn't like the idea of this man knowing more about her family's concerns than she did. It made her feel like the outsider. It also threw a glaring spotlight on her deficiencies as a granddaughter. She didn't come home often enough, didn't keep up with the local news, didn't call as often as she should. The list of venial sins went on, adding to her feelings of guilt. Still, she couldn't keep herself from asking the sixty-four-thousand-dollar question.

"And just what do you think those reasons are, Mr. Doucet?" she queried, looking up at him.

His face remained impassive. "Ask Gifford, if you want to know. I don't get involved in other people's lives."

"How convenient for you. You have no one to worry about, no one to answer to except yourself."

"That's right, sugar."

"Then what are you doing bringing me out here when you would clearly rather have come alone?"

Lucky scowled at her, his black brows pulling together like twin thunderheads above his eyes. When he spoke his voice was soft and silky with warning. "Don' you go tryin' to get inside my head, Dr. Sheridan."

Serena rolled her eyes. "God forbid. I'm sure I'd rather fall into a snake pit."

One and the same thing, *chérie,* Lucky said to himself, but he refrained from speaking that thought, knowing it was the kind of statement a psychologist would pounce on. He was managing just fine. If everyone would just butt the hell out of his life, he would be great.

"How come you don' know Gifford's reasons for comin' out here?" he asked, going on the offensive. "Don' you ever talk to your grandpapa on the telephone? Mebbe you don' care what goes on down here. Mebbe you don' care about this place or Chanson du Terre, eh?"

"What kind of question is that?" Serena bristled, rising to the bait like a bass to a fly. "Of course I care about Chanson du Terre. It's my family home."

Lucky shrugged. "I don't see you livin' there, sugar."

"Where I live is none of your concern."

"That's right. Just like it's none of my concern if someone wants to

44

come in and flatten the place with bulldozers. It's not my family what's lived and worked on that land two-hundred-some years."

Serena stared up at him, feeling as if she'd been hit in the chest with a hammer. "What do you mean, flatten the place? What are you talking about?"

"Chanson du Terre, angel. Your sister wants to sell it to Tristar Chemicals."

"That's absurd!" she exclaimed, laughing at the sheer lunacy of the statement. "Shelby wouldn't want to sell Chanson du Terre any more than Scarlett O'Hara would put Tara on the market! You obviously *don't* know my sister. It would never happen. Never."

She went on chuckling at the idea, shaking her head, trying to ignore the terrible certainty in Lucky's eyes as he stared down at her. The look was meant to assure her of the fact that he knew many things she didn't have a clue about. A part of her rejected the notion outright, but another part of her churned with a sudden strange apprehension.

At any rate, there was no time to question or argue the issue, because as they rounded a bend in the bayou there came the sudden deafening explosion of a shotgun—firing at them.

Chapter Five

Serena had no trouble managing a scream this time. She shrieked, dropping to her knees on the floor of the pirogue and covering her head with her arms as buckshot hit the bayou in front of them, spewing muddy water and bits of shredded lily pad everywhere.

Her first thought was that they were being set upon by one of the honest men Lucky had been poaching from. Perhaps even the rightful owner of the crawfish squirming in the onion sacks two feet from her nose. She expected to hear another volley of shots and wondered if Lucky had a gun tucked away someplace to defend them with. But the initial *boom* faded away. In the ensuing silence, she lifted her head a few inches and peeked out between her fingers.

Gifford stood on the bank, legs spread, the smoking gun cradled loosely in his big hands. He was a tall, well-built man who didn't look anywhere near his age except for his thick head of snow-white hair, one lock of which insisted on tumbling rakishly across his broad forehead. With his square shoulders and trim waist, he still looked fit enough to wrestle a bear and win. His bold features were set in a characteristically fierce expression—bushy white brows lowered, square chin jutting forward aggressively. His nose was large and permanently red from years spent in the fields under the relentless southern sun.

"Goddammit, Lucky!" he bellowed, his voice a booming baritone that rivaled the shotgun for volume. "I thought you were that bastard Burke!"

"Naw," Lucky called back calmly, poling the boat forward as if getting shot at didn't affect him in the least. "You might wanna shoot me anyway, though, when you see what I brought you."

Serena rose up on her knees, snapping her head around to give him the evil eye before turning back toward her grandfather. She pushed her hair out of her eyes with one hand, hanging on to the side of the pirogue with the other to steady herself. Conflicting emotions shoved together in her chest like a log jam as she looked at the man who had essentially raised her. With adrenaline still pumping through her veins and the sound of the shotgun blast still ringing in her ears, anger took precedence for the moment.

The pirogue slid in beside a weathered dock with gnarled pilings and pitted planks. Serena didn't even wait for the boat to settle. She clambered out of it, awkward in her haste as she pulled herself up onto the rickety wharf. The pirogue scooted away as she pushed off from it and she slipped and hit her shin but managed to keep from falling back into the muddy shallows. Dirty, disheveled, with blood seeping into the previously immaculate white cotton of her pant leg and her hair tumbling in disarray around her shoulders, she stormed for shore, limping.

"Dammit, Gifford, what the hell do you think you're doing? Shooting at people! My God!"

Gifford scowled at her. "Jesus Christ. What the hell kind of language is that for a lady to use?"

"The kind I learned from you!" Serena shot back. She planted herself in front of him, her hands on her hips, staring up at him with as much defiance as she could muster.

"Well, hell," Gifford muttered. There wasn't any way around that one. He cracked the shotgun open and extracted a shell, which he slipped into the breast pocket of his faded chambray workshirt. "I'll bet you don't use that kind of language up in Charleston."

"I'm not up in Charleston."

"For once," he said with a snort. "What are you doing out here?" he asked, frowning down at Serena again. "I sure as hell never expected to see you riding around the swamp in a pirogue."

"Believe me, it's not my idea of fun," Serena said, shooting a glare Lucky's way. "I can think of a lot better things to do with my free time and much more pleasant company to do them with."

"She takes exception to my temperament," Lucky said with a sardonic smile as he approached, an onion bag of crawfish swinging from his fist.

"Among other things," Serena muttered.

Lucky stopped beside her, dropped the bag at his feet, and lit the cigarette dangling from his lip, his eyes on Serena the whole time. She could feel his gaze burning into her as hot as the flaring tip of his cigarette. Color rose to tint her cheeks.

He tilted his head back and blew a thin stream of smoke into the air. "Guess I'm gonna have to go back to charm school for a refresher course," he drawled laconically.

"Don' you believe him, Miz 'Rena," Pepper Fontenot said with a gravelly chuckle as he ambled toward them from his lawn chair. Pepper was a thin, wiry man with the same pitch-dark skin and light eyes as his sister, the formidable Odille. He had somehow managed to sustain a very merry personality despite having lived with Odille his entire life, and wore his wide smile as comfortably as he wore his faded old coveralls. He slapped Lucky on the shoulder. "He charm the hide off a 'gator, dis one, if he be of a mind to."

Serena arched a brow at Lucky. "He must not have been of a mind, then."

"Mebbe it was the company," Lucky said through his teeth.

Quelling the juvenile urge to stick her tongue out at him, Serena turned back toward her grandfather. "You might tell me you're glad to see me," she said, not quite able to hide her hurt at his cool reception.

"I might say it once I find out what you're doing here."

"What *I'm* doing here!" she exclaimed, splaying a hand across her chest. "I'm here because you took off without a word of explanation to anybody. I come down for a visit and the first thing I'm told is that you moved yourself out here two weeks ago and haven't been heard from since. What was I supposed to do? Say, 'Oh, gee, too bad I missed him' and just go on with my vacation? My God, Gifford, you could have been dead for all we knew!"

"Well, I'm not," he snapped. "If that's all you came to find out, you

48

can go on home now. You aren't going to inherit for a while yet if I can help it."

"What kind of a rotten thing is that to say?"

"It's the kind of thing a man starts saying when he's nigh onto eighty with a bum ticker and a couple of ungrateful granddaughters."

He snapped the shotgun closed with a decisive click, turned, and walked away.

Serena stood there, dumbfounded, watching him walk up the slight incline toward the cabin. Every time she saw Gifford in the flesh she was stunned by how badly she wanted his love and approval and how badly it hurt when he didn't offer them freely. It was as if the instant she encountered him, the child in her revived itself.

She was tired and frustrated, hungry and dirty. All she wanted to do was snuggle into her grandfather's embrace and let go of the determination that had gotten her this far. She wanted to be able to tremble and have Giff soothe her fears away as he had when she'd been a little girl, but that wasn't an option. She wasn't a child anymore, and Gifford hadn't been sympathetic to her fear of the swamp for a long, long time.

When she hadn't gotten over it after what he thought was a reasonable amount of time, his understanding had metamorphosed into a subtle disapproval and disappointment that had colored their relationship ever since. He thought she was a coward. Watching him walk away, she wished he could have realized how much courage it had taken her to get this far.

"Yeah, there's just nothin' quite so heartwarmin' as a family reunion," Lucky muttered, his eyes also on Gifford's back as the old man walked away.

Serena glared at him. "Butt out, Doucet." She stomped after her grandfather, her espadrilles squishing in the damp, spongy dirt that constituted the front yard.

The cabin was a simple rectangular structure covered with tan asphalt shingles. It was set up a few feet off the ground on sturdy cypress stilts to save it from the inevitable spring flooding. The roof was made of corrugated tin striped with rust. A stovepipe stuck up through it at a jaunty angle. The front door was painted a shade of aqua that hurt the eyes. There were no curtains at the two small front windows.

The cabin had never contained any amenities, certainly nothing that could have been considered "decorating" unless one included mounted racks of antlers. Serena doubted that had changed since the last time she'd been out here. The hunting lodge was one of those male bastions where anything aesthetically pleasing was frowned on as unmanly. Gifford undoubtedly still used the same old tacky, tattered furniture that hadn't been good enough for the Salvation Army store twenty years earlier. The floor of the two-room structure was probably still covered with the same hideous gray linoleum, the kind of indestructable stuff that promises to last forever and unfortunately does.

Serena wasn't going to find out immediately. Gifford didn't go to the door of the cabin. He climbed partway up the stairs, then turned around and plunked himself down with his gun across his lap as if he meant to block the way. Serena's step faltered just long enough so that the two old blue tick hounds that had jogged out from behind the woodshed could jump up on her and add their paw prints to the front of her shirt. She groaned and shooed them away, scolding them.

"You used to love them dogs," Gifford grumbled, scowling at her disapprovingly. "I suppose they don't allow hounds like that up in Charleston."

Serena shook a finger at him as she came to stand at the foot of the steps. "Don't you start that with me, Gifford. Don't you start in on how Charleston has changed me."

"Well, it has, goddammit."

"That's not what I came out here to discuss with you."

Gifford swore long and colorfully. "A man can't get a scrap of peace these days," he said, addressing the world at large. "I came out here to get away from people, not to form some pansy-ass discussion group."

Serena ignored his protest and pressed on. "It's not like you to just take off, especially this time of year. There's too much work to be done around the plantation."

He rolled his big shoulders and looked down at his feet. "That's what I've got Arnaud for. He's the manager, hell, let him manage. Tired old men like me are supposed to take off and go fishing."

"When you knew I was coming to visit?" Serena pushed the hurt away with an effort and gave an unladylike snort. "Since when are you a tired old man?"

"Since I figured out I don't have an heir who gives a rat's ass about everything I've broke my back for."

"Oh, for heaven's sake, Gifford!" she snapped. "What are you talking about?"

"I'm talking about you living eight hundred miles away and your sister ready to sell the old place at the drop of a hat. That's what I'm talking about."

"What is this nonsense about Shelby wanting to sell Chanson du Terre?" she demanded irritably. "I've never heard anything more ludicrous in my life. Ever since we were little girls she's talked about growing up and getting married and living on the plantation. She wouldn't dream of selling it!"

"Well, that just shows how out of touch you are with your own family, young lady," Gifford announced piously.

"Oh, for the love of Mike!" Serena cut herself off abruptly, not trusting herself to say anything more until she reined her temper in a notch. She clamped her mouth shut and paced back and forth along the base of the stairs, her arms banded tightly across her as if to keep herself from exploding.

"Honestly, I don't know what to think," she muttered more to herself than to Gifford. "People telling me Shelby's lost her senses and wants to sell Chanson du Terre. Shelby tells me she thinks you've gone senile—"

"Senile!" Gifford launched himself off his step like a rocket, shooting up to his full height. His craggy face turned an unhealthy shade of maroon. "By God, that tears it! Is that what you've come out here for, Serena? Is this a professional visit? You out here to see if the old man's lost his marbles? Then y'all can get that candy-ass lawyer husband of Shelby's to have me declared incompetent, sell the old place, and live off the sweat of my carcass— By damn— By God—I won't have it!"

He clutched the railing with one hand and the shotgun with the other and hissed a breath in through his teeth, struggling suddenly for air.

Serena rushed up the steps, her own heart thundering in alarm. "For God's sake, Gifford, sit down!"

He complied without argument, his knees buckling, backside hitting the old step with a thump. The tension went out of his muscles. His wide shoulders sagged and he drew in a ragged deep breath. He fished around in his shirt pocket for a pill, pulling out the shotgun slug and tossing it carelessly aside.

Serena kneeled at his feet, shaking all over. She pressed her hands against her lips and struggled not to cry, realizing for the very first time just how old he was, just how mortal. She watched him stick a little pill under his tongue and held her breath as his color faded slowly from red to pale gray. He seemed to age twenty years before her eyes, his incredible inner fire dimming like a flame that had been abruptly turned down.

"You all right, Giff?" Lucky said, his dark voice shot through with tension. Serena realized with a start he was on the step right behind her. He leaned down to get a look at Gifford's face, laying a hand on her shoulder in a manner that might have been intended as comforting.

Gifford muttered one of his more virulent oaths.

Pepper stuck his head in under the stair railing and flashed a smile of relief. "He kin cuss like dat, he all right. He stops cussin', him, den you ax him if he be dead."

"Smartass," Gifford growled.

Pepper gave a hoarse laugh and withdrew to snatch the squirming bag of crawfish away from the inquisitive coon hounds that were sniffing and pawing at it.

Serena felt herself sag with relief. She couldn't stop herself from reaching a hand up to touch her grandfather's knee, just to reassure herself. "You ought to go in and lie down, Giff. We can talk later."

"I don't need to lie down," the old man snapped. "Just a little dizzy spell, that's all. Christ, I don't know who wouldn't be dizzy with all this going on around them. It makes me so damn mad, I can't see straight half the time. I make one remark about selling, and your sister, who couldn't sell ice water in hell, runs right out and finds a buyer. Judas H. Priest. And where are you? Off shrinking heads in Carolina, as if there aren't enough lunatics in Lou'siana to go around."

"We can talk about it when we get home," Serena said softly.

There were a hundred questions to be asked. Why hadn't Shelby called her when Gifford had left? Why had she denied knowing the reason Gifford had left? Why would Gifford ever have mentioned selling the plantation and why would Shelby agree to it, much less find a buyer?

Feeling a little like Alice waking up in Wonderland, Serena pushed herself to her feet and wiped the remaining tears from her eyes. The questions would have to wait. She wouldn't quiz Gifford now and run the risk of giving him another attack. It could all be sorted out once they were back home. And the sooner the better.

She turned around to look back at the dock. Gifford's bass boat was tied up on the side opposite Lucky's pirogue. "Pepper, would you please get the boat ready?"

Pepper shook his head, smiling at her much the way Lawrence

Gauthier had earlier. "Oh, no, *chère*. Me, I kinda like bein' alive. You ax Giff 'bout it, he don' wanna go nowhere."

Serena turned back to her grandfather. He refused to look at her. "Gifford, please. You can't stay out here."

"I sure as hell can."

She turned to Lucky.

He shrugged and physically backed away from the conversation. "It's a free country."

"I don't believe this," Serena said angrily, raking her hair back from her face with trembling hands. "Dammit, Gifford, you nearly had a heart attack right before my eyes. You can't stay out here!"

"I can do whatever I damn well please, young lady," he said, forcing himself to his feet. He swayed a bit, but gripped the rail with a white-knuckled fist and locked his knees. "I won't have you or your sister or anybody else trying to run my life."

Serena cast one last glance at Pepper and Lucky, looking for help but finding none. Pepper shuffled his feet and dodged her gaze, staring down at the bag of crawfish. Lucky merely stared back at her, saying nothing, offering nothing. She shook her head. "I think you've all gone mad."

"Well then, why don't you just go on back to Charleston, where you won't have to worry about all your crazy relatives," Gifford said coldly. "Outta sight, outta mind. You don't care what all goes on down here."

Serena held up a hand to cut him off, pressing her lips together and blinking hard to ward off more tears of frustration. "I won't discuss this with you now, Gifford. I won't."

"Fine. Then go on and get out of here. Leave me in peace."

"I'm not going anywhere," she announced. "I'm staying right here until I convince you to come home."

"The hell you are. I won't have you," Gifford barked. "Lucky, you take her on back to Chanson du Terre."

Lucky backed away another step, brows drawing together ominously low over his eyes. "Forget it. I ain't running no goddamn ferry service. I'm not takin' her all the way back to Chanson du Terre. It's gettin' dark. I've got things to do."

"Then she can stay with you at your place, 'cause she sure as hell ain't staying here," Gifford declared. "I came out here to get *away* from ungrateful women."

"Stay with *him!*" Serena said with horror.

"Stay with *me!*" The idea nearly made Lucky choke.

They regarded each other with a kind of terror that didn't go unnoticed by Gifford. The old man raised an eyebrow.

"She's not stayin' with me," Lucky said emphatically. "It's out of the question. Absolutely out of the question."

His house was his sanctuary. It was the space he had created for himself to heal in, to have some measure of peace. It was his private refuge, the last stronghold of his sanity. The last person he wanted breaching those walls was this woman, a woman he wanted beyond all reason, a woman whose face haunted his mind with memories of the pain and betrayal of another.

"*Non. Non,*" he muttered, shaking his head. "*Sa c'est de la couyonade.*"

Gifford snorted. "So you think I'm foolish too? By God, the two of you deserve each other. You can sit around over coffee tonight and compare notes on ways to avoid your responsibilities."

Lucky wheeled around, stomping up three steps to thrust a warning finger in Gifford's face. "You're skatin' on thin ice, old man," he said through his teeth. "I don' owe you. I don' owe Chanson du Terre."

"Oh, that's right," Gifford drawled sarcastically. Lucky's ferocious look didn't impress him; he was too old to be frightened by the idea of his own mortality. "You don't owe anybody anything. You're your own man. Good for you, Lucky. You can pat yourself on the back after the swamp silts up and everything dies."

"Don' you talk to me about responsibilities, Gifford," Lucky snapped. "You've got your own. And where are you? Out here fishin' and takin' potshots at Tristar reps. How the hell is that gonna solve anything?"

"I've got my own way of dealing with the situation."

"*Mais, yeah,*" Lucky said with a harsh laugh. "By *not* dealing with it."

Serena stepped between them. "Excuse me. Do I get a say in this matter?"

Both men scowled at her simultaneously and answered in thunderous unison. "No!"

She fell back a step in utter disbelief.

Lucky jumped off the stairs and started pacing again. He knew Gifford—mules had nothing on him when it came to stubbornness. If he said he wasn't letting Serena stay with him, he meant it. He'd leave her on the doorstep all night if it came to that. The idea went against

Lucky's grain on a fundamental level where he'd long ago thought he'd given up all feeling.

He glanced at Serena out of the corner of his eye and mentally swore a blue streak. She was just as proud and stubborn as her grandfather. She'd stood toe to toe with the old man. She'd been on the brink of tears with worry over him. She obviously loved him. And old Giff had given her an emotional buffeting for her trouble. She looked like a hothouse flower that had been thrust outdoors during a thunderstorm—bedraggled, dirty, exhausted.

And Gifford was bent on turning her away.

Damn.

It wasn't that he *cared* about her, Lucky assured himself. It wasn't that he *wanted* to get involved. It was none of his business how Gifford treated his granddaughter. For all he knew, she deserved to be left out on the porch all night. The extenuating circumstances were what concerned him—another example of the way other people's affairs kept drifting into the path of his life. This swamp was his world. He couldn't bear the idea of seeing it destroyed.

He heaved a sigh and raked his hands through his hair. What were his options? He wanted Gifford to deal with the Tristar problem before something catastrophic happened, like Gifford shooting Len Burke or Shelby succeeding in selling the place to a company with a record as environmental rapists. That meant getting Gifford to go back to face the situation. Serena had resolved to get him to return, and heaven knew she had the determination to convince him, given enough opportunity. That meant keeping her near the old man and away from her sister's poisonous influence. And that meant . . .

Hell and damnation.

He examined the dilemma from another angle. How long could it take Serena to talk Gifford into going home? A day or two. Three at the outside. How much harping could a man take, after all? Lucky decided he wouldn't actually have to stay with her if she was in his house. He could easily spend that much time out in the swamp. He had plenty of other things to keep him occupied. Still, he didn't like the idea of being cornered into doing something.

He stopped his pacing, turning his head to glare up at Gifford. "All right," he said, his voice low. "I'll keep her."

Gifford successfully fought off a smile.

Serena's jaw dropped.

For a long second no one said anything. The tension building in the air was enough to make the coon hounds whine and trot away in search of a safe haven.

"Keep me?" Serena questioned softly, glaring at Lucky. *"Keep me!"* Her voice rose several decibels. She planted her hands on her hips and leaned over him, enjoying the height advantage for once. "You most certainly will not keep me!" She whirled toward Gifford, her face livid. "I will not stay with this man! I hardly know him and what I do know about him is hardly flattering. For heaven's sake, Gifford, you can't really expect me to stay with him!"

"Who knows what I might expect," Gifford said, putting on a wounded air. "I'm just a crazy old man waiting to die."

"Stop it!" Serena spat out. She stared up at him in the fading afternoon light and felt a big ball of fear swell up in her chest like a balloon. He had that same look he'd had on his face when she'd been seventeen and the sheriff had brought her home after catching her and two other honor students splitting a jug of cheap wine under the bleachers at the football stadium.

Her voice softened to a whisper. "Gifford?"

He shook his head. "Don't you even ask me, Serena. I'm so mad right now I could spit brass tacks. You think you can just come breezing in here and fix everything up with a sentence or two because you've got a sheepskin from Duke and a fancy practice up in Charleston. You don't know what's going on here and you don't care. You just want to put all the parts back in their places and get on with your vacation." He shook his head once more and blew out a breath. His color was heightening again, a flush creeping up from his throat into his face like mercury rising in a thermometer. "Go on, get out of here. You'll be all right with Lucky."

He turned and trudged up the rest of the steps, letting himself into the cabin without looking back. Serena felt stunned, as if someone had hit her between the eyes with a rock. Well, she'd gotten what she deserved, hadn't she? In his usual no-nonsense style Gifford had cut through to the heart of the matter. She *had* thought she'd come out here and simply set things straight, put her world back on track, rearrange things to her satisfaction. She had inherited that take-charge manner from Gifford. She used it to great success in her everyday life back in Charleston. But they weren't in Charleston.

Damn this place. She closed her eyes and rubbed her hands over her face, erasing what was left of her makeup.

"I'm sorry, Miz 'Rena," Pepper said, climbing the stairs to stand

56

beside her, his wriggling, clicking crawfish sack hanging down from his fists. "You know old Giff. He gets in a temper, him, there's no tellin' what he say. He don' mean half."

Serena tried without much luck to muster a smile. "Does that mean you'll run me home after all?"

He frowned, something that looked completely foreign to his face, as if his mouth didn't quite know how to turn that way. "Can't. Dat old boat, she's not runnin'. Lucky, he bring the part, but dat don' make her run. Take me a coupl'a days to fix."

Serena hadn't thought it possible for her spirits to sink any lower. She'd been wrong. They seemed to fall now from their last toehold into a bottomless black pit. It must have been a painful thing to watch, because Pepper made another attempt to frown. He shuffled his feet on the worn tread of the step, working up to making a run for it.

Why, oh, why had she let her temper goad her into coming out here without thinking it through, without first finding out exactly what was going on? Now she was stuck in this god-awful place. Turned out by her own grandfather. Turned over to the care of man who wouldn't know a scruple if it bit his handsome butt.

She turned her bleak gaze to Lucky. He stood absently scratching the head of one of the coon hounds as he watched her, his expression inscrutable. In the long, sinister shadows seeping across the ground as the sun slid away, he looked more dangerous than ever.

"Get in the boat, *chère,*" he said softly. "Looks like we're stuck with each other for a little while longer."

Chapter Six

"Come on," Lucky said, nodding toward the pirogue. "I'll bring you back tomorrow and you can have all day to hound him."

Serena followed him reluctantly to the water's edge. She looked out across the bayou and at the black forest that seemed to be looming ever larger as the light faded. Fear started to claw its way past the last wall of her resistance.

"I'll pay you anything if you just take me home." The words were out of her mouth before she was even aware of thinking them, but she didn't try to take them back. They were true. She could have managed staying at the cabin with Gifford and Pepper, but the idea of staying with a stranger—a dangerous stranger—and having him see her fear . . . she couldn't do it. At that moment she would have given him the keys to her Mercedes if he would have agreed to take her back to civilization. She wanted a long hot bath, a meal, some aspirin, and an explanation from her sister—not necessarily in that order.

"Anything?" Lucky arched a brow and gave her a slow, wicked smile as he considered. "That's tempting, sugar, but I just plain can't take you back tonight. I have a previous engagement."

Serena ground her teeth and forced the word through them. "Please."

Lucky bent and lifted the box of motor parts out of the bow of his boat, setting it aside on the bank. "Look, angel," he said as he straightened, resting his hands just above the low-riding waist of his fatigue pants. "I'm sure you think I'm gonna take you back to my place, tie you to the bed, and ravish you all night long, but I've got more important things to do. You'll just have to content yourself with fantasizing."

Serena gave him a look of complete disgust. He ignored her, wading out and pushing the pirogue away from the shore.

"Come on, sugar, *allons.* Get in the boat, or you can spend the night with Gifford's coon hounds out in the woodshed."

What choice did she have? Serena knew her grandfather. He was fully capable of leaving her to spend the night outside. He seemed angry enough to do it. Not even the idea of sharing a house with Lucky Doucet seemed as terrible as the idea of being out alone all night.

Dragging her tattered cloak of pride around herself once again, she lifted her nose and walked out onto the dilapidated dock to get in the boat.

They headed away from Gifford's and deeper into the wilderness. The bayou narrowed to a corridor flanked on both sides by what looked to be impenetrable woods. Cypress and tupelo trees stood in dark, silent ranks in their path like a natural slalom course. Dusk had fallen, casting everything in one last dusty glow of surrealistic light.

Serena sat, trying to keep her back straight, trying to keep from crying. Now that the confrontation with Gifford was over and the anger had subsided, pain rushed in unabated. She had come for him. Couldn't he see that? How could he accuse her of being so callous as to be thinking only of her inheritance? She had never even thought about him dying, much less what he would leave her.

Gifford dying. In her mind she relived the horror of watching him turn purple and collapse. She couldn't bear the thought of losing him. She especially couldn't bear the thought of losing him now when he seemed so angry with her, so disappointed.

Tears welled in her eyes and she blinked them back furiously. She would not cry now. She would not cry in front of Lucky Doucet and give him yet another reason to sneer at her. She couldn't let go and cry now, anyway, because she was afraid that once she started, she wouldn't be able to stop and she had too much yet to face before this day was over.

That was hardly a cheerful prospect, she thought, fighting another wave of despair. She already felt as if she'd been dragged by the hair for eight hundred miles and brutally dismembered. The person she had been just yesterday was no longer recognizable; she had been dismantled by this place and its people and the memories and emotions they evoked. She was exhausted from the ordeal, but she clung to her one last shred of strength and dignity and fought back the tears.

Lucky stood behind Serena, watching the little tremors that shook her shoulders. He could hear her catch a breath and knew she was trying valiantly not to cry. Proud, stubborn little thing. He felt something twist in his chest and did his best to ignore it.

He was having a hard time maintaining his image of her as an ice bitch. The woman who had tried to hire his services had been a professional woman, prim and cool, consummately businesslike in her designer suit, not a hair out of place. That woman had been easy for him to dislike. But that guise was long gone now, and her efforts to appear calm and in control were no longer irritating but touching—or they would have been had he been susceptible.

She hiccuped and sniffled and swatted at the mosquitoes that were rising off the water in squadrons to swarm up around her head, and Lucky clenched his jaw against the very foreign urge to feel sympathy.

"I hate this place," Serena announced, smacking at the mosquitoes with both hands. The swarm dispersed and regrouped to mount another sortie. She hiccuped and sniffed again, sounding perilously close to bawling. Her voice trembled with the effort to hold the tears back. "I have *always* hated this place."

Great. Lucky frowned. The fate of the swamp was coming to rest on the shoulders of a woman who hated it.

He eased the pirogue to a halt and secured the pole. He stepped gingerly around Serena, narrowly avoiding having her hit him in the groin as she slapped at the mosquitoes. He snatched up the wad of *baire* he kept in the front of the boat and tossed the sheer netting over her like a dust cover over an old chair.

"Now you can stop your squirming before you capsize us and serve us up to the 'gators for dinner."

Serena shuddered at the mention of alligators, but didn't look at the water for evidence of any. "Thank you for your concern," she said dryly. "Why aren't the mosquitoes after you, enormous, half-naked target that you are."

"They like your perfume. Very uptown tastes, these skeeters have.

Mebbe you'd like to take some of them back to Charleston with you, *oui?*"

"Don't you start in on me," she warned, her voice hoarse from the big knot of emotion lodged like a rock in her throat. "You don't know anything about it."

"I know Giff needs you here," he said, taking up his stance behind her once again. The pirogue slid forward. "That is, if you care anything about your heritage. Mebbe you don't. You say you hate this place. Mebbe you'd like to see it poisoned and ruined, yes?"

"Gifford would never allow such a thing to happen."

"Gifford won't have any say in the matter if he doesn't take charge of the situation soon. He thinks it'll just go away if he stays out here and shoots at the Tristar rep every time he comes around."

"You make it sound like he's running away from the problem. Gifford Sheridan never ran from a fight in his life."

"Well, he's runnin' from this one."

"It's ridiculous," Serena insisted. "If he doesn't want to sell to Tristar, all he has to do is tell them no. I don't understand what the big problem is."

"Me, I'd say there's a lotta things here you don' understand, sugar," Lucky drawled.

Not the least of which was *him,* Serena thought, plucking at the edge of the mosquito netting. The man was a jumble of contradictions. Mean to her one minute and throwing mosquito netting over her the next; telling her in one breath he didn't involve himself in other people's affairs, then giving his commentary on the situation. She wouldn't have credited him with an abundance of compassion, but he was rescuing her from having to spend the night outside, and, barring nefarious reasons, compassion was the only motive she could see.

She wondered what kind of place he was taking her to. She didn't hold out much hope for luxurious accommodations. Her idea of a poacher's lair was just a notch above a cave with animal hides scattered over the floor. She pictured a tar-paper shack and a mud yard littered with dead electricity generators and discarded butane tanks. There would probably be a tumbledown shed full of poaching paraphernalia, racks of stolen pelts and buckets of rancid muskrat remains. Certainly it would be no better than Gifford's place. She couldn't imagine Lucky hanging curtains. He struck her as the sort of man who would pin up centerfolds from raunchy magazines on the walls and call it art.

They rounded a bend in the bayou, and a small, neat house came into view. It was set on a tiny hillock in an alcove that had been cleared of trees. Its weathered-cypress siding shimmered pale silver in the fading light. It was a house in the old Louisiana country style, an Acadian house built on masonry piers to keep it above the damp ground. Steps led onto a deep gallery that was punctuated by shuttered windows and a screen door. An exterior staircase led up from the gallery to the overhanging attic that formed the ceiling of the gallery—a classic characteristic of Cajun architecture. Slim wooden columns supporting the overhang gave the little house a gracious air.

Serena was delightfully surprised to see something so neat and civilized in the middle of such a wilderness, but nothing could have surprised her more than to hear Lucky tell her it was his.

He scowled at the look of utter shock she directed up at him through the mosquito netting. "What'sa matter, *chère*? You were expecting some old white-trash shack with a yard full of pigs and chickens rootin' through the garbage?"

"Stop putting words in my mouth," she grumbled, unwilling to admit her unflattering thoughts, no matter how obvious they might have been.

A corner of Lucky's mouth curled upward, and his heavy-lidded eyes focused on her lips with the intensity of lasers. "Is there something else you want me to put there?"

Serena's heart thudded traitorously at the involuntary images that flitted through her mind. It was all she could do to keep her gaze from straying to the part of his anatomy that was at her eye level.

"You've really cornered the market on arrogance, haven't you?" she said, as disgusted with herself as she was with him.

"Me?" he said innocently, tapping a fist to his chest. *"Non.* I just know what a woman really wants, that's all."

"I'm sure you don't have the vaguest idea what a woman really wants," Serena said as she untangled herself from the *baire* and tossed it aside. She offered Lucky her hand as if she were a queen, and allowed him to hand her up onto the dock, giving him a smug smile as her feet settled on the solid wood. "But if you want to go practice your theory on yourself, don't let me stop you."

Lucky watched her walk away, perversely amused by her sass. She was limping slightly, but that didn't detract from the alluring sway of the backside that filled her snug white pants to heartshaped perfection. Desire coiled like a spring in his gut. He might not have known what

Miss Sheridan really wanted, but he damn well knew what his body wanted.

It was going to be a long couple of days.

He pulled the pirogue up out of the water and left it with its cargo of suitcases and crawfish to join Serena on the gallery. He didn't like having her there. This place revealed things about him. Having her there allowed her to get too close when his defenses were demanding he keep her an emotional mile away. He might have wanted her physically, but that was as far as it went. He had learned the hard way not to let anyone inside the walls he had painstakingly built around himself. He would have been safer if she could have gone on believing he lived like an animal in some ancient rusted-out house trailer.

"It's very nice," she said politely as he trudged up the steps onto the gallery.

"It's just a house," he growled, jerking the screen door open. "Go in and sit down. I'm gonna take the sliver out of that foot of yours before gangrene sets in."

Serena bared her teeth at him a parody of a smile. "Such a gracious host," she said, sauntering in ahead of him.

The interior of the house was as much of a surprise to her as the exterior had been. It consisted of two large rooms, both visible from the entrance—a kitchen and dining area, and a bedroom and living area. The place was immaculate. There was no pile of old hunting boots, no stacks of old porno magazines, no mountains of laundry, no litter of food-encrusted pots and pans. From what Serena could see on her initial reconnaissance, there wasn't as much as a dust bunny on the floor.

Lucky struck a match and lit a pair of kerosene lamps on the dining table, flooding the room with buttery-soft light, then left the room without a word. Serena pulled out a chair and sat down, still marveling. His decorating style was austere, as spare and plain as an Amish home, a style that made the house itself seem like a work of art. The walls had a wainscoting of varnished cypress paneling beneath soft white plaster. The furnishings appeared to be meticulously restored antiques—a wide-plank cypress dining table, a large French armoire that stood against the wall, oak and hickory chairs with rawhide seats. In the kitchen area mysterious bunches of plants had been hung by their stems from a wide beam to dry. Ropes of garlic and peppers adorned the window above the sink in lieu of a curtain.

Lucky appeared to approve of refrigeration and running water, but

63

not electric lights. Another contradiction. It made Serena vaguely uncomfortable to think there was so much more to him than she had been prepared to believe. It would have been easy to dislike a man who lived in a hovel and poached for a living. This house and its contents put him in a whole other light—one he didn't particularly like to have her see him in, if the look on his face was any indication.

He emerged with first aid supplies cradled in one brawny arm from what she assumed was a bathroom. These he set on the table, then he pulled up a chair facing hers and jerked her foot up onto his lap, nearly pulling her off her seat. He tossed her shoe aside and gave her bare foot a ferocious look, lifting it to eye level and turning it to capture the best light. Serena clutched the arm of her chair with one hand and the edge of the table with the other, straining against tipping over backward. She winced as Lucky prodded at the sliver.

"Stubborn as that grandpapa of yours, walkin' around half the day with this in your foot," he grumbled, plying the tweezers. *"Espèsces de tête dure."*

"What does that mean? Ouch!"

"You're a hardheaded thing."

"Ouch!" She tried to jerk her foot back.

"Be still!"

"You sadist!"

"Quit squirming!"

"Ou-ou-ouch!"

"Got it."

She felt an instant of blessed relief as soon as the splinter was out of her foot, but it was short-lived. Serena hissed through her teeth at the first sting of the alcohol, blinking furiously at the tears that automatically rose in her eyes.

"Your bedside manner leaves a lot to be desired," she said harshly.

Lucky raised his eyes and stared at her over her toes. The corners of his mouth turned up. "Yeah, but my manner *in* bed won't leave anything to be desired. I can promise you that, *chère.*"

Serena met his hypnotic gaze, her heart beating a wild pulse in her throat as his long fingers gently traced the bones of her foot and ankle. All thoughts of pain vanished from her head. Desire coursed through her veins in a sudden hot stream that both excited and frightened her. She didn't react this way to men. She certainly shouldn't have been reacting this way to *this* man. What had become of her common sense? What had become of her control?

With an effort she found her voice, but it was soft and smoky and she barely recognized it when she spoke. "That's no promise, that's a threat."

Lucky eased her foot down and rose slowly. His fingers curled around the arms of Serena's chair and he tilted it back on its hind legs, his eyes never leaving hers as he leaned down close.

"Is it?" he said in a silken whisper, his mouth inches from hers. "Are you afraid of me, *chère?*"

"No," she said, the tremor in her voice making a mockery of her answer. She stared up at him, eyes wide, her breath escaping in a thin stream from between her parted lips. The molten heat in his gaze stirred an answering warmth inside her and she found herself suddenly staring at his mouth, that incredibly sensuous, beautifully carved mouth.

"You're not afraid of me?" he said, arching a brow, the words barely audible. He leaned closer still. "Then mebbe this is what you're afraid of."

He closed the distance between them, touching his lips to hers.

The heat was instantaneous. It burst around them and inside them, as bright and hot as the flare of the lamps on the table beside them. Serena sucked in a little gasp, drawing Lucky closer. He settled his mouth against hers, telling himself he wanted just a taste of her, nothing more, but fire swept through him, his blood scalding his veins. One taste. Just one taste . . . would never be enough.

Her mouth was like silk soaked in wine—soft, sweet, intoxicating. His tongue slipped between her parted lips to better savor the experience. He stroked and explored and Serena responded in kind, reacting on instinct. Her tongue slid sinuously against Lucky's. His plunged deeper into her mouth. The flames leapt higher.

A moan drifted up from Serena's throat, and her arms slid up around Lucky's neck. She could feel herself growing dizzy, as if her body were floating up out of the chair. Dimly she realized Lucky was rising and pulling her up with him. His arms banded around her like steel, lifting her, pulling her close. His big hands slid down to the small of her back and pressed her into him.

He was fully aroused. His erection pressed into her belly, as hard as granite, as tempting as sin. She arched against it wantonly, reacting without thought. A growl rumbled deep in his chest, and he rolled his hips against her as he changed the angle of the kiss and plunged his tongue into her mouth again and again.

He stroked a hand down over the full swell of one hip. Cupping her buttock, he lifted her to bring her feminine mound up against his hardness. She made a small, frightened sound in her throat and need surged through him like a flood. He wanted her. God, he wanted her! He wanted to take her right here, right now, on the table, on the floor. It was madness.

Madness.

Sweet heaven, what was he doing? he wondered, finally hearing the alarm bells clanging in his head. What was she doing to him? He set her away from him with a violence that made her stumble back against the chair she'd been sitting in. She stared at him, her eyes wide and dark with a seductive mix of passion and fear. Her hair tumbled around her shoulders in golden disarray. Her mouth, swollen and red from the force of his kiss, trembled. She stared at him as if he were something wild and terrifying.

Wild was exactly what he was feeling—out of control, beyond the reach of reason. His chest was heaving like a bellows as he tried to draw in enough oxygen to think straight. He speared his hands into his hair and hung his head, closing his eyes. Control. He needed control.

Control. She'd lost control—of the situation, of herself. Serena swallowed hard and pressed a hand to her bruised lips. How could this have happened? She didn't even *like* the man. But the instant his mouth had touched hers she had experienced an explosion of desire that had melted everything else. She hadn't thought of anything but his mouth on hers, the taste of him, the strength of his arms, the feel of his body. Shivers rocked through her now like the aftershocks of an earthquake. Heaven help her, she didn't know herself anymore. What had become of her calm self-discipline, her training, her ability to distance herself from a situation and examine it analytically?

You wanted him, Serena. How's that for analysis?

She shook her head a little in stunned disbelief. "I think I would have been safer with the coon hounds," she mumbled.

Something flashed in Lucky's eyes. His expression went cold. *"Non.* You're safe in this house, lady. I'm out of here."

He turned and stormed into the next room. There was a banging of doors that made Serena wince. When he reappeared he was wearing a black T-shirt that hugged his chest like a coat of paint. He shrugged on a shoulder holster. The pistol it cradled looked big enough to bring down an elephant. Serena felt her eyes widen and her jaw drop.

"It's not hunting season." She didn't realize she had spoken aloud, but Lucky turned and gave her a long, very disturbing look, his panther's eyes glowing beneath his heavy dark brows.

"It is for what I'm after," he said in a silky voice.

He pulled the gun and checked the load. The clip slid back into place with a smooth, sinister hiss and click. Then he was gone. He slipped out the door like a shadow, without a sound.

Serena felt the hair rise up on the back of her neck. For a long moment she stood there, frozen with fear in the heat of the night. With an effort she finally forced her feet to move and went to the screen door to look out.

The night was as black as fresh tar with only a sliver of moon shining down on the bayou. The water gleamed like a sheet of glass. She thought she caught a glimpse of Lucky poling his pirogue out toward a stand of cypress, but in a blink he was gone, vanished, as if he were a creature from the darkest side of the night, able to appear and disappear at will.

"Heaven help me," she whispered, brushing her fingertips across her bottom lip. "What have I gotten myself into now?"

Chapter Seven

The pirogue cut across the inky surface of the bayou as softly as a whisper on the wind. Mist drifted like smoke among the smooth dark trunks of the trees. The air was heavy with scents, like a courtesan's perfume, sweet, almost palpable—honeysuckle and jasmine, verbena and wisteria, all mingling with the darker metallic scent of the water and the decaying growth that lay beneath it. Intertwined with scent was sound—the chirp and trill of insects, the song of frogs, the call of an owl and the whoosh of its wings as it left its perch. In the distance an alligator roared, a nutria screamed. Night feeders had come out to hunt and be hunted.

Lucky let his boat drift toward the shelter of a massive live oak that overhung the water's edge. The bank had been eaten way to the gnarled roots of the tree and formed a tiny cove that was deep enough to keep the boat afloat. It provided natural cover with the canopy of the tree spreading out wide and low, its ragged beards of moss hanging down like a moth-eaten curtain. It was the perfect place to wait.

He dug a cigarette from the pack in his shirt pocket and lit it, taking a deep, soothing drag. The tip flared red in the gloom of the night. The match hissed as it hit the surface of the water. Tension hummed inside him like an overloaded power line. Tension for the job he was here to do, but a greater part of it was sexual frustration. He'd never wanted a woman so badly in his life. Never. Not even in his youth when his hormones had roared in perpetual high gear. Not even after he'd spent a year in a Central American prison. He had never wanted a woman more than he had wanted Serena Sheridan in that blinding flash of heat. He was still shaking with the intensity of it. He was still half hard.

Damn her. *Why* her? Of all the women on the planet, why her? How could it be possible for him to look at Serena and remember Shelby's duplicity and still want her?

She wasn't Shelby. He knew that. Shelby would never have come after Gifford. She would never have stood nose to nose with the old man and matched him temper for temper. Shelby's methods of getting what she wanted fell more into the eyelash-batting and pouting categories. No, in terms of personality, the sisters were nothing alike. Shelby was all calculated flirtation and coy charm. Serena was all business and sass. Still, he didn't want to want her. She was dangerous to his sanity, reminding him of the past and the affair that had set his life on a near-disastrous course.

He had surrendered to Shelby's charms, succumbed to her, and lost himself. He was a junior at the University of Southwestern Louisiana in Lafayette, young and hot and full of himself, caught up in the idea of taking the world by storm, determined to show everybody what he could do. The big brooding kid everyone watched with a wary eye was going to be the first Doucet to get a college education. He was going to be a biologist. Having Shelby Sheridan on his arm—and in his bed—was another feather in his cap. He had the world by the tail that spring. Then it turned around and knocked him senseless.

He was nothing but a means to an end, a tool for Shelby to get what she really wanted—John Mason Talbot IV. Talbot was balking at the idea of marriage. Shelby took up with Lucky to provoke jealousy. A simple, time-honored plan. The fact that she had gotten pregnant with his baby had been an inconvenience easily dealt with just as soon as Talbot put his ring on her finger.

Lucky could still taste the bitterness. He hadn't loved Shelby as much as he had loved the idea of her. When she dropped him, the blow to his youthful ego was terrible. When he found out about the aborted pregnancy, the cut went to his very core. Shelby had shattered

69

his pride with careless ease and gone on with her life as if nothing had happened at all, while pain and humiliation drove him to abandon school and all his grand plans.

With youthful drama he dropped everything and joined the army, sending his life down a path that led to a gray place of shadowed existence, where there was no good or evil, only missions and objectives, a place where his soul was stripped away from him a little bit at a time.

Thirteen years passed and he could still feel the shame of having been played for a fool by a pretty dark-eyed blond belle.

And now he was being tempted by another.

He swore in French and flung the butt of his cigarette away. As if he didn't have enough trouble already, he had to go stirring up old nests of resentment. Maybe that was it. Maybe it was revenge he wanted when he looked at Serena. Or maybe he was complicating matters unnecessarily. Maybe it was just sex.

Hell, he could handle sex. It would be fabulous between them. He already knew that. The instant he'd touched his mouth to hers he'd been wild to get inside her. And she'd lost that cool control of hers and responded to him with all the fire she had previously reserved for sarcasm. Yeah, he could handle sex with Serena Sheridan. The idea of having all that cool beauty and inner heat beneath him and around him damn near made him burn up from the inside out.

It was an emotional entanglement he wanted to avoid. He was smart enough to keep that from happening. He wouldn't let Serena get that close to him. He wouldn't let anyone get that close, not even his family. He didn't have anything left to give anyone. He guarded what was left of his soul like a miser.

The distant buzz of an outboard motor broke in on his thoughts. Lucky came to attention, following the sound carefully. It wasn't too far off—over on the next bayou and nearing the fork that branched into the little no-name stream he was on. He was exactly where he needed to be. A nasty smile unfurled across his dark face. He pulled a pair of infrared goggles from his gear bag, put them on, then took up his *baire* and draped it over himself, pulled his gun, and waited.

Serena couldn't sleep. She hadn't tried. Her exhaustion went bone deep, but the fear went deeper. She was alone. It didn't seem to matter very much that she was in a house with a roof over her head. She was still in the swamp, alone. In the ordinary course of things she thought of herself as a strong, competent, self-reliant individual able to handle most anything that might come her way. This she couldn't quite handle. Even after all these years the memories were too strong. Every sight, every sound, every smell only brought them into sharper focus. She would have given her left arm for a Valium. Just one. Anything to dull the little knives that were splitting her nerve endings.

"Pull yourself together, Serena," she muttered aloud, tightening her arms across her chest in a symbolic gesture as she paced the width of the dining room. "If your patients could see you now, they'd pack up their neuroses and go shrink shopping."

A skittering sound rattled across the gallery just as she passed the screen door. She shrieked and bolted sideways, banging her knee and stubbing her toe on a table leg. She swore a litany of curses under her breath and limped around the table.

In the time since Lucky had left she had done little else but pace. She had washed up in the tiny spotless bathroom, found a comb and restored some order to her hair. She'd made a sandwich with a spongy slice of Evangeline Maid white bread and peanut butter and eaten on the move, too keyed up to sit. Really, she'd been too keyed up to eat, but she knew from experience that not eating properly only magnified her paranoia. So she had walked and chewed, hiking over every inch of the first floor of Lucky's house.

There was nothing much to distract her from her fear. There was no television, no radio, no stereo. She spotted a CB radio on a shelf in the kitchen, but she had no idea how to work it. She couldn't even amuse herself by unpacking and repacking her suitcase because it was still outside.

She assumed Lucky had taken her luggage out of his pirogue. It probably wouldn't do for a poacher to be caught toting silk lingerie and a supply of makeup. Other swamp boys might get the wrong idea. But even if he had left her bags on the dock, they weren't going to do her any good because there was no way in hell she was walking out to get them. The ground was literally crawling out here at night. In her imagination she could picture herself trying to tiptoe across yards of writhing reptilian bodies.

"Stop it!" she snapped as a spasm of fear ran down her back and a wave of it rose up in her throat as thick and sour as grease.

From somewhere in the far distance beyond the front door came the *crack! crack!* of what sounded like gunfire.

Lucky.

"Oh my God," Serena whispered. Her eyes teared up and she lifted a trembling hand to her lips. What if he were shot? What if he were killed? What if whoever did him in came looking for God knew what?

Her heart thudding like a paddle ball behind her ribs, she crept toward the door, straining her eyes to see something in the stygian blackness beyond. For a moment all she could hear was the blood roaring in her ears, then the raspy screech of frogs. Something screamed, a terrible blood-chilling sound that might have been an animal in its death throes or a woman on the brink of hysteria. The sound tore across the night like a knife ripping through silk and then it was gone, leaving an eerie stillness in its wake. Serena sucked back a sob and moved quickly away from the door and into the next room.

She resumed her pacing, picking up speed as she walked a path from the front window past the old horsehide sofa to the bed and back. The sore on the bottom of her foot had gone past the point of pain to numbness. She wished for the pain back; it would have been some-thing else to think about besides this awful choking fear.

She tried to think about the situation at Chanson du Terre, but there were still too many pieces missing for her to make any sense of it. Thoughts of her last few moments with Lucky drifted through her head, but she shooed them away. She didn't yet want to consider the ramifications of getting that close to man who claimed to be crazy and carried a gun.

Her toe connected with something solid hidden under his bed as she turned the corner to pace back toward the front window. Hesi-tantly, she turned to face the bed. It was a mahogany half-tester with delicately carved details. A thick curtain of mosquito netting was draped back from the headpiece. The coverlet was an exquisite exam-ple of Cajun weaving in soft brown cotton with narrow indigo stripes.

The idea of Lucky, pagan and barbaric, stretched out naked on this elegant bed stirred the embers of desire deep inside her. She could see him, dark skin against white sheets, his stallion's mane loose across the pillow, his golden eyes staring up at her, hot and mesmerizing.

Serena shook her head in amazement. How could she want a man who was so contrary to her idea of what a modern man should be? She knew there were women who wanted to be dominated, women who would have melted into puddles at the feet of a man like Lucky Dou-cet. She was not among them. She had always held to the idea of equality between the sexes. Lucky was a throwback to the heyday of male chauvinism. She didn't trust him, didn't like him, didn't respect him. How could she want him?

Her gaze roamed over the bed again, and heat unfurled like a dozen ribbons in her belly, tickling, tantalizing.

Tearing her thoughts away from sex, she dropped to her knees on the woven rug beside the bed and lifted the edge of the coverlet. There were several large cardboard boxes stashed away and she reached for one, stopping herself just as her fingertips grazed the edge. She could find something she would be better off not knowing about. Or she could find something that would give her a clue to who Lucky Doucet really was. She nibbled her lip in indecision but jerked the box toward her as another strange scratching sound drifted in through the window.

The carton was packed with books.

"God, who would have guessed he even knew how to read," she muttered to herself.

Her fingers drifted lightly over the spines of the hardbound volumes that had been so carefully packed. They were largely college-level text books on biology. There was a collection of Shakespeare, several tomes on art history, and a set of small, very old-looking volumes with French titles in faded gold print. Serena carefully lifted out one of the science books and turned back the cover. It smelled musty and sweet and the pages stuck together as she turned to the title page and read the handwritten note in the upper righthand corner:

Etienne Doucet. USL. 1979.

College. She tried to imagine Lucky walking the hallowed halls of USL, going to class with books in his arms, but could picture him only in army fatigue pants and no shirt, climbing up into a tower with an assault rifle. But he'd been a student, and a serious one, if these books were anything to go by. Why then was he making his living by nefarious means?

"I'm over the edge. I might do anything."

"He's been living like an animal out in the swamp ever since he got out of the army. Folks say he's half crazy."

How did a student of science and the arts make the jump to the military and from the military to here? What had happened? What events had shaped him into the tough, sullen man he was today?

Her mind working on the question, Serena replaced the book and shoved the box back under the bed. She perched herself on the edge of the bed and sat there for a long moment, thinking, her gaze drifting around the room as she tried to make sense of the enigma that was Lucky.

The stillness crept in on her by degrees. By the time she was fully aware of it, it seemed absolute. The night that had seemed almost raucous with sound was suddenly silent. The eeriness of it felt like fingers tracing down her back.

She felt totally vulnerable. If someone outside the house were bent on coming in, the only thing to stop an intruder was a screen door. She thought she heard the scrape of a boot on the gallery floor, but the sound was gone so quickly she might have imagined it. The fear that had temporarily abated rushed back like a flood tide. There was more than snakes and alligators to be wary of in the swamp at night. The faces of the men Lucky had confronted at Mosquito Mouton's came to mind with nauseating clarity, and the big man's threat came back loud and clear—*I'll get you* . . .

Serena blew out the kerosene lamp on the nightstand, dousing the room in blackness. Grabbing a heavy brass candlestick, she crept on tiptoe toward the front wall. Lucky could fight his own fights, she was sure, but if his enemies came looking for him, she was not interested in being made a secondary target for their violence.

She pressed her back against the wall beside the window and strained to hear. Nothing . . . a faint thump . . . or was that just her heartbeat? She inched her way toward the door, breath aching in her lungs, candlestick raised in a white-knuckled fist.

A hand grabbed her arm from behind.

She didn't have time to draw breath to scream before she'd been spun around and pinned to the wall. A large hand clamped over her mouth and a heavy male body pressed into hers, his weight holding her with ridiculous ease. The candlestick dropped from her grasp and clattered to the floor.

"You lookin' to put a few dents in my head, sugar?"

Serena went limp against the wall. The tension ran out of her, leaving the trembling afterglow of fear. Lucky. He dropped his hand from her mouth and eased back from her, an amused smile twitching his lips. The smile died the instant Serena launched herself at him.

"You bastard! Of all the rotten things to do!"

He caught her by the wrists and held her off. "Hey, cool out!"

"I will not cool out!" She aimed a kick at his shin, but he dodged it easily, which only made her angrier. "If you had any idea how frightened I was to begin with— Damn you!" she raged, tears of terror swelling over the dam of her lashes. She kicked again and won the satisfaction of hearing him grunt as her toe made contact. "If you had any idea . . ."

It all caught up with her then. The fear, the memories, the episode with Gifford, her exhaustion, the futility of trying to hurt Lucky all rushed up on her and hit with the strength and finesse of a freight train. She stopped struggling against him. His grip relaxed and she jerked her arms back, pulling free. She turned toward the door and pressed her hands over her face as the last brick in her wall of resolve crumbled.

She didn't want to be there. She didn't want to be frightened. She didn't want to have to deal with any family problems. She didn't want to have to deal with a man like Lucky.

Tears came very much against her will, but she didn't have the strength to stop them. They rolled like pearls down her cheeks.

Lucky watched with something akin to horror. The sound of a woman crying flipped a panic switch inside him. He could deal with her smart mouth and her cool reserve and the temper she had just unleashed on him, but tears . . . *Dieu!* And these were the real thing, not some phony whimpering designed to win her something. These were real tears, and it was plain she didn't like having him see them. She kept her back to him, her shoulders rigid as she tried in vain to fight them off. He stood there helpless, his hands jammed at his waist. The image of her standing on the pier at Gauthier's came back to him —the way the color had suddenly washed from her face as she'd looked down at his pirogue, the impression he'd had of inner fragility. It was there again, that sense that something inside her had cracked.

He couldn't help but feel empathy. He knew what it was to feel strength give way inside, to feel darkness creeping in like cold black ink. It didn't matter how many times he told himself he wouldn't get involved with her beyond the physical sense. It didn't matter how detached he told himself he was. He couldn't ignore this kind of pain.

"Hey," he said, coming to stand directly behind her. He rested a hand on her shoulder and held on, gentle but firm, as she tried to shrug him off. "What'sa matter, *chère?* Did I scare you that bad? I didn't mean to. I don' like comin' in the front door. It's an old habit that's saved my miserable hide more than once. Saved me from gettin' a goose egg this time," he said, pushing at the candlestick with the toe of his boot.

"It's not that," Serena whispered miserably. She shook her head and tried to sniff back the tears, but they still squeezed out to dribble down her face. She felt too defeated to cling to her pride. It served no purpose anyway. Why not tell him and get it over with? He probably thought the worst of her as it was, and what did it matter if he did? She didn't have to answer to him.

"It's this place. The swamp," she said. She brushed her hair back from her face and stared out the door at the shades of darkness beyond. "It terrifies me."

"Is that why you never went out to get your bags?"

Serena nodded. "I'm sure it seems completely stupid to you, but going out there in the dark is one of my worst nightmares."

"Why is that?" Lucky asked, backing a step away from her and letting his hand drop from her shoulder. "Why do you hate this place so? Is it too dirty for you? Too primal? It offends your sophisticated sensibilities that much?"

The bitterness in his voice touched Serena's raw nerves like acid. She jerked around to face him, glaring up at him through her tears. "Stop it. I'm sick of your reverse snobbery. Stop putting me down because I prefer to live in a city and hold a regular job and wear a complete set of clothes. You don't know anything about me. You don't have any idea why I hate this place."

"Then tell me." He spoke it like a challenge, told himself he didn't care what the answer was, and waited to hear it just the same.

Serena blew a long sigh of resignation between her lips. Wrapping her arms around herself, she turned once again to face the door. "When I was seventeen I got lost out here," she began, relating the tale in a voice carefully devoid of emotion. "My sister and I and some friends came out for the day in Giff's bass boat. We were just fooling around, having fun. We had packed a picnic lunch and we stopped off at a little clearing to eat. I wasn't sure where we were, but the boy driving the boat said he was, so I didn't worry about it.

"Shelby and I started getting on each other about something. I don't even remember what it was. We were always like that—bickering over little things, always taking opposite sides of an issue no matter how trivial. Anyway, when we got ready to leave, I realized I had forgotten my jacket in the clearing and went back alone to get it. Shelby talked the boy who was driving the boat into leaving me there."

"She left you there. Alone." Anger simmered in Lucky's gut, hot and furious. *Shelby.* "The bitch."

Serena made a dismissive gesture with one hand, then tucked it

76

back against her. "It was just a spiteful joke. She didn't mean for anything bad to happen."

"Didn't she?" Lucky said flatly.

"No. Of course not. She was just mad at me and wanted to give me a scare. They went off in the boat, intending to come back and get me in an hour or so, but a storm blew up.

"It was one of those days. The sky was blue one minute and black the next." She could still see it clearly in her mind's eye—the clouds rolling in across the swamp, gray and black with a strange yellow tinge, like noxious smoke boiling up out of a hundred factory chimneys. She could still taste the air, could still feel the weight of it pressing on her the moment before the storm broke. She could still hear the deafening thunder, the vicious cracks of the lightning as it ripped across the sky.

"It rained so hard it looked like ice coming down in sheets. It stormed for hours, and when the thunder and lightning finally quit, it just kept on pouring. I got scared. I knew no one would be able to come and get me with a boat the way it was raining. I thought if I got pointed in the right direction, I might be able to find my way back. I was wrong."

She stopped there, unable to talk about what it had been like to walk on and on, following swelling streams that ran one direction and then another, turning so many times she'd had no idea whether she had been going toward home or hell. She couldn't talk about the terror of spending the night with no shelter, no supplies, no food. She couldn't put into words what it had felt like to crouch on a tree stump as that dark water swirled up toward her, driving a trio of cottonmouths up to share her perch.

The pressure building inside her as she relived the memories forced the false sense of calm from her voice. "I don't remember a lot of what happened," she said in a tremulous whisper. "I blocked a lot of it out. I remember being cold and wet . . . and so afraid, I thought I'd choke on it . . . shaking so hard with fear that I almost couldn't walk. I remember the look on Gifford's face when they found me."

"How long did it take?"

"Two days."

Lucky swore under his breath. He had grown up on the bayous, fishing and hunting with his father and brothers, exploring just for the sheer joy of it. It was nothing for him to spend days in this wilderness. He knew every plant, every animal, every insect, every inch of mud and water. But he could imagine the kind of girl Serena had been—a soft, pretty debutante, member of the country club and cheerleading squad—and he could imagine her terror. The swamp was an unforgiving place, a place of natural beauty and natural violence. It didn't suffer fools gladly. Serena had been thrown into it completely unprepared. Considering the circumstances, that she had survived was a miracle.

And it had all been Shelby's fault.

It was Shelby's fault Serena was standing before him now, her fierce pride in tatters, trembling as if she were being given jolts of electricity at regular intervals. She had had this fear inflicted on her by her own sister, her twin. That was unthinkable to Lucky. Whatever else he might have done in his life, he had never intentionally hurt one of his own family members. But Shelby had. Shelby, who didn't care whom she hurt as long as she got what she wanted.

Anger surged through him now as he stared down at Serena. Anger and an emotion he refused to recognize as protectiveness. She stood with her back to him, but he had shifted to one side so he could see a little of her face over her shoulder. She looked impossibly young and sad standing there with her hair down around her shoulders and no makeup on her face.

"I was in the hospital for a week," she said. "Suffering from exposure and snakebite. As you can see, I never did quite get over it." She gave a little laugh, but it held no humor, only pain and frustration and a sense of shame. She sniffed and shrugged. "Now you know my disgraceful little secret: The calm, cool psychologist has a phobia she can't overcome."

Lucky closed his eyes and folded his arms around her, holding her because he knew how badly she needed comforting. He could hear it in her voice and he couldn't keep from responding. He pulled her back against his big, solid body and marveled absently at how perfectly she fit.

Serena didn't fight his embrace. She wasn't sure what it meant, this show of caring from such a hard man, but she accepted it. She let herself lean back against his strength and soaked in the feeling of safety his arms inspired. In that moment it didn't matter how they'd fought or how different they were from each other. He was just a man offering her compassion when she needed it badly. She turned her head and pressed her cheek to his chest, listening to the solid thud of his heartbeat.

"This is why you didn't want to come out here in the pirogue, *oui?*" he asked softly, resting his cheek against the top of her head without even realizing it, certainly without recognizing the tenderness of the gesture.

"I didn't want to come out here, period."

"Why did you?"

"Because I had to. Somebody had to."

"That you're so afraid of the swamp—why didn't you tell me this sooner?"

"And give you another reason to sneer at me? No thank you. Frankly, I didn't think my fears would be of any interest to a man like you."

"We've all of us got fears, *chère,*" he murmured almost to himself.

She looked up at him over her shoulder, arching a brow. "Even big, bad Lucky Doucet?"

Lucky said nothing. It was one thing to have Serena confess to him. It would be quite something else to turn the tables. He wouldn't, couldn't, let her get that close to him. He had worked too hard to pull himself together to let some lady shrink dissect him.

"What are you afraid of, Lucky?" she whispered, her dark eyes glowing with intelligence and curiosity. There were tear tracks on her cheeks and her mouth looked soft and vulnerable.

"Nothing," he murmured, turning her in his arms, "nothing." He lowered his mouth to hers.

He kissed her deeply, parting her lips expertly and sliding his tongue into her mouth in a gesture of possession. She tasted salty and sweet and so damn good his mind nearly went numb from it. He stroked his hands over the unbound silk of her hair and down her back to the subtle curves of her hips.

He hadn't stopped wanting her in the time he'd been gone. The fire had merely been banked, not put out. The flames leapt to life as her mouth moved beneath his, as her body moved against his. He had pulled away the first time, but he had no intention of pulling away now. He wanted her. It was desire, nothing deeper, nothing more complex than the basic story of a man wanting a woman, of a male needing a female.

With one hand splayed across the small of her back, he pulled her hips tighter against his. With his other hand he found the hem of her top and slipped beneath it to stroke the smooth satin of her skin. With deft fingers he unsnapped the front catch of her bra and cupped a breast. The fullness of it surprised him. The feel of her nipple hardening at the brush of his fingertips excited him.

He dragged his mouth from Serena's lips to her jaw to her ear. She shivered as he traced the delicate shell with the tip of his tongue and trembled when he whispered to her, his voice as dark and hot as the night.

"I want your breast in my mouth, *chère*. I wanna taste you. I wanna feel your nipple between my lips."

A whimper caught in her throat.

"I wanna be inside you. I wanna feel you around me, tight and hot and wet."

Serena's mind reeled with the seductive images he was conjuring. She could feel her temperature rising, sexual desire like a fever in her blood. It was exhilarating, intoxicating, frightening. Her body pressed against his, making its own desires known even as her mind grappled for control.

He kissed her throat, letting his teeth graze the skin. Serena caught her breath against the moan that threatened, but she couldn't stop herself from arching her neck to give him better access. He whispered a more explicit request in her ear, then sucked gently at the soft petal of her earlobe.

"No," she barely managed to say between gasps. It sounded more like a question than an answer. "No," she said more forcefully.

Lucky rolled her nipple between thumb and forefinger, tugging subtly at the turgid peak. He raised his head a fraction and stared down at her, his eyes heavy-lidded and dark with passion, the thin band of amber ringing the pupils as warm as the light from the lamp on the table.

"Yes, *chère*," he whispered.

Serena's gaze drifted to his mouth, that incredible, sensuous mouth, gleaming wet and red from their kiss. She stared at it, imagining it at her breast, tugging, sucking, his tongue laving her nipple while his fingers stroked her most sensitive flesh.

"No," she murmured, the word barely a breath moving from her lips. "I hardly know you."

"You know I'm a man. I know you're a woman. What more do we need to know?"

"We don't even like each other."

Lucky growled low in his throat as his mouth moved toward hers. "I'm likin' you just fine right now, sugar." He kissed a corner of her mouth, probing gently at the cleft of her lips with the tip of his tongue.

"J'aime te faire l'amour avec toi," he breathed the words against her lips. *"Bien, ma chère, casse pas mon coeur."*

He might have been saying anything. He might have been telling her she was uglier than a mule, but the words, spoken in his smoky voice and flavored with their rich French accent, had their desired effect just the same. Serena felt her common sense further diluted by desire. A languid weakness floated through her arms and legs. She leaned heavily against Lucky and his scent filled her head—musky and warm and indisputably male.

He kissed her again, filling her mouth with his taste. His fingers left her breast to encircle the wrist of her right hand. He drew it down from where it rested flat against his chest and pressed it to the shaft of his manhood, letting her feel his length, his hardness. Serena moaned, a sound that managed to combine longing and admiration.

He moved against her hand, nuzzled her cheek, nipped her ear. "That's all for you, angel. Let me give it to you, *chère.*"

Serena let her fingers flex hesitantly. Another wave of heat flashed through her. Oh, God, she wanted him. She wanted a man she'd only just met, a man who was a mystery to her, a man whose overwhelming masculinity frightened her on a fundamental level.

She turned her head away to draw in a deep breath, and her gaze hit the butt of the semi-automatic pistol that nestled against his ribs. Her heart skipped a beat, then rushed into double time as she looked beyond the gun to his biceps. An ugly two-inch-long gash was carved in the flesh and a line of dried blood trailed from it.

He was a dangerous man. A criminal. A man without scruples.

Shaking from the conflict that raged inside her, Serena pushed herself back from him. "You're bleeding."

"What?"

"Your arm. The one next to the gun," she said pointedly. "It's bleeding."

"It's nothing." Lucky reached for her.

Serena stepped back, crossing her arms in front of her, still avoiding his gaze. "Not to me it's not."

He reached out slowly to touch her hair, lifting a golden lock to rub it between his fingers. "If I put a Band-Aid on it, will you go to bed with me?"

"No."

"Why not?"

"Because I don't indulge in meaningless sexual flings with men I barely know," she said, struggling to resurrect her façade of calm.

Lucky watched her lift her chin and straighten her shoulders and resented like hell the ease with which she seemed to throw off the need that still pounded through him. "You mean you'll fuck a man only if you think he'll put a ring on your finger," he said brutally.

"That's not what I said."

"*Mais non,* but that's what you meant."

"That isn't what I meant," Serena argued. "I don't believe in casual sex. I don't go to bed with men who have no intention of investing emotionally in a relationship just because they happen to be well hung. *That's* what I meant," she said bitingly. "Are you going to try to tell me you're in love with me?"

Lucky forced a laugh. "Not a chance."

Serena clenched her jaw against the unexpected stab of hurt his words inflicted. Of course he wasn't going to say it—not now, not ever. Nor did she want him to. "That settles it, then, doesn't it?"

"Only for tonight, sugar," he said, hooking a finger beneath her chin and tilting her head back. He bent his head and brushed a mocking gentleman's kiss against her lips. *"Bonsoir, chérie.* Sweet dreams."

Serena watched him saunter out the front door. She had no idea where he was going. She told herself she didn't want to know. At any rate, she was too exhausted to care. She'd been put through an emotional wringer, and every muscle and bone ached with it.

Avoiding even a glance at the bed, she curled herself into one corner of the sofa and tried not to think about Lucky, his heat, his passion . . . the way he had held her when she'd told him she was afraid. . . .

Chapter Eight

Serena sat in the pirogue, shading her eyes from the fierce morning sun that had come up like a ball of fire to burn off the low-lying fog. It was not yet noon and already the heat was as oppressive as a fur coat in July. She had dressed in a sleeveless white cotton blouse and khaki walking shorts, but even these summerweight garments wilted and clung to her and made her think longingly of a swim suit and a quiet day at the beach.

Adding to her discomfort was the knowledge that Lucky was standing behind her. She could feel him glowering down at her, and she straightened her back to show she wouldn't be intimidated by his evil mood.

She had gone searching for him at seven-thirty, eager to get to Gifford's—partly because she didn't quite trust herself to be alone with him. She had slept all of two hours after they had parted company the night before. And those two hours had been full of erotic dreams starring Guess Who. Just the memory was enough to make her blush. She didn't want to begin to decipher its meaning.

Lucky Doucet was trouble; he was an outlaw. The fact that he had a body to rival Adonis's couldn't enter into the argument. She couldn't get involved with him. She kept repeating that to herself like a mantra, but every time she thought she had herself convinced, her mind would sneak in the memory of the way he had held her after she'd told him about getting lost in the swamp. For that moment he had been gentle and tender and compassionate. . . .

He had been none of those things when she found him that morning. After searching the galleries back and front and finding only a trio of baby raccoons playing on the steps, she made her way up the exterior staircase to the attic.

Lucky stepped out and slammed the door shut behind him as she neared the landing, glaring at her with bleary, bloodshot eyes. His jaw was shadowed with morning beard. His hair was loose and disheveled, falling to his shoulders in unruly blue-black waves.

"What the hell are you doin' up here?" he demanded, his voice low and as rough as gravel. "I don' want you comin' up here. You got that?"

"Why?" Serena questioned, arching a brow. "Is this where you keep the bodies?"

"C'est pas de ton affaire," he muttered. "Never you mind what I keep up here. It's nothin' for a pretty shrink to go sniffin' through. You're a helluva lot better off not knowing."

The mere suggestion made Serena curious. What was he hiding? Stolen goods? Illegal liquor? Drugs? Guns? It could have been any of those things, all of them, or something even worse.

"I'm sure I don't care what you keep in there, Mr. Doucet," she said with as much cool as she could muster. "I only came up here looking for you."

He moved down to the step below hers, putting them nearly at eye level. Giving her a look that was at once calculatedly cruel and seductive, he lifted a hand to cup her cheek and brought his mouth down close to hers.

"Change your mind, sugar?"

"Certainly not." Making a disgusted face and leaning back to escape his breath, she fanned the aroma away with her hand. "You've been drinking."

"Heavily," Lucky said, straightening away from her. "You oughta try it sometime. Loosen you up. From what I've seen, you could stand it."

On that infuriating note, he turned and descended the stairs, his heavy boots barely making a sound on the wooden treads. Serena followed at a discreet distance, her mind wrestling with the conflicting facets of the man and with the conflicting emotions he aroused inside her. Her overriding thought was that the sooner she got to Gifford's, the sooner she would be free of Lucky Doucet and the strange spell he seemed to have cast over her.

While she sat at the table waiting impatiently, Lucky went through his morning ablutions without haste, shaving, showering, emerging from the bathroom barechested, wearing a pair of jeans that were nearly white with age. His wet hair was slicked back into its queue and bound with a length of leather boot lace. A scrap of red bandanna was tied around his right biceps, hiding the ugly wound he had acquired the night before.

Serena's gaze fastened on the makeshift bandage, and she felt something twist in her stomach. She told herself it was revulsion at the reminder of how this man made his living, but she knew that wasn't the whole truth. A part of that knot could be directly attributed to fear of what might have happened to him if the bullet had gone high and inside. He would have been dead and there would have been no chance left for anyone to reform him.

She shied away from the direction her thoughts were taking. That path was a dead end, a fast track to heartache.

"I suppose you'll tell me the other guy looks worse," she said, still staring at the bandage and the massive arm it was bound to. Looking at it at least kept her eyes off his chest and the taut, hard muscles of his stomach.

Lucky looked down at the bandanna as if getting grazed with a bullet had slipped his mind. He flicked a speculative glance at Serena. "*Mais yeah,* but then, he was an ugly son of a bitch to start with."

"Shouldn't you have a doctor look at that?"

"You're a doctor," he said, his voice low and rough, his eyes capturing hers. He braced his hands on the arms of her chair and leaned down until his mouth hovered a breath away from hers. "You wanna look at it?"

"No," Serena murmured, tensing against the waves of heat rippling through her. He was much too close: His body gave off an electrical charge that shorted out her common sense and stimulated the primitive instincts buried beneath her sophisticated façade. His clean male scent filled her nostrils, and she caught herself wondering what it would be like to kiss him when he tasted like toothpaste instead of tobacco.

85

"No?" he questioned softly, arching one black brow. "Is there some other part of me you'd care to examine, Dr. Sheridan?"

Her memory leapt at the opportunity to remind her of the way he had molded her hand to his erection. Serena bit back a curse, but she couldn't stop the heat from rising in her cheeks.

"Just say the word, sugar," Lucky announced. "Your wish is my command."

Serena broke away from the beam of his gaze and spoke through her teeth. "I wish you would stop wasting time on crude seduction routines and take me to Gifford's."

He backed away from her, his expression cold and closed. "You'll get there."

"When?"

"When I'm damn good and ready to take you."

He proceeded out onto the back porch, where he set down a dish of dry cat food for the baby raccoons, shooting Serena a look that dared her to comment. She stood at the back door, watching quietly as the little bandits gamboled around his big feet, vying for his attention, playing with his shoelaces. Lucky grumbled at them in French, but made no move to kick them away. He looked annoyed and embarrassed and Serena felt a most disastrous weakening in the heart she was trying to steel against him.

"It's just easier to feed them than have them in my garbage all the time, that's all," he said defensively. "It's not like they're pets."

The words had barely left his mouth when one of the coons sat up on its hind legs and snickered at him, reaching up with its front paws to bat at his pant leg.

"Why not just shoot them?" Serena asked sweetly. "You could save up all their little hides and make yourself a shirt."

Lucky narrowed his eyes and growled at her, but the effect was ruined when another raccoon reached from its perch on the gallery railing for the shiny button on Lucky's jeans. He arched away from it, scolding it in rapid French. The little coon sat back and whinnied at him, and he reached out grudgingly to scratch it behind one triangular ear.

Serena felt her heart give a traitorous thump. The big bad poacher had a soft spot for little animals. She reminded herself that even Hitler had had a pet, and she forced herself to go back to the table to wait.

Only after a breakfast of fried catfish and a bottle of beer did Lucky give any indication of being ready to take her to Gifford's.

"I've got better things to do than play chauffeur," he grumbled as he poled the pirogue away from the shore.

Serena shot him a look over her shoulder. "You know, I'm sick of hearing you complain. If you didn't want to get involved in this, you could have left me at Gifford's yesterday. Why bring me here if you're too busy to take me back?"

He arched a brow above the rim of his mirrored sunglasses with insulting lasciviousness. "Do you really have to ask, sugar?"

She narrowed her eyes speculatively. "You know, I think you do that on purpose."

"What?"

"Make obnoxious sexist remarks. I think you do it to make me angry, to throw me off the topic. Why is that, Lucky? Are you afraid to have a real conversation with a woman?"

"I'm not afraid of anything," he said too vehemently, giving the push-pole a mighty shove. "I'm sure as hell not afraid of you."

They traveled on in a silence that was as thick as the muggy air.

No shotgun blast greeted them this time as they rounded the bend to Gifford's cabin. Gifford sat on the steps tying fishing flies. Pepper Fontenot sat in a ratty old green and white lawn chair in the yard with a gutted outboard motor on a tarp at his feet. The clamorous sounds of a Cajun band blasted out of a portable radio on the gallery.

"Hey, Giff, what'sa matter with you? You run outta shells or somethin'?" Lucky hollered as he piloted the boat alongside the rickety dock.

Gifford pushed himself to his feet and jammed his big hands at his waist. "Hell, I ain't wasting good buckshot on you, Doucet."

"What about me?" Serena called. She waited for Lucky to pull the nose of the pirogue up on shore and exited from the bow, preferring to step on land rather than risk her neck on the rotted pier again.

Gifford gave her a long, hard stare as she came to stand at the foot of the steps. "I figured you'd be on your way back to Charleston by now."

Serena swallowed down the hurt and met his gaze head-on. "I told you, I won't leave this swamp until you do. I want you to come back to Chanson du Terre with me."

"And I told you, I'm not going. You're not bossing me around, little girl. I don't give a toot how many degrees you have. You can't hightail it out of Lou'siana first chance you get, then come on back and try to run things on the weekend."

87

She didn't back down. Lucky watched her take it on the chin. He cursed Gifford for being so hard on her, then told himself he didn't care. He leaned a hip against the newel post and lit his fourth cigarette of the morning, sucking smoke down a throat that was already raw.

He felt like holy hell. Even in the best of circumstances he never slept more than a couple of hours at a stretch because of nightmares, but the previous night had been worse than usual. What little sleep he'd gotten had been plagued with memories of pain and betrayal. As if his conscious mind hadn't been doing the job well enough, his subconscious had seen fit to remind him that beautiful women were the cause of most of his problems. First Shelby, then Amalinda Roca, the lovely little viper whose duplicity had helped to land him in a Central American prison.

He had finally given up on the idea of sleep and had proceeded to attempt to drown his foul mood and sexual frustration with whiskey, succeeding only in giving himself a colossal hangover. Now his head banged in syncopated rhythm with the gash in his arm where Mean Gene Willis had managed to nick him.

"You look like hell," Gifford said, his hard gaze still on Serena. His voice had lost some of its edge, betraying his true concern as he took in the dark crescents beneath her eyes. He glanced at Lucky to distract himself from his guilt. "You both look like hell."

"Mebbe they both been *raisin'* hell," Pepper suggested, chuckling merrily at the dark looks his comment received from both Lucky and Serena. Gifford only raised a bushy white brow in speculation as he studied them.

Serena felt a blush rise to her cheeks at the memory of the near miss of the night before. There but for the grace of God and Smith & Wesson . . . If the sight of Lucky's gun hadn't brought her back to reality in a cold rush, she may well have had something to blush about now. Dropping her head, she made her way up the steps, past her grandfather and onto the gallery.

"I could use a cup of coffee. Pepper, do you still make it strong?"

"Black as dat bayou and strong 'nough to curl your purty blond hair, *pichouette*," Pepper said, flashing his teeth.

"Sounds like heaven," Serena mumbled, letting herself in the front door.

Gifford remained on the steps, staring down at Lucky. "What have you got to say for yourself? You been fooling 'round with my little girl?"

Lucky slid his sunglasses on top of his head and gave Gifford a belligerent look. "What would you care, old man? All you wanna do is give her the sharp side of your tongue. You're the one left her with no place to stay last night."

"I got my reasons."

"Like you got your reasons for holin' up out here?" Lucky shook his head and muttered an expletive. "Cut her some slack, Giff. She came, didn't she?"

"Yeah, she came, and she'll leave again too," Gifford drawled, nodding. "First chance she gets. She don't give a damn about what happens here. The girl oughta have some respect for family, for tradition."

Lucky snorted. "You got a funny way of teachin' respect. Dump her out in the swamp to spend the night. She'd probably cut your heart out if you had one."

The idea that Gifford had known about Serena's fear and played on it infuriated Lucky. And the rise of his protective instincts made him even angrier. He swore again, tossed his cigarette butt to the dirt, and snuffed it out viciously with the toe of his boot. "I oughta just wash my hands of the lot of you. It's nothin' but trouble, this business."

"Me, I hear you got 'nough trouble wit' dat Perret boy and dat big ugly son Willis," Pepper said, rocking back on the hind legs of his lawn chair. His light eyes sparkled like aquamarines in his dark face.

Lucky scowled at him. "Where'd you hear that?"

"Me, I heard dat wit' my ears, I did." The old man chuckled at his little joke, not heeding Lucky's ferocious glare in the least.

"Yeah, well, you keep your ears out of it or they might just get shot off."

The end of his warning was punctuated by the sound of the screen door slapping shut, the soft "pop" sounding like a toy gun. Serena made her way across the small gallery, trying to concentrate on the steam rising from her coffee instead of the conversation she'd heard plainly through the screen while she'd been inside.

"Are you going to make this easier on all of us and explain to me what's going on, Gifford?" she said, lowering herself carefully to sit on the top step.

Gifford looked down at her and frowned. "Shouldn't have to be giving you an update like some kind of goddamned foreign correspondent."

Serena sighed heavily, feeling too exhausted to even bring her cup to her lips so she could draw on the amazing elixir that was Pepper

Fontenot's coffee. "Gifford, please. You've made your opinion of my life abundantly clear. Yes, I'm living miles away. People do that, you know. They grow up, they move on, they make their own lives."

"You've got no sense of tradition."

"I won't be a slave to it, if that's what you mean. I appreciate the history of Chanson du Terre, but I'm not going to become a planter to keep it going. Shelby is the one who always planned to carry on the tradition in one way or another. My career has taken me elsewhere. That doesn't mean I don't care about Chanson du Terre or you. I love you both," she said, looking up at him with fierce earnestness in her wide dark eyes. "Is that the confession you were looking for? Are you happy now?"

"Hardly," the old man grumbled. Still, he backed up a step and sat down beside her. "If you cared about the place, things would never have come to this."

"And just what is 'this'? What's going on?"

He hesitated a long time, considering and discarding options. Serena didn't rush him, but sat patiently, sipping her coffee. Finally, he heaved a sigh and plowed a hand through his white hair, leaving short strands standing on end.

"Some hotshot political people have got it into their puddin' heads Mason Talbot is destined for political stardom. They want him to run for the legislature next year. He's just pretty enough and stupid enough to get elected too. He'll make a nice little puppet for the oil kingpins. His daddy may have lost his fortune in the bust, but he hasn't lost any of his connections. I'm sure old John Talbot would love to have a son in the governor's mansion one day."

"Mason running for office," Serena murmured, a troubled frown drawing her brows together. "I can't believe Shelby didn't mention it to me."

"Seems to me there's quite a few things Shelby didn't mention to you, *chère*," Lucky commented darkly.

Serena shot him a look of annoyance and turned back to Gifford. "I don't see what this has to do with Chanson du Terre."

"Think about it, Serena. Shelby has her heart set on Mason going to Baton Rouge. They won't need the plantation. The state the place is in right now, all it is is a liability. But if I were to sell it now and advance her her inheritance, that would give Mason enough money to buy his way into any office he wanted.

"Everybody knows it's advertising wins elections nowadays. Plaster

Mason's pretty face on billboards, on television, on the sides of buses, nobody's gonna care that he's got cotton for brains."

Serena felt compelled to stick up for her absent brother-in-law. She had always liked Mason. He was too laid back for Gifford's taste and he might have been more fluff than substance, but he had a good heart. "Mason has got more than cotton for brains. He graduated from law school fifth in his class."

Gifford gave a snort that eloquently spoke of his regard for lawyers in general. "Don't mean he's got a lick of sense. All it means to me is he has a nose for loopholes and technicalities. Hell, that hound over there can sniff out a coon fast as dammit, but that don't mean he's Einstein."

It was pointless to argue with him, and they had gotten off the most important topic, so Serena steered them back with effort. "You said yesterday you'd mentioned something to Shelby about selling. Why would you do that if you don't want to sell?"

He scowled at his boots and looked uncomfortable. When he spoke, it was as grudgingly as a schoolboy owning up to sticking gum on his teacher's chair. "Hell, I was just makin' noise. We've been having a rough spot here—cane smut last year, too much rain this spring, production costs are up, that damned gas tax gets us coming and going. I was just grumbling is all, trying to see if I might raise a little interest in Shelby for something besides redecorating the house while she's staying in it. So I say over dinner one night, 'By God, if all I'm gonna do is work myself to death on this place so some stranger can come in and take over, I might as well sell it and go to Tahiti.' Faster than I could spit and whistle, she had a Tristar rep nosing around the place."

Serena frowned as she listened. It had seemed unlikely to her that Shelby would want to sell Chanson du Terre, if not because of a sense of tradition, because it had always represented status in the community —something Shelby prized almost above all else. But if she had set her sights on an even higher plateau and saw selling the place as a means of achieving that end, that was a different story. Shelby's talent for rationalization was unsurpassed in Serena's experience.

"Why Tristar Chemical?" she asked.

Gifford shrugged wearily. "I don't know. There's probably some connection through Mason's family. How else would she have found a buyer at all? Since the oil bust, the market down here is soft as butter. Shelby couldn't sell igloos to Eskimos to begin with. Mason only let her have that office space downtown to placate her. You know I love her, but she's a silly little thing and always has been. The only reason she went into real estate was so she could dress up, look important, and go to the chamber of commerce meetings."

"So you don't want to sell the place," Serena said, uncomfortable with the topic of her twin. "Tell the Tristar people no and be done with it."

"They don't take no for an answer," he grumbled. "That damned Burke is like a pit bull. I can't shake him for love or money."

Serena fixed her grandfather with the stern look she'd learned from him. "Gifford Sheridan, in all my life I've never known you to back down from a fight."

He frowned at her. His square chin came up a notch. "I'm not backing down from a fight."

"Then what are you doing out here?" she asked, exasperated.

He raised his head another proud inch, looking as stubborn and immovable as the faces on Mount Rushmore. "I'm dealing with it my own way."

They were back to square one. Serena squeezed her eyes shut for a second and concentrated on the needle of pain stabbing through her head. She took a sip of coffee, hoping in vain that the caffeine would bring her energy level up. Instead, it churned like acid in her stomach and made her feel even hotter and more uncomfortable than she had been to begin with.

Of course, Gifford's obstinance wasn't helping. Nor was having Lucky's steady gaze fastened on her. He stood at the foot of the steps, staring at her through the opaque lenses of his sunglasses, an unnerving experience in the best of circumstances. The only thing that might have made it worse was if he hadn't been wearing the glasses. She couldn't think of anything more disturbing than the heat and intensity of those amber eyes.

Pepper broke the tense silence, rising lazily from his chair. Without a word to anyone he ambled down to the edge of the bayou and stood for a moment, apparently admiring the view. When he turned to come back, he looked up at Giff and said, "Company comin'. Me, I hears dat ol' Johnson outboard wit' the bad valve."

Gifford swore, pushing himself to his feet and turning for the cabin. He returned with his shotgun, the twelve-gauge cracked open so he could shove slugs into it as he pounded down the steps and across the yard.

"Gifford!" Serena set her coffee cup down and ran after him. "Gifford, for heaven's sake!"

He managed to get one shot off before she reached him. The buckshot hit the water, sending up a spray just off the port bow of the game warden's boat. Perry Davis's voice crackled at them over a bullhorn.

"Goddammit, Gifford, put the gun down!"

Gifford lowered the shotgun but wouldn't relinquish it to Serena when she tried to pull it away from him. She ground her teeth and counted to ten and tried to call on her years as a counselor to cool her temper. Nothing helped much. She was furious with Gifford and she knew she was simply too close to him to ever be completely rational and objective in dealing with him.

The engine of the game warden's boat cut and the hull bobbed on the dark water a few feet from shore. Perry Davis stood behind the wheel, looking outraged and officious, his baby face flushed. Beside him was a middle-aged man, big and raw-boned with a fleshy face and a head of slicked-back steel-gray hair. He wore navy slacks and a striped necktie that had been jerked loose and hung like a noose around the collar of his sweat-stained blue dress shirt.

"You keep shooting at people and I'm gonna have to arrest you, Gifford," Davis threatened, switching off the bullhorn.

Lucky, who had come to stand on Serena's left, gave a derisive snort. "You don't arrest nobody else. Why start with him?"

The game warden worked his mouth into a knot of suppressed fury. "Maybe I'll start with you."

Lucky pushed his sunglasses up his nose and gave Davis a long, level look, smiling ever so slightly. "Yeah? You and what army?"

"I'll get you, Doucet. I can promise you that," Davis said, thrusting a warning finger in Lucky's direction. "Crazy bastard like you running around loose. Folks aren't gonna stand for that forever."

Serena could feel the tension humming around Lucky like electrical waves. The muscles in his jaw worked. He never took his eyes off Perry Davis and he never said another word. Yet, even from a distance of several yards, Davis felt compelled to back away; he moved to the back of the boat on the excuse of looking at the motor, trying to appear as if he had casually dismissed Lucky and their conversation. Gifford took advantage of the silence.

"Burke, you turn yourself around and get out."

The big Texan let a phony grin split his meaty features. "I can't do that, partner. We've got business to discuss."

"I've got nothing to say to you that can be said in front of a lady," Gifford retorted. "I'm not interested in your offer. Go on back to Texas before I shoot you full of holes."

"Gifford," Serena said, schooling herself to at least appear calm and under control. "Why don't you invite Mr. Burke in? I'm sure we can settle this business amicably with a little plain talk."

Burke gave an exaggerated shrug. "The little lady has a head on her shoulders, Gifford. I've said that all along. Isn't it about time you listened to her?"

It occurred to Serena that the Tristar rep had mistaken her for Shelby, but she didn't have the chance to correct him.

"I don't have to listen to anybody!" Gifford shouted, color rising in his face from his neck up. "I'm not senile, by God. I can make up my own mind. And if there's gonna be any plain talk, it's gonna come from the business end of old Betsy here," he said, raising the stock of the shotgun to his shoulder.

"Gifford!" Serena shouted, lunging toward him.

He squeezed the trigger as she knocked him off balance. The shotgun bucked as another deafening explosion rent the air. Water sprayed up against the hull of the game warden's boat, dousing Burke and Davis with a rain of mud and shredded vegetation. The two men ducked, covering their heads with their arms, then came up swearing.

Burke pointed a warning finger at Gifford. "I've had it with you, Sheridan. You're a crazy old man. There's been plenty of witnesses to that. I can get the sheriff out here. You can't just go around shooting at people who want to do business with you."

"Hell," Gifford said, wading out into the water, his fierce gaze fixed on Burke. "I said a long time ago they ought to open season on Texans. This state wouldn't be in the mess it's in if we'd a kept you greedy sons of bitches on the other side of the border!"

Serena eyed the muddy water with distaste, a tremor of fear snaking down her spine. Then she looked at her grandfather's back as he advanced toward the game warden's boat and forced herself to take the first step in, her shoes sinking into the muddy bottom. She grabbed Gifford by a belt loop on his jeans and tried to pull him back toward shore.

Burke had turned hot pink; his eyes bugged out of his head as if someone had suddenly pulled his tie tight enough to cut off his wind. "Keep it up, Sheridan! Come on, say a few more lines like that one! They'll sound real good at your competency hearing!"

Gifford tried to launch himself toward the boat, but Lucky stepped in front of him and planted a hand on his chest.

"*C'est assez.* Go on up to the house, *mon ami*," he said softly. "Go on."

The old man stood for a moment, grinding his teeth, his weight on his forward foot, his big hands twisting on the shotgun. The only other sound was Beausoleil playing "*J'ai Été au Zydeco*" on the portable radio with inappropriate joy.

"Gifford, please," Serena whispered behind him, pressing her cheek to his broad back as her feet sank deeper into the goo.

"Come on, Giff," Pepper said from the bank. "He ain't worth the trouble."

Gifford snarled a curse, jerked around, and waded back to shore. With Pepper whispering and gesturing animatedly beside him, he headed for the cabin.

Lucky's gaze settled on Serena. She was up to her knees in the bayou. The color was draining from her face and her eyes looked huge as she stared at him.

"*Foute ton quant d'ici,*" he murmured. "Go on, *chère,* get away from here. I'll take care of this."

She backed away slowly, grimacing as the mud sucked at her shoes.

Lucky turned and advanced on the boat, wading right up alongside it until he was waist-deep in the muddy water. "This is no way to do business, M'sieu Burke," he said, his low, rough voice just above a whisper.

Burke leaned down, bracing his hands on the side of the boat, his gaze intent on Lucky's face. "You tell your friend to start cooperating, then, son," the Texan said, also speaking softly, as if the weight of the subject required a tone of conspiracy. "My company has gone to a lot of trouble to choose that site, and they mean to have it."

"Is that supposed to be a threat?"

"It's a fact, son."

The words hit him wrong. Burke's tone, his voice, his accent, his air of command, all conspired against him in Lucky's mind. For a split second he was back in Central America taking orders from a big Texan who had sold him down the river, a lieutenant colonel who had been using his covert operations team to make himself a bundle. Lucky had uncovered the man for the traitor he was, but not before spending a year in hell. That all came back to him in a flash, and the reins of control slipped a little through his mental fingers.

"You know, there's a lotta things I'm not too sure of," he said to Burke, a chilling smile curving his mouth. "But there's one thing I do know for certain." In the blink of an eye the smile was gone. He grabbed the knot of Burke's tie and gave it a yank, pulling the man down toward him so they were nose to nose. "I'm not your son."

The Tristar rep was over the side of the boat and diving headfirst into the bayou before he could register a protest. He landed in the water like a whale and came up spitting mud.

"You hadn't ought to lean over the side that way, *mon ami,*" Lucky said, wading casually toward the shore. "You might fall in. You fall in, there's no tellin' what might get you in this water."

As if he had conjured it up by magic to illustrate his point, a water snake slid out of some reeds near the bank. Burke swore and scrambled to get back over the side of the boat. Davis helped him, grabbing him by the back of his pants and hauling him up, shouting at Lucky all the while.

"I mean it, Doucet! I've had it with you running roughshod! Your days out here are numbered."

Lucky made a face and waved him off. Serena met him on the bank, glaring up at him. Color had come back into her cheeks, he noticed.

"Can't you show respect for anybody?" she asked sarcastically.

"*Mais yeah,*" he said flippantly. "My *maman,* my *papa,* the Pope. Len Burke ain't the Pope, sugar. I don't think he's even a good Catholic." He gave her an infuriating indulgent look. Behind them the motor of the game warden's boat roared to life, then faded into the distance.

"That's it," Serena declared, stopping in her tracks. She threw her hands up in a gesture of defeat. "I've had it. There's something about this place that drives people over the edge. I can't stand it. Gifford is going around shooting at people. You— You're—" She couldn't finish the sentence, she was so upset. She gave in to the urge to stamp her foot. It seemed she could control little or nothing out there—not the situation, not her fears or her passions or her temper, least of all her guide.

"This whole situation is just ridiculous," she said, pacing a short stretch of bank, her arms crossed tightly against her. "Why didn't Shelby call me? Why didn't she just explain all this to me to begin with?"

"Gee," Lucky said with mock innocence. "Could it be she didn't want you to know? Could it be she thought she might pull off the deal without having you know a thing about it until it was too late?"

Serena shot him a look from the corner of her eye. "Oh, for Pete's sake, you make it sound like a big conspiracy."

"That's because it *is* a big conspiracy, sugar," he said, leaning back against the trunk of a massive live oak. He shook a cigarette out of the pack from his shirt pocket and dangled it from his lip without lighting it.

"Don't be ridiculous," Serena snapped. "You're trying to tell me Shelby is in league with the Tristar people to drive her own grandfather from his land?"

Lucky shrugged. "*C'est bien.* You got it in one. It's a sweet deal. She gets a nice fat commission on the sale and her inheritance besides. On top of that, she and the politically ambitious Mr. Talbot bring industry to a town with a depressed economy. There's nothing like a local hero in an election year, you know."

Serena planted herself squarely in front of him, settling in for the argument. "You're way off base. In the first place, Mason doesn't have an ambitious bone in his body. If he were any more laid back, someone would have him interred."

"You heard your grandpapa, *chère.* The powers that be want Talbot in office. His daddy wants him in office. Shelby wants him in office. You think he's gonna tell all those people no? You think Shelby would let him?"

"You make my sister sound like Lady Macbeth. Shelby is hardly that calculating or devious."

Lucky knew exactly how devious and calculating Shelby could be, but he didn't give voice to his own experiences. He used Serena's instead. "Isn't she? Are you forgetting what you told me last night? She left you out here alone. You could have been killed."

"That was an accident, a joke that went wrong."

"Was it?"

Serena dodged his steady gaze. He was dredging up old hurts inside her and they had no place here. Besides, no one had been more relieved than Shelby when Serena had been found after her ordeal. Her sister had wept at her hospital bedside and had begged her forgiveness . . . and she had thrown her fear of the swamp, the fear that had resulted from that incident, up in her face time and again since then.

Serena shrugged off the grain of doubt trying to insinuate itself into her mind. Her feelings toward her twin were complicated enough already; she didn't need Lucky's dark suspicions adding to the morass.

"Stop trying to turn me against my own sister," she said irritably. "I'm sure you have every reason to be paranoid, considering the kind of life you lead, but I refuse to fall into that kind of thinking."

"You shrinks have a word for that too, don't you?" Lucky said, arching a brow. "Denial?"

"Talk about denial," Serena grumbled, changing the subject as she resumed her pacing. She threw a fuming look up at the cabin. "I can't believe Gifford. He says he's dealing with this *his* way. He's not dealing with it at all. He's making me—"

She broke off as the realization hit her like a brick square in the forehead. Making her deal with it *was* his way of dealing with it. He wanted to force her into caring more about the plantation. He wanted her to take up the banner and fight for the cause, and in doing so revive her sense of tradition and duty. God, he had even lured her into the swamp, the place she had lived in fear of for fifteen years.

"That old fox," she muttered, planting her hands on her hips. "That old son of a boot."

He had manipulated her as neatly as a chess master, and now there was no honorable way out. She was involved and she would have to do her best to resolve the situation or lose face with Gifford again. She might have run the risk of incurring his wrath, but she couldn't bear the thought of facing his disappointment in her. He had bet on that and won, the old horse thief.

"Take me back," she said suddenly, turning toward Lucky. "Take me back to Chanson du Terre. I have to talk with Shelby. I'll straighten this mess out as best as I can. But if Gifford thinks he can guilt me into staying here forever, he can just think again."

Chapter Nine

Lucky dropped her off at his house, telling her he would be back in an hour to pick her up and return her to Chanson du Terre. Serena watched him pole away, then let herself inside. It was silent and cool. One of the baby raccoons peered in the back door at her, its long front paws pressed to the screen. When Serena moved toward it, the coon whinnied and scampered away, its claws clattering on the wooden floor of the gallery, making the exact sound that had scared her witless the night before.

She set her suitcases by the front door, then raided Lucky's small refrigerator and made herself a ham sandwich, taking great care to make certain the kitchen was as spotless when she was finished as it had been to begin with. When that small task was accomplished, she still had forty minutes to wait.

Her mind turned to the question of what she would find awaiting her at Chanson du Terre. It all seemed so unlikely. Mason running for office. Shelby plotting against Giff. The plantation's existence threatened.

Bulldozers, Lucky had said. Tristar would raze the place to make room for labs, offices, manufacturing facilities, warehouses. The possibility, as remote as it was, hit Serena in a tender spot. That old house had borne silent witness to a lot of history. It had seen the last days of French rule in Louisiana, the golden era before the war. Yankees had camped on the lawn, and the staircase still bore the marks where a drunken officer had ridden his horse up it. It had survived the Reconstruction and the Great Depression. Had it survived all that only to fall victim to greed?

No. Of course not. The current situation would be cleared up and life would go on at Chanson du Terre with Gifford ruling the roost as he had for nearly sixty years.

And when Gifford was gone and Shelby was off in Baton Rouge and Serena was back in Charleston . . . what then?

"Oh, no, you don't," Serena muttered, pushing herself up from her place at the table. This was exactly what Gifford wanted—to rouse her sentimental streak.

Instead, she turned her mind to another puzzle—Lucky. She wandered the two rooms of his cottage, trying to discern as much as she could about him from the things she found. It was an exercise in perception and reasoning, she told herself, not simple curiosity about the man.

What she found in examining Lucky's lair was almost nothing. Utilitarian furnishings that happened to be antique. Nothing frivolous, nothing personal, nothing more revealing than a respect for his heritage and a need for order. He kept no books in sight, no magazines, no photographs, no art on the walls. But that in itself was a revelation. He was a man in hiding. His house was hidden. In his house, everything personal was hidden. He let nothing of his inner self show if he could help it at all.

Why was that? It didn't seem like a wholly natural reticence. It seemed more as if he had carefully constructed a maze of walls around himself for protection. What would a man like Lucky need protection from? He seemed so tough, so self-reliant. And yet there were the contradictions. He gave food to orphaned raccoons. He had defended her to Gifford. He had held her when she had felt miserable and afraid.

She opened the tall door of the armoire in the dining room. The shelves of the cupboard were stocked with only the kind of things one would expect to find in a dining room. Serena groaned a little in disappointment and hesitated a moment before crossing into the other room, which was, with the exception of the quality of the furnishings, barren as a monk's cell.

"Jackpot," she whispered as she swung open the door of the large armoire that stood opposite the foot of the bed.

The closet had a column of cubbyholes along the left side, with an area for hanging clothes on the right. A set of three deep drawers created the base. She glanced over his wardrobe, which consisted of jeans, fatigue pants, T-shirts, and an army dress uniform with a chest full of decorations. The uniform interested her, but the smaller shelves on the left drew Serena's immediate attention.

They held framed photographs. The Doucet family captured at all different times of their lives. There was a sepia-toned wedding picture of his parents—a handsome, smiling couple gazing at each other with love. There was a battered black and white snapshot of his father standing with his hand on the shoulder of a gangly boy who was proudly displaying a trophy-size fish and a gap-toothed grin. Lucky, she assumed, looking much younger and lighter of heart. There were more recent photos of other members of the clan, unmistakable by their resemblance to one another, children of various ages, chubby babies in frilly baptism gowns, and grade-schoolers taking first communion in their Sunday best with their faces shining and their cowlicks slicked into submission.

Serena felt her heart melt a little as she looked at the photographs. Lucky had a family and he loved them. He wouldn't have gone to all the trouble of framing the pictures if he hadn't cared deeply. Why did he isolate himself from them? Shelby had said his parents were nice people, respectable people. Did Lucky feel unworthy of them because of the life he led? Or was there something else that made him feel separate?

She reached out to touch the photograph of Lucky and his father, brushing her fingertips over the smiling face of the boy he had been. What had happened to that boy to put shadows in his eyes? What events had turned him into the dangerous, brooding man he was today?

A yearning to know that was deeper than professional curiosity ached inside Serena. She wanted to know Lucky's secrets, wanted to reach past them to offer him something—solace, comfort. This longing wasn't wise, and it brought her no joy, but she didn't try to deny it. She just stood there, hurting for him, hurting for herself, wishing to God she had never left Charleston.

"Mom sent over a chocolate cake and some cookies and two loaves of French bread she baked today. I just set 'em on the counter."

Serena shrieked and jumped back from the armoire as if it had suddenly come alive. She swung around with a hand over her heart to keep it from leaping out of her chest. Standing at the entrance to the room was a boy of about thirteen, beanpole-thin in jeans that were too short and a T-shirt that proclaimed Breaux Bridge to be the crawfish capital of the world. His eyes were dark and round with excitement.

"You ain't Lucky," he blurted out. "But Lucky sure is."

The instant the remark registered in his brain he flushed a shade of red that rivaled the color of the baseball cap he wore backward on his head.

Serena laughed, more out of relief than anything. "You startled me," she said, pushing the door of the armoire closed. "Lucky's not here right now. He should be back in about half an hour. I'm Serena Sheridan."

"Will Guidry." He came forward hesitantly, started to offer her his hand but stopped midway to check it for dirt. Finding it relatively clean, he stuck it out in front of him again, looking as if he fully expected contact with her to give him a painful shock.

"It's nice to meet you, Will." Serena gave his hand a firm shake and released it. "Would you care to wait for Lucky to come back?"

"Um—well—no—that's okay," the youth stammered. He jammed his hands into his pants pockets and shuffled his oversize feet, staring down at them as if they were the most amazing sight he'd come across recently. "I was just leavin' off some stuff. Mom says she knows he won't take nothing—" He grimaced and corrected himself. "Won't take *any*thing for runnin' them poachers off our crawfish nets, but she said the least she could do was bake him somethin' nice seein' as how he lives out here all alone—" He broke off and winced again, as if some unseen etiquette monitor was smacking him with a switch every time he goofed up. "I mean, he *did* live alone until you— But then, maybe you aren't—I mean, this could just be— Aw, hell—I mean, *heck*—"

Serena stared at him, everything inside her going still. "What did you say?" she asked softly, ignoring the boy's red-faced embarrassment. "Did you say 'running poachers off'?"

Will shuffled his sneakers and shrugged, giving her a look that told her he suspected she might be a little odd. "Well, yeah. That's sorta what he does."

"But I thought—" Serena cut herself off, snapping her mouth shut with an audible click.

She had thought what Lucky had wanted her to think. She had taken one look at him and assumed he was an outlaw, and he had let her believe it, had reinforced that image every chance he'd gotten. This was certainly her day to feel like a fool.

"We been havin' some trouble, you know," Will said somberly, scratching his bony elbow. "My dad's gone down to the Gulf to look for work, so it's just Mom and us kids to home. Poachers figured our nets would be easy pickin.' Lucky showed 'em different."

"Lucky," Serena murmured. Big bad Lucky Doucet. Savior of orphaned animals. Defender of the defenseless. Not poaching, but chasing poachers away from the nets of women and children.

"He's some kind of man," Will said happily. "But I guess you already know that." His gaze dropped abruptly and he turned red again. He was at the age where nearly everything struck him as a sexual innuendo, and every social blunder seemed catastrophic. He looked at Serena with horror. "I didn't mean that you'd *know*. I meant, you know . . ."

"I know," she said absently, still too stunned to take much pity on the poor kid.

If Lucky wasn't a poacher, then why had he let her believe he was? And why the antipathy between him and the game warden? Maybe they simply didn't like each other. Maybe Lucky didn't think Perry Davis was doing a good enough job. There could have been any number of reasons, not all of them good. Just because he wasn't a poacher didn't mean he wasn't guilty of something. There was still the matter of the illegal liquor and the room upstairs he didn't want her to see.

"Anyhow," Will said, gulping down his embarrassment. "I oughta be goin'." He shuffled backward toward the door, swinging a long, bony arm in the direction of the kitchen. "I just left the stuff on the counter."

"Yes, thank you. I'm sure Lucky will appreciate it," Serena said, resurrecting her manners and her smile. "It was nice meeting you, Will."

He blushed and shrugged, ducking his head and grinning shyly. "Yeah, you too. See ya 'round."

He bolted out the front door and loped across the yard to a canoe beached on the bank of the bayou. Serena wandered out onto the gallery and waved to him as he paddled away. Even from a distance she could see him blush. Adolescence. What hell. She shook her head in a combination of amusement and sympathy, and wondered what Lucky might have been like at that age.

As if she didn't have enough to figure out about the grown man. If he wasn't a poacher, then what was he? A bootlegger? A gun runner with a heart of gold?

Her gaze drifted across the porch to the stairs that led up to the overhanging *grenier,* the forbidden room.

Never you mind what I keep up here. . . . It's nothing for a pretty shrink to go sniffing through. . . . You're a helluva lot better off not knowing.

She was better off not knowing, or he was safer if she didn't know?

She was on the steps before she could tell herself not to go on. Whether it was a need to understand the man that compelled her, or a need to justify her attraction to him, she didn't try to discern. In fact, she tried not to think at all. Almost as if they belonged to someone else's body, she watched her feet ascend one step at a time, watched her hand reach for the doorknob and turn it, watched the door swing back.

Nothing could have prepared her for what she saw. Not in her wildest imagination had she suspected this. She thought she had been prepared for anything—crates of guns, bales of drugs, boxes of stolen goods—but she hadn't been at all prepared for beauty, for art.

The room was ringed with paintings. Canvases, stacked three deep, leaned back against the walls. An easel took center stage in the open, airy room. On it was propped a work in progress.

Serena wandered into the room, gazing all around her in a daze. Unlike the first floor, the attic was not divided, but was one large room with windows at either gable end and skylights punctuating the ceiling on the north side. The light that filtered in through the blinds was soft and dusty-looking, spilling onto the floor in oblong bars of gold. There was a long workbench against one wall, loaded with jars of brushes and tubes of paint, sketch pads, pencils, paint-spotted rags. A heavy sheet of canvas served as rug and dropcloth, covering a large area of the wooden floor surrounding the easel. The smell of oil paint and mineral spirits hung heavy in the air like cheap perfume.

So this was Lucky's deep dark secret. He was an artist.

Serena walked around the edge of the dropcloth, trying to take in the paintings propped against the wall. They depicted the swamp as a solitary place of trees and mist, capturing the stillness, the sense of waiting. They were beautiful, hauntingly, powerfully beautiful, filled with a dark tension and an aching sense of loneliness. They were magnificent and terrifying.

She stood before one that featured a single white egret, the great bird looking small and insignificant among the columns of gray cypress trunks and tattered banners of gray moss and smoke-gray morning mist. She stood there in the hot, stuffy room and felt as if the painting were drawing her in and swallowing her whole. She could feel the chill of the mist, could smell the swamp, could hear the distant cries of birds.

All the paintings shared that ability to draw the viewer into the center of the swamp and the center of the artist's anguish. They were extraordinary.

"Oh, Lucky," she whispered as understanding dawned painfully inside her. She closed her eyes and pressed her hands to her face.

This was what he hadn't wanted, for her to see beyond the façade of macho bravado, not because he was ashamed of what she would find, but because it was too personal, too private. He wasn't a man who would easily share his inner self; she'd known that all along. But she had never suspected his inner self would be so tender, so full of pain and longing.

Hugging herself, she looked at a painting of a storm building over the swamp. An angry sky churned in a turmoil of gray, green, and yellow above the stillness of the bayou. Tears rose in her eyes.

He had told her more than once he didn't want her prying into his life. He was nothing more than her unwilling guide and unwilling host. But she had pushed and prodded, excusing her behavior as professional curiosity, telling herself she had a right to know just how dangerous he really was, and in doing so she had violated the most basic human right—the right to inner privacy.

She turned to leave and jumped back, sucking in a startled breath as her heart vaulted into her throat. Lucky stood at the open door, staring at her. He was perfectly still, but there was a terrible sense of raw tension vibrating in the air around him. His eyes flashed like lightning warning of a coming storm.

"I'm sorry," Serena whispered. She realized dimly that she was trembling. "I shouldn't have come in here."

"No, you shouldn't have," he said, his voice low and thrumming with fury.

He stared at her, struggling to hold himself from flying into a rage.

What he did in this room he did for himself. This had been his solace, his salvation when he came back from Central America. He spent hours in this room, healing, focusing on his canvases to keep his mind together and to vent what was trying to tear him apart. These paintings were his most private feelings, the pain he couldn't escape, the fear he wouldn't acknowledge. Having someone see them was like stripping his soul bare and putting it on public display. It was unthinkable. And now it was inescapable.

"I didn't mean to pry," Serena said stupidly.

"Of course you did," Lucky snapped. He strode into the room and began throwing cloths over the paintings, his movements jerky with anger. "That's what shrinks do best, isn't it? Dig into people's heads, dig out their secrets."

"I was only trying to see if you were doing something illegal. I have a right to know who I'm staying with," she said, the words sounding self-righteous and foolish even to her.

He wheeled around suddenly and grabbed her by the arms, jerking her up against him, bending over her so that she had to arch her back to look up at him. "You don't have any rights out here," he growled. "You don't belong here. This isn't polite society, Shelby. There are no rules except my rules."

"Serena." Her name trembled on her lips. She stared up at him, at the wild look in his eyes, genuinely afraid of him for the first time. *I'm over the edge. . . . Folks say he's half-crazy. . . .* "I'm Serena, Lucky," she said softly, her heart pounding as she watched him struggle to pull himself back from that edge.

Lucky blinked at her, his mind sliding back from the darkness and chilling as he realized what she had said. He straightened and let go of her abruptly. She stumbled against the easel, setting the canvas on it rocking.

"I know who you are," he said bitterly. Plowing his hands through his hair, he began to pace the width of the room like a caged tiger, his head down, eyes burning bright with fury and pain and fear.

"Damn you. Damn you," he muttered as the breath soughed in and out of his lungs in gusts. So much had been taken from him—his youth, his innocence. It seemed all he had left was his pride and his privacy, and the woman standing there staring at him with doe eyes full of fear was stripping him of both. He didn't want her interference. He didn't want the reminder of his past she brought him. He didn't want the fire she set in his blood. Damn her, *damn her!*

106

Serena reached out to steady the easel, steadying herself at the same time. She watched Lucky pace, watched the storm of emotions raging inside him and witnessed the awesome battle to contain those emotions within him. As she watched, her fear receded and was replaced by something stronger—the need to reach out to him.

"Lucky, I didn't mean any harm," she said softly. "I'm very sorry. Really, I am."

He stopped abruptly and looked at her sideways, his eyes as bright and hot as molten gold. A savage smile cut across his dark face. "You're sorry. You invade my life, invade my privacy, drag me into your battles, and all you have to say is that you're sorry. Use me to your own end and excuse it all with an apology. Very civilized. Very proper. *Dieu,* isn't that just like the Sheridan girls?"

The words rang in his ears like the clashing din of cymbals. If he could have reached out and grabbed them back, he would have, but they hung there. Serena met his gaze, her face filled with dawning awareness and questions.

"How well do you know Shelby?" she asked carefully, not wanting to hear the answer.

"Well enough to know better than to let her twin take me for the same ride."

Serena was unprepared for the stab of jealousy that pierced her at the thought of Shelby and Lucky together. It didn't seem possible. She didn't want to believe it, but she didn't have much choice.

"I'm not Shelby," she said, drawing her armor of cool poise around herself. "I'm nothing like Shelby. I'm sorry if she hurt you, but I won't pay for her sins, Lucky."

"Forget it," he muttered. "It was a lifetime ago."

He could see she had more questions, but before she could voice them, he jerked his head around and resumed his pacing, dismissing the subject as if it hadn't been the one pivotal event that had changed his life's course.

"What did you think you would find up here, *ma petite?* Contraband? Guns? Drugs?"

"You let me think you were a poacher," Serena said evenly. "Why, Lucky? Why let me think you're something bad when you're not?"

To keep you away. To keep from getting hurt. He pressed the heels of his hands to his temples as if to hold the thoughts in as they swelled and throbbed behind his eyes. When he started toward her, he roared, an animal cry of impotent rage and guilt and fury. Serena jumped, but held her ground, waiting for an answer. Lucky lunged at her, pulling himself up just a hairbreadth in front of her.

"You look at me and see something bad. That's because I am," he insisted.

"I've seen what you wanted me to see, not who you really are."

"*Mais non, chère,*" he said bitterly. "You've seen all there is."

"That's a lie. What about this?" Serena raised a hand toward the half-finished canvas on the easel. "You wouldn't have let me see this. There's nothing bad here. Your paintings are beautiful and touching, Lucky. Why wouldn't you let me see them? Do they show too much?"

Snarling an oath, he pushed past her, grabbed the canvas off the easel, and hurled it across the room like a giant Frisbee. It hit the leg of the workbench with a loud crack, the stretcher snapping in two along one side of the canvas, ruining it.

"Cloth and pigment," Lucky spat out. "That's all it is. I do it to pass the time. Don't read anything into it, Dr. Sheridan," he warned, leaning over her again. "Don't look for symbolism or metaphors. Rest assured, the only way I want to touch you is with my hands," he said, pulling her against him with barely leashed violence.

"This is how I want to touch you, *chère,*" he whispered savagely, sweeping his hands over her hair, down her back to her hips. His fingers pressed into her flesh, stroking roughly, caressing without tenderness. "This is the only way I want to touch you." He brought one hand up to cup her breast through the sheer fabric of her blouse. "This is all I have to give you, all I'll let you take."

He lowered his mouth the rest of the way and kissed her hard.

She should have pushed him away. Common sense told Serena to push him away. Common sense told her that poacher or artist, Lucky Doucet was a man with problems, a man who wouldn't share himself. He'd given her fair warning on that score. All he wanted was this, the physical, the sexual. He wanted desire and nothing more. Even that need he gave in to grudgingly, angrily. He wanted her, but he didn't like it. She wanted him and it confounded her. She was too smart a woman to fall into the trap of wanting a man who would never give of himself. She was too slick and polished to want a barbarian, too in need of control to surrender it utterly.

She should have pushed him away. But she didn't. Couldn't. She wanted his touch, his kiss. He had awakened an instinct in her that had lain dormant even through marriage. Now it roared with life, with hunger. It frightened her and thrilled her, and she surrendered without a fight because no matter how wrong her common sense told her it was, the woman in her said it was right.

The woman in her, who had never known true passion, yearned for it now, with this man, this warrior with the soul of an artist. She had held herself in check with the idea he was a criminal, but he wasn't a criminal. He was a man with hidden fears. He was a man who covered his tenderness, his inner loneliness, his goodness with a mask of toughness and danger, a man who needed love but would never reach out to take it.

Serena didn't push him away. She melted against him.

Lucky groaned helplessly as her mouth softened beneath his. He hadn't meant this to happen. He had meant to push her away, to frighten her, to repel her, to chase her so far away she wouldn't want to come within an emotional mile of him. But the instant her resistance melted, so did his anger. Need swept over him like a tidal wave. He needed to touch her, to taste her, to hold her. He wanted to lose himself in her. It was madness, he knew, but such sweet madness he couldn't resist.

He raised his head a scant inch and looked into her eyes. What he saw was a mirror of his own bewilderment, need, and wariness of that need.

"I want you," he murmured, untangling the overwhelming knot of emotions to the root of the problem. "I want you, Serena."

"I know."

Her words were little more than shadows of sound passing between her lips, lips that were swollen from his kiss. Her braid had come loose and her hair fell around her shoulders in disarray, a shaft of light from the window above turning it the color of spun gold. She was temptation personified, a temptation Lucky had no intention of resisting.

"I stopped last night," he reminded her. "I'm not stopping this time, *chère.*"

Serena could feel him, hard and urgent against her belly, and she knew he meant what he said. A primitive thrill shot through her at the thought that he meant to take her, to claim her as males had claimed their mates from the dawn of time. He lowered his mouth to hers again, sipping, tasting, testing her. Serena framed his face with her hands and pressed her lips more solidly against his, letting him know she had no intention of stopping him.

She met the thrust of his tongue eagerly as reason and logic shut down and instinct took control. He filled her mouth with the taste of him, surrounded her body with his heat and raw power. She slid her arms around his neck and gasped as her breasts flattened against the granite wall of his chest.

Lucky pulled her lower body tight against his with one hand and slid his other hand between them, seeking and finding the open throat of her blouse. He needed to touch her skin, needed to see her. The top button gave way as he curled his fingers into the fabric and pulled downward. One by one the buttons surrendered, falling to the floor.

He trailed his kiss down her jaw to her throat, stripping the blouse from her shoulders and discarding it. His thumbs hooked under the straps of her bra and he drew them down off her shoulders, peeled the cups away to reveal her breasts to his touch, his gaze, the hunger of his kiss.

Serena cried out as he took one turgid peak into his mouth and sucked strongly. She tangled her fingers in the black silk of his hair and pressed him closer as heat swept through her.

Together they sank to their knees on the rumpled canvas drop-cloth. Serena leaned back, arching into the heat of Lucky's mouth. It was exquisite—the pull of his lips, the rasp of his tongue, the feel of his hand kneading her other breast. Her own hands moved restlessly over his broad shoulders, gathering the fabric of his T-shirt into her fists.

He pulled away and tore the garment off, flinging it aside, never taking his eyes from hers. His gaze was searing, hot, wild with desire. It took her breath away to look at him, at the intensity of his face and the perfection of his body. His body was a living sculpture of muscle. He looked to Serena like the consummate male animal, hungry and un-tamed, intent on one purpose.

She made a sound of surprise when he snatched her into his arms again, then moaned at the contact. They met flesh to flesh, soft white skin to hard, tanned muscle, woman to man. She trembled at the power of just touching him, and excitement swirled through her at the thought of being possessed by him.

He kissed her roughly, wildly, his arms banding her to him, his hands sweeping down her back, pressing her hard against his arousal, then finding their way around to the button of her shorts. The baggy khaki shorts fell to pool around her knees. She gasped into his mouth as he caught his fingertips in the waistband of her panties and jerked the scrap of silk and lace from her hips, tearing it free.

He whispered to her as he smoothed one hand over her bare hip and the delicious roundness of her buttock, kneading, squeezing, lifting her. While the fingers of his other hand slid into the nest of dark blond curls at the juncture of her thighs, seeking the heat and silken softness that lay beyond, he murmured against the shell of her ear— words of sex, words of praise, words in a language she didn't understand.

Serena tried to catch her breath to whisper his name, but couldn't. He stroked her intimately, knowingly, wringing another gasp from her as he slid a finger into her heat to test her readiness. Her hips moved against the pressure of his hand, inviting him, begging him silently.

Lucky raised his head and looked down at her. Her eyes were closed, her lips parted. Her back arched as she moved against him, thrusting her full breasts upward. With her hair tumbling around her shoulders she looked like a wanton angel. There was no sign of her infuriatingly cool control. There was no hint of polished sophistication. She was a woman who wanted a man, wanted *him,* and her body was making no secret of the fact. She moved against his hand, caught up in sensation, the soft petals of her feminine cleft dewy and warm.

Desire roared inside Lucky like an inferno, licking at his sanity, pulsing in his groin. He'd never wanted a woman like this. Never. He wanted her with every fiber of his being and she was hot and ready for him, her body begging him to take her. His nostrils flared like a stallion's scenting a mare, his head filling with a mix of expensive perfume and the subtle musk of arousal.

He pulled back from her and tore at the fastening of his jeans, fumbling with the button and struggling to get the zipper down over his erection. His manhood sprang free into Serena's waiting hands. She closed her fingers around him, measuring the length and thickness of his shaft. She stroked downward, opening her hand to cup him gently, then drew her hand slowly back up, tightening her fingers until he was throbbing. He pulled in a breath as her thumb brushed across his velvety tip.

She pressed her lips to his chest and flicked the tip of her tongue across one nipple, and Lucky lost what was left of his control. It tore away from him on a wild animal groan that started in his chest and worked its way up the back of his throat. He had to have her now. Sooner than now.

He lowered Serena onto her back and mounted her, attempting to enter her fully with a single thrust, the need to claim her as his overwhelming. She cried out and dug her fingernails into his back, her body tensing against his intrusion.

111

"Oh, sweet heaven," Lucky groaned, bracing himself on his elbows above her, fighting his natural urge to bury himself in the tight wet glove of her body. "Take it all, baby," he pleaded. "Please, *please,* Serena! All of me. All of me."

"Oh, Lucky," she gasped. "I can't. You're too—"

"Shh . . ." he whispered, brushing his lips tenderly against her temple. "Just relax for me, *chère,*" he went on seductively, schooling his own body to sink down against her. "Relax. It's gonna be all right. It's gonna be so good. Just relax for me, sugar. That's it. That's right."

She moved hesitantly beneath him, taking another inch, then tightening around him, taking him to another level of ecstasy. Lucky checked his passion ruthlessly, reining in the urge to drive himself into her, to bury himself to his hilt. He brushed her hair back from her cheek and kissed her slowly, deeply, sinking into her a little at a time as her body relaxed beneath his.

"You're tighter than a fist," he whispered breathlessly, his lips brushing hers. He struggled to hold himself still against the gentle rippling of her woman's body as it adjusted to accommodate him. *"Mon Dieu,* don't those men up in Charleston know what to do with a beautiful woman?"

Serena didn't answer him. She couldn't. She was beyond speaking, beyond telling him she couldn't even remember the name of the last man she'd gone to bed with because it had just been permanently erased from her mind. All she could think of was Lucky. All she could feel was Lucky, filling her, stretching her, kissing her. She stroked her hands over the sweat-slick muscles of his back, stroked a finger down the valley of his spine. Her hands cupped his taut buttocks and pulled him deeper into her as she tilted her hips to accept him fully.

His big body pressed down against her and he began moving slowly, easing in and out of her, gaining speed and strength with each thrust, until he was lifting her hips off the floor each time he drove into her. Serena arched against him, straining to meet him, straining toward something she had only guessed at before now. It was unlike anything else she had experienced, this feeling of intense excitement that grew like a bubble inside her, pushing away sanity, pushing aside her need for control. It was at once frightening and exhilarating, sweeping her away on a wave of sensation.

She clung to Lucky as if he could anchor her to the real world. She wrapped her arms around him, wrapped her legs around his lean hips.

And still the wild sensation grew, hotter and brighter and more intense, swelling until it burst into a million brilliant shards.

"Lucky!"

Lucky felt her climax, heard her cry his name, then his own consciousness dimmed as he exploded inside her. He arched into her with a hoarse cry, unable to think, unable to comprehend anything except the exquisite pulsing of her body around his. The moment was so sweet, so perfect, so golden that for an instant all the darkness was banished from his soul and he felt clean and whole and at peace for the first time in a long while. He clung to the feeling, clung to Serena, holding her to him as if he might be able to absorb some of the goodness he'd found in her.

Reality returned by slow degrees, coming to him as if out of a mist. The paint-stained dropcloth. The feet of his easel. The stripes of filtered daylight falling through the blinds. The woman beneath him.

He looked down at Serena and felt something squeeze painfully in his chest. She was crying silently, her head turned to the side, the teardrops leaking out through the barrier of spiky lashes. He'd hurt her. He'd taken her like a stag in rut. He'd felt how tight she was and still he'd let his own need overwhelm him and banged the living daylights out of her. *Dieu,* what kind of an animal had he become?

As many times as he'd told himself he didn't care about anyone or anything, Lucky couldn't stomach this. He'd been raised to treat women gently and with respect. Despite the cynicism that had taken root inside him over the years, the idea of a man physically abusing a woman, overpowering her with his strength, was abhorrent to him. The idea of hurting Serena, brave, proud Serena, whose regal mask hid secret fears, cut deeper than he wanted to admit.

His hand was trembling slightly as he brushed her hair back from her temple. "Serena? Serena, I'm sorry—"

"Don't be," she whispered. "I'm all right."

"I hurt you. I was too rough. I—"

"No. That's never happened for me before," she said, breaking in on his apology with her confession.

Lucky went still above her as comprehension dawned. "Never?"

She turned her head and gave him a tremulous smile. "Not like that. I didn't have any idea it could be like that. I've never been very good at sex."

Nothing could have aroused Lucky more strongly or more immediately save having her tell him she was a virgin. Knowing he had taken her somewhere no other man ever had was the next best thing. Possessiveness surged inside him and for once he didn't try to fight it or deny it. She was his. He felt it on a fundamental, instinctive level. She was his.

Still snug in the silken pocket of Serena's womanhood, his body stirred strongly and her body tightened around him in automatic response. He stared down at her, feeling caught in the grip of a powerful emotion he couldn't name. She looked up at him, her eyes dark and liquid, her lips parting softly as her breath caught.

"Oh, *ma jolie fille,*" Lucky said, lowering his head to gently nuzzle her throat. "That might have been your first trip to heaven, but it sure as hell won't be your last."

Chapter Ten

He'd had the dream a hundred times. He was crawling through a sewer tunnel under the private prison of self-styled general and drug kingpin Juan Rafael Ramos, the fumes choking him, the screams of prisoners in the interrogation rooms coming to him through the stone walls like the eerie cries of tortured souls from another dimension.

He had planned this escape since the day he had regained consciousness after his first "questioning" by Ramos's men. He had concentrated on the plan every time they tortured him, focusing his mind on freedom instead of the excruciating pain, had visualized it in his mind over and over through the endless hours in a dark, dank cell. Now the end of the tunnel was literally in sight. His fingers threaded through the rusted grate and pushed it out. On the other side, standing in a ball of bright light were Ramos, Amalinda Roca, and Lieutenant Colonel R. J. Lambert.

He lunged for Lambert first and killed him with a rough metal shank. Blood gushed from the body like water from a fire hydrant and pooled around him, thick and warm and shoulder-deep. He could hear a woman's laughter, and he turned toward it slowly, his movements hindered by the fluid rushing around him. Amalinda hovered above him, her long hair flowing around her like streamers in the wind.

The instant he recognized her her face contorted grotesquely into a monster's snarling countenance with fangs dripping venom. Her fingers transformed into snakes that wrapped around his throat and pulled his head under the swirling current of blood, drowning him. He could feel the pressure, the pain in his lungs, the panic rising in the back of his throat—

Lucky jerked awake, gasping for air and looking wildly for the source of the pressure on his chest. A woman lay with her cheek pressed over his heart, her hair spilling like a curtain of silvery silk over his dark skin. Shelby. No, no, he told himself, working to keep another rush of ugly memories at bay. Not Shelby. Serena.

It took him a long moment to sort reality from the nightmare, to realize who Serena was and where they were. Fragments of thought and emotions swirled like dust at the edges of his mind, and he painstakingly selected the appropriate pieces and frantically attempted to push the rest aside.

Serena. Safety. Home.

She lifted her head and blinked sleepily, looking up at him in silent question. Lucky said nothing. He eased out from under her and left the bed, padding naked to the front window.

A cold sweat filmed his skin. His hair was damp as he ran his fingers through it, slicking it back from his face. He was shaking— perhaps not visibly, but inside he was shaking violently and his heart beat like thunder. He braced his hands against the frame of the open window, trying to get a breath of fresh air, trying to hang on as fear tore at the edges of his sanity. It crawled up the back of his throat to choke him, and he coughed and gripped the window frame harder as he fought the sensation back down.

They were old companions, the nightmares and their aftermath, the shaking, the blinding fear that maybe this time he wouldn't be able to push the darkness back from the edges of his mind, the weariness, the regret. The thing he wanted most was to lie down and escape from it all with sleep, but he knew he wouldn't sleep again this night. The dreams were too terrible, too vivid, too seductive in their attempts to pull him over the edge.

He wouldn't sleep again this night because he was afraid, and because he was afraid he was ashamed. A stronger man could have slept. A better man wouldn't have been plagued by demons the like of these.

Knowing Serena was there to witness it all made the shame a hundred times worse and he called on his deep reservoirs of anger and self-protection to deflect it.

Serena watched him from the bed. She couldn't see his face, but the pale moonlight spilling in through the window washed silver over his shoulders and back as he stood with his head lowered. Every muscle was tense, taut, perfectly delineated from its neighbor. His back rose and fell as he struggled for breath. She had no idea what kind of nightmare had driven him from sleep to this mental ledge he was clinging to now. All she knew was that she wanted to help. She wanted to reach out and offer him her strength as he had offered his the night before.

She found Lucky's T-shirt among the tangle of clothes on the floor beside the bed and pulled it on. It fell to the middle of her thighs as she slipped from the bed and went to him.

"What's wrong?" she asked quietly. For a long moment the only sounds that answered her came from outside—the chirrup of frogs and insects, the distant whinny of a raccoon.

"*Rien,*" he said at length, then shook his head impatiently as he realized he hadn't answered her in English. "Nothing."

She reached out to lay a hand on his arm. "Lucky—"

"Nothing!" He roared, turning on her. It was a tactical error. Serena didn't back away. Instead, she looked up into his face and read it as plainly as a college professor might have read a grade-school primer. Lucky turned away to stare out the window again, schooling his voice to a calmer tone. "It's nothing to do with you. Just some leftover stuff from my stint in Central America."

"What were you doing in Central America?"

A sardonic smile twisted his mouth. "Well, I wasn't down there with the Maryknoll Fathers, that's for sure."

"The army?"

"Yeah. Doin' a little job for Uncle Sam. It was nothing."

"We don't get nightmares from nothing."

"*Pas de bêtises,*" he muttered.

"If you want to talk about it, I might be able to help," Serena said softly, her eyes warm with concern.

Lucky forced a laugh. "You can't even help yourself," he said, almost wincing at the deliberate cruelty of his words.

Serena ignored his verbal strike. He was scared and hurting; lash-

117

ing out was a natural response. "It's easier to solve other people's problems."

"Yeah, well, forget it," he growled.

She shrugged and crossed her arms in front of her. She looked all of nineteen standing there swallowed up in his T-shirt, her hair down, her skin smooth and flawless in the moonlight. Lucky felt a fresh stirring of desire and a dangerous tenderness. They added to the burden of all the other emotions he was shouldering at the moment, and he wondered if he would be able to shrug them off before he buckled beneath the load.

"All right," Serena said, nodding. "I just thought—"

"What?" Lucky snapped. "You thought what? That just because I've spent half the night inside you that gives you the right to open up my head to see what kind of snakes are in it? Think again, angel."

Serena wanted to argue with him. She wanted the right to ask him what haunted his dreams. She wanted to know everything about him. She wanted him to share that information with her willingly, but she knew he wouldn't any more than he would have shared his paintings with her. He would have been happier if she had gone on believing he was a criminal.

Maybe she would have been happier too. She would have stayed her distance from the man she had first believed him to be.

She turned and looked back at the bed they had shared the last few hours. Day had faded into night. Between bouts of lovemaking they had found their way down from the *grenier,* trading the hard floor of Lucky's studio for the comfort of an old-fashioned mattress stuffed with Spanish moss and fragrant dried flowers and herbs. Lucky had made love to her again slowly, tenderly, drawing out the anticipation and the climax, taking her to yet another height she had never before scaled. Her body was still alive with the sensations, her every nerve ending humming in awareness of the man standing beside her.

"Don't read anything into it," he muttered, following her gaze. "It's just sex."

Serena's mouth twisted in a wry, rueful smile. "Gee, thanks for making me feel like a cheap one-night stand."

"It's nothing personal."

"Oh. I see," she said dryly. "I'm just one in a long line of cheap one-night stands. That makes me feel a lot better. You sure know how to flatter a girl, Lucky."

"If you wanted pretty words, you came to the wrong man. There's nothing pretty inside me."

Serena thought of the haunting beauty of his paintings but said nothing. He hadn't appreciated her seeing them, and he wouldn't appreciate her seeing anything else that was buried beneath his tarnished armor either.

"I'm just being honest with you, chère. Isn't that what you shrinks always want? Honesty? The straight line?"

Serena said nothing. The awful fact of the matter was that deep down she would rather have had him lie to her tonight. She felt so raw emotionally; so much had happened in the last two days, she would have been glad to have a man hold her and tell her she meant the world to him even if it wasn't true. But she would have been a fool to think this man would do it. Lucky wouldn't let anyone that close to him, not even in a lie.

She walked away from him, moving gingerly. Unaccustomed to sex, her body ached in muscles she'd forgotten she had. She went to the screen door and looked out at the bayou. The fear that had assaulted her the night before was conspicuously absent tonight. Other things had taken precedence over it—thoughts of Gifford, Shelby, the very real and physical presence of Lucky. Lucky, her hero, her antihero, her lover.

She'd never taken a lover before. She'd never even known a man like Lucky before—hard, haunted, dark, and complex. It all seemed so unreal, being in this place with this man. She felt as if she didn't know herself anymore. She had a wild urge to look into a mirror to see if she even resembled the person she had been two days before.

"Are you all right?" Lucky asked.

He had moved to stand behind her. She could feel the heat of his body and didn't resist the urge to lean back into him. His arms folded around her automatically, offering comfort he would never voice.

Serena sniffed, a wry, weary smile tugging at one corner of her mouth. "Sure. I have my whole life turned upside down on a regular basis. Doesn't everyone?"

"You could leave. Go back to Charleston. Make Gifford deal with this on his own."

"No. Unlike you, I *am* obligated to other people. I may live my life apart from them, but that doesn't mean I can just shut them out. I can't walk away from this until it's over."

Lucky listened to the mix of resignation and conviction in her voice

119

and wondered how he could have ever confused her with her sister. The only thing they had in common was a pretty shell. Serena's hid a core of integrity and a deep well of strength she was having to draw on again and again, thanks to Shelby and Gifford. She was at once tough and fragile, a combination that touched him in a way he didn't want to admit. And it hurt him to think she was going to lose what was left of her innocence before everything was done here—hurt him in a place he hadn't believed he could be touched.

Out of a strong sense of self-preservation he denied the feelings. What he felt for Serena was desire and nothing more, he told himself. A desire that seemed insatiable. It stirred in his gut again like the glowing coals of a fire that could be banked but not extinguished.

He bent his head and brushed his mouth against her cheek and her temple. "Can I have you until it's over?" he murmured, his hands moving restlessly upward, over her ribs and stomach to her breasts.

Serena shivered from the heat of his touch and the coldness of his words. No pretense of love or affection. Just the bald, blunt truth. She tried not to let it bruise her heart. Lucky was no man for a long-term commitment. If she wanted him at all, she would do well to take a page from his book and see it as an opportunity for great sex and nothing more. An adventure, an odyssey she could look back on later when she returned to Charleston and sanity, and marvel at the recklessness of it.

At any rate, she didn't think she had a choice. She wanted him whatever way she could get him. Her body was responding to his now as if they had been lovers for weeks instead of hours. Heat rose inside her, inflaming the tips of her breasts as his fingers rubbed them through the soft cotton of the T-shirt. It seared her core as she felt his erection press into her back and throb relentlessly in the tender flesh between her legs. He turned her in his arms, pulling the T-shirt up so she would fit against him skin to skin.

"I can't get enough of you, *chère,*" he whispered, tasting her lips with soft, ardent kisses. "I want you again."

Serena ducked her head against his chest. "I don't think I can."

Lucky hooked a finger under her chin and tipped her head back. What he saw in her face wasn't rejection but embarrassment, and he smiled softly in understanding.

"Me, I've got just the thing for that, sugar," he said seductively, leaning down to nuzzle her cheek. "Come on back to bed and let ol' Lucky kiss it and make it better."

They left for Chanson du Terre while the mist still hovered over the bayou like thin wisps of cotton batting, giving the swamp its most primitive air. It looked like the dawn of time, when the earth was still cooling beneath the waters. Dinosaurs would not have appeared out of place.

It was easy for Serena to imagine they had slipped through a hole in the fabric of time and had fallen into earth's prehistory, that she and Lucky were the only woman and man on earth. It was an uncharacteristically romantic notion, but she didn't try to chase it away.

She took in the scenery silently as Lucky poled the boat. She still wasn't comfortable with the swamp—she doubted she ever would be —but her perceptions had changed subtly after having seen Lucky's paintings of this place. She glimpsed it now a bit through his eyes, and she tried to understand both the swamp and the man better.

Both were filled with secrets. Both were cloaked with an air of mystery and shrouded in isolation and loneliness. It was no wonder Lucky had taken refuge here; the swamp understood him. Serena wondered if she would ever be able to comprehend him fully, if she would ever be able to unlock his secrets or if he would remain as much a puzzle to her as the swamp.

The yearning to know more about him yawned inside her like a sudden crack in her block of knowledge that needed filling with details. She wanted to know what he'd been like as a boy, why he'd left college, what incidents had sown the seeds of cynicism in him. The questions buzzed on the tip of her tongue, but Serena didn't give them voice. It was foolish to encourage the desire to deepen their relationship. Lucky had set the bounds very clearly and concisely: they could share each other's body for the duration of her stay, offer the rudiments of friendship on occasion, but nothing more.

"What are you thinking?"

Serena jerked her head up in surprise, looking at Lucky with what she supposed was an unfortunately guilty expression.

"Nothing," she mumbled. She wasn't much of a liar. The word was probably emblazoned in red across her cheeks. Lucky frowned at her and she changed the subject before he could comment. "I'm not looking forward to dealing with this situation at Chanson du Terre. I don't feel it's my place to interfere."

He planted the push-pole, and the pirogue slid forward. "You said yourself, you don't have a choice."

"I know, but I don't have to like it or feel comfortable doing it. I feel like an outsider butting in. Shelby is going to resent it in a big way."

"There are more important things at stake here than Miz Shelby's feelings," Lucky said acridly.

Serena twisted around on the seat of the pirogue to get a better look at him. His jaw was set, his eyes trained on some point in the middle distance. His face gave nothing away.

"Is your family close?" she asked.

Lucky flinched inwardly. Was his family close? Oh, yes, they were close, like the woven threads in homespun Cajun cloth . . . with one exception—him. He had kept his distance since returning, though he knew it puzzled them and hurt them. They were good people, his parents, his brothers and sisters, too good to risk tainting them with his experiences and his problems. He visited his parents dutifully if not often, and he saw the others from time to time, but he remained the loose thread in the fabric of the Doucet clan. The one that had come unraveled, he thought with bitter humor.

"Lucky?"

"*Oui*," he said shortly. "They're close."

"I've never been fortunate enough to say that about my sister and me. What's going to happen with the plantation isn't likely to help matters in that respect."

"As I said, *chèrie*, there are bigger things to consider."

He steered the pirogue to the shore. Serena looked around them. They were in what seemed to be the heart of the swamp. There was no sign of civilization, certainly no sign of their destination. There was nothing much visible except black water and dense forest. She lifted a brow in silent question when Lucky glanced down at her.

"I need to show you something."

He hopped out of the pirogue and pulled the nose ashore. Serena remained stubbornly in place as he offered her his hand.

"Where is this thing you need to show me?" she asked suspiciously.

"Down this path," he said, motioning toward the woods.

Serena saw no evidence of Lucky's path. All she could focus on was the wild tangle of trees and underbrush and the knowledge of what might be under the underbrush. The old fear rose to the surface of her feelings like oil.

Lucky gently cupped her chin in his hand and turned her face up so she would look at him instead of the forest. "Don' be afraid of this

122

place, *chère,"* he whispered. "You're with me. You're mine now. I won' let anything hurt you."

Staring up into his hard face, Serena felt a strong elemental connection with him, a bond that had been forged without their knowledge or consent as they had come together in passion. She was his, Lucky Doucet's lady, bound to him in the most fundamental of ways. He would protect her as well as possess her, as males had protected their females for eons.

"You trust me, *chérie?"*

"Yes," she answered. *With my life if not my heart.*

She trusted him. It would have been unthinkable just two days earlier. She would never have believed a man who seemed so unscrupulous, so untamed, a man who defied authority and solved his problems with violence would be trustworthy on any count, but she knew now that there was so much more to Lucky than what met the eye. He was like a diamond in the rough—hard and dark on the outside, a multitude of facets within.

She took his hand and allowed him to help her from the boat. As soon as her feet touched shore he swept her up in his arms and carried her to the place he wanted her to see. The path he followed was overgrown with ferns and thorny dewberry bushes and crowded on both sides by trees. The swamp was doing its best to eradicate the evidence of man's past intrusion. For the most part, Serena saw no trail at all, but Lucky walked on as steady and sure as if he'd been strolling down Main Street in town.

He took her to a small clearing at the edge of another stream. The clearing was framed with hackberry and magnolia trees, the magnolias scenting the air with the heavy perfume of their last few blossoms. The opposite bank of the stream was dotted with white-topped daisy fleabane and black-eyed susans. Silhouetted against the rising sun were a doe and twin fawns that had come to drink.

Lucky stood Serena down in front of him, keeping her within the shelter of his arms. He pointed to a raft of water hyacinth that stretched from bank to bank.

"That stuff can choke a bayou to death," he said softly. "One plant can produce sixty-five thousand others in a single season. It blocks the light from getting to the plants beneath it and they die. The phytoplankton the fish feed on goes, and so go the fish. The pond weeds the ducks feed on die and the ducks leave. Man introduced that plant here by accident."

123

He turned slightly and pointed to a stand of cattails along the far bank where the head of an animal that resembled a beaver was visible between the reeds. "There's a nut'ra. They were brought to Lou'siana in the thirties for breeding experiments. Some got away. Now there's so many down in the marshes, they're eatin' the place up. They chew the grass down to nothin' in places where the oil companies won't let trappers in. Without the grass roots to hold it together, the marsh soil breaks up and washes away, and saltwater leaches in from the Gulf and poisons everything. Man brought the nut'ra here.

"You look at this place and think it's a world away from anywhere," he said. "But right here are two examples of man's intrusion. The swamp might seem an unforgiving, indestructable place, but it's a delicate place of checks and balances. Man could destroy it in the blink of an eye."

"Why are you showing me this?" Serena asked, looking up at him over her shoulder.

"I just wanted you to understand before you go back to deal with Shelby and Talbot and Tristar. It's not just Chanson du Terre ridin' on this, angel, and it's not just your relationship with your sister or Gifford. It's a whole ecosystem," he said, staring out at the wilderness as if he felt the need to memorize every aspect of it before it was too late. "This swamp is dying already a little bit at a time. Silting up from the big channels that were built to keep the Mississippi from flooding farm land that never should have been farm land to begin with. Tristar has plans to dig their own navigation channel. That'll bring in more silt. *Le bon Dieu* only knows what they'll dump out here where nobody can see. They have a rap sheet of environmental crimes as long as your arm."

Serena listened carefully, taking in not only his words but the sentiment behind them. This wasn't Lucky the erstwhile poacher talking, it wasn't Lucky the tough guy. This was Étienne, the student of biology, the boy who had grown up on these bayous, learning their secrets. "You love this place, don't you?"

Lucky said nothing for a long moment. This swamp was his home, his salvation, the solitude that had helped him heal when he'd been clinging to the ragged edge of sanity. The silence grew heavy, weighed down with the importance of his answer.

"Oui," he said at last. "I know you hate it, but this place is my life."

His admission touched Serena in the most tender corner of her heart, and she felt a dangerous rise of emotion pressing against the

124

backs of her eyes. This was the first part of his inner self Lucky had shared with her willingly, candidly.

No matter how foolish her brain told her it was, her heart embraced this small piece of hope greedily. She turned in Lucky's arms and hugged him, wanting something she didn't dare name and feeling in that moment that she would do anything to save this place, no matter how much she feared it, just to be able to give something to Lucky that went deeper than desire.

Chapter Eleven

"Can't you *do something,* Mason?"

Shelby paced the width of the small study her husband had taken for his own use when they had moved temporarily into Chanson du Terre. It was a dark cubbyhole of paneled walls and wood floor, filled with masculine leather furniture and shelves of musty books. Portraits of stern men from the last century stared down disapprovingly from the walls. Shelby ignored them, crossing her arms tightly beneath her breasts as she paced and listened to the click of her heels in the silence.

Mason looked up distractedly from the papers on the desk, shoving his glasses up on his nose. There was a bland, slightly vacuous look in his eyes as he took in Shelby in her new red and black suit. "I'm not sure what it is you want me to do, darlin.'"

Shelby bore down on him, her dark eyes flaming with impatience. She braced her hands against the desk, her fingers newly manicured and decked with a garnet and diamond ring. "You heard what Burke had to say. He thinks we should have Gifford declared incompetent."

"Now, Shelby," Mason said, smiling benignly. He abandoned the papers he'd been going over and folded his hands neatly on top of

126

them. "I have explained to you before why that won't work. In the first place, how would that look if I had my wife's grandfather declared incompetent so I might profit from the sale of his estate? That wouldn't do, sweetheart. The voters frown on that sort of thing. Secondly, Serena would never agree to it."

"Serena." Shelby spat out her sister's name like a curse as she pulled back from the desk to resume her pacing. "Blast her. Why did she have to come back just when things were looking so good for us? She's going to ruin everything for me. She always does."

Mason tut-tutted at her from behind his smile. "Have a little faith, sugar plum. Serena may very well see reason when she hears the whole story."

"She'll side with Gifford," Shelby snapped, smoothing a stray hair back toward her neat French twist. "I'm sure he's been filling her head with nonsense. And who knows what that Lucky Doucet has been telling her."

"Why should he be telling her anything? She only hired him to take her out to Gifford's."

"Well . . ." she stalled, dodging her husband's vaguely curious stare. "Well . . . because he's crazy, that's why."

Mason shook his head. "You're getting all riled up for nothing."

"One of us had better get riled up. If we don't raise some cash soon, we're going to be in trouble, Mason. You need funding for your campaign and we have to close on the new house soon."

"It would help if you could get the old one sold."

Shelby stopped in her tracks, pressing a hand to her heart and looking wounded, as if her husband's suggestion had been a stake driven into her. "I am trying to sell the house, Mason. It isn't my fault the Loughtons' financing fell through at the last minute. It isn't my fault the market is soft right now."

"I know it isn't your fault, pet," Mason hurried to assure her. "Of course it's not. I was just wishing out loud, that's all."

He did the rest of his wishing in silence as he thought of the credit card Shelby had run to its limit even before she'd bought this new ensemble. He had a terrible sinking feeling the red leather pumps were exorbitantly expensive, but he said nothing. Previous suggestions for Shelby to curb her spending habits had been met with hysteria.

"I'll tell you what I wish," Shelby muttered, putting on her most effective pout. "I wish I were an only child and that Gifford would come to his senses. That's what I wish."

"You worry too much, peach," Mason said. "Things will work out. You'll see. They always do."

There was a sharp rap at the door, and Odille Fontenot slipped into the room. Her bony frame was painfully erect, her light eyes and thin mouth fierce and disapproving, as always. Her hair was a distressed ball of salt-and-pepper frizz around her head. She wore a cotton house-dress in a bright flowered print that was subdued somehow by her general aura of gloom. It hung shapelessly from shoulders as sharp and thin as a wire hanger.

"You ought to wait to be invited in, Odille," Shelby said defensively, not certain what the housekeeper might have overheard. "Your manners are atrocious. If you worked for me, I'd fire you for insolence."

Odille sniffed indignantly. "Me, I don' work for you. Day I work for you, day I lose my mind."

Shelby puffed herself up like an offended pigeon. "Of all the impertinence!"

"Was there something you needed to tell us, Odille?" Mason intervened tactfully.

Odille's narrow eyes shifted from Mason to Shelby and back. "Miz 'Rena home," she announced ominously, then turned and stalked out without waiting to be dismissed.

Serena appeared a moment later. She'd left her bags by the door and gone directly in search of her sister, intending to clear up a few things immediately.

"Shelby, Mason, I think we need to have a talk," she said as she stepped into the library.

"Serena!" Shelby gushed with a great show of worry. She rushed forward, wringing her bejeweled hands. "Are you all right? We were just worried sick about you! Anything might have happened to you out in the swamp with that madman!" Her gaze flicked over Serena's shoulder. "Did Gifford return with you?"

"No, he didn't."

Mason came around from behind the desk, moving with the grace of breeding, a smile of welcome beaming across his face like the sun. He was attractive in the mild, unassuming way of all the Talbots. He wore a rumpled blue oxford shirt and an air of good-natured distraction that had an immediate calming effect on Serena. She managed a smile as he reached for her.

"Serena, darlin,' it's so good to see you," he said, giving her a

128

brotherly hug, then standing her back at arm's length to get a good look at her. "I'm sorry I wasn't here to greet you the other day. I'm afraid my practice is a taskmaster. And then Shelby informed me you'd gone off on your own after Gifford." He shook his head in reproach. "I must say, you had us concerned."

"The situation with Gifford seemed to demand immediate attention."

"Gifford. Yes." He nodded, arranging his features into an appropriately grave expression as he tucked his hands into the pockets of his tan chinos. "Well, Shelby tells me she didn't get a chance to explain things adequately before you rushed off."

"As I recall," Serena said dryly, giving her sister a pointed look, "Shelby made no attempt to explain."

Shelby summoned up the same wounded look she'd bestowed on her husband earlier and directed it at her sister. "That's simply not true, Serena! I practically begged you to stay so we could chat!"

"You told me you didn't know why Gifford had gone into the swamp."

Mason stepped in to arbitrate like a born diplomat. "I think what Shelby meant was that we're all a little baffled as to why Gifford left instead of staying here and dealing with the situation in his usual straightforward manner. Things are in a bit of a tangle, as you may have gathered."

"Yes, I figured that out somewhere in between shotgun blasts," Serena said sardonically. "Can we sit down and discuss this from the top?" she asked, moving toward one of the big leather chairs.

Mason made an apologetic face as he consulted his watch. "I'm afraid I can't at the moment, Serena. I've got a meeting with a client at two. I really must rush now or I'll be late." He consulted his reflection in the glass doors of a bookcase, buttoning the collar of his shirt and pushing up the knot of his regimental tie. "There will be ample time to go over it all tonight at dinner. Mr. Burke is coming, as well as Gifford's attorney. We thought perhaps Lamar might have some sway over Gifford in the event you weren't able to bring him back."

Serena heaved an impatient sigh. She had wanted to tackle the problem immediately, the sooner to finish with it, but that wasn't going to be possible now. She looked at Mason and wondered if there really was a client. Her brother-in-law gave her another earnest, apologetic smile before he kissed Shelby's cheek and left, and she chided herself for hunting for conspiracy and deceit where there probably was none. Mason had never been anything but sweet to her.

"And I just have a million things to do today!" Shelby declared suddenly. She bustled around the desk, straightening papers into stacks. "I have an open house to conduct at Harlen and Marcy Stone's. Harlen is being transferred to Scotland, of all places. Imagine that! And John Mason has a soccer game and Lacey has her piano lesson. And, of course, I'll have to oversee the dinner preparations.

"I asked Odille to fix a crown roast, but there's no telling what she might do. She's a hateful old thing. John Mason hasn't slept for two nights since she told him his room is haunted by the ghost of a boy who was brutally slain by Yankees during the war."

Serena sank down into a chair and dropped her head back, her sister's bubbling energy making her acutely aware of her own fatigue.

Shelby stopped her fussing, turning to face her twin with a motherly look of concern. "My stars, Serena, you look like death warmed over!" Her eyes narrowed a fraction. "What happened to you out there?"

"Nothing."

"Well, you look terrible. You ought to take a nice long soak and then have a nap. I'd tell Odille to slice some cucumber for those horrid black circles under your eyes, but she'd probably take after me with a knife. She's just that way. I can't imagine why Gifford keeps her on."

"Why didn't you tell me about Mason possibly running for office?" Serena asked abruptly.

Her sister gave her a blank look. "Why, because you never gave me a chance, that's why. You just had to run off into the swamp before I could explain a thing. And now I have to run. We'll tell you all about it over dinner." Her face lit up beneath a layer of Elizabeth Arden's finest. "It's the most excitin' thing! I'm just tickled!" She checked the slim diamond-studded watch on her wrist and gasped delicately. "I'm late! We'll talk tonight."

"We certainly will," Serena muttered to herself as the staccato beat of her sister's heels faded down the hall.

As the quiet settled in around her, she thought longingly of Shelby's suggestion of a bath and a nap. She thought about lapsing into unconsciousness in the chair she was sitting in. But in the end she forced herself to her feet and went outside in search of James Arnaud, the plantation manager.

130

Chanson du Terre had once been a plantation of nearly ten thousand acres, but it had shrunk over the decades a parcel at a time to its current two thousand acres. Rice and indigo had been the original money crops. Indigo still grew wild in weedy patches here and there in ditches around the farm. There had been a brief experiment with rice in the 1800s, then sugarcane had taken over. For as long as Serena could remember, the fields had been planted half with cane, a fourth with soybeans, and a fourth allowed to lie fallow.

Growing cane was a gamble. The crop was temperamental about moisture, prone to disease, vulnerable to frost. The decision of when to harvest in the fall could be an all-or-nothing crap shoot, with the grower putting it off to the last possible day in order to reap the richest sucrose harvest, then working round the clock to bring it in. Once the freeze came, the cane in the fields would rot if not harvested immediately.

Gifford had always said sugarcane was the perfect crop for the Sheridans. They had won Chanson du Terre on a gamble; it seemed only fitting to go on gambling. But the gamble hadn't been paying off recently.

James Arnaud, found swearing prolifically at a tractor in the machine shed, informed Serena that the plantation was caught in a downward spiral that showed no promise of reversing itself any time soon. Arnaud was a short, stocky man in his forties who possessed the dark hair and eyes of his Cajun heritage and a volatile temper to match. He had been manager of the plantation for nearly a dozen years. In that time he had proven himself worthy of Gifford's trust time and again. Serena knew he would tell her the truth, she just hadn't realized how grim that truth would be.

Much of the previous season's crop had been lost to disease. Heavy spring rains had hurt the present crop's growth in several fields where drainage was an ongoing problem. As a result, there was no extra cash to replace aging equipment and they had been forced to cut back on help. All in all, Arnaud thought it was more than most seventy-eight-year-old men would care to deal with, and he said he wouldn't blame Gifford a bit if he did indeed sell the place and go to Tahiti.

What they needed, Arnaud said, was an influx of money and possibly a new cash crop to rotate with the sugarcane. But money was as scarce as hen's teeth, and Gifford was resistant to change.

Serena walked away from the conversation more depressed than she had been to begin with. Even after this business with Tristar Chemicals had been settled, the ultimate fate of the plantation would still be up in the air. She would go back to Charleston. Shelby and Mason would go off to Baton Rouge. Gifford would remain; an aging man and an aging dream left to fade away.

She walked along the crushed-shell path with her hands tucked into the pockets of her shorts, her wistful gaze roaming over the weathered buildings, looking past the pecan orchard to a field of cane. The stalks were already tall and green, reaching for the sky. In her memory she could almost smell the pungent, bittersweet scent of burning leaves at harvest time, when machines the size of dinosaurs crept through the fields and workers bustled everywhere. Harvest time was one of her favorite childhood memories. She had loved the sense of excitement and urgency after the long, slow days of summer.

It had been a good childhood, growing up here, she reflected as she climbed the steps to the old gazebo that was situated at the back of the garden behind the big house. She slid down on a weathered bench, glad for the shade, and leaned back against the railing, staring up at the house. Odille came out the back door wearing an enormous straw hat with a basket slung over her arm, and brandishing garden scissors and a ferocious scowl as she headed for a bed of spring flowers. At a corner of the house John Mason crept around a pillar, intent on scaring the living daylights out of Lacey, who was sitting on the grass playing with dolls. It was the kind of scene that brought memories to the surface— hot spring days and the unencumbered life of childhood in the shadows of Chanson du Terre.

It was the only home Serena and Shelby had ever known growing up. Their parents had settled in immediately after their wedding. An only son, Robert Sheridan, their father, had been groomed from an early age to take Gifford's place at the helm of the plantation. Serena couldn't help but think how different things would have been if he had lived. But he hadn't. He had died in a plane crash the day she and Shelby had turned fifteen.

His wife had preceded him to the grave by ten years. Serena barely remembered her mother except in random adjectives—a pretty smile, a soft voice, a loving touch. She remembered that her father had been devastated by her mother's death. She could still hear the terrible sound of his crying—wrenching, inconsolable grief confined to his bedroom while ladies from their church had placated everyone else with tuna casseroles and Jell-O. There had been no second marriage, no more children, no sons to carry on the line or take up the reins of the plantation.

What was it like to love someone that much? To love so that death meant the death of one's own heart. Serena couldn't imagine. She had never known that depth of emotion with a man, had never expected to. In her work she'd seen too many crumbled relationships to believe the other kind came along very often.

Her thoughts drifted to Lucky. She told herself it was only natural. She'd just spent a long hot night in his arms. That didn't mean she was thinking of him in permanent terms. But she couldn't help but wonder if he had ever known that kind of love. He would deny being capable of it. Of that she was certain. He didn't want anyone to know there was a heart under that carved-from-granite chest. Why? Because it had been broken, abused?

He had known Shelby, had been involved with her to some extent. Every time she thought of it, Serena felt a violent blast of disbelief and jealousy. Had they been lovers? Had they been in love? Was it Shelby who had bred that distrust of women in him? The idea brought a bitter taste to her mouth. It was yet another perfectly logical, practical reason for her not to get involved with Lucky Doucet, but she had taken that ill-advised step anyway. She had seen all the warning signs and plunged in headfirst in spite of them.

What a mess, she thought, a long sigh slipping between her lips. She picked absently at a scab of peeling paint on the railing and shook her head. She'd left Charleston with nothing on her mind but thoughts of a pleasant vacation and had fallen into a plot worthy of a Judith Krantz novel.

That was another reason she had left Chanson du Terre to begin with. In Charleston she had no complicated family relationships to deal with. She didn't have to wonder if her own sister was up to no good. She didn't have to look at her ancestral home and wonder what would become of it after two hundred years of Sheridan stewardship ended. She didn't have to worry about falling short of Gifford's expectations. She didn't have to watch him grow old. She could come back for the occasional dose of nostalgia and leave before it became necessary to deal with anything as unpleasant as past hurts and old fears.

"You can't hightail it out of Lou'siana first chance you get, then come on back and try to run things on the weekend."

Gifford's voice still rang in her ears. The old reprobate. He had hit a nerve with that line, had scored a bull's-eye, sticking the dart right smack in the center of her guilt. And even while he'd been doing it, he had been maneuvering her so she would either have to deal with the problems or dig her guilt a deeper hole. He had her right where he wanted her, in the last place she wanted to be, dealing with questions she had never wanted to face.

"Serena, I don't believe you've met Mr. Burke from Tristar Chemical," Mason said smoothly. He came forward, innocuous smile in place, and took her gently by the arm as she entered the front parlor.

"We haven't been formally introduced, no," Serena said, extending her hand to the big man in the western-cut suit. "I'm afraid you mistook me for my sister the other day out at Gifford's, Mr. Burke. I'm Serena Sheridan."

Burke let his eyes drift down over her, taking in the subtle lines of her figure revealed by the straight cut of her toffee-colored sleeveless linen sheath. He pumped her hand and grinned. "By golly, who'd a guessed there'd be two this pretty? It's a pleasure, *Miss* Sheridan?" His brows rose with a hope that made Serena loath to answer his implied question.

"Yes," she murmured. She extracted her fingers from his meaty grasp and managed a twitch of the lips that passed for a smile. His gaze homed in on her breasts like radar.

"Now, what was a lovely young thing like yourself doing out in that swamp anyway?" he asked, settling a too-familiar hand on her shoulder.

Serena shrugged off his touch on the excuse of reaching up to smooth her fingers over her loosely bound hair.

"Serena is here on a visit from Charleston. She was trying to persuade Gifford to return so we might all deal with this offer in a proper manner," Mason explained.

"And did you?"

"No, unfortunately not," Serena replied. "As you no doubt realize by now, Mr. Burke, my grandfather can be a very stubborn man."

"It goes a might beyond stubborn, if you ask me," Burke said, baring his teeth. "I have my doubts about his sanity."

"Do you?" Serena arched a brow. "Are you a psychologist, Mr. Burke?"

"No—"

"Well, I am," she said, her tone as smooth and cool as marble. "And

I can assure you that while Gifford may be unreasonable and cantankerous, he is very much in control of his faculties."

Burke's face turned dull red. His nostrils flared like a bull's and his chest puffed out. Mason intervened with diplomatic grace.

"Would you care for a drink, Serena?"

"Gin and tonic, please," she said with a sweet smile, resisting the urge to lick a finger and chalk up a point for herself.

"Coming right up. And can I freshen that scotch for you, Len?"

Frowning, Burke followed him across the room to the antique sideboard that served as bar and liquor cabinet. Serena took the brief moment of solitude to survey the room. It looked exactly as it always had—taupe walls trimmed in soft white, faded Oriental carpets over a polished wood floor, heavy red brocade drapes flanking the French doors that led onto the gallery. The furniture was too formal to invite relaxation. It was a room Gifford never set foot in unless forced. He called it a place for entertaining people he didn't really like. How appropriate that they were gathering here, Serena thought as her gaze wandered over the people assembling for dinner.

Mason was already looking the part of the junior senator in a crisp shirt and tie and dark slacks, not quite as rumpled or distracted as he usually seemed. He made harmless small talk as he dug ice cubes from the bucket with tiny tongs. She had never thought about it before, but he would probably make a successful politician with his mild good looks and genteel manner.

Burke, in spite of the expensive cut of his suit, struck her as a man who wasn't afraid to get his hands dirty. He had the predatory air of a man who had clawed his way up to his present status and had no intention of going back down. He wore a gawdy diamond pinky ring and a boulder-sized chunk of turquoise on a bolo tie, flaunting the rewards of his labors like a warrior brandishing the trophies of battle.

Serena hadn't liked what she'd seen of him at Gifford's, and her instincts were telling her not to like anything about him tonight, but she tried to be objective. It wasn't a fatal character flaw for a man to be vulgar or pompous or sexist, and she had to admit he'd had a right to his temper of the day before—Gifford had been shooting at him, after all. Still, there was something about him that made her uncomfortable. Something about his narrow eyes and the set of his mouth. Gifford had said the man wouldn't take no for an answer. Serena wondered what lengths he might be willing to go to to achieve his objective.

Shelby breezed in from the hall then, resplendent in an ultrafeminine dress done in a dark English-garden print with a square ivory lace collar and a flowing skirt. Her hair was neatly confined in an old-fashioned ecru snood that perfectly completed the picture of refined southern womanhood. The scent of Opium drifted around her in a fragrant cloud.

"Mr. Burke! How delightful to see you again!" She preened and sparkled, treating him to her most flirtatious smile as she came forward and offered him her hand.

"It's a pleasure, as always, Mrs. Talbot," Burke said, treating her to the same once-over he had Serena. "I've just had the chance to meet your lovely sister as well."

Shelby's smile tightened as she shot a look at Serena. "You're looking a little better tonight, Serena. Not quite as haggard as before."

"Why, thank you," Serena said, fighting a wry smile. She accepted her drink from Mason and sipped it, enjoying the bite of the gin a little more than she probably should have. This crowd was enough to drive anybody to drink. The room hummed with undercurrents.

"I've just been down to the kitchen to check on things," Shelby said, batting her lashes at the big Texan. "We're having a lovely ham. I do hope you like ham, Mr. Burke. Our Odille's ham gravy is simply sinful!"

"What happened to the crown roast?" Serena questioned innocently.

Shelby flashed her a dark look. "That didn't work out as I'd hoped."

"Pity."

"Well, now," Mason said expansively. "We're just waiting on Lamar and then we can go in."

Shelby pouted, stirring the swizzle stick of the drink her husband handed her. "That doddering old fool. I don't understand why Gifford retains that man. It's an embarrassment that he won't let his own grandson-in-law handle his legal affairs."

"Now, Shelby," Mason cajoled. "Lamar has been Gifford's attorney since God was a child. I certainly wouldn't expect him to dissolve an old loyalty like that."

"Well, I would," Shelby said, fussing with one pearl earring. "What must people think? That he doesn't trust you to handle his affairs? It's disgraceful. I only hope it doesn't have an adverse affect on your campaign."

136

Mason smiled at her benignly. "I'm not concerned about it, darlin.' Don't you be."

"I'm sure securing new jobs for the community will more than outweigh it, Mrs. Talbot," Burke said smugly, swirling the ice in his glass. "Bringing industry to a stagnant economy could take Mason here a long, long way."

"Aren't you forgetting something, Mr. Burke?" Serena said mildly. "Our grandfather has no intention of selling his property to Tristar."

Burke flushed again, his eyes narrowing. Shelby shot daggers at her sister with her eyes. Mason flashed a big politician's smile and said, "I do believe I hear Lamar's old Mercedes coming up the drive."

Lamar Canfield was eighty if he was a day, a southern gentleman lawyer from the old school. He was a small, neat man with large dark eyes and thin white hair that now grew only on the sides of his head. He was dressed meticulously in a blue seersucker suit and starched white shirt with a jaunty striped bow tie at his throat and a fine Panama hat in his hands.

"Shelby! How good it is to see you again!" he said, beaming a smile as he came forward with the grace of Fred Astaire to take Serena's hand and plant a courtly kiss upon her knuckles.

"I'm Serena, Mr. Canfield," she corrected him gently.

He pulled back, beaming a broad smile, his eyes gleaming with a sparkle that had set more than one female's heart aflutter in his day. "Yes, of course you are, my darling," he said without missing a beat. "How lovely to have you home for a visit. You don't return often enough, you know," he chided her, tilting his head in a look of reproach.

Serena couldn't help but smile at him. She had always liked Lamar. He was all flirtation and show and he had the voice of a snake-oil salesman—smooth and exaggerated, rising and falling dramatically. He displayed all the airs and mannerisms of a completely charming charlatan, all presented with a twinkle of amusement in his dark eyes that suggested he didn't take himself or anyone else too seriously.

"How doubly fortunate for us gentlemen to have the company of both our lovely Sheridan ladies," he said, turning and bowing to Shelby, who regarded him with wary petulance, for once not swayed by a compliment. He straightened and turned his hat in his hands, directing his attention toward Serena once again.

"Are you back to stay, perchance, Serena? Heaven knows there is an abundance of warped minds in the immediate area. You could certainly keep yourself entertained."

"No," Serena said a bit hesitantly. "I'm just here for a visit, I'm afraid."

Lamar looked at her speculatively from under his lashes and clucked his tongue.

Mason stepped forward. "Lamar, you've met Mr. Burke from Tristar, if you'll recall."

"Yes . . . of course," Lamar drawled, dragging the words out and letting them trail away as if they pained him. "You're that man from Texas, aren't you?" He pronounced it *takes-us*, though whether he had done so as a deliberate slight or whether it was simply his extravagant drawl was impossible to tell.

Burke gave him a stony look, rattling the ice in his scotch.

Odille slipped into the room then and cast a baleful glare over them all as she announced dinner.

"Odille, my love!" Lamar said brightly. "Charming as ever. Tell me what I might be able to do to entice you away from Gifford's employ."

Odille sniffed indignantly, squeezing her light eyes into slits of disapproval. "Nothin.' "

"Locquacious, isn't she, Shelby?" Lamar said, arching one brow as he took Serena's arm and tucked it through his.

Dinner was served in a formal dining room that had changed very little in a hundred years. They were seated at a mahogany table that had hosted planters from antebellum days. They used silver that had spent the war in a gunnysack in the bottom of the well to keep it safe from Yankee plunder. The oil painting on the wall above the sideboard portrayed a Sheridan standing on the lawn of Chanson du Terre, holding the reins of a prized race horse; a brass plaque on the frame dated it to 1799.

"Such a lovely home," Lamar remarked idly as he cut his ham. "So gracious and full of history."

"Yes," Serena agreed. "It would be a pity to see it destroyed."

"There are more things to consider here than architecture," Mason said. "Chanson du Terre is a graceful old home, I grant you, but should it be placed ahead of the welfare of an entire community?"

"That's a good point, Mason," said Burke. He looked across the table to Serena. "You don't live around here, Miss Sheridan. Maybe you don't realize how hard the oil bust hit. People moved out of Lafayette by the convoy. Many of those who remained in South Louisiana were faced with unemployment. The new Tristar plant will employ two hundred fifty people to start with and eventually many more."

"But at what cost to the environment, Mr. Burke?" Serena asked. "I understand your company has a rather bad reputation in that area."

Burke's eyes went cold. A muscle in his jaw twitched. "I don't know where you get your information, but it simply isn't true. Tristar has never been convicted of anything regarding violations of pollution standards."

Serena lifted a brow, singling out the word "convicted." Tristar had never been convicted, that wasn't to say they had never been charged or had never committed any crimes. They had simply never been convicted, a fact that made her wonder what lengths they may have gone to to keep blemishes from their record. If Len Burke was an example of the kind of man they hired to make their acquisitions, she could well imagine the sharks they retained on their legal staff to help them work around inconveniences like EPA regulations.

Her gaze moved to Mason, the fledgling politician whose campaign would rely heavily on Tristar. She wondered if he realized just how neatly he was being maneuvered. Tristar was providing him with a platform on which to run. Directly or indirectly they would be providing him with funding. Had it occurred to him that eventually they would call in those markers?

"Isn't it true Tristar would dig a navigation canal that would contribute to the demise of the swamp?" she asked.

Burke snorted and shook his head. "You'd put a few acres of worthless mud and snakes ahead of the lives of the people around here?"

"The swamp isn't worthless to everyone," she said quietly, thinking of the look in Lucky's eyes as he'd shown her his special place that morning. "It's an ecosystem that deserves respect."

Shelby laughed without humor. "My, you're the last person I would have expected to hear that from, Serena. Why, you've hated the swamp as long as I can remember. You moved all the way to Charleston to get away from it."

Serena regarded her sister with a look that barely disguised anger and hurt. "Be that as it may," she said, "we are getting ahead of ourselves, aren't we? The fact remains Gifford has strong feelings about heritage and tradition. He would prefer to see Chanson du Terre continue on as it always has."

"How can it?" Shelby asked, tearing a biscuit into bite-size pieces.

She looked askance at her twin. "Are you going to come back from Charleston and farm it, Serena?"

"Of course not."

"Then what do you suggest? Mason's future lies elsewhere. Who else is left to run it?"

"Shelby's right," Mason said. "Even if Gifford doesn't sell now, he'll only be delaying the inevitable. He's going to have to retire in the not too distant future. He'll be forced to sell in the end. Taking Tristar's offer now is the only practical thing to do. It's a very generous offer, certainly more than Chanson du Terre is worth as a going concern."

"The place is falling down around Gifford's ears," Shelby remarked. "You can't help but have noticed. The house is in need of major restoration. Why, just look at the ceiling in this room for example."

All eyes traveled upward and widened at the sight of the heavy brass chandelier hanging down from the center of a sagging, water-stained, peeling spot of plaster. It looked as if one good tug could bring the whole expanse crashing down on their heads.

"There are other alternatives to selling," Serena said, bringing them back to the matter at hand. "The land could be leased to another grower. The house must qualify for historical status; there's the possibility of grant money being available to restore it."

"But to what end?" Mason questioned. "When Gifford passes on, I trust he will leave the place to you and Shelby equally and Shelby has already stated she no longer wants it. Are you prepared to buy her out, Serena?"

"If you are, perhaps you'll just run along and get your checkbook, darlin,' " Shelby suggested archly. "I have a life to lead and I'd sooner get on with it than wait."

Serena's mouth tightened as she looked at her sister. "What happened to your dedication to the preservation of southern antiquities, sister?" she queried bitingly through a chilling smile. "Did that committee meeting conflict with your facial appointments?"

Shelby slammed her fork down on the table and straightened in her chair, her mouth tightening into a furious knot. "Don't you talk to me about dedication, Serena. You're the one who lives eight hundred miles away. You're the one—"

"Now, ladies," Mason interrupted with the borrowed wisdom of Solomon shining in his eyes behind his glasses. "Let's not regress to pointing fingers. The fact is neither of you will take over the running of the plantation. What we must concentrate on is how to deal with Mr.

Burke's offer and how to deal with Gifford. Might you have any suggestions in that area, Lamar? Lamar?"

Canfield had dozed off over his mashed potatoes. Shelby rolled her
eyes. Burke huffed in impatient disgust. Odille, making the rounds
with a fresh gravy boat, gave the old attorney a bony elbow to the
shoulder. He jerked awake, confusion swimming in his eyes as his gaze
searched the table and settled on Serena.

"A lovely meal, Shelby," he said with a smile. "Thank you so much
for asking me out."

Serena groaned inwardly. If there had been any hope of finding a
valuable ally in Gifford's attorney, it had just faded away.

"There's no place for sentiment in business," Burke announced,
helping himself to another mountain of sliced ham. "The place will be
sold in the end. Y'all might as well face the facts and take the money."

"It's not our decision to make, Mr. Burke," Serena said tightly.

He gave her a long look. "Isn't it?"

"What are you saying?"

He lifted his shoulders and looked away from her toward Mason
and Shelby. "Just that Tristar's offer is firm. We want this piece of
property. If you want to collect on that, I suggest you strengthen your
powers of persuasion where your granddaddy is concerned—one way
or another."

The addendum had all the nasty connotations of a threat. Serena
sat back in her chair, her gaze on Burke as he shoveled food into his
mouth. Gifford had been right; a simple no was not going to deter the
Tristar rep. She wondered as she caught her sister looking her way just
what it was going to take to put an end to this business once and for
all, and whether there would be anything left of her family when it was
over.

Chapter Twelve

Serena changed into her nightgown feeling as if she hadn't slept in a month. Dinner had been an exhausting ordeal, not to mention depressing. And with no progress for the trouble. Burke was still set on acquiring Chanson du Terre; Shelby and Mason were still bent on selling it to him. She was still caught in the middle.

She had been glad to escape to the quiet and comfort of her bedroom. The room hadn't been changed at all in the time she had lived away from Chanson du Terre. Like the rest of the house, it seemed to possess a stubborn agelessness that defied change. The walls were papered in a delicate vine and flower pattern over a background of rich ivory. The rug that covered the floor had been trod upon by generations of Sheridan feet. The cherry bed and its hand-tied net canopy had offered rest to the weary a century before. Serena found the idea comforting. The sense of constancy appealed to her, especially now, when she was feeling tired and uncertain about so many things. She could at least look around her room in the soft light of the bedside lamp and feel welcomed.

Belting her white silk robe around her, she went to stand in the open doorway leading onto the gallery, leaning against the frame as if she hadn't the strength left to support herself. The night beyond was dark and starless, the air heavy with the promise of rain and the scents of wisteria and honeysuckle. How many other Sheridan women had stood in this exact spot and looked out into the night, pondering their futures? How many would do so in years to come? None, if Len Burke got his way. And if Burke didn't get his way . . . ?

A soft knock on the door roused Serena from her tormented musings. She turned as Shelby stuck her head into the room.

"May I come in?"

A shrug was the only answer Serena could muster. She was exhausted. The prospect of yet another conversational wrestling match with her sister was not inviting.

Shelby came in and closed the door behind her, leaning back against it, an uncertain look in her dark eyes. She had shed her pumps and let her hair down, making her look young and sweet in her feminine dress. She still wore an array of expensive rings on her dainty hands and demonstrated her hesitancy by twisting her topaz around her finger.

"I'm only trying to be practical, Serena," she said with a suddenness that made it seem as if she had launched into the middle of the conversation instead of the beginning. "I should think you, of all people, would appreciate that. You've always been practical."

"Practicality isn't the issue," Serena said, coming away from the gallery door, sliding her hands into the deep pockets of her robe.

"Well, it should be. For heaven's sake, Serena, think about it!" Shelby insisted. She moved around the room with short, brisk strides, compulsively straightening things that didn't need straightening. "The place will have to be sold eventually. Here we have a buyer ready to hand us money on a platter, and I can tell you as a real estate professional, they don't come along every day. There's nothing but good in this for everyone, and Gifford is standing in the way just to be stubborn!"

"He's worked this land all his life," Serena pointed out calmly, playing the devil's advocate out of habit and necessity. "He doesn't want to see it all wiped away."

Shelby stopped her fussing and shot her sister a narrow sideways look, her mood flashing from businesslike to petulant to shrewd. "He's manipulating you."

Serena didn't argue the point; it was true. She was too caught up watching her sister's chameleon qualities, at once fascinated and horrified by rapid changes. They pointed toward problems Serena found herself wanting to deny.

"He's just that way," Shelby went on, absently rearranging things on the dresser to suit her own tastes. "He's in his glory now, holding all of us hostage. He's a stubborn old man."

"Would you give up your children for the sake of someone else's livelihood?" Serena asked.

Shelby turned toward her, offended and incredulous. "Give up my children? Don't be ridiculous! Of course not, but it's hardly the same thing."

"It is to Giff. This land is as much a part of him as we are. Why should he be expected to give it up?"

Shelby's face flushed and she stamped her foot on the rug. Her hands balled into fists at her side. "Because it's what everyone else wants! Because it's going to happen anyway. For pity's sake, why doesn't he just give in?"

"Because he's Gifford."

"Well, something has to be done, Serena," she announced vehemently as she resumed pacing. "He's just being unreasonable and it's hurting us all. I told you I thought he was going senile and I believe it. And I'm not the only one who thinks so."

Serena thought back to Burke's threats of a competency hearing and frowned at her twin. She refrained from pointing out that a man who had the ability to manipulate so many people so neatly couldn't possibly be senile. Instead, she simply said, "I will not see Gifford declared incompetent, Shelby. Don't even think about suggesting it."

"It would serve him right," Shelby said sourly, her lower lip jutting forward in a pout.

Serena was appalled by the suggestion and the attitude that accompanied it. She may not have been especially close to or fond of her sister, but still she didn't want to believe her own flesh and blood, her own twin capable of such callous selfishness. She stared at Shelby now, disgust and disbelief stark on her face. "I can't believe your greed would push you to something so ugly."

Shelby's eyes flashed wildly. Serena thought she could almost hear her sister's control crack. "Greed? Greed!" Shelby shouted, stepping toward Serena. Her lovely ivory complexion turned a mottled red. Every muscle in her body seemed to go rigid. "How dare you accuse me of greed! You're the greedy one! You and Gifford. Greedy and selfish! I want only what's best for everybody!"

Right, Serena thought. Businesswoman of the Year. Mason in the legislature. A healthy bank account and the unending gratitude of those who would profit from the deal. She didn't say any of those things, however. She stood silent, staring at her sister, a sick churning in her stomach.

Shelby paced back and forth along the length of the bed, huffing and puffing like a toy train. "Isn't this just like you?" she said bitterly. "You waltz in from Charleston and take Gifford's side just to please him and then you'll waltz back out and not give a damn that you've ruined everything for everyone else. You won't have to deal with it. You don't live here. You don't care. The rest of us have responsibilities here."

"You don't seem to feel any responsibility toward Gifford or your family home or the environment," Serena pointed out, knowing she would have been better off saying nothing. But she couldn't seem to find the cool restraint she used when confronted by an overwrought patient. She couldn't maintain objectivity with her own family, and the only way she could distance herself from them was in the physical sense. The minute she came back here she felt sucked into an emotional maelstrom, a thick familial quicksand that pulled her down from her safe perch above it all. It was a humbling experience and an exhausting one. She gave in to it now as her temper rose and her control slipped away.

"You know what the petrochemical industry has done down here already," she argued. "Fouling land and water—"

"Feeding people, providing jobs, keeping towns alive—"

"—elevating the cancer rate, destroying animal habitat—"

"Oh, for the love of Mike!" Shelby threw her hands up in exasperation. "You sound like those lunatics up in Oregon, or wherever they are, harping on the loggers for scaring off a bunch of owls that don't have sense enough to go live someplace else. And all for a place you hate to begin with!"

Serena pulled herself back from the ragged edge of anger and sighed, crossing her arms defensively. "Just because it's not a place I like to be doesn't mean I want it wiped off the face of the earth. There are people who still make their living out there, you know."

Shelby sniffed indignantly. "Poachers and white trash. If you ask me, Tristar would be doing us all a favor getting rid of them."

Serena rolled her eyes. "A very charitable attitude."

"Practical. Practical," Shelby reiterated with a decisive nod. She calmed visibly as she put on her businesslike persona again, folding her hands primly in front of her. "It's the practical thing, Serena. And if you have no interest in staying here anyway, I don't see why you don't just side with us and get it over with. It's best for everyone. It's best for Gifford, if you come right down to it.

"He's seventy-eight years old and he's got a heart condition, for heaven's sake," she said, warming to this new angle of showing concern for someone else. "He shouldn't be out in the cane fields. He shouldn't have to worry himself sick over the weather and the insects and the price of diesel fuel and whether or not that old John Deere is going to make it another season. He should be taking it easy. He shouldn't have to think about anything but going fishing with Pepper and swapping stories with the men down at Gauthier's.

"He almost went bankrupt last year, you know," she added, looking genuinely saddened. "Many more things go wrong this year and he will. What good will all his stubborn pride do him then? It would kill him to go under. He can avoid it now, go out with dignity."

Serena said nothing. Her sister's arguments were valid. They made perfect sense. They were neat and tidy and left no loose ends—except Gifford's heart's desire and the fate of Lucky's swamp. And how did one compare those things to the fate of a town? Was two hundred years of heritage more important than two hundred fifty jobs? Were a few jobs worth ruining a delicate wilderness that could never be replaced?

"I don't know," she murmured half to herself.

She sat down on the foot of the bed and leaned against a slender post, twining her arm around it like a vine. She stared at her reflection in the mirror above the dresser, looking for answers that weren't forthcoming. She felt as if she had the weight of the world on her shoulders, and all she wanted to do was shrug it off and walk away, but she couldn't. She couldn't walk away from Chanson du Terre or her need to please Gifford or her complicated relationship with her sister.

"I don't know what to do," she whispered, a feeling of bleak desolation yawning inside her like a cavern.

The image in the mirror was duplicated as Shelby sat down beside her. They looked less like twins now, Serena thought, because she herself looked like hell. There were dark crescents beneath her eyes and she was pale and drawn. The emotional war was taking a toll on her. Shelby was bearing up better under the strain with the aid of a full compliment of expensive cosmetics. She looked less troubled by the burden of it all, perhaps because she shouldered none of the load. Shelby had always possessed the convenient ability to shift blame elsewhere, so while she may have been frustrated with the current situation, she felt it was all someone else's fault. Serena had no doubt her sister slept like a baby. For all her talk of accepting responsibility, responsibility rolled off Shelby like water off a duck's back.

"My, you look all done in," Shelby said softly, and her brows knitted in one of her rare shows of genuine concern.

She didn't look directly at Serena but assessed her appearance via the mirror, as if she were obsessed with their likenesses. It was a disturbing thing, and Serena forced herself to stand up and move to avoid it. She went to the French doors again and stood with her back against the frame.

"You didn't tell me you knew Lucky Doucet," she said mildly, watching out the corner of her eye for a reaction.

Shelby jerked around in surprise, a multitude of emotions sweeping over her face like clouds scudding across the night sky. "What did he tell you?" she asked guardedly.

"Nothing much," Serena conceded.

Apparently feeling safe, Shelby rose to her feet and moved in a leisurely manner, smoothing the bedspread, straightening the skirt of her dress. "I went out with him a few times back when I was dating Mason to make Mason jealous," she admitted without remorse. "It was a long time ago. I never think about it. I mean, for heaven's sake, look at what became of him. I'm embarrassed to admit I ever knew him. Why did you want to know?"

"No reason."

"Good Lord, Serena," she said with genuine alarm. "You're not involved with him, are you? He's dangerous. Why, you can't imagine the things people say about him!"

Serena expected she could imagine quite vividly what the average person would have to say about Lucky. They would look at him and see exactly what he wanted them to see, and "dangerous" would only just begin to cover it. She had wondered if he had let Shelby see some other side of him. Obviously he hadn't.

It frightened her to think how happy that made her. This was dangerous territory—thinking she might be the one woman to reach beyond his barriers and touch his heart, taking joy in the knowledge that her sister had not been there before her. It was foolish. She had enough trouble without trying to take on a project like the reformation of Lucky Doucet. All he wanted from her was sex.

"He mentioned that he knew you," she said. "I was just curious, that's all."

"Oh." Shelby shrugged and headed for the door. "Well, it was nothing," she said, reducing the affair down to the level of importance it held for her. Lucky Doucet had served his purpose. She had gotten what she wanted. Nothing else mattered. "Good night."

"Good night."

Serena watched her sister go. Nothing had been resolved. They had gone another circuit on the merry-go-round of their relationship once more, suffering through emotional ups and downs only to return to the place they had started.

She sighed as the door clicked shut and gasped in the next breath as someone grabbed her from behind. One brawny arm went around her waist and hauled her back into what seemed like a rock wall, and a hand clamped over her mouth, effectively snuffing out the scream that tore its way up the back of her throat.

"All dressed up for me, sugar?" Lucky said, his lips brushing her ear, his left hand moving restlessly over the silk that covered her belly. "You shouldn't have."

"Damn you," Serena told him as he pulled his hand away from her mouth. She tried to twist around in his arms so she could hit him, but he held her in place with ridiculous ease. "You scared the hell out of me."

"Yeah, you oughta be scared of me," he muttered, nuzzling the side of her throat.

He made that kind of comment again and again to convince her of the blackness of his character, but Serena was no longer willing to buy it. Now that she had caught glimpses of the real man, she was no longer willing to believe the myth. Her heart had, with a will of its own, set itself on that man beneath the dangerous façade. However futile it might have seemed, she wanted to latch on to the goodness she knew was inside him and draw it out.

That he still wanted to keep her away from who he really was made her angry—angry with him and angry with herself. Of all the men in the world, why did this one have to be the one to capture her heart? Two days earlier she hadn't even *liked* him. She wasn't sure she liked him now, but she couldn't escape the fact that she had fallen in love with him. It seemed impossible and foolishly romantic and very unlike the Serena Sheridan who lived a sane and orderly life in Charleston. But they weren't in Charleston and she wasn't the same person who had left there, she reminded herself with weary resignation.

"Stop it," she said, her exhaustion with the whole situation showing in her voice.

"Stop what? This?" He rubbed his beard-roughened cheek against her skin again, breathing in the scent of her. "Or this?" he asked, sliding his dark hand down over her belly to the juncture of her thighs where he stroked her boldly through her clothes.

Serena moaned at the sensations that burst and flowed inside her like floodwaters from a dam. In the span of one night Lucky had conditioned her body to respond to his without reserve. She wanted him instantly, wanted nothing more than to lie down and welcome him into her, to love him with every part of herself. But she forced herself to pull away from him, fighting to retain some small scrap of control, some tiny piece of sanity.

He let her go, chuckling wickedly, and sauntered over to her dresser, where he idly picked up and examined a perfume bottle as he watched her in the mirror from beneath his lashes.

Serena tightened the belt of her robe, staring hard at his reflection. "Stop trying to scare me away from you," she said.

"Was that what I was doing?" He made a face of surprise. "Me, I thought I was on my way to gettin' you in bed."

"You know what I mean."

He shrugged and refused to comment, devoting more attention to her toiletries than to her argument. Frustration swelled inside her, but she refused to vent it, knowing that goading her was one of his favorite methods of keeping her at bay.

"What are you doing here? No poachers to thwart tonight?"

He gave her a black look by way of the mirror and picked up a tube of moisturizer. "How was dinner?"

"Enlightening. Burke says Tristar has never been convicted of anything regarding pollution."

"Oh, no," he drawled. "Just like they've never been convicted of bribing government officials or transporting illegal substances to unlicensed dumping sites. But if he said they've never done it, he's a liar."

"He doesn't seem ready to give up on the idea of building here."

"I'm sure he's not. They'd get a perfect site on the edge of nowhere, acres of dumping grounds in their backyard, and an eager young politician to boot." He shook his head as he fingered the carved back of a rosewood hairbrush. *"Mais non,* he's not gonna give up."

Serena moved to stand beside him, her gaze on his long artist's fingers as they touched her things. "What else can he do?" she asked. "Gifford says he won't sell and he means it. There's nothing Burke can do. Gifford can't be forced into selling."

The instant she said it she remembered the look in the big Texan's eyes as he'd sat at their dinner table and told them Gifford would have to be persuaded. He struck her as a man who got what he wanted by whatever means were necessary, and her grandfather stood between him and his goal. How hard might he push? To what lengths might he be willing to go?

She pushed the disturbing questions from her mind and went to stand at the open door again, looking out into the night as if she might see an answer shining like a star in the darkness. "He says the plant would employ two hundred fifty locals to start."

"That's bullshit," Lucky said. "A hundred, mebbe. Seventy-five, probably. The rest would be company men. There aren't a lotta chemists and engineers standin' around on street corners here lookin' for jobs."

"Still, that's more jobs than Gifford can provide. The boost to the local economy would be tremendous."

"And the damage to the local environment would be devastating." Serena sighed and brought her hands up to rub the tension from her forehead. "It's not as simple as I thought it would be."

"It is simple," Lucky argued adamantly. "It's stupid simple. Black and white. Good guys and bad guys."

Serena turned and faced him. "Which are you, Lucky? I thought you didn't care about anyone or anything. You tell me you're a bad guy, then I find out you're out playing Lone Ranger in the night. You let me think you're some bad-ass poacher, then turn around and spout environmentalist propaganda at me. Who are you really?"

"Trust me, sugar," he said. "You don't wanna know."

She met his scowl without flinching. "I *do* want to know."

"I told you before, Doc," he said darkly, raising a finger in warning. "Don' go lookin' inside my head. You won't like what you find."

Serena stared at him, taking in the fierce set of his jaw, the intimidation in his stance . . . the brief flicker of uncertainty in his eyes—a wariness of her or of himself?

She could feel the dangerous desire to reach out to him shifting through her, a need to know that went beyond curiosity. A smart woman would have taken heed of his warning. A smart woman would have kept her distance. He had drawn the boundary line between them, and like a fool she stepped across it again, figuratively and literally, moving toward him, needing to know, needing to touch him.

"And what would I find in your heart?" she asked softly as she closed the distance between them.

"That I haven't got one," he said, his face carefully blank.

Serena shook her head. "I don't believe that. You go out of your way to help people. My God," she said, gesturing to the bandanna still tied around his injured arm, "you risk your life to help people."

"Don' make me out to be some hero," Lucky snapped, just barely resisting the urge to back away from her. "I get paid back for what I do."

"In French bread and cookies?"

"In privacy. People wander into my life and I get them out. That's all I do. That's all I care about," he insisted, his inner tension crackling in his low, rough voice.

"Is that what you tell yourself, Lucky? You're a liar."

"It's the truth." He brought his hands up to take Serena by the shoulders, his fingers pressing on silk and tender flesh as if he might be able to physically force his opinion on her. His heart pounded with the necessity of it, the urgency of it. He leaned over her, his eyes as bright as a zealot's. "I'm a devil, not a saint, and whatever heart I might have had once got ripped out by the roots a long time ago, sugar. Don' go lookin' for things that aren't there."

Serena said nothing, but lifted a hand and splayed it across his chest, her fingers small and white against the black of his T-shirt. Her eyes locked on his as they both felt the frantic pounding behind his ribs, the evidence that shattered his lie more than any words could have.

Lucky gave a snarl of frustration and rage and battled within himself as fear swelled like a balloon inside him. He kicked it down, checked it ruthlessly, hardening himself against it with an effort that trembled through him like an earthquake. He gave Serena a shake.

"I don' give a rat's ass if you don' believe it," he said in a voice like smoke. "You wanna go diggin' through your psych books for explanations, do it on your own time. I didn't come here to get analyzed; I came here to get laid."

His mouth swept down on hers, hard, seeking to punish, but he

151

was met with no resistance, no fear. She was soft and sweet, yielding to him, melting against him, and that undid his anger as nothing else could have. He softened the kiss, making a sound of surrender in his throat as her lips parted beneath his in invitation. The kiss deepened and he felt himself going under, losing himself. His heart pounded and he clutched Serena to him, his mind swirling with the question of whether she was the stone that would sink him or the branch that would save him from drowning.

Neither, he told himself. She could be neither because this was desire and nothing more. She couldn't hurt him; she couldn't heal him. She could give him pleasure and he could help her forget her problems for a few hours. It was simple. Stupid simple. Black and white.

"I want you," he whispered against her mouth.

He brushed his lips against her temple and turned her in his arms so she faced the mirror above the dresser. Serena stared at their reflections—Lucky, big and masculine behind her, his arms around her, his head bent down, his eyes on hers in the glass; and herself, dainty and feminine in his shadow, golden and white beside his darkness. She watched as his fingers untied the belt of her robe and stood motionless as he drew the garment back off her shoulders and let it fall to the floor. The gown she wore beneath it was silk and lace, a sheer white mist clinging to the curves of her body and hanging past her knees.

He stroked his hands down the front of her, cupping her breasts through the lace cups, kneading her stomach through the silk, sliding down over her hips, tracing every curve and line that expressed her femininity. He lowered his mouth to her shoulder, nibbling at her flesh, catching the narrow strap of the gown in his teeth and drawing it down. Serena watched as he feasted on her skin, kissing, nipping, licking, devouring every exposed inch. She bent her head to the side to give him access to her throat and moaned as he took it, his mouth moving fervently along the ivory column. He caught the other strap of her gown with his fingers and drew it down, then peeled the lace bodice away from her, letting it pool in a drift of white at her waist. He captured her breasts in his hands, lifting and squeezing them, plumping them together and flicking his thumbs across her nipples.

Serena's breath caught in her throat. She'd never been a party to anything so erotic. Her eyes, heavy-lidded and dark with passion, were locked on the image in the mirror. Lucky's big, tanned hands kneading her breasts, her nipples thrusting out swollen and red between his

152

fingers. Arousal seared through her, hot and thick as she watched her own seduction and experienced every sensation at the same time.

He slid one hand down her rib cage and over her belly, pressing the white silk of her gown taut over her feminine mound. Serena leaned back against him, letting her thighs part as he slid his hand between them. He caressed her through the silk, moving the cool slick fabric against her most sensitive heated flesh. Then the gown was gone and through the haze of desire she watched his fingers stroke through the delta of tawny curls as the fever of need intensified inside her. With one arm banded across her ribs, he lifted her up against him and her head lolled back against his shoulder, rolling from side to side as he eased a finger deep into the warm, wet channel of her womanhood.

"Watch," he whispered. "Watch," he said, his voice as smooth and smoky as whiskey, as seductive as a siren's song. "This is what I want from you, *mon ange.*"

His eyes locked on hers in the mirror. He stroked her deeply, rhythmically, in time with her harsh breathing. Serena moaned and moved against his hand, her control gone, her instincts overwhelming her as Lucky took her closer to the edge.

She chanted his name, the words catching in her throat as she struggled for breath. Her breasts rose and fell in the image in the mirror. Her stomach quivered. Lucky's hand moved against her groin. His eyes watched her from beneath the rim of dark lashes, smoldering amber, hot and bright. Her gaze fastened on his mouth, blatantly sensual, carnal, his lips moist and parted slightly as he whispered to her.

"Vien, chérie, vien, vien, vien . . ."

Her climax hit her like a wave, breaking over her, knocking the breath from her. Her body stiffened in his arms and she would have cried out, but Lucky twisted her around and fastened his mouth over hers. He kissed her hungrily, savagely, bending her back over his arm, his free hand tangling in her hair as it spilled behind her.

In the next instant they were on the bed, Serena lying back on the cool sheets, Lucky with one knee on the mattress and one foot on the floor as he tore his T-shirt off and flung it aside. His jeans followed. He came to her magnificently naked, magnificently aroused, lowering himself over her and plunging himself into her in one smooth move that lifted her off the bed.

Serena arched up against him, taking everything he would give her and knowing in her heart it wouldn't be enough. She gave him her body, let him fill her again and again with the essence of what made him male. She welcomed the driving power of his thrusts, delighted in the feel of his muscled back beneath her hands, the hot musky scent of his body, the smoky taste of his kisses, but she longed for something more.

She looked up into his face and saw the torment there, the strain as he gave her his body and fought to withhold his soul. For an instant she could look into his eyes and feel the terrible struggle going on inside him, and it tore at her heart. There was no place here for reason or self-control. All she could give him was her love, no matter how foolish it seemed, no matter that she knew he wouldn't want to take it, no matter that she was certain her heart would get broken in the end.

As he moved powerfully over her and inside of her, she wrapped her arms around him and pressed her cheek against his chest, hanging on for dear life as longing tore through her shield of logic once and for all. She was in love with a man for the first time in her life, helplessly, hopelessly in love. He took her on a breathless climb to passion's very summit and soared with her over the edge, his big body straining against hers, his arms crushing her to him. And she let herself believe in that one brilliant moment that he could love her too.

Chapter Thirteen

She looked like an angel. Her hair spilled golden and silky across the pillow. Her lashes lay like tawny lace fans against her cheeks. Her mouth was soft and rosy, relaxed in sleep. Lucky looked down at her, something twisting painfully in his chest as he reached out to touch her but stopped himself, his fingers a scant inch above her face.

She was giving and caring, strong and brave, everything he'd ever given up on finding in a woman, and he couldn't allow himself to indulge in anything other than her body. That, of course, was heaven itself. What he felt when he was inside Serena was incredible. She took away the coldness, chased back the darkness, made him feel alive instead of caught in some bleak plane of existence. He could take her five times a day and never get enough of her. He'd never felt such an insatiable yearning for a woman, had never had his needs met with such sweet absolute surrender.

He wouldn't have believed it possible of the woman he'd first encountered in Gauthier's, but that cool, controlled woman wasn't who Serena really was. Too bad for him, he thought, his mouth twisting in a wry parody of a smile.

Serena wasn't cold and hard. She was a warm, golden temptation. Heaven was losing himself in her, hell was knowing he couldn't stay. She would want too much from him. She would want things he couldn't give. He couldn't let her get that close.

In the first place, he was terrified of what she would see—the things he'd done, the things he'd seen, the cold blackness that surrounded his soul and crept in on his mind. In the second place, he was terrified of what would happen. He had spent the past year putting himself back together, painstakingly reconstructing himself from the fragments Ramos's hell had left him in. Now those fragments balanced one against the other like a house of cards. One wrong move and it would all come crashing down.

He needed his peace, his solitude, his art. That was all. He had stripped his life down to those bare essentials because he couldn't tolerate anything more. He couldn't be around people because their presence irritated him, like air blowing across an exposed nerve. By necessity his focus had to remain inward, concentrating on holding himself together. He couldn't need a woman whose job was to poke around inside people's minds, ferreting out their secrets, taking them all apart to see what made them tick.

He slid from the bed without disturbing Serena, stepped into his jeans and zipped up, leaving the button undone. He dug a cigarette from the pocket of his T-shirt, hung it from his lip, and wandered across the room to the French doors that still stood open. Thunder rumbled in the distance, an appropriate accompaniment to everything that was going on inside him and around him; a portent of a coming storm within and without.

He had a bad feeling about this business with Chanson du Terre. He had from the beginning and it was only getting worse. Opposing forces were pushing against each other, building pressure. Something was going to have to give. Digging a match out of his pocket, he lit his cigarette and inhaled deeply, wondering which side would give in first.

Gifford Sheridan was an old man. Ferocious and hardheaded, to be sure, but an old man nevertheless. If he had a son to inherit or a granddaughter who wanted to stay, things might have looked better. As it was, the deck was stacked against him, against Chanson du Terre, against the swamp.

On the other side stood Tristar and Len Burke. Burke, who reminded Lucky too much of his old nemesis, Colonel Lambert, a man who had known no boundaries when it came to getting what he wanted. Where would Burke draw the line? And what of Shelby? Lucky knew all too well how far she was willing to go to get what she wanted.

Mason Talbot struck him as little more than a pawn to be used by Tristar and Shelby. He was too laid back to instigate anything. Too dimwitted in Gifford's opinion. But he would have his uses. He would make a perfect figurehead to rally the town around in favor of economic growth. And once Tristar was in place and Mason was ensconced in the legislature in Baton Rouge, he would make a very attractive spokesman for the chemical industry.

Lucky's gaze drifted back to the bed and Serena, who was frowning and mumbling in her sleep, her hand sweeping against the mattress where he had lain. The load had been dropped squarely on her slender shoulders, and while she seemed determined to uphold her grandfather's wishes, would she only be delaying the inevitable? She had said Gifford's ploy wouldn't hold her here. What would happen when she left?

"Lucky?" she whispered, rousing herself like a sleepy kitten. Blinking against the soft light, she sat up and combed back a handful of honey-gold hair from her eyes. Lucky watched and said nothing, savoring the sight of her as she drew the ivory cotton sheet up demurely over her breasts, a gesture that struck him as sweetly incongruous considering everything they'd done together in bed.

She tilted her head and blinked at him. "What are you doing?"

"Havin' a cigarette," he said. He took a deep drag and exhaled a plume of smoke in demonstration.

Serena frowned as she slid from the bed, wrapping the sheet around her like a Grecian gown. "You smoke too much," she chided him softly as she padded across the faded carpet. She cuddled against him, not waiting for an invitation, but sliding her arms around his lean waist and nuzzling her cheek against his bare chest. She tilted her head back to look up at him. "You shouldn't smoke at all. It's bad for you."

Lucky couldn't hold back a soft, incredulous laugh. He stared down into her earnest face, something like wonder rising inside him. He couldn't remember the last time he'd given a moment's thought to his health. Not because he doubted his own mortality, but because he didn't care. For a long, long time he'd felt as if he had nothing left to lose, including his own life. When he first returned from Central America, he spent night after night staring at a 9mm Beretta, his death awaiting him in a sleek black casing filled with hollow-point ammunition. The only thing that kept him from sticking the thing in his mouth and pulling the trigger was the knowledge of what it would have done to his parents, who were staunchly Catholic.

He had lived with death as a constant companion and now Serena stood looking up at him, warning him of the dangers of smoking.

"Why is that funny?" she asked, looking annoyed with him.

Lucky sobered. "It's not."

He turned without leaving her embrace and crushed his cigarette in a decorative china cup sitting on a stand. "Happy?"

"Hardly." Serena sniffed. "That was my great-grandmother's tea-cup."

"This old house is full of stuff like that, isn't it?" he asked, looping his arms loosely around her. "Antiques, heirlooms, family treasures passed down and down."

"Yes," Serena answered, her own gaze wandering over a dozen things in this room alone that had seen generations of Sheridans come and go. "It's like a microcosm of history. It ought to be renovated and opened to the public as a museum."

"Instead, it could be razed and lost forever."

She looked up at him, her brows pulling together over troubled dark eyes. "Could we not talk about it for a while? I'm so tired."

Lucky ran a hand over her hair, an unexpected wave of sympathy sweeping over him. He would have liked to have taken her away from all the problems, protected her, kept her all to himself for a little while, but that wasn't an option. He knew he should have steeled himself against the tenderness stirring inside him as he looked down at her, but he gave in to it for an instant, leaned down, and kissed her. She looked tired. She looked confused and battered. What could it hurt to offer her a little comfort?

Her lips were soft and warm beneath his. Eager, yearning. She clung to his kiss as if it might intoxicate her past thinking. She pressed herself against him as if she wished to be absorbed directly into his body. The desire to protect her rose up even stronger inside him and he tried to push it back. He couldn't be anyone's savior; he had all he could do just to hold himself together.

When he lifted his head he touched her cheek and murmured regretfully, "I'm sorry, *chère*. I know you didn't ask for this fight."

"It's mine by birthright, I suppose," Serena said, drawing away from him. She wandered in the little pool of lamplight, absently touching objects on the table and dresser with one hand and clutching the sheet to her breasts with the other.

"It's ironic, you know," she added, trying unsuccessfully to smile. "I left here because I thought my life was somewhere else, because I didn't think I'd ever become my own person if I stayed. And here I am . . ." She gestured to the room, to the house in general, looking around her with a vague sense of bewilderment. "Here I am. They say you can't go home again. I can't seem to get away."

"You'll be able to get away permanently if your sister has her way," Lucky said, watching her with a hawkish gaze. "Is that what you want —to be out from under the burden of your heritage forever?"

Serena looked around at the room, feeling the personality of the great house bearing down upon her. She was too tired to fight it. Resignation flowed through her and her shoulders sagged. She would be forever tied to this house in a way time and distance couldn't alter even if she wanted them to. This was her home. It would always be her home. Chanson du Terre was where her roots were and they went two hundred years deep.

"No," she said softly.

She didn't want to see the old house destroyed. She didn't want to see strangers living here. She didn't want Tristar Chemical building a processing plant where the old slave quarters stood in silent testimony to past lives. She didn't want to see high wire fences surrounding what once had been cane fields. She wanted Chanson du Terre to be owned by a Sheridan; she just didn't want it to be her.

"Then you'd better be ready for a fight, sugar," Lucky said. "Len Burke means to have this land. He'll fight dirty to get it and your sister will be there right beside him."

"It's not Shelby I'm worried about."

He gave her a guarded look. "Don't underestimate her, Serena. I don't think you realize what she might be capable of."

Serena shrugged off his warning and the niggling doubts that had taken seed in her own mind over the past few days. Shelby was flighty and selfish, but she wasn't ruthless. "She's my sister. I think I probably have a better idea of what she's capable of than you."

"Did you think she was capable of abandoning you in the swamp?"

The jab found its target, hitting the nerve with stinging accuracy, but Serena stubbornly shook it off. "We've been over that ground before. She didn't intend anything bad to happen. Shelby doesn't think

159

things all the way through. She doesn't consider all the consequences of her actions, just the immediate effect."

Don't count on it, sugar, Lucky thought, but he kept the idea to himself. He supposed it was only natural for Serena to have a blind spot where her twin was concerned. What kind of person could look at their own flesh and blood and see evil? He only hoped that blind spot didn't keep her from seeing something truly dangerous before it was too late.

The explosion came just before dawn. It rattled the windows and shook the foundation of the old house. Serena was able to smell smoke before she was fully conscious. She shot up and out of bed, the instinct to flee danger pumping adrenaline through her bloodstream.

It took several seconds for her brain to catch up, sorting through the questions of where she was and what was the source of the danger. Her room was dark and in the aftermath of the blast the only sound was the rumbling of thunder. For a moment she thought that might have been all that had awakened her, but then the scent of smoke came again. It drifted in through the open French door, carried on a strong cold breeze that heralded the coming storm.

Grabbing her robe and throwing it on hastily, she rushed to the open door and looked out across the gallery and across the yard. A ball of orange glowed in the distance, and flames licked up the side of the machine shed. Shouts cut through the silence and men arrived at the scene, their shapes silhouetted against the brightness of the fire.

Serena whirled toward the bed, suddenly thinking of Lucky, but he was gone. His absence struck her like a physical blow, but there was no time to contemplate where he had disappeared to, or when or why.

She grabbed clothes out of the wardrobe without looking and jerked them on, not bothering with underwear. She stepped into her tattered espadrilles and ran out onto the gallery, down the steps, and across the garden, flying as fast as her legs would take her toward the building that was already engulfed in flames.

Workers were directing hoses at the conflagration by the time she got there, but to no avail. Fire was devouring the building. James Arnaud rushed back and forth between the workers, shouting to be heard above the roar, telling them to concentrate on wetting down the part of the enormous old wooden shed that wasn't already ablaze.

"What happened?" Serena yelled, grabbing his arm and his attention as he paced past her.

"Hell if I know," he snapped, his thick dark brows set in a V over furious eyes. "I heard the blast and came running. It was probably lightning. All I know is we've got most of our equipment in there and we're gonna lose it all if we don't get this fire put out!"

"Has anyone called the fire department?"

"They're on the way and they'd better get here fast. We might as well piss on this building for all the good we're doing."

He shrugged her off then and went to help with the seemingly futile business of dousing the shed. Serena stood back helplessly, watching, squinting into the brilliance of the flames, the heat searing her cheeks even from a distance.

Above them the sky lit up with a network of white lines, and thunder boomed like cannon fire. Thick, rolling storm clouds were illuminated in the fluorescent glow of the lightning, black and swollen like enormous sponges.

"Come on, rain," she shouted.

Mason came running from the house in pajamas and a robe, his thin brown hair standing up, his glasses askew. He wore a pair of polished oxfords but no socks.

"My God, this is terrible!" he said, tugging on the belt of his robe. He stared up at the blaze, the flames reflecting eerily in the lenses of his glasses. "I've called the fire department. They're on their way."

"I was just praying for rain," Serena said. Fat drops splashed down on them from above and she turned her face up to the heavens.

Mason stared at the fire as it consumed the huge shed like an angry, voracious beast, devouring the walls, lapping at the heavy equipment within. "All that machinery. I hope to heaven Gifford's insurance is up-to-date."

The rain began to fall harder. In the distance came the sound of sirens.

Mason took Serena by the arm. "We ought to get out of the way. There's nothing we can do here."

She reluctantly backed away from heat, feeling helpless as she thought of Gifford. She felt as if she were failing him somehow. It was absurd, she knew, but that didn't stop the old feelings of inadequacy from surfacing. Somehow she should have been able to prevent this. She should have been able to stop the destruction.

The rain came beating down now, cold and hard, soaking through the silk blouse she'd grabbed at random, matting her hair against her head, blurring her vision. Still the flames leapt into the night sky, roaring and crackling, mocking mother nature's efforts to put them out. There came a splintering sound and part of the roof caved in, sending a cloud of orange sparks billowing upward. Mason pulled harder on Serena's arm.

"Serena, come on!" he yelled urgently. "There's nothing we can do. It's not safe here!"

He dragged her back a few more steps. Lightning lashed across the sky. Thunder exploded in a deafening blast. The wind picked up, shaking the trees and bending the tongues of flame that shot up from the burning building. The rain came harder in a fierce downpour, finally shrinking the fire, tamping it down. The first of the fire trucks roared up the driveway. Mason pulled Serena back another few steps.

"Let's go!"

They hadn't taken three steps toward the house when the second explosion came. In the periphery of her vision Serena saw the ball of flame burst through the ravaged wall of the building. From that point on what took only a split second in reality registered in her brain in slow motion—men running, fire rolling outward, lumber and shrapnel hurling in every direction.

She later remembered opening her mouth to scream, but not hearing anything. The invisible force of the explosion hit her in the back and flung her to the ground like a rag doll with Mason right beside her. She hit the ground with a bone-jarring bounce, gravel and crushed shell digging into her skin. Then everything went blessedly black.

"Total loss," the claims adjuster said with the gravity of one imparting the death of a loved one. He stood in the doorway of the dining room, clipboard in hand, a small, apologetic man of forty-five with receding dark hair and eyes like a spaniel. There was soot on his hands and forearms and one big smudge of it across his high forehead.

He had arrived practically on the heels of the fire department, along with the neighbors. A fire was a major event in these parts, an occasion for people to gather and gawk and offer support to those who had suffered a loss. There was no two-week wait for the insurance man because chances were he would be standing there watching as the last of the rafters fell into the ashes.

"A total loss," he repeated morosely. "The building and everything in it. It's still smoldering in places."

"Cool!" John Mason exclaimed, scrambling down from his seat. "I'm gonna go see it!"

Shelby scowled at her son. "You most certainly are not. You stay away from there, John Mason. Just look what happened to your father and your aunt Serena!"

Serena sent her nephew a meaningful look. She sat in her chair, still trembling, her ears ringing, pain biting into her body in various places. There were cuts and scrapes on her hands, knees, chin. Her cheeks and forehead wore a dark blush from the heat of the fire. She had yet to make it to the shower, and her hair hung like damp strings around her head. She still wore her ruined fuchsia silk blouse and red slacks.

All in all, she didn't make a pretty picture, and Mason had fared little better. She looked over at her brother-in-law as he sat staring down into his coffee cup with a vacant expression. His fine hair stood up in little shocks around his head. His robe was torn and dirty. There was a cut on his left cheekbone that stood out like a line of red ink against his ashen skin.

Serena imagined they both looked as if they had been mugged and left for dead, but they had to count themselves lucky. Two of the men who had been struggling to fight the blaze were now in the hospital, seriously injured by flying debris from the second explosion.

"Gifford had his insurance paid up, didn't he, Mr. York?" she asked, unsure whether she was whispering or shouting. She felt as if she were wearing cups over her ears.

York regarded her with his spaniel's eyes, looking like he was afraid she might call him a bad dog and send him away. "Yes," he said hesitantly. "The premiums were paid up. There's no problem with that at all."

"Are we to take it there *is* a problem elsewhere?"

"Er—well—" He shuffled his feet, then glanced down quickly to see if he tracked in mud. "I'm afraid, yes, there is."

"Oh, for pity's sake!" Shelby snapped as she poured herself a second cup of coffee. "Spit it out."

She sat in Gifford's place at the head of the table, prim and lovely in a green silk dressing gown, her hair twisted neatly in back, looking as if an explosion and fire were nothing to disturb her normal daily routine.

York swallowed hard. "Well, I was just on the scene with the fire

163

marshal, as y'all know, and there seems to be little doubt but that this was arson."

"Arson?" Serena said in disbelief, a chill going through her. She shook her head, rejecting the possibility and all its ramifications. "No. It was lightning."

York looked woebegone. "Ah—well—begging your pardon, Miss Sheridan, it wasn't. The fire was deliberately set. There really isn't any question of it. It was quite a sloppy job. You see," he said, becoming more animated at the prospect of sharing some of his expertise, "there was one big hot spot in the southwest corner of the shed and trailers leading out from it. That is to say, lines indicating a fuel path. There was alligatoring in the charred wood, giving the indication of rapid, intense heat, and signs of spalling in the concrete floor. It's very apparent that someone poured gasoline or a like substance all around and simply lit it up. And from what we could tell by the remains of the one tractor, a fuel path led directly to it. I'd have to say someone meant it to blow up."

Serena sat back in her chair, pressing one hand to her lips and banding the other arm across her aching ribs. No one at the table said anything. She looked across at the chair Len Burke had occupied the night before, eating their food, drinking their wine, telling them that Gifford would have to be persuaded to sell—one way or another.

"You understand that until this matter is cleared up, my company won't be able to make a payment on your claim, I'm afraid. I'm sorry," Mr. York said, sounding reluctant once again. Delivering bad news was evidently not his forte. He squeezed his clipboard. "I really am sorry."

"Mr. York," Mason said, mustering a faint version of his affable politician's smile. "Surely you don't believe one of the family is responsible for this horrible crime?"

"Oh, no, well—er—that isn't my place to judge. There will have to be a full investigation, you understand."

"But Mr. York," Serena said, trying to pull her mind away from thoughts of Burke, "some of that equipment will have to be replaced immediately. How do you suggest we do that if your company isn't going to make good on the claim?"

York appeared to give earnest thought to the question, making a series of faces that caused the soot smudge on his forehead to wriggle like a shadow puppet. Finally he looked her in the eye and she thought he might burst into tears. "I don't know," he said. "I'm sorry. Really I am."

After several more rounds of questions, explanations, and apologies, the claims adjuster took his leave to have a second look at the rubble with John Mason hot on his heels.

"What a horrid little man," Shelby said, selecting a muffin from the basket Odille brought in as if it were her most important task of the day. "No wonder his wife is having an affair with the vice president of the bank."

Serena shot her a look. "Shelby, for heaven's sake, we have more pressing issues to discuss."

"Serena's right, sweetheart," Mason said gently.

"What's an affair?" little Lacey asked, staring owlishly up at her mother.

Shelby beamed a smile and stroked a hand over her daughter's blond curls. "That's something cheap, trashy women do, darling. No need to worry your pretty head about it."

"E-vil," Odille intoned dramatically, drawing back from the table with the empty coffee urn clutched in her long, bony hands. Her turquoise eyes burned like blue flame, settling on each face in turn. "Dat's what come dis house. E-vil. Lord have mercy on us all."

On that ominous note she backed out of the room, her thin mouth stretched into a line of supreme disapproval.

"My God," Shelby sniffed in affront, pulling together the lapels of her dressing gown. "I don't know why Gifford keeps that woman on."

"She's a witch," Lacey said nonchalantly, reaching for a muffin. She dug one out of the basket and scampered out of the room, calling for her brother.

Serena rubbed her temples and sighed. "Arson. Your Mr. Burke sending Gifford a little warning?"

There was a beat of stunned silence, then Mason came to life.

"Oh, Serena, you can't possibly believe Len Burke had anything to do with this!" he said with an incredulous laugh. "Mr. Burke is a respectable businessman representing a respectable company. You can't honestly believe he's an arsonist!"

Serena looked at her sister and brother-in-law with grave eyes. "Well, I certainly wouldn't want to believe the alternative."

"That one of us might have done it?" Mason said, arching a brow above his glasses. "Really, Serena, you've been spending too much time with your patients; you're becoming paranoid. Shelby and I were in bed. I don't mind saying I highly resent your entertaining such an

165

insulting notion. Just because we're in favor of selling doesn't mean we'd burn the place to the ground."

"My stars, Serena, is that what you really think of us?" Shelby said, her agitation building visibly as she stirred sugar into her coffee. Dots of color bloomed on her perfect cheekbones; her mouth tightened into a thin line. She glared at her sister, her demeanor of calm vanishing as instantly as mist. "Accusing your own sister and brother-in-law! I don't know what's become of you up in Charleston. You're like a stranger to us!"

Serena pressed two fingers to her temples and sighed heavily. She was battered and exhausted. She felt as if all her tools for dealing with people had been stripped away from her. Certainly her energy for dealing with her twin's endless dramatic mood swings had been.

"Shelby, can we please dispense with the constant theatrics?" she said through her teeth. "I didn't mean to accuse you. I was only saying that Mr. Burke would stand to benefit by this fire. It could have been set as a warning or with the express purpose of destroying the machinery. Either way, Gifford is out of money he can't afford to lose."

"Well, I think it's preposterous," Shelby pronounced indignantly. "I find Mr. Burke perfectly charming."

Serena couldn't find the strength to roll her eyes.

"The fire might not have had anything to do with the sale of the property," Mason pointed out. "Gifford has cultivated his share of enemies over the years. Why, not a month ago he had to let go of some of his hired men. It caused hard feelings, I can tell you. Then again, plenty of people stand to gain by Tristar coming here, Serena," he said, contemplating his coffee. "This is a small town; I imagine word is out by now. Gifford is preventing people from getting jobs. Someone might have decided to persuade him to change his mind."

Serena pushed herself up from the table, her eyes on Mason, an unpleasant smile turning the corners of her mouth. "My, what an interesting choice of words."

"What are you going to do?" Shelby asked, looking up at her with suspicion.

"First, I'm going to take a long, hot shower. Then I'm going to go out into the swamp and get Gifford to come back here if I have to drag him by his hair."

Lapsing into unconsciousness seemed like a more attractive choice, but Serena didn't see that she could afford the luxury of sleep. Forcing herself to plant one foot in front of the other, she pushed open the dining room door and left.

Shelby stared after her, waiting in breathless silence for the sound of a door down the hall closing.

"Well, that's just wonderful," she said sulkily. "She's going to bring Gifford back here. That's all we need. Damn her, why couldn't she just stay out of this?"

Mason reached for a muffin. "Don't worry yourself about it, peach. This could turn out just fine. Gifford is bound to get disheartened sooner or later. If he comes back and sees the kind of damage that fire did, realizes what he's going to have to go through to replace the equipment and so on . . . he may just give up."

"I certainly hope so, Mason. I certainly hope so."

Serena let herself into her room, aching to fall across the bed and cry herself to sleep. Instead, she turned and nearly fell into Lucky. He grabbed her by the shoulders in a grip that could have bent iron and held her at arm's length, his gaze sweeping over her, wild and intense.

"*Mon Dieu*," he muttered breathlessly. "Look at you. Are you all right?"

"Oh, I'm fine except for the heart attack," she said sarcastically. "Is there something intrinsic in your makeup that compels you to frighten people? Did someone sneak up on you during your potty training or something?"

Lucky swore under his breath, letting go of her and turning to pace the bedroom floor. He ran a trembling hand over his hair and rubbed the back of his neck as he struggled to school his breathing to normalcy. "I heard about the fire. Explosion. People being taken to the hospital."

Serena bit back the flippant remark that sprang instantly to her tongue. She stood back and studied Lucky as he paced. He'd been afraid for her. It was clear in his eyes and the set of his mouth. It was clear in his struggle for control of his emotions. She made no comment but felt a flare of something like hope in her breast. The granite man who cared about no one had been frightened for her.

"I'm all right," she said quietly. She let her knees give way and sank down on a little Victorian dressing stool, toeing off her ruined espadrilles and starting on the buttons of her blouse. She watched Lucky move back and forth along the bed, tension rolling off him like steam as he forceably calmed himself. "Where were you?"

167

"I had business to take care of."

"You certainly have strange working hours."

"I have a strange life," he admitted dryly. "You may have noticed."

Serena arched a brow. "What? Everyone I know lives in a swamp and picks their teeth with a commando knife."

She dismissed his dark look and started to shrug off her blouse, but stopped herself as she realized two things simultaneously—she wasn't wearing anything underneath it and Lucky's eyes had suddenly settled, hot and glowing, on her chest. It wasn't that she felt modest around him. But a wild sensation fluttered in her middle. A deep, primal fear combined with excitement that took no notice of her need for control. Nor did it seem to care that the path it wanted to drag her down led to heartache. She managed to head it off at the pass and pushed herself to her feet, ignoring the protests of her aching legs.

"I have to take a shower," she said, her fingers clutching her blouse together between her breasts.

Lucky stared at her. All the anxiety he had felt channeled itself into the one emotion he could understand and deal with—lust. When he'd heard about the explosion he'd nearly gone wild with thoughts of Serena lying burned and twisted among the rubble. Now she stood before him, looking bedraggled and a little bit afraid, but alive. Her dark eyes were wide and soft as she stared up at him.

He closed the distance between them with two long strides. His fingers pulled the blouse from her hand and peeled the two halves back as he pulled her gently into his embrace. With reverent care he bent and pressed his lips to each scratch that marred her face.

"I have to take a shower," she mumbled again, her breath catching as Lucky's mouth settled on the pulse spot in her throat. "I have to go to Gifford's." She gasped and arched her back as his hand carefully claimed her breast, but tried valiantly to hold on to her train of thought. "Will you take me?"

Lucky raised his head, his smoldering gaze capturing hers, an unconsciously tender smile turning one corner of his sensuous mouth. "Oh, yeah, *chère*. I'll take you. Absolutely."

Chapter Fourteen

"Arson!" Gifford exploded, his weathered face turning an alarming shade of red. "By God, that tears it! That just tears it! I don't know what the hell this world is coming to. People got no respect for nothing anymore."

He set aside the shotgun he'd been cleaning and rose from his lawn chair to pace in agitation. His hounds lay on the ground, one on either side of the chair, watching him move back and forth with their droopy eyes and somber expressions.

"That bastard Burke. I'll have his head on a pike before this is over. And that smarmy little Clifton York too," he said, jabbing the air with a forefinger for emphasis. "The nerve of that little weasel, refusing to pay the claim."

Serena thought of the apologetic insurance adjuster and felt a pang of sympathy. "Mr. York is only doing his job."

"Practically accusing me of burning my own property," Gifford ranted. "By God, I'd eat dirt before I'd stoop to something so low. No Sheridan ever behaved in such a reprehensible manner—not counting the ones that got kicked out of the family, of course."

"Of course," Serena confirmed dryly. She stood before him with her arms crossed over the front of her wilting pink cotton blouse and her knees locked to keep her legs from buckling beneath her. The early morning storm had turned the cabin's meager yard to a soft ooze that squished up around the sides of her calfskin loafers. This trip was taking a heavy toll on her footwear on top of everything else. If she stayed much longer, she was going to have to go around in bedroom slippers.

"There was a time in this country when a man's honor meant something," Gifford announced, as upset with having his reputation impugned as he was with having someone burn his machine shed to the ground. He planted his feet, jammed his hands at the waist of his jeans, and glared down at Serena as if it were all her fault standards had fallen to such an appalling level.

"I'm sure it's nothing personal," she said. "It's a clear-cut case of arson. Until they figure out who did it, the company can't pay."

Gifford snorted. A shock of white hair tumbled across his forehead. His eyes were fierce. "Until they figure out who did it. A blind halfwit could figure out who did it. Burke is responsible. Goddamn Texan. This state ought to have border regulations."

"Burke has an alibi," Lucky said unexpectedly. "He was at Mouton's."

Serena turned toward him, unable to hide her surprise. He was leaning indolently against the trunk of a big live oak, his eyes hooded and sleepy. He looked like a panther, all leashed strength and quiet intensity, waiting for some unsuspecting deer to wander past.

"How do you know that?"

He gave her a look that was flat and unreadable. His big shoulders rose and fell in a lazy shrug. "Because I was there too, sugar."

He'd left her bed to go to Mosquito Mouton's. Serena did her best to stem the rush of hurt. She had no hold on him, she reminded herself. Regardless of what her heart wanted, Lucky had clearly defined their relationship as just sex. Having agreed to those terms, she had no right to be angry with him or feel hurt that he hadn't chosen to hold her all night.

Business, he'd said. She wondered what kind of business one conducted at Mouton's in the wee hours of the morning. She wondered if it was the same kind of business he had been conducting the last time he'd been there—starting brawls, threatening people with knives.

"Of course he has an alibi," Gifford said with disgust. "A man like

Burke does his own dirty work when he's coming up through the ranks, but he hires it out as soon as he can. It wouldn't be any mean feat to hire some local piece of trash to start a fire. People will do anything for a dollar these days."

"Unfortunately, no one saw anything," Serena said. "Whoever did it managed to get away either before the first explosion or during the confusion afterward. I know I never thought of looking for a car or for anyone running away from the scene."

"Maybe they never left the scene," Lucky said quietly.

Serena sighed, blowing her breath up into the sweat-damp tendrils of hair that stuck to her forehead. She could feel Lucky's eyes on her, but she didn't look at him. They had already had this argument on the way to Giff's. She didn't for a minute believe Shelby had started the fire. It was simply impossible for her to picture Shelby slinging gas cans around and rigging machinery to blow up. But there may well have been a hired man capable of being bought off—by Burke, Serena insisted. Or the perpetrator may have been an outsider compelled by God knew what, a man who had simply blended in with the rest of the men while they had struggled to save the building.

"Well, there's no use speculating," she said at last. "The point is, this business is getting way out of hand. You have to come back home, Giff. I mean it this time."

Gifford lifted one bushy white brow. "Why? So you can cut and run?"

Serena refused to flinch. She stood toe to toe with the old man and said calmly, "So you can face up to your responsibilities."

"Why should I be any better at it than you are?" he asked sarcastically. "Hell, I took my lessons from you, little girl. I didn't want to deal with it, so I left."

"Stop it," Serena snapped. She could feel the reins of her temper sliding through her exhausted grasp. Even in the best circumstances she had trouble dealing with Gifford in a controlled and rational manner. He knew exactly which buttons to push and he pushed them with a kind of malicious glee that infuriated her even further. She looked up at him now and held her anger in check with sheer willpower. "You stop trying to lay all this guilt on me, Gifford. I've had it with your manipulation."

"Oh? You *are* going back to Charleston, then?" he said with cutting mock-surprise. "Leave your old grandfather to deal with arsonists and strong-arm tactics and treason among his own ranks."

Serena ground her teeth and spoke through them. "I'm not going anywhere."

Gifford stared at her long and hard. "Neither am I."

The pressure built between them for another few seconds as their gazes locked and warred. Then abruptly Serena's temper erupted like a volcano. She kicked the lawn chair and let fly a very unladylike curse that sent the coon hounds scurrying for safety under the cabin.

"Damn you, Gifford," she shouted, her hands knotting into useless fists in front of her. "How can you be so stubborn!"

"It's a family trait."

"Don't you dare be glib with me," she warned, shaking a finger at him. "This is serious."

"I know exactly how serious it is," Gifford said softly, abandoning his theatrics for cold, hard sobriety. "I know exactly what's at stake here, Serena. I wonder if you do. You think I'm just being a contrary old fool. You think I'm enjoying all the havoc I'm wreaking on everyone's lives. I'm trying to save something that's been a part of this family for *two centuries*."

"By sitting out here in the swamp?"

He shook his head, his impatience and weariness showing in his dark eyes and the set of his mouth. "You don't get it, do you? I swear, for someone so intelligent you can be as thick as a red Georgia brick. I'm not talking about saving Chanson du Terre for the moment. I'm talking about it living on after me."

Serena took in his words and their meaning, tears of anger and hurt and frustration rising in her eyes. She knew exactly what he meant. "You can't make me want to come back here, Gifford. You can't force me to want to stay."

"No," he said softly. "But I can make you see what the consequences will be if you don't. I can put it all in your hands. You can have the power of Caesar—does it live or does it die. Do two hundred years of heritage go on or do they get ground to dust. It will all be up to you, Serena. Sell it or save it."

There it was. The cards were on the table. No more games. No more silent manipulation. He was laying it all at her feet and the thing she wanted most to do was turn and run. Serena stared up at him through a wavy sheen of tears and hated him at that moment almost as much as she loved him. She couldn't turn away. He meant too much to her. She couldn't stand the idea of disappointing him, of having him look at her and see a failure and a coward.

As a psychologist she could pick each of those thoughts apart, dissect them and diagnose them, and recommend therapy. But as a granddaughter, as a woman, she could only stand there and experience it. She felt as helpless and impotent as a child. She couldn't step back from it to examine it with the cool, objective eye of a neutral third party. She couldn't simply watch the storm from a safe distance. She was in the middle of it and there was no honorable way out.

"You think about that for a minute," Gifford said, his face as stern and set as if it had been carved from granite. "Then you come on inside the cabin. There's something that needs to be taken care of before you go back."

He walked away, calling softly to his hounds. Serena stood facing the bayou, fighting the tears, trying to concentrate on the sound of footsteps and dog toenails on the worn boards of the gallery, the slam of the screen door, the sound of Marc Savoy singing on the radio, the call of an indigo bunting somewhere in the treetops nearby. Arms bound tight across her middle, she stared out at the muddy water and the profusion of spider lilies that grew along the opposite bank, and forced herself to hang on to the very last scrap of her pride and control.

Lucky watched her, everything inside him aching for her. Every feeling he had thought dead had been resurrected in the past few days and they ached and throbbed now, hypersensitive in their rebirth. He didn't welcome their return. It was easier, safer, not to feel at all. He resented their intrusion on his emotional isolation. He resented Serena for arousing them so effortlessly. But he couldn't look at her now and feel anger. Nor could he turn away. He couldn't look at her now and see how the calm, controlled woman from Charleston had been broken apart in a matter of days and not feel something—sympathy, empathy, compassion. . . .

He pushed himself away from the tree and went to stand behind her. He wrapped his arms around her, silently offering his strength, rocking her gently in time with the Cajun waltz that floated out through the cabin's screens.

Serena turned her face to his shoulder and squeezed her eyes shut against the tears, forcing two past her lashes to roll down her cheek and soak into Lucky's black T-shirt. The temptation was strong to just let go, to cry, to put the burden on his broad shoulders and ask him to take care of her problems the way he had taken care of Mrs. Guidry's poachers, the way he took care of the orphaned raccoons. But she didn't. Couldn't. He didn't want her problems. He had problems of his own. He didn't want involvement and he didn't want love. That knowledge made it all the more bittersweet to have his arms around her now, when she needed so badly to have someone to lean on.

Maybe he would change. Maybe he felt more for her than he wanted to admit. Maybe, when this business with Chanson du Terre was over, he would let her near enough to help him with the demons that haunted him.

And maybe pigs would fly.

She wasn't doing herself any favors falling into the trap of "there but for the love of a good woman" thinking. She and Lucky had been thrown together by circumstances, had given in to physical needs, and when it was over they would go their separate ways—he into his swamp and she . . .

"I guess I'd better go in and see what new treat Gifford has in store for me," she said, sniffing back the tears she wouldn't let fall. She turned in Lucky's arms and looked up at him, knowing with a terrible crystal-clear clarity that she had somehow, somewhere fallen in love with him. The thought hit her with a violent jolt every time it came. This big, brooding warrior with his panther's eyes and hooker's mouth, with his dark soul and heart of gold, had captured a part of her no other man ever had. Too bad he didn't want it.

They were greeted at the door of the cabin by the smell of warm beignets and strong coffee. While the battle of the Sheridans had been raging in the yard, apparently Pepper had been inside slaving over a hot stove. The old black man greeted Serena with a sad smile and a pat on the shoulder.

"You come on over here, Miz 'Rena. You looks like you could use some my coffee."

Serena tried to smile. "Could I have you inject it directly into my bloodstream, Pepper? I feel like I haven't slept in a month."

"Po' Miz 'Rena," Pepper muttered, shooting a damning glare at Gifford, who sat at the battered red Formica-topped table with a long envelope in front of him.

Serena pulled out a chrome-legged chair and sank down on a green vinyl seat that had cracked and torn and been repaired with duct tape. Gifford had taken the seat by the window that looked directly out onto the yard, and she wondered if he had seen Lucky holding her, but she dismissed the thought. Despite the way Gifford made her feel, she was no longer sixteen years old and under his guardianship. If she chose to have an affair with a man who looked and acted like a pirate, that was her own business.

She glanced around the cabin as Lucky took a seat and fished a cigarette out of his shirt pocket. Pepper kept up a running monologue in the background, drawling on pleasantly about the crawfish catch as he gathered up mismatched mugs and a big white enamel coffeepot. The coon hounds lay sprawled on the floor like rugs, looking up at Serena with mournful eyes. The furniture seemed haphazardly arranged around their gangly forms, worn and tattered armchairs with stuffing poking through in spots. The walls were unadorned except for mounted antlers and a gun rack grotesquely fashioned from a pair of deer forelegs.

Serena had always thought the cabin looked like her idea of a prison camp barracks with its tarpaper walls, pitted linoleum floor, and absence of niceties. It hadn't changed a lick in twenty-five years. It was the same floor, the same furniture, the same outdated appliances, the same arrangement of foodstuffs on the single shelf above the single cupboard, the same old round-edged black radio playing Cajun music and herbicide ads. Even the condiments on the table looked the same.

Gifford tapped his envelope against the tabletop, drawing Serena's eye away from the half-empty bottle of Tabasco sauce. It was a standard white business envelope with the return address printed in neat black script in the upper left-hand corner: LAMAR CANFIELD, ESQ. ATTORNEY AT LAW.

"This is yours."

"What is it?" she asked suspiciously, loathe to reach out and touch the thing. She'd had enough unpleasant surprises to last her.

Gifford pushed it across the table. "Look at it. Go on."

She looked from her grandfather to Lucky, who was frowning darkly at the old man, and back to the envelope. Feeling as if she were about to take a step that couldn't be taken back, she picked it up and withdrew the folded papers. The document was ridiculously simple considering the power it wielded. It granted her power of attorney over Gifford's affairs, including the disposition of Chanson du Terre. It was stamped and signed on the appropriate lines in Gifford's bold hand and Lamar's, and it had been dated nearly three weeks previous. All it needed was Serena's signature to make it official.

Serena stared at it, feeling manipulated and used. It really was in her hands—a power she didn't want over a home that wouldn't let her go. Her first impulse was to throw the papers back in Gifford's face, but she didn't. Instead, she folded them neatly and put them back in the envelope. Without a word she stood and walked out.

"Why don't you put a little more pressure on her, Giff?" Lucky said sarcastically. "Then we can all stand around and watch her crack."

"She'll bear up," Gifford said, lifting his chin. "She's a Sheridan."

"So's her sister."

The old man sniffed and looked away, absently lifting a hand to rub the ear of a hound that had come to silently beg for attention.

Pepper clucked in disapproval as he slid down onto the chair Serena had vacated. "Ain't no wonder she don' stay 'round here, you all the time pushin' her 'round dis way, dat way. Me, I'd go on to Charleston too."

Gifford scowled at his friend. "Then why don't you?"

" 'Cause if'n I left, there wouldn' be nobody 'round to listen to all your cussin' 'cept Odille, and she'd up'n kill you one fine day."

"Smartass."

Lucky ground his cigarette out in the blue tin ashtray on the table, crushing it with short, angry jabs, then skidded his chair back and stood up.

"I don' like your tactics, old man," he said in a low, tight voice. He was reacting on instinct, he knew, not with any kind of rationale. Serena had been hurt and upset and that brought all those long-dormant protective feelings rushing to the fore. He didn't like it, but that didn't keep it from happening.

"I did what I had to do."

"Without a thought to how Serena would feel about it."

Gifford arched a brow, his dark eyes speculative. "Since when do you give a fig about other people's feelings?"

Lucky said nothing. There was an answer lodged somewhere in his chest, but he refused to let it out or even look at it. He simply gave Gifford a long, disturbing look, then slipped out the door.

Serena was standing on the steps, looking out at the bayou, the infamous envelope tucked under one arm, her arms crossed over her chest. She looked pale and drawn, the dark smudges beneath her eyes a stark contrast to the youthful effect of the ponytail she wore. Lucky slid an arm around her and tilted her sideways against him.

"I don't want to go back just yet," she said in a small voice.

"Je te blâme pas," Lucky murmured, rubbing his hand up and down her arm. "I don't blame you, sugar."

"Can we go to your place?"

176

"*Oui.* If you like."

"I need to get away for a while."

She closed her eyes and pressed her head against him, and he felt that strange swelling, twisting feeling in his chest again.

"I'll take you away, *mon 'tite coeur,*" he said softly, and led her down the steps toward his pirogue.

Storm clouds were rushing in from the Gulf again as the pirogue slid in beside Lucky's dock. Fat and black, like dyed balls of cotton, they rolled north, thunder rumbling behind them. In a minute it would be raining, pouring, Serena thought as she looked up at the sky. And the minute after that it might be sunny and calm. The weather here seemed forever unsettled, unstable, adding to the impression of the swamp being a prehistoric place. Now, as the leaden clouds poured across the sky above, silence settled like a suffocating blanket all around. The trees went still. The birds went silent.

The rain started to fall as they crossed the yard, and by the time they had entered the house it was pounding down on the tin roof and splashing in through the window screens. Serena moved to close a window, but Lucky pulled her away.

"Let it rain," he said, walking backward and drawing her with him toward the bed.

She looked up at him uncertainly. "But the floor—"

"It's cypress; nothing can hurt it."

They undressed each other to the accompaniment of the thunderstorm, slowly and quietly as the rain pounded down outside and the cool moist breeze blew in through the windows.

"I need you," Serena whispered, head back, eyes closed against the weariness and turmoil that ached through her like a virus. She needed Lucky to sweep it all away, if only for a little while. She wanted to lose herself in the bliss of belonging to him, even if it was only temporary.

"I'm here," he said, reaching behind her to release the clasp from her hair.

She sighed as he ran his fingers through her unbound tresses, spreading them across her bare shoulders. Rising on tiptoe, she returned the favor, pulling the leather lace from his queue and combing her hands through his curling black mane. He bound his arms around her, holding her high against his body, and kissed her slowly and deeply, then stood her away from him.

177

"Viens ici, chérie," he whispered, sliding across the bed, holding his hand out to her.

Serena stared at him for a moment, mesmerized. He looked wild and dangerous, but she reached out and took his hand, welcoming its solid strength as she welcomed the strength of his arms when she settled herself on the bed and into his embrace.

They made love slowly as the rain fell. Lucky took complete command, letting Serena lie back to simply enjoy. He kissed her again and again, long, slow, deep kisses that left her breathless and languid. He lavished attention on her breasts, sucking gently at her nipples for what seemed like hours. Slowly he made his way down her body, kissing her everywhere with lingering, leisurely kisses, tasting her stomach, the point of her hip, the inside of her knee.

Lying between her legs, he slid his hands beneath her buttocks and lifted her slightly. He settled his mouth against her intimately, caressing her with his tongue, drinking in the taste of her. Serena arched her back and sighed at the exquisite pleasure. Desire swirled through her, building like the storm wind outside, sweeping her away to a place where there was nothing but herself and Lucky and this vibrant heat that burned inside her and exploded through her as he took her over the brink.

The shock waves were still pulsing when he slid up over her, caressing her body with his. She cried out when he entered her, not in pain, but in ecstasy as her muscles clenched and held him deep within her, caressing him, coaxing him toward his own completion.

Lucky ground his mouth against Serena's, catching her soft, wild sounds, giving her his tongue and the lingering sweet taste of her own body. The old bed creaked as he moved against her. Thunder rumbled overhead and rain hammered down on the tin roof, but those things receded into nothingness. Chanson du Terre, the past, the present, all faded away.

All Lucky could think of was Serena, her softness, her heat, the way she fit around him as tight as a silken glove, the way she welcomed him into her body and held on to him as if she would never let him go. All he could think of was giving her pleasure and letting that pleasure sweep him away.

He moved within her, slowly, gently, holding back his own release as he lured her toward another. Her hips moved against his. The tempo of her breathing quickened. He slipped a hand between them and rubbed his thumb against her most sensitive flesh, and she cried his name again as her ecstasy crested, taking Lucky with her. His body shuddered and stiffened as he poured his seed into her. He tightened his arms around her and thought he'd never felt quite so alive.

He turned onto his side as his muscles began to relax, and sank gratefully into the mattress. Physically, he was tired. Emotionally, he was exhausted from the constant war between feeling and trying not to feel. He gathered Serena close against him and wondered if she could sense him shaking inside.

Outside, the storm had passed. The thunder was rolling away to the north, leaving behind only the gentle sound of the rain. Inside, the storm of passion had passed and Serena lay in Lucky's arms, spent, too tired to face the feelings their lovemaking had kept at bay—all the emotions Gifford's actions had jerked loose, the pressure he had put on her, the conflicts over what needed to be done, the questions about family loyalty, the memory of the fire and all it meant. As he had promised, Lucky had taken her away from all that for a brief time, but now it all came rushing back.

The tears came as quickly as the spring shower had, and she let them fall without bothering to hide them or apologize for them. Lucky held her close, stroking her hair, brushing his lips against her temple. He whispered to her in French, soft words, comforting words, his low, purring voice almost as tangible a caress as his hand. It was just the respite she needed. Quiet compassion. Sheltering. Tender solace. The kind of consolation offered on an unspoken plane of understanding, offered with empathy, offered by a soulmate.

Serena felt her heart swell painfully at the thought. What they had was temporary, tenuous, a slice of their lives that seemed taken out of context. It was like a hothouse flower that had been forced to burst open overnight. Feelings had been magnified and time-accelerated. She wondered if what they had would die as quickly as it had come to life.

She knew the answer. It wrung a few extra tears from her heart and brought the words to her lips even though she knew she shouldn't say them. She shouldn't have become involved with him to begin with, but it was too late to change that and she couldn't change what was in her heart, no matter how pointless it was.

She sighed with a sense of fatalism and murmured against the base of his throat, "I love you."

The words ran into Lucky's heart like the blade of a knife. His hand stilled in the act of stroking her hair. Every muscle in his body tensed in rejection. "Don't," he said automatically.

179

Serena sat up, pulling the sheet over her breasts, and looked at him, her expression as carefully blank as his. "Don't what? Don't love you or don't say it out loud?"

He shook his head as he climbed out of the bed and reached for his jeans. "Don't," he repeated as he pulled up the zipper. "Don't say it. Don't think it."

Serena watched him as he prowled the room, reading his unease in the set of his muscular shoulders and the tempo of his stride. He walked with his head down, eyes hooded, his hair partially obscuring his profile.

"Why not?" she asked, keeping her voice even.

He shot her a sideways glance. "Because it isn't true. You can't love me. You don't know me. This"—he gestured toward the bed—"this is just sex."

"Not for me, it isn't."

Lucky wheeled on her, his expression cruel, his eyes tormented. "Well, it is for me," he shot back, taking an aggressive step toward the bed. "How's that, baby?" he asked sarcastically, raising his hands in question. "Is that what you wanted to hear? You're a great lay, but that's all it is."

The pain was instantaneous. Serena told herself she'd asked for it, but that hardly dulled the sting. Even seeing the tumult of contradictory emotions in Lucky's eyes wasn't much of a balm. This was his line of defense and he would cling to it to the bitter end. He didn't want to believe there could be something more between them even when he knew it already existed. He was afraid of it. He didn't want her seeing beyond his armor, didn't want her to touch him.

"It's just sex," he repeated half under his breath as he retreated to pace along the foot of the bed.

"I don't believe you."

"I don't care."

"If you don't care, why does it upset you so much to hear me say I love you?"

He stopped in his tracks and turned his face to her with a look that would have chilled most men. "Don't play shrink games with me, Serena."

She didn't deny the charge, but shrugged and lifted her chin. If she'd been in possession of her common sense, she would have let the matter drop. But then, if she'd been in possession of her common sense, she never would have gotten into the pirogue with him at Gauthier's dock.

"I love you. That's how I feel. I needed to say it. I don't see why you're so upset," she said defensively. "I didn't ask you to say it back."

Lucky snorted. *"Mais non,* but you expected me to."

She stared at him, feeling an acute sense of sadness like a stone in her chest. "No. I didn't."

He swore in French and turned toward the window. "I can't give you what you want, Serena," he said, ignoring her answer. "I don't have it in me."

"Oh, I think you have it in you. You're just afraid to give it."

"No," he said, staring out at the rain. "It's not there. It's gone. There's nothing there. I can't be the kind of man you need."

"What do you know about the kind of man I need?"

"I know he isn't me."

"What if you're wrong?"

He wheeled on her, letting all the frustration and pain and rage surface in one explosion of feeling. "What do you know about me?" he roared. "Nothing! You've pieced together some fantasy profile, made me out to be a hero when I'm nothing. I'm nothing but a man hanging on to his sanity by his fingertips. I'm nothing but a trained killer who might go off the edge in the blink of an eye. I don't have anything inside me but nightmares. Is that what you want? Is that the kind of man you need?"

Eyes wild, nostrils flaring, he stalked to the bed in a half crouch, meeting Serena at eye level. "You wanna have a peek inside the man you think you love, Doc?" he whispered. "You wanna know what makes me run?

"I spent a year in a private prison in Central America. My commanding officer arranged it because he was dirty and I was on to him. Our mission down there was one of those little soirées our government doesn't own up to. They told my family I was killed in a training accident. And for a year I sat in a filthy, rat-infested cell in total darkness. The only time they took me out was to torture me.

"Do you know what that does to a man's mind, Dr. Sheridan? Do you know what that leaves him with?" He straightened and slowly backed away. "Nothing. Nothing. I don't have anything to give you. I live for myself, by myself, and that's the way I like it. I don't want your help and I don't want your love. The only thing I ever wanted from you was your body."

181

He turned away from her and went back to the window, feeling bleak and empty.

Serena sat there for a long moment, absorbing his words, aching— not for herself, but for Lucky, for the sensitive young man who loved his family, the scholar, the artist who had had his life systematically destroyed. She hurt for the man he was now, tormented, frightened, alone. She wanted so badly to reach out to him, but she knew he would only push her away.

"If you wanted me to believe you were nothing but a heartless bastard, you should have left me at Gifford's that first night," she said, a part of her wishing he had done just that.

"You got that right," he answered derisively. "I should have left you. But don't tell me I led you on, sugar. I told you from the first what this would be."

"Yes, you did." And from the first it had been a lie. They had come together in passion and anger and need, but it had never been as simple as "just sex." Never.

"Then keep your pretty words to yourself," he muttered. "I don't want to hear them. I have no need of your love."

Serena wanted to cry. She'd never seen a man more in need of love. He pulled himself away from people, hid from the world. He had retreated to the solace of his swamp to heal his own wounds, but they weren't healing. They lay open and raw, and he retreated further still to some desolate place within himself. Her foolish heart ached to help him. The woman in her yearned to be the one to make a difference. But the psychologist knew it wouldn't happen and she knew why, small consolation though that was.

She didn't have the strength to fight the inevitable. All things considered, it seemed best to make the break there and then. Going on would be an exercise in futility, like beating her head against a brick wall. She had lost any kind of perspective that could have maintained a sexual relationship between them even if she had been able to stomach that kind of affair. And God knew she had other problems to take care of. She would chalk this up to being in the wrong place at the wrong time with the wrong man.

As she moved to gather her clothes, she studied Lucky, still standing framed by the curtainless window, and wondered bleakly how the wrong man could seem so right.

He turned and watched her, cast in a mix of silver light and black shadow that made a perfect portrait of him. "Where do we go from here?"

Serena paused as she buttoned her blouse, considering options and answers, and decided to take his question at face value. "Chanson du Terre."

Chapter Fifteen

It was a long ride back. As Lucky stood silently behind her, Serena sat in the pirogue taking in the sights and sounds of the swamp. This would be her last trip through this wilderness that had haunted her for so many years. She had no intention of coming back for Gifford again. He had pushed things too far. Next time he would have to come to her. And as for any other reason she might venture out here, there wasn't any, she told herself, refusing the urge to turn around and look up at Lucky.

She focused instead on the swamp, looking past her instinctive fear at the primitive beauty, the delicacy, the place that Lucky loved. The rain had passed and the sun had returned with a vengeance, turning the place into a natural sauna. Moisture rose like steam from the surface of the water and dripped from the lacy festoons of Spanish moss. Wildflowers glistened, brilliant spots of color among the drab grays and browns. Serena wondered if Lucky had ever painted it this way.

They held their silence by tacit agreement until the landing at Chanson du Terre came into sight.

"What are you gonna do?" he asked quietly as he steered the boat in an arch for the dock.

"End it," Serena said, still facing forward, her eyes on the big house. "Send Burke packing. See that the matter of the fire and insurance claim are settled."

"And then?"

She didn't answer him for a long moment. The pirogue snuggled in along the dock and settled. Finally she turned and looked up at him as she rose to her feet. "Why should you care, Lucky? You got what you wanted."

Lucky said nothing, but he stood wrestling with the emotions twisting inside him. He didn't care, he told himself. She could go back to Charleston, where she belonged. It didn't matter to him. He would have his swamp and his peace and no Sheridans to upset the placid surface of his life. He ignored the pain in his chest as Serena stepped from the boat and walked away without looking back. He didn't need her, couldn't need her, and that was the end of it.

With strong strokes of the push-pole he moved his pirogue away from the dock and turned south for Mouton's. It was going to be a good night for getting drunk and raising hell.

Serena crossed the yard slowly, her attention on the white Cadillac parked beside Shelby's BMW. Burke's, no doubt. As Giff had said, the man was as tenacious as a pit bull. And as charming. She wondered how he would take the news of her decision. Not well. He didn't strike her as a graceful loser.

Shelby was liable to take it badly too. She didn't like having her plans interfered with, particularly when personal glorification was at stake. She saw selling the plantation as the one and only means to achieve her goal of putting Mason in the legislature and putting herself on a public pedestal all in one fell swoop. She wouldn't be happy about having that means taken away from her. Added to that frustration would be the old feelings of competition between them. Gifford had played favorites, giving Serena the one tool that would have made all of Shelby's dreams come true.

Serena cursed Gifford for putting the land above all else. She cursed herself for coming back. But the die was cast now. The hand had been dealt and there was nothing to do but play it out.

They were gathered in the front parlor. Shelby was resplendent in a sleeveless red silk dress with a snug bodice and full skirt. Her hair was curled back neatly in a style that made her look like a movie star from the Carol Lombard era. Mason was in another one of his junior-senator outfits, charcoal slacks and an ivory shirt with the tie of some illustrious British regiment slightly askew at his throat. Burke wore the same western-cut suit he'd worn the previous night, but had opted to forgo the bolo tie. They turned as one toward Serena as she entered the room, their faces registering various expressions of surprise.

Shelby frowned. "My word, Serena, is this how people dress for dinner in Charleston? You look a mess!"

Serena glanced down at her rumpled cotton blouse and black walking shorts that were creased and wrinkled. A quick peek in the gilt-framed mirror on the wall showed her hair escaping the bonds of its clip.

"Yes, I do look a mess. I'm sorry, but I just now got back from Gifford's," she said, trying to mentally dismiss the afternoon spent with Lucky as easily as she omitted it from the conversation. "You'll forgive me, Mr. Burke, for not being more presentable," she said coolly. I'm tired and I'd rather not take the time to freshen up."

"Gifford didn't return with you?" Mason asked, his brows lifting above the frame of his glasses.

"No."

"What did he have to say about the fire?"

"Suffice it to say, he was upset."

"But he didn't come back here to deal with it?" Burke said gruffly. He chewed on the end of his cigar and made a face like a bulldog. "Damned strange, if you ask me."

"I didn't ask you," Serena said, too exhausted to adhere to the code of southern hospitality.

She watched his reaction with clinical interest. His jaw hardened. His eyes narrowed. She got the strong impression he didn't like taking guff from women.

Mason looked scandalized at her lack of manners. "Serena! Mr. Burke is concerned with Gifford's mental state, as are we all."

"I'm well aware of what Mr. Burke is concerned with. As to Gifford's mental state, I can assure you all he is as shrewd as ever."

"He's behaving like a madman," Shelby muttered, pouting. She lifted one bejeweled hand to play with the diamond pendant that hung from a gold chain around her neck. "Stringing us all along, delaying the business proceedings. Mr. Burke is a busy man. He can't wait forever."

"He doesn't have to wait at all," Serena said, lifting the envelope she

186

held so that everyone focused on it. "Gifford has granted me power of attorney. I am to act on this matter as I see fit."

Shelby gave a dramatic gasp, hand to her heart, but Serena pushed on, eager to get it over with and in no mood for her twin's theatrics. "I don't see fit to sell this property to Tristar Chemical. Mr. Burke, I'm sorry your time here has been wasted."

Burke turned scarlet. He pulled the cigar from his mouth and pointed it at Serena's face. "Now, wait just a goddamn minute. You can't do that."

"The courts would beg to differ. I didn't want the responsibility of this decision, but I have it and I've made up my mind."

"I don't believe this," Burke muttered. He wheeled on Mason. "This deal was as good as done, Talbot. You talk some sense into her or you can kiss your trip to Baton Rouge good-bye."

Mason looked nervous. He turned toward Serena, his affable smile contorting a little with uncertainty. "Serena, let's not be hasty. I don't believe you've had time to take all the factors into consideration. There's a great deal at stake here."

Serena gave him a level look. "I know what's at stake, Mason. I think I see it more clearly than you do."

"You!" Shelby snapped suddenly, drawing everyone's immediate attention. She glared at Serena, her knuckles turning white as she clutched a tumbler of scotch. She took a step forward. "What do you know about anything? What do you know about having to live here? We're trying to do what's best for everybody."

"You're trying to line your pockets and buy Mason a seat in the legislature," Serena said succinctly. "I have the power to stop you from sacrificing our heritage for your greed, and I'm using it. It's as simple as that, Shelby. I didn't want it to come to this, but I don't have any choice."

Shelby advanced another step. Her perfect complexion was turning red in splotches that rose from the collar of her expensive dress to her hairline. "You self-righteous little bitch," she spat out. "How dare you come waltzing back here, waving your morals like a banner, telling us what to do! We never asked for your interference."

"No, you didn't," Serena said, wondering if Lucky hadn't been right about them trying to get the deal through without her finding out about it until it was too late.

"Then why didn't you just stay out of it? Why didn't you just stay in your neat, clean little world in Charleston, ignoring us the way you always have?"

"I'm sorry," Serena whispered, feeling her connection to her sister growing thinner and more brittle by the second. All she could think of was that it shouldn't have come to this.

"Sorry?" Shelby sneered, taking another step closer. "Sorry!"

She flung her glass to the floor, heedless of the scotch that soaked into the rug in a dark stain. Stepping forward, she struck out with both hands, giving Serena a shove that sent her stumbling backward. Serena didn't try to defend herself physically or verbally. Words would do her no good; Shelby was well beyond seeing reason. Her rage was a tangible feeling in the air, like electricity building before an explosive storm. Serena watched in fascinated horror as the storm was unleashed.

"You don't see anything!" Shelby said, her voice rising in pitch and volume with each word as her control slipped further and further through her grasp. "You don't care about this place. You never have. All you're doing is playing up to Gifford so he'll give you everything that ought to be mine!" She gulped a breath, half crying, her mouth twisting grotesquely as her fury built uncontrollably. "You're trying to ruin everything for me just like you always have! God damn you! I wish you'd never been born!"

Serena stood motionless, not even trying to block the stinging slap her sister delivered. Shelby turned and fled the room, choking and sobbing. Serena didn't move. She stood in the electrified silence, struggling with her feelings, knowing at that moment that any slim hope she had held out for closeness with her twin had just been shattered.

Burke and Mason looked on, both men looking distinctly uncomfortable in the wake of female wrath. Mason recovered first, coming forward to gallantly offer his immaculate linen handkerchief. Serena took it, staring at it stupidly.

"There's blood," he said, eyes downcast. "The corner of your mouth."

She dabbed it, but refused to look at the stain on the handkerchief. It was bad enough to know it was there. She focused instead on the envelope she still held and wondered if Gifford had any idea what he'd done.

"Serena," Mason said softly. "I realize you have a certain sentimental attachment to Chanson du Terre, but I've heard you say on more than one occasion that you wouldn't change your life because of it. We've discussed the practicality of selling, particularly now, when the plantation isn't doing well to begin with and the market is so bleak. And now there's the fire damage to consider—"

"Yes, what about that fire damage?" Burke interrupted. "Can Gifford afford to cover the loss himself?"

Serena lifted her eyes and fixed them on the Texan. "I think, Mr. Burke, the only aspect of the fire you need to concern yourself with is whether or not your name can be attached to it."

He didn't appear the least bit shocked by her accusation, which was as good as an admission of guilt to Serena.

"I wasn't anywhere near here when the fire started," he said, glancing idly at the end of his cigar. It had gone out. He frowned and went on calmly. "I've got witnesses. It won't do you any good to try to prove otherwise." His eyes hardened to stone as he stared down at her and repeated with emphasis, "It won't do you any good at all."

Serena arched a brow. "Is that a threat, Mr. Burke?"

"It's a fact, sweetheart."

She gave him her coolest look, not letting him see her questions about how far he might be compelled to go to get what he wanted. After a moment she stepped back from him and said, "I believe I've had enough of your company to last me, Mr. Burke. It's been a very long and trying day. I'm going to call it an evening. Mason will show you out. And since your business here is finished, I won't expect to see you back again. Good night." She nodded to her brother-in-law. "Mason."

She felt their eyes on her back even after she'd slipped out the door.

"What do you propose to do about this, Talbot?" Burke demanded in a low, rough voice, his glare bearing down on Mason like a spotlight. "You blow this deal and you can just bend over and kiss your political ass good-bye."

"Now, Len," Mason said in his most soothing tones. He gamely resurrected his smile and turned toward the sideboard to pour his guest a drink. "I'm sure I can get Serena to see reason. She just needs a little time, that's all. She's allowed Gifford to manipulate her. Once she realizes that and looks at the situation from a fresh perspective, I'm confident she'll see things our way."

Burke gave him a long cold look. "She'd better."

Shelby paced the bedroom, her agitation showing in every step. The room was a shambles. At the peak of her rage she had tipped over every chair, torn the coverlet from the bed, pulled every article of clothing from the closet and dresser and flung them everywhere. Her path was now littered with designer-label suits and dresses that had been worn no more than twice. She ground the delicate fabrics beneath the heels of her pumps as she stalked the floor.

"Damn her. Damn her. I hate her!" she ranted, snatching a bottle of Chanel from the dresser and hurling it against the wall. It shattered, immediately engulfing the room in a sickening cloud of fragrance as the perfume soaked into the wallpaper in an oily stain.

Mason sat on the edge of the bed with his hands clasped lightly between his knees. He watched his wife's awesome display of temper with a properly concerned look knitting his brows and curling down the corners of his mouth. She whirled toward him, her eyes wild, her face contorted in a mask of rage.

"Do something!" she screamed, then lowered her voice to a hissing whisper. "Do something, damn you! Don't just sit there looking pretty while Serena ruins everything I ever wanted!"

"Now, Shelby sweetheart, calm yourself—"

"Don't tell me to calm myself. If everyone calmed themselves as often as you said, we'd all be catatonic. This isn't the time to be calm! This is the time for action. We have to do something. Our future is riding on this."

"I know that, peach," Mason said, his gaze drifting wistfully over the expensive wardrobe Shelby had trampled into the floor.

"Of course, if you made more money in your law practice or if your parents hadn't lost their fortune in that silly oil bust, we wouldn't be in this mess."

Mason hummed a noncommittal note.

"I wish we could just pretend Serena had never come here," she muttered, resuming her pacing. She ran her fingers through her hair again and again, dislodging pins that fell silently into the drift of fabric she waded through. "I wish she would just disappear. Gifford should have given that power of attorney to me. It's my future that's tied to this place, not Serena's. He should have given it to me, but no, he gave it to her and she doesn't have sense enough to see what's right."

"Let's not fret over it now," Mason said softly, standing and reaching for her hand. He drew her across a bright pink suit that still bore the price tag and pulled her into his arms. "Let's sleep on it," he said, brushing his lips against her temple. "It'll all work out, peach. You'll see."

"Yes," Shelby said, suddenly utterly calm as she leaned against her husband. "I will see."

Chapter Sixteen

"Telephone call, Miz 'Rena," Odille announced as she stepped into the dining room.

Shelby's head snapped up from a brooding contemplation of her crawfish bisque. "Honestly, Odille, you know better than to interrupt dinner—"

"It's all right," Serena said, pushing her chair back from the table with unseemly haste. "I was finished anyway."

She dropped her napkin over the plate she'd barely touched and turned to the housekeeper, who was giving Shelby a smug glare. "I'll take it in the hall, Odille. Thank you."

Walking out of the dining room and into the hall, Serena felt as if she'd just left a pressurized chamber. She'd never been so glad to escape a meal in her life. The day had been an especially trying one. She'd spent hours with the insurance investigator and the state fire marshal going over the particulars of the fire, walking through what was left of the machine shed. She'd spent another few hours on the telephone in Gifford's office soliciting aid in the form of equipment from neighboring planters. Then there had been the trip to the bank to

191

really brighten the day. In addition to these pleasant chores she'd had to contend with Shelby's fire and ice moods and Mason's diplomatic lobbying for her to change her mind about selling the land.

Dinner had been the crowning glory. How anyone in that dining room had managed to choke down a single bite of food was beyond her. Serena was more than happy to have an excuse to get away. She could have kissed Odille's feet for interrupting.

She stopped at the hall table and picked up the receiver, expecting to hear the voice of one of the planters she had spoken with that day.

"This is Serena Sheridan. How may I help you?"

"You got it backward," the man said in a hushed voice. "I want to help you."

A chill ran down Serena's spine. Her hand tightened on the receiver. "Who is this?"

"A friend."

The voice was dark and rough, not the voice of a friend, but the voice of a stranger. Serena steeled herself against the tingles of fear running through her and spoke in the most businesslike tone she could manage. "Look, either you give me your name or I'm hanging up."

"You're not interested in information that could tie Burke to your fire?"

Serena's heart picked up a beat. She swallowed hard. "I'm listening."

"Meet me at the back edge of that cane field that runs along the bayou in half an hour."

"Isn't there some other way of doing this?" she asked. The idea of meeting an anonymous caller in the middle of nowhere held no appeal at all. "Can't you tell me what you know now?"

"You can't see evidence over the phone, lady," he answered impatiently. "Do you want it or not? It's no skin off my nose if the insurance company never pays off."

In the end Serena agreed to the meeting. She decided she would have James Arnaud follow her at a distance in case there was trouble. She didn't like the idea of meeting the man behind the voice, but she couldn't take the chance of dismissing evidence that would clear the way for the claim to be settled. The future of Chanson du Terre rode on getting that money. The plantation had become Serena's responsibility. She would do whatever she had to do.

She left the house without a word to anyone and walked to

Arnaud's house only to be informed by a gum-chewing teenage daughter that the manager had gone to the hospital to visit the two men who had been injured in the explosion. Serena thanked the girl and wandered down the drive, wondering what to do. She could ask one of the other hired men to go with her, but she had no way of knowing which one of them might have been Burke's accomplice. She thought about skipping the meeting, but there was no guarantee her informant would try again.

The claim had to be settled. There was no question of that. Gifford wouldn't be able to cover even a fraction of the cost to replace the machine shed, let alone the machinery that had been burned inside it.

There was no choice for her to make. Taking a deep breath and squaring her shoulders, she set off for the rendezvous spot with determined strides.

No one was waiting for her when she arrived ten minutes later. Serena found herself standing at the end of the canebrake, shifting her weight nervously from one foot to the other. She didn't like being there. Even if it had been the middle of the day, she wouldn't have liked it. This particular field wasn't far from the plantation buildings, but the buildings were out of sight, giving one the impression of total wilderness. The money-green stalks of cane were already tall and grew thickly across the field to the south. To the north, Bayou Noir made a dog-leg cut into Sheridan property, partially isolating this field from the others. The mass willow trees along the bank of the bayou increased the sense of isolation.

Even at high noon this wasn't a place she would have chosen to be. It wasn't noon. The sun had begun its fireball descent. It would be night soon and she stood alone at the end of an equipment lane between a cane field and a black bayou, listening to the melodious call of a red-winged blackbird as the setting sun spilled orange light over everything.

She swung around, her breath catching hard in her throat at a rustling in the tall reeds along the bank. A blue heron rose, eerily silent, its long, spindly legs stretching out behind it as it sailed away. Serena forced herself to exhale slowly. It wasn't an alligator. It wasn't a snake.

It wasn't her informant.

Serena stroked her fingers along the canister of Mace inside her purse. Her ex-husband had given it to her as a gift when she'd begun her pro bono work at the mental health clinic. Romantic devil. The neighborhood where the clinic was located was a bad one, and she occasionally worked late. Paul had been concerned for her safety and Serena had to admit there had been times when she'd been concerned herself, but she had yet to use his gift. She touched it now only to reassure herself. She didn't really believe she would need protection.

She had already considered the possibility of a trap and dismissed it. Burke wouldn't be foolish enough to try something so close on the heels of the fire. It would point directly to him. Still, it didn't hurt to be prepared.

She heaved a long sigh and scanned the ground around her, looking for snakes. There were long black indigo snakes out here that hunted mice among the cane stalks. They weren't poisonous, but she had no desire to encounter one just the same. There were cottonmouths along the bayou that came out at night and copperheads that commanded the floor of the woods. The idea of them made her skin crawl and fear knot at the back of her throat. They wouldn't come looking for her, Serena reminded herself, doing her best to swallow the impending panic attack.

Where was her damned informant?

The sound of an outboard motor idling down drew her attention to the north. She tried to peer through the tangled ribbons of willow branches to make out the boat and its occupant, but it was impossible to see well. Already the light was fading along the bayou, and all she could make out was bits of color and shape.

She had for some reason assumed the man would be coming the same way she had, by foot down the lane. In the back of her mind she had decided he was an employee of Chanson du Terre. She had imagined he had chosen this spot for the meeting because it was near the plantation buildings and yet secluded enough so they wouldn't be seen. She had given no thought to the bayou or a boat, and she cursed her lack of foresight as a sudden chill swept over her from head to foot.

"Well, lookee here, Pou," Gene Willis said, a leering smile twisting the hard line of his mouth as he parted the weeds and willow branches and stepped into the clearing. Pou Perret scuttled along at his heels like a pet weasel, his droopy eyes darting furtively all around, his mustache twitching as if he were scenting the air for danger. "If it ain't Lucky Doucet's lady. Fancy meetin' you here, Miz Sheridan."

Serena eyed the pair warily, her hand closing around the Mace. She recognized them from Mouton's. She doubted she would ever get the scene out of her head: Lucky with a knife in his hand, this big red-haired man lunging for him, the little scruffy one swinging a broken bottle, a wild gleam in his eye. They might have been the kind of men one would hire to start a fire or commit any number of other criminal acts, but they didn't seem like the sort to come forward with information—unless it was for a price.

"How much do you want for the information?" she asked, trying to sound calm and businesslike despite the way she was beginning to tremble from the inside out.

"You hear that, Pou?" Willis went on smiling, sauntering closer. He moved with all the grace of a bear and looked nearly as strong. Serena's gaze focused on his hands. They were huge and ugly, raw-looking with fingers like sausages. "The lady wants to pay us. I can't remember the last time a *lady* wanted to give me anything, can you?"

Pou apparently took it as a rhetorical remark. He said nothing, but Serena could feel his eyes on her, hot and feral like an animal's. He moved slowly toward her and to her right, his hands behind his back.

"Isn't that what you came here for?" she said, trying to buy time. She forced herself to stand her ground and gripped her can of Mace with a sweaty hand. "Money?"

Willis grinned, an expression that had undoubtedly looked evil even when he'd been in the cradle. One sinisterly arched red brow climbed his forehead while the other hung low over a narrow eye. "No, Miz Serena. We're already gettin' paid. And hell," he added with a nasty laugh, "this is a job I'd do for free."

They were moving closer, slowly, menacingly. Serena took a half step back. Fear climbed high in her throat. "I'll pay you double." She wasn't sure how they were supposed to be earning their money, but she was fairly certain it would be worth paying them double *not* to do their jobs.

Pou shot a glance up at Willis, looking for a reaction. Willis pretended to consider her offer, humming and making an exaggerated face. After a minute he shook his head and smiled at her again.

"Naw, I don't think so," he said, rubbing one of his ugly hands across his massive jaw. "You see, the perks of this job are so much better than money. Ain't that right, Pou?"

Perret flinched a little at the sound of his name, tearing his gaze off Serena once again to look up at his partner. "Jesus, Willis, let's just do it," he whined, suddenly nervous again. "Me, I don' wanna be hanging 'round here if that son of a bitch shows up. He'll kill us!"

"If you're looking for Lucky, he could be here any minute," Serena said. It wasn't much of a threat, but she was beginning to feel a little desperate.

Willis just smiled and inched a little closer. "Nice try, sweetheart, but I know exactly where Doucet is. He's at Mouton's with a whiskey bottle and a peroxide blonde who could suck the brass off a doorknob. I don't think he'll be joining us any time soon. Too bad for him. He's gonna miss one hell of a party."

Serena felt a painful lurch in her middle at the thought of Lucky with another woman. Her concentration broke for just an instant, and in that instant Gene Willis reached out and grabbed her, his big ugly hand manacling her left wrist.

She reacted instantly, pulling the Mace from her purse and hitting the button as she swung it wildly toward Willis's face. He knocked her hand aside with a swift, hard blow that numbed her arm to the elbow and sent the can and her purse sailing, but he was a split second late. The spray caught him in the left eye and he let her go and reeled backward, howling like a wounded beast.

Serena turned and ran. Her heart was in her throat. Her blood roared in her ears. Her body felt as if it belonged to someone else, someone who didn't realize the kind of danger she was in. Her legs wouldn't move fast enough. Her lungs wouldn't draw enough breath for her to scream. She ran down the lane, stumbling because the loafers she wore weren't designed for flight.

Behind her she could hear Willis swearing and shouting at his partner, "Get her, damn you!" Then came the pounding of feet.

She couldn't hope to outrun him. The lane stretched before her, looking longer and longer with not a building in sight. Her only options were to jump in the bayou and swim for it or try to lose herself in the cane. The cane led back to people. She thought of the indigo snakes and hesitated. There was no other choice. As Perret's footfalls rushed up on her, she veered suddenly to the left, diving for the cover of the sugarcane.

Perret tackled her from behind, his shoulder hitting her in the middle of the back, driving her forward and knocking her off her feet. She hit the ground with a thud that jarred every part of her. Her captor landed on top of her, the force of his weight blurring her vision and knocking the air from her lungs. Before she could even think of moving he had his knee planted between her shoulder blades, pinning her to the hot, moist earth.

He used a dirty bandanna for a gag, tying it roughly behind her head, incorporating strands of hair into the knot so that no matter how still Serena tried to be, it pulled. Tears of fear and pain flooded her eyes as Perret bound her hands tightly behind her back. They rose up in her throat and she choked and gagged, discovering very quickly that she wouldn't be allowed the luxury of crying. The bandanna with its foul, sour taste hindered not only speech but breathing and swallowing.

Perret rose and pulled her up with him, using the gag like a bridle on a horse. He curled his fingers into the back of it, pulling it unbearably tight, twisting her hair along with it, and jerked her to her feet and steered her back toward Willis.

The big man had regained his feet, but stood half doubled over, one hand pressed to his injured eye. The glare in his good eye was murderous, and Serena suddenly understood why self-defense instructors preached cooperation rather than aggression. Whatever Willis had had in store for her was nothing compared to what was going through his mind now.

She tried to stop before she got too close to him, but Perret shoved her forward and she had no way of catching herself. Willis knocked her to her knees with a single backhanded blow across the face that brought more tears and the taste of blood.

"You bitch," he growled, clutching at his eye. "You're gonna pay for this. You're gonna pay till you wished you'd never been born a woman."

Serena managed to turn and raise herself up as he swung his foot at her. The kick caught her shoulder instead of the side of her head. Pain exploded through her at the blow and then again as she went facefirst to the ground, unable to break the fall.

"Get her in the boat," Willis ordered, and staggered away, still rubbing at his eye.

Perret once again took hold of her makeshift bridle and hauled her to her feet. They loaded her with a minimum of ceremony into a battered aluminum-hulled boat with a massive outboard motor hanging off the back. It was the kind of thing poachers might use, Serena suspected, with enough horsepower to outrun the game warden—or the odd Lone Ranger. The boat was loaded with traps and tarps, empty whiskey bottles and crushed beer cans. There were a number of small holes in the side above the water line that may well have been caused by bullets. It reeked of swamp water and fish. Perret forced her to sit on the bottom on a wadded-up piece of damp black canvas with her back against the side of the boat, the unadorned edge biting into her spine. Then Pou started the motor and piloted them away from the bank while Willis attempted to flush the Mace from his eye with beer.

The fear that rose inside Serena threatened to swallow her whole. She could feel it growing stronger, clawing at her, tearing at her mind as the boat carried her away from Sheridan land. She wanted to scream, but the screams caught in the back of her throat and choked her. She wanted to run, but there was nowhere to run to; there was nothing around her but black water and swamp.

God, they were taking her into the swamp! The terror she normally felt at the prospect of going out there doubled, then tripled. She better than anyone knew how easy it was for a person to become lost. By the time anyone realized she was missing, it would be virtually impossible to find her. Willis and Perret could do anything they wanted. There would be no witnesses. There would be no one to hear her screams. Suddenly her future looked worse than anything her nightmares had ever conjured.

She wondered wildly what their orders were. What exactly had Burke paid them to do? Scare her into selling? Get her out of the way while he made a deal for the land? Use her as a hostage with Chanson du Terre as her ransom price? It seemed unlikely. Too dangerous to Burke and to Tristar. That left only one possibility. Burke would get her out of the way—permanently.

That deduction brought another wave of fear. Tears gathered in her eyes, but she fought them back. Control. That was her only hope—to keep her head, to keep her cool, to look for the opportunity to escape.

With effort she forced the fear back, compressed it and shoved it into a mental compartment and shut the door. Fear would get her nothing. It was a waste of time and energy. It would do her no good to cry and shake. It would do no good to wish for a rescuer. Lucky wasn't going to swoop down from a tree and save her. He was at Mouton's drowning his sorrows, and she was on her own. She could save herself or she could be tortured and killed. It was as simple as that.

Still trembling, she forced herself to look around and take in land-marks. If she concentrated hard enough, she might be able to memorize the route they were taking and retrace it once she managed to get away. She thought it was the same way Lucky had gone to get her to Gifford's, but she wasn't sure. It was growing darker by the second, making it very difficult to see, and the bayou branched off too many times for her to be certain of the turns.

The swamp closed in around them, dark and silent beyond the

puttering of the motor. Perret slowed the boat to a crawl as he negotiated the way among a stand of cypress. Willis sprawled in one of the boat's two bucket seats, facing Serena. He had stopped using the beer from his cooler to rinse his eye and had started drinking it instead.

Serena could feel his gaze on her, lingering on her breasts. She tried to shrug it off, but the feeling clung as tenaciously as the mosquitoes that were feasting on the exposed skin of her throat and face. She had worn a long-sleeved blouse and slacks, knowing better than to go out into the fields at dusk uncovered, but she had forgotten Lucky's warning about her perfume. She had dabbed some on after her shower, needing to feel feminine after a day of grubbing around in the ashes of the machine shed, and hadn't thought to wash it off before leaving the house.

Willis slid down from his perch to kneel on the tarp in front of her. Serena eyed him warily. His left eye was nearly swollen shut, giving him an even more monstrous appearance than before. Beer had spilled unheeded over his shirt, adding to the sour stench of his sweat. He raised a hand and brushed his rough-skinned knuckles along her jaw, smiling like a snake in the fading light.

"They don't call that Cajun bastard Lucky for nothing, do they?" he said. "You're some fancy piece."

Serena fought the urge to shrink away from his touch. An animal like Willis would feed on fear. She bit down on the gag and schooled her features into what she hoped was a blank mask.

"What would a lady like you see in that coonass trash anyway?" he asked, his eyes roaming over her as if the answer might be written somewhere on her body. His leering grin spread across his thin, hard lips and his good eye lit up. "I'll bet he's hung like a stallion. Do proper ladies like you go for that? A man with the right kind of tool for the job? Who would'a guessed?"

He chuckled, apparently as amused by her lack of response as he would have been by a protest.

"You know," he went on, still stroking her ja   ᵇ in Angola I had a picture of a pretty blonde on th⟋ to dream about doing her every night. She lo⟋ only she was naked."

He lowered his hand from her chin to th⟋ silk blouse and popped it open with a fli⟋ Bile rose in Serena's throat, but she sv⟋ button gave way and another. She bit⟋

stared straight ahead as Willis opened her blouse and feasted his eyes on her breasts.

"Nice," he whispered, leaning closer. He traced the lacy edge of her bra once, then again, this time dipping his finger inside the fabric to caress the slope of her breast. "I can hardly wait to see the rest."

Serena couldn't stop the involuntary shiver that rippled across her skin. The thought of this man putting his big ugly hands all over her body, touching her softest, most private flesh, was utterly repulsive.

Willis caught the reaction and gave a laugh that held more menace than humor. He engulfed one breast in his hand and gave it a squeeze that bordered on painful.

"You might as well get used to it, Lady Serena, 'cause ol' Pou and me are gonna have you every way there is before we're through with you."

She nearly vomited at the mental images his warning conjured. Serena had counseled rape victims. She'd heard tales of abuse that had made her wonder what kind of God allowed such atrocities. Details came back to her now, vivid and horrible. She flicked a glance over the side of the boat at the inky water and wondered fleetingly if she wouldn't be better off drowning herself now.

It was then that they finally reached their destination. Perret guided the boat in alongside a ramshackle dock and cut the engine. Willis hefted himself and his beer cooler out of the boat and started up the incline toward the cabin, leaving Serena for his lackey. Pou's eyes fastened on the open front of her blouse and he reached out to touch her, but pulled back at the sound of Willis's voice.

"Wait till we get her inside," he ordered. "Goddamn mosquitoes are driving me nuts."

The cabin looked abandoned. A tar-paper shack on stilts, it was the sort of place Serena had imagined Lucky living in before she'd seen his house. The yard was little more than mud and stringy grass. It was littered with junk—beer cans and bottles, tires, an old refrigerator with the door hanging open. There was a rusted car of indeterminate age sitting some distance away in a stand of weeds.

A car. That had to mean there was a road. But what good would a road do her if she was on foot? They would run her down just as they had before. Her only hope would be to lose herself in the woods.

What a hope—to lose herself in the dead of night, bound and ⟨gag⟩ed, in a wilderness that terrified her. Her old fear stirred strongly, but the new one was even worse. She had survived the swamp before; she would not survive what Willis and Perret had in store for her.

Willis had gone inside. Perret steered her across the yard, his fingers wound into the back of the gag again, pulling her hair. He was a small man, only about as tall as she was and thin, anemic-looking. His chest had a sunken look and his dirty jeans clung low on nonexistent hips. He wouldn't be nearly as strong as Willis, but he was quick. If she could manage to get free of him, she would have to do a better job of escaping than she had the first time.

Serena stepped up her pace toward the cabin so he was no longer shoving her along, but quickening his step.

"You in a hurry, *chère?*" he asked, laughing, displaying an alarming array of crooked rotten teeth. "Me too."

Sticking her right foot out to trip Perret, Serena pulled up abruptly and twisted her upper body sharply away to the left. One second Perret was chortling like a fiend, enjoying his dominance over her, the next second he was on the ground, tangled among a mess of old tires and rusty chicken wire.

Serena wasted no time looking back to see if he was coming after her. She dashed into the woods and ran blindly, dodging trees at the last second, stumbling over roots. She zigzagged, cut back, turned again, and ran on. Branches cut at her face and tore at her clothes. There was no light, only darkness and the blacker shapes of trees. She slammed her shoulder into one and had to stop and double over while pain rocked through her.

Crouching there against the trunk of a persimmon tree, she took quick stock of her various aches, all of them renewed by this latest blow. Her hands had started to go numb behind her back, but she was very aware of her right forearm where Willis had struck to dislodge the can of Mace. It felt as if it had been hit with an ax handle. Her left shoulder had taken Willis's boot and now the tree trunk as well, and it throbbed relentlessly. Her muscles had started to cramp from the awkward position of her arms. There were a dozen assorted pains, but at least she was alive and free. For the mom

Her breath soughed in and out of her lung
The cloth had loosened somewhat from Perret
thought she might be able to work it free. She
the trunk of the tree and rubbed her cheek
the bandanna down. The hard, scaly bark o
but she persisted. Progress came gradually

201

of her mouth. Still knotted into her hair in back, it hung like a noose around her neck. She leaned over and spat, trying in vain to get the taste of it out of her mouth.

Something slithered in the underbrush to her right, and Serena bolted, straining to see in the velvet darkness. She could hear the movement but couldn't tell what it was or precisely where it was. Memories crowded in her mind and tears rose up the back of her throat as she scanned the darkness all around, wondering wildly what awaited her. The swamp came alive at night, alive with hunters and the hunted.

"God, that's me," she whispered, tears of despair stinging her eyes.

She didn't have the benefit of natural camouflage most animals of the swamp possessed. She had to stand out like a beacon in the night in her white blouse and khaki slacks.

Some distance behind her she could hear someone crashing through the growth. As she forced herself to press on, she wondered if Perret had come after her on his own or if Willis had joined him. She changed directions again and started running.

If only she could see. If only she had the use of her hands. If only she weren't so damned scared. If only Lucky were there.

Lucky. She wondered if she'd ever see him again. It seemed a stupid thing to think of, all things considered, but she wondered if he had any idea how much she loved him. She wondered if she'd had any idea herself before now. Running for her life put a lot of things into perspective, and she found herself making promises to God. *If I get out of this, I'll patch things up with Shelby, I'll forgive Gifford, I'll give more to charity, I'll try harder to reach Lucky.*

She would see him again if she kept running. She had to believe that. If she kept running, everything would turn out all right. She would be safe, Burke would get caught, she would see Lucky again. If she kept running. If she got away.

The night air was like fire in her lungs. She could no longer hear anything except her own breathing and the thunderous beating of her heart. Her head was pounding. The damp, musty scent of the forest filled her nostrils. The spongy ground seemed to dip and rise beneath her feet. She felt completely disoriented, almost dizzy, hanging somewhere between hysteria and delirium.

She thought that if she could somehow get to Lucky's house she could use his CB radio to call for help or maybe she could find his gun. But she didn't make it to Lucky's house. An exposed root caught the toe of her loafer and pitched her headlong into the blackness. She landed on her face at the booted feet of Mean Gene Willis.

Chapter Seventeen

"Come on, sweet stuff, let's go somewhere we can have us a little private party."

Lucky regarded the blonde draping herself over his left side with ill-concealed impatience. The woman had no self-control and less sense of danger. She had approached him the instant he'd settled himself behind the corner table at Mouton's, too stubborn or too stupid to notice that everyone else in the place was giving him a wide berth. As well-endowed as she was in other respects, she had obviously gotten severely short-changed in the brain department. The woman couldn't take a hint. He had snarled and snapped at her, but the efforts had bounced off her shield of stupidity, leaving her unmoved.

It was aggravating. He hadn't come looking for an easy lay; he'd come looking for trouble. He had come in to soak his temper in cheap booze and hope some big fool would strike a spark to it and pick a fight with him. He felt a need to hit something. It was what he'd done the night before, and it was what he planned to continue to do with his nights until he got it out of his system.

The blonde had other ideas.

She leaned against him, tilting her head back and squeezing her breasts together with her upper arms to best display her cleavage. The black tank top she wore seemed to have been intended for a flat-chested twelve-year-old. It rode up well above the waistband of her skin-tight jeans and made it abundantly clear to one and all that she found wearing a bra too restricting. She seemed to have difficulty keeping her eyes open, probably due to the thickness of her blue eye shadow and the weight of her false lashes. Her silvery-blond hair—brown at the roots—had been teased and tormented into a frightening confection and lacquered into place with enough spray to put a hole in the ozone the size of Lake Pontchartrain. The earrings dangling from her lobes looked like small chandeliers.

Lucky heaved a sigh of disgust. The woman had no class. She smelled like dime-store perfume and stale smoke, and she'd drunk most of his whiskey. She was pretty enough in a cheap, hard sort of way, and she had a body that had undoubtedly turned a head or two, but she roused nothing in him except irritation. She might have done better if she'd shown a little style, a little cool, if she'd presented herself as a . . . lady. Like Serena.

He swore a vicious oath in French and tossed back what was left of his drink. What did he need with a *lady?* What did he need with a woman who wanted to touch his rawest nerves and memories? She was nothing but trouble. She would never let him alone. She would never allow him the emotional distance he needed to maintain. He'd told her from the beginning what she would get from him, and still she'd dug for more. She wanted love and he wanted nothing to do with it. End of story.

So why was he brooding about her? a mocking inner voice asked. Why was he wondering how she had handled Burke and how she was bearing up with Shelby? Why did he want to know if she had exhausted her supply of strength, if she was in need of a shoulder to lean on?

He swore again and shrugged the blonde off, reaching for the bottle of whiskey on the table before him. The blonde—her name had gone in one ear and out the other—sat back with a coy look and helped herself to his cigarettes.

"You're a tough guy," she observed, blowing smoke at the ceiling in a pose that was calculated to show off her profile. "A loner." Her shoulders swayed, and unencumbered breasts bounced in time to the frantic Zydeco tune blasting from the jukebox.

Lucky shot her a sardonic look. "What are you? Einstein's daughter?"

She went on with her seduction routine as if he hadn't spoken. "I like a tough guy. I don't mind a little adventure, if you read me."

"Like a book."

"So-oo-o . . ." She drew the word into three syllables, squirming a little on her chair and giving him a dazzling smile, raising her carefully plucked eyebrows in question.

Lucky's answer was forestalled by the arrival of Skeeter Mouton. Skeeter pulled up a chair on Lucky's right and settled his bulk on it, mopping the sweat off his forehead with a bar rag. A smile lit up in the center of his beard like a crescent moon, but it didn't reach his dark eyes.

"Hey, Lucky, where you at?"

Lucky ignored the greeting and poured himself another drink. "You been waterin' the whiskey again, Skeeter."

The bartender clutched his heart dramatically. His round face tightened in a wounded expression. "Me? *Mais non!* Madame Mouton, she keeps the books, she waters the liquor. How can you accuse me of such a thing when me, I come all the way over here to give you information?"

"Information 'bout what?"

"Your two friends."

It was on the tip of Lucky's tongue to tell Mouton he didn't care what Willis and Perret were up to. He was all through fighting other people's battles. From now on he was adhering to a strict code of isolationism. No more damsels in distress. No more plantations to save. He was living for himself; the rest of the world could go to hell. But Skeeter went on, oblivious of Lucky's inner thoughts.

"They had them a little meetin' s'afternoon."

"Who with?" Not that he cared. He was just mildly curious, that was all. He directed his gaze across the crowded smoky room to where Len Burke sat deep in angry conversation with Perry Davis. "With him?"

Mouton shook his head. *"Non.* The big oil man, he been right here the whole time. The other two, they got a call and went out, come back a while later smilin' like 'gators and throwin' money 'round. This was all just before you got here. You walk in, they slip out the side."

"So?"

The round man shrugged and rolled his eyes, digging a folded bill out of a pocket on his apron. He waved it under Lucky's nose as if the smell of it might rouse him to show greater interest. "So this is the bill they tipped their waitress with. 'Toinette, she was just showin' it to me 'cause she never had a tip so big. She 'bout fainted." He gave a snort of disapproval. "A twenty-dollar tip. Talk about!"

Lucky glanced at the bill in irritation. It was crisp and new, the kind of money decent people carried. In his experience, trash like Willis carried money that looked as dirty as the kind of deals that brought it to them. If Willis was leaving fresh twenties for cocktail waitresses, then it was a good bet there were lots more where this one had come from. He would have had to come into a tidy sum to inspire that kind of generosity. Gene Willis wasn't known for his philanthropy.

" 'Toinette, she says Willis had a roll of those as thick as a 'gator's tail. Me, I don' figure he got 'em sellin' Bibles and he ain't been on the bayou since the night you shot up his boat full o' holes, so he didn' get 'em from stealin' crawfish. Somebody payin' him this kinda money . . ." Mouton shrugged and mopped his forehead. "Must be some kinda dirty job, *oui?*"

Lucky stared at the bill, rubbing the stiff paper absently between his fingers. This could have been the final payment for starting the fire, but if so, Willis and Perret would still be here, swilling Mouton's watered whiskey and playing *bourré* in the back room; the night was young. *Non.* This was payment for something else, something they were undoubtedly doing that very minute.

"You don' know what they were up to?"

Skeeter shook his head, frowning. "No good, dat's for sure. Willis, he said somethin' 'bout meetin' a lady. I didn' pay him no mind. What lady would meet with the like of him?"

Shelby, Lucky answered mentally. Serena was right, her sister would probably not have started the fire herself. The job was too dirty and physical. Shelby would have considered it well beneath her. But she wouldn't have hesitated to pay someone else to do it. And now she was paying them for another job.

"They took outta here, headed up the bayou." Skeeter tilted his head, his dark eyes twinkling as he chuckled. "You sure put the air-conditioning in dat one, *cher.* Willis, he ain't never gonna get all them bullet holes patched up."

The blonde, who had remained blessedly silent for all of five minutes, perked up suddenly at the mention of Willis's name. She leaned across the table toward Skeeter, making certain to twist herself around so Lucky could have another look at her amazing cleavage. "You know Mean Gene? He's a rowdy son of a bitch, ain't he?"

She threw her head back and gave a laugh that bore an unfortunate resemblance to the braying of a mule.

Lucky turned on her slowly, his eyes glittering. The dangerous look had caused more than one man to back away from him. The blonde just gave him a wink and a grin.

"How do you know Willis, *chère?*" he asked, his voice silky.

"Well, shoot, I know him *every* way." She gave her donkey laugh again and slapped Lucky on the arm. "He's the one set me on to you, Ace. Said he reckoned you'd be needin' a woman 'cause yours was goin' someplace." She flashed him her brightest smile and ran her hand up his thigh. "Remind me to thank him later."

Everything inside Lucky went cold and still. He murmured a prayer in French and stood up slowly, like a man in a daze, his hands clutching the edge of the table.

Chapter Eighteen

The powerboat roared through the swamp at a speed that wouldn't have been prudent even in daylight. The water was an obstacle course of snags and deadheads and cypress knees that were hidden now by the high water level. Lucky opened the throttle a little more and eased the wheel right, then left to narrowly avoid hitting a log. He focused straight ahead, trying to channel all his energy into navigating the boat. He knew this swamp better than anyone. All he had to do was focus, visualize the path and react mentally a split second before he needed to react physically.

He had run out of Mouton's like a man with the devil at his heels, stopping at his pirogue only long enough to grab his gear bag before commandeering the craft he was piloting now. He wore his infrared glasses, which allowed him to make out something of his surroundings, but not enough considering the speed he was traveling. The 9mm Beretta was strapped to his shoulder. He would have liked to have his rifle, but it wasn't something he kept in the pirogue and there was no time to go get it.

He had known the instant the pieces had come together back at

Mouton's that time was of the essence. What he'd found at the Chanson du Terre had confirmed his worst fears. Odille had seen Serena leave the house and walk down the lane toward Arnaud's. The Arnaud girl had watched her walk off toward the bayou. At the end of the service lane along the bayou Serena's purse had been lying abandoned, a can of Mace not far away.

Willis and Perret had her. Lucky thought he had a good idea of where they would take her. Willis had a place where he kept his fighting cocks. It was supposed to be a secret hideout, so they would undoubtedly feel perfectly safe taking Serena there. They wouldn't count on Lucky knowing the place. They wouldn't count on him turning down the attentions of the blonde either. He would have the element of surprise. He only hoped he wouldn't be too late.

The thought of Willis and Perret with their hands on Serena filled his head with a red haze, and he had to make a conscious effort to pull back from the image. Rage was ready to consume him. He could feel it roaring at the edges of his control, ready to sweep in and obliterate all else. He had to keep it leashed. He wouldn't do Serena any good if he came tearing in like a wild animal.

He called on old skills and instincts, reached deep within himself for a sense of dead calm. This was a mission. He would get the boat through the swamp. He would find Willis and Perret. He would kill them for touching his woman.

His woman.

He was in love with Serena Sheridan. He had been able to deny it before, but knowing Serena was in jeopardy put everything into perspective. What he felt for her went deeper than desire. It had from the first. That knowledge brought no comfort or joy to Lucky's heart. In fact, what it made him feel was bleak and desperate. He could offer her nothing. He was little more than a shell of man, just managing to get himself from one day to the next. How could he take on the responsibility of love, of a wife? He didn't want it, couldn't handle it. Love changed nothing.

He cursed it as he swung the wheel of the boat to dodge a cypress knee at the last second. The only thing this love was doing was distracting him from his task. If he wasn't careful, it would get both himself and Serena killed.

The bayou took a slow bend to the east, and Lucky throttled down, instantly cutting the roar of the motor. He would go on foot from here. Guiding the boat in along the bank as close as he could, he shut it off and stuffed the key in the pocket of his fatigue pants. He tied the boat to an overhanging willow branch and jumped to shore.

As silent as a stalking cougar he moved through the woods, his mind playing back fragments of other missions. For the briefest instant he could smell the rain forest, hear the distant sounds of guerrilla gunfire. He felt his mind start to slip, but he pulled it back with an effort. If ever there had been a time for him to hang on to his sanity, it was now. He pulled the Beretta from its holster and cradled its familiar weight in his hand as he made his way through the dense growth.

It was a warm, still night. The air was heavy with the scent of honeysuckle and mud. The songs of frogs and insects combined into one high-pitched hum that floated across the whole swamp. Lucky strained to catch other sounds, thinking Willis might have stationed Perret somewhere as a lookout, but all he heard was the normal range of rustlings and squawkings that filled the nights. There were no shouts, no screams.

The last thought raised a knot in Lucky's throat. *Bon Dieu,* he couldn't bear the idea of Serena suffering at the hands of men like Perret and Willis. They were little more than animals—cruel, cunning, base. They would enjoy terrifying her simply because that was their nature, but they would take added pleasure in hurting her because they knew she was his. They would make her pay for everything he'd done to thwart their poaching business.

For one excruciating second he had a clear picture in his mind of Serena tied down, her face twisted in pain, a scream tearing from her throat, tears streaming from her eyes. His vision blurred and he pressed the heels of his hands to his temples and forced back the image and the terrible rush of fear that accompanied it.

He would kill Shelby for this. The thought drifted like smoke around the dark edges of his mind. She had bought her own sister's death. Serena had been an inconvenience to her, just as his baby had been an inconvenience to her, nothing more than a stumbling block in the path of her goal. The idea brought a rush of hatred burning through him. He gritted his teeth and fought it under control. This was no time for emotion. He needed to pull himself into the eye of the storm, be calm, detached, focused.

He stopped and leaned back against the trunk of a tree for a moment, willing his body to relax. Taking a long deep breath, he cleared his mind of everything but cool white light.

Serena stumbled through the door of the cabin and fell across the dirty linoleum floor as Willis released her. The only light in the place came from behind the cracked yellow shade of an ancient black iron floor lamp in one corner. The room was filthy and smelled of mice and urine. A low green sofa squatted above the pitted linoleum floor with stuffing and springs sticking up through the cushions. A coffee table made from a heavily shellacked slab of wood sat in front of it. On the opposite side of the room stood a bed with a rusty iron headboard and footboard. There were no sheets, just a thin mattress covered with stained ticking.

Not the kind of place she had ever imagined staying in, let alone dying in, Serena thought as she struggled to her knees. Her gaze swept around the room automatically looking for an escape route. There was a back door, but it looked an awfully long way away as Willis stepped in front of her. He reached down and hauled her up off the floor by her sore arm and shoved her onto the bed.

"Make yourself comfortable, sweetheart," he said, chuckling.

"It's kind of hard to be comfortable with my hands tied this way," Serena said, blocking the pain as she pulled herself into a sitting position on the edge of the mattress. "You might as well untie me. I know when I'm beaten. I obviously can't get away from you."

"That's right." Willis bent over the coffee table, then turned to face her with a whiskey bottle in one hand and his revolver in the other. A smile of smug triumph twisted his mouth. "You can't get away. And with your hands tied, you can't get a hold of a gun either, and you can't scratch our eyes out while we have our little bit of fun. Nice try, Miz Sheridan, but no go. I like you just the way you are."

He took a swig from the bottle, whiskey dribbling down his chin as he swaggered toward the bed. Serena watched him warily, trying to gauge his level of intoxication. He'd had several cans of beer on the way. He may have been drinking before that as well. If he drank enough, he might not be able to participate in the festivities, but there was still Perret to contend with.

He stood in the doorway with the shotgun in his hands, laughing nervously as he watched Willis advance on her. Serena was almost more afraid of him than she was of Willis. Willis was cruel and calculating, but Perret had a wild gleam in his eye when he looked at her that made her think he was teetering on the brink of a dangerous kind of frenzy.

Willis sat down beside her, his thigh pressing against hers, his hip brushing her hip. He braced himself upright with the whiskey bottle against the mattress and leaned over into Serena's face. The smell of his breath and the sour scent of his body was enough to make her want to draw back, but she held her ground. As long as she kept her mind working and the fear at bay, she had a chance. The second she buckled under the weight of terror, she would be lost; they would be on her like wolves on a lamb.

"See, if I untied you," Willis said, his mouth a scant inch above hers, "then you might just try to stop me from doing this."

He brought the pistol up, and Serena's heart lodged in her throat as he drew the end of the barrel slowly along her jawline, down her throat, over her breastbone. He traced the lacy edge of her bra, the cold steel pressing into the flesh of her breast. A shudder passed through her from head to toe, and Willis smiled and chuckled.

"You like that, Lady Serena?" he asked, stroking the gun barrel across her nipple. "You'll like this even better."

Serena breathed a sigh of relief as he set the .38 aside on the bed, but gasped in the next instant as he grabbed her by the hair and pulled her backward onto the mattress. He leaned over her, looking like something from a horror movie with his twisted smile and one eye swollen shut. Chuckling low in his throat, he raised the whiskey bottle over her. Serena tensed and squeezed her eyes shut, waiting for the blow, but none came. Whiskey splashed onto her chest, soaking into the fabric of her bra and running in rivulets down her sides. The scent of it filled her nostrils.

Willis bent over her and took her nipple into his mouth, sucking hard at her through the wet silk. He jammed a knee between her thighs, forcing her legs to part and lowered himself onto her, grinding his erection against her.

Serena fought the tears that stung the backs of her eyes as the last of her hope was crushed beneath the weight of Gene Willis. She'd had her chance to escape, and she'd blown it. She wished they had simply killed her. She wished that the last thing she was to endure on this earth wasn't defilement and debasement. She didn't want to die with rape as her last memory.

Close your eyes and think of England. That was the line Victorian women had been schooled to remember in the face of sexual relations. *Close your eyes and think of Lucky.* The tears pressed harder for release as Willis sucked noisily at her breast and thrust himself against the apex of her thighs. Serena bit her lip until she tasted blood. Revulsion

213

shuddered through her and rose in her throat to gag her. This was violence in one of its ugliest forms.

"Hey, who says you get her first?" Perret demanded, suddenly looming up behind Willis. His droopy eyes were narrowed and his mustache twitched as he worked his jaw angrily from side to side. The shotgun was still clutched loosely in his hands and his fingers twisted on the stock and barrel.

Willis raised his head from Serena's breast, but didn't deign to look at his partner. "I say I get her first," he said, his tone low and dangerous.

Serena watched Perret with interest as his face flushed and his mouth moved back and forth as if he were working up the nerve to spit the words out. The feral gleam in his dark eyes intensified as his gaze fastened on her chest and the wet fabric that covered her breasts. "You said before, I'd get her."

"The hell I did," Willis grunted. He ground his hips against Serena's and began to lower his head again, dismissing the man behind him.

"You did!" Perret insisted. "You said I could have her first."

"Looks to me like his promises don't mean very much," Serena said. Her deflated hopes lifted a fraction. Her skill with minds and words was the only weapon she had. If she could turn the two men against each other, she might yet have a slim chance to live through this ordeal, and a slim chance was better than no chance at all.

Willis scowled at her. "You shut up."

"Why should I listen to you?" she countered. "He's the one with the shotgun."

"That's right," Pou said militantly, his hand stroking up and down the barrel of the gun. "Me, I got the shotgun, Willis. Get off her. I wanna do her first."

"Go to hell."

"I can shoot you, you lyin' bastard!" He swung the barrel of the shotgun around as if he had every intention of making good on his threat, but instead of pulling the trigger, he jabbed the nose of the gun in Willis's back.

Willis swore through his teeth. "All right. Jesus, let me up."

Perret stepped back and lowered the gun. Willis rose slowly, adjusting his jeans, glaring at the smaller man. In a quick move that belied his cumbersome size, he snatched the shotgun away by the

214

barrel and swung the stock end at his partner like a baseball bat, narrowly missing Pou's head as he ducked back.

"You stupid coonass trash!" Willis shouted. "You can't even get her from the goddamn boat to the house without screwing up! You can damn well wait your turn!"

"You said I got her first!" Perret shouted back.

Serena watched them argue. They yelled back and forth, issuing threats and insults, all the while inching away from the bed and toward the other side of the room. Nothing stood between her and the front door. She could make another run for it. She doubted she would get away, but there was a chance. Perhaps they would shoot her instead of chasing after her, too, and that seemed infinitely preferable to suffering the kind of violation they had planned.

She leaned forward, bracing herself to make a running start. Willis turned suddenly and set the shotgun beside the door. He sent an angry glance Serena's way.

"All right, all right," he snapped, waving his hands in Perret's face to shut him up. "We'll flip for first chance."

He dug a quarter from his pocket and Perret snatched it away from him to make sure it wasn't two-headed. Willis grabbed it back and sent it into the air with a flick of his thumb.

Serena sprang from the bed and lunged for the door.

Perret wheeled toward her.

The quarter never landed.

The back door of the shack swung open. A shot exploded through the air and the coin vanished. Serena's heart leapt into her throat as she jerked around and saw Lucky standing there. He was danger personified in fatigue pants and a black T-shirt, mud smeared across his face and arms, a sleek black gun clutched in his hands.

Perret screamed as if he were seeing an apparition from hell. Whirling toward the door, he reached out for the shotgun propped against the wall. The gun in Lucky's hands bucked once and Pou screamed again as a bullet tore into his shoulder. He fell headfirst through the screen door and landed sprawled on the steps whimpering and crying.

Willis lunged for Serena, one brawny arm catching her around the neck. The momentum of his body carried her backward and to the floor, and they landed against the side of the bed, sending it skidding sideways. The .38 was in his hand and swinging in Lucky's direction before Serena could blink. Acting on adrenaline and instinct, she shoved backward with all her might, throwing Willis off balance. His shot went into the ceiling, sending down a rain of disintegrated Sheet-rock.

Serena twisted out of his grasp and hurled herself toward the door, scrambling to get up from her knees. Her ears were ringing from the deafening sound of the shots and the pulse roaring in her veins. She didn't hear Willis behind her, but she felt his meaty hand close on her ankle and yank her leg out from under her. As she fell she turned her shoulders and saw Willis coming down toward her, the gun pointed at her head.

Everything went into slow motion then, time stretching out with its weird elasticity. The gun bore down on her, and behind it Willis's face, ugly and distorted with rage. His mouth opened as he shouted some-thing at her she couldn't hear. Then Lucky flew in out of nowhere. He hit Willis like a freight train and they both went sprawling across the pitted linoleum, Willis's gun flying out of his hand and spinning across the floor like a top.

Lucky hauled Willis up off the floor by his shirtfront and slammed him back against the wall of the cabin. He had dropped his own gun and pulled his knife, pressing the deadly edge of the blade to the man's throat.

Willis's whole body trembled visibly. His face turned gray, and sweat popped out on his forehead and ran down his face like water on the waxy skin of a pumpkin. In a harsh whisper he invoked the names of various members of the holy family as he stared bug-eyed into the face of death.

"Oh, I wouldn' be callin' on them, *cher*," Lucky said, chuckling softly. A frightening smile lit his panther's eyes and curled the corners of his lips. He caressed Willis's throat with the blade of the knife. "Me, I got a feelin' you're not exactly on the A list up there."

Willis swallowed convulsively, his Adam's apple scraping the razor edge of the knife. "Jesus, Doucet," he whispered frantically. "I'm not armed. This is murder."

Lucky's eyes were cold and bright. "You think I care? There isn't gonna be enough of you left for anyone to prove it. You touched my woman, Willis. I'm gonna kill you. I just wish I could take my time doin' it."

"Lucky." Serena's voice floated to him from across the room. Trem-ulous and soft, it barely penetrated the edge of his consciousness, like a voice from another dimension. "Lucky, don't do it."

He glanced at her as she came into the periphery of his vision. There were scratches all over her face and neck. Her blouse was torn and dirty and hung open down the front. There was a bloody cut at the corner of her mouth and her lower lip was swollen. Her eyes, her beautiful, soft doe eyes were filled with terror and pain. The maelstrom of his fury surged through Lucky with renewed force.

"He did this to you," he snarled through his teeth.

Serena said nothing, terrified that her answer would push him over the edge. She could see a part of him fighting to keep the wild rage at bay. The rage flashed in his eyes and rippled in his muscles; his whole body was rigid with it.

He turned back to Willis. "I'll see you in hell, Willis," he whispered, his voice silky-soft. "But you're gonna get there a long way ahead of me."

He let the knife bite into the man's skin. Several drops of blood beaded on the blade and ran down it to drip like teardrops onto Willis's shirt. Willis's mouth trembled as he let out a pitiful whimper.

Lucky stared at the blood as the scent of it filled his nostrils. Images whirled in his mind—Colonel Lambert, Amalinda Roca, Shelby. He saw each of their faces in the bright red drops, their eyes wild, mouths laughing. He saw fragmented pictures from his past—other enemies, other battles, other deaths. He felt the cold black ooze seeping in around the edges of his mind, threatening to wash in on him like a wave and sweep him away forever. His hand tightened on the hilt of the knife. Willis sucked in a breath.

Then Serena's voice came again, like a siren's call. "Lucky, no. Leave him for the sheriff. He isn't worth it." She stepped closer, looking up at him with her battered face, tears swimming in her eyes. "Please, Lucky," she whispered. "I need you. I love you."

"He hurt you," he said, enunciating each word with painful deliberation. He kept his eyes on the knife. The storm raged inside him, pulling at him, tearing at him, and the blackness swirled at the edge of his mind like blood. "He hurt you."

"Not as much as this will."

The knife bit a little deeper. Willis made a strangled sound in his throat. Blood trickled across the blade. Lucky stared at it, fascinated, horrified. The blackness swept in a little closer, dimming his vision. He was tired of fighting it. It would be so much easier for everyone if he just let it take him once and for all.

Serena's voice came to him again, so softly it was as if she had somehow spoken the words inside his head. "I'm safe, Lucky. You saved me, now save yourself. Don't do this."

A part of him wanted to let the knife go deeper. In his mind's eye he could see the blood flowing, swirling up to drown him, just like in his nightmare. It would wash over him and then he would be gone, no more battles to fight, no more betrayals to endure, no more love to forsake. His hand trembled on the hilt. He could feel his control bending, bowing under the weight.

"Hang on," Serena whispered. "Please hang on, Lucky."

She stared at him, tears streaming down her face, afraid that if she blinked she would lose him. She could feel the tension vibrating around him. His fierce gaze was on Willis, but she didn't think Willis was what he was seeing. The expression in his eyes was something that came from looking inward and seeing the things one feared most. The most deadly struggle going on in the room was the one Lucky was waging with himself, and if he lost it, Serena had the terrible feeling he would be lost forever. A part of her would not have mourned for a second if Gene Willis had met his end, but revenge was nowhere near worth the price it was going to cost her.

"Hang on, Lucky," she said again, drawing on some deep reservoir inside her for calm. "You can beat it."

"I'm tired," he whispered, his eyes bleak and afraid as he looked through the face of Willis.

"I know," Serena said, taking another half step toward him. "I know you're tired, but you're stronger than you know. You're better than you know. You can beat it for good. Pull back from that edge. Please, Lucky, for me, for your family, for yourself. Pull back. You can do it. I know you can."

Lucky stared at the blade of the knife, at the blood dribbling across it. He could feel himself teetering on the precipice, the ground crumbling beneath his boots. The abyss of madness beckoned, but on the other side Serena lured him back with strong, soft words, with the love he wanted so desperately to hang on to, the love he knew he could never keep. The pressures of the conflict built within him like steam until he was shaking from the force of it, as if he might explode at any second, and it kept building and building.

With a great roar of anguish he pulled the knife back and plunged it into the wall beside Willis's head. He pushed himself away from his captive and Willis crumpled to the dirty floor in a dead faint.

Lucky stepped back, swaying unsteadily on his feet as the darkness rushed to the outer boundaries of his mind and vanished in a blinding flash of light. He turned toward Serena, feeling strangely weak and disoriented, as if some vital electrical force had been suddenly drained from his body.

Serena tried to smile at him through the rain of tears streaming down her face. "I've never been so glad to see anyone in my life," she whispered.

Lucky drank in the sight of her, feeling her every cut and bruise as if it were his own. He wanted to heal her. He wanted to take her back in time and protect her from this nightmare and prevent her from witnessing what she had just witnessed. He wanted a lot of things at that moment—to be stronger, to be whole, to be the kind of man who could have had a future with a woman like Serena—but he contented himself with knowing she was alive and safe, and he pulled her into his arms to prove it to himself.

"*Merci Dieu*," he whispered, burying his lips in her hair. His whole body was trembling from the internal battle he had just been through. His breath came in shallow gasps. Tears squeezed through the barrier of his lashes. He tightened his arms around Serena as if he were trying to absorb her into his being. "*Je t'aime. Je t'aime, ma douce amie.*"

I love you. Serena pressed her cheek to his chest and cried with a mixture of joy and relief and belated fear. Lucky loved her. She was safe. He was safe. They would have a chance at tomorrow together. But there was so much more left to face and so many feelings still to be dealt with, not the least of which were her feelings about what she had experienced tonight. They rushed to the fore now that she was in the shelter of Lucky's arms.

"I've never been so afraid," she mumbled against his chest as the tears came harder.

"I know. I know, *mon chérie*. It's all right now. Everything's all right. You're safe." He pressed fervent kisses to her temple, her cheek, her lips, trembling at the sweet taste of her. He couldn't get enough of just touching her, holding her, breathing in the faint scent of her perfume. With one shaking hand he began to carefully brush the leaves and twigs from her hair.

"Lucky?"

"*Oui.*"

"I really like having you hold me," Serena said, twisting a little in his iron grasp, "but do you think you could untie me first? I'd kind of like to hold you too."

Lucky pulled back abruptly, swearing in French. He turned Serena around and dealt with the cord that bound her hands. She almost cried at the pain as feeling came rushing back into her fingers and her shoulders were allowed to sag forward, but decided she was too glad to be alive to cry about it.

They dealt with Willis and Perret quickly. Lucky dragged Pou back inside and grumbled while Serena did a cursory first aid job on the man's bullet wound. Then he bound both men hand and foot and tied them each to a bedpost.

"Let's get out of here," he said when the task was accomplished and the two thugs sat on the floor glaring up at him. "I'll bring the sheriff back later for these two."

Serena nodded. Now that the danger had passed, she was feeling the effects of what she had been through. She ached all over and felt vaguely dizzy and rubber-legged. Lucky seemed to sense her fatigue and without a word swept her up in his arms. With long, purposeful strides he carried her away from the shack and into the woods.

He wound his way through the tangle of dark forest silently, surely. Serena put her arms around his neck and laid her head against his shoulder, marveling at the sense of safety she felt with him in this place she had feared for so long. But gradually the feeling of safety gave way to a subtle foreboding.

Lucky hadn't spoken a word since leaving the cabin. Serena thought she could actually feel him withdrawing from her. He might have, in a moment of intense emotion, told her he loved her, but she had the terrible feeling that love was something Lucky was more likely to shy away from than embrace. He had told her before that he didn't want her love, that he didn't have anything left inside him to give her. The discovery that he was capable of feeling would not be welcome to a man who had sentenced himself to emotional exile.

She sighed wearily at the thought that while the battle for her life was over and won, the battle for her heart was a long way from being over.

"Hey, it's a real boat," she said in a weak attempt at levity as they emerged from the woods at the edge of the bayou and she saw the powerboat sitting in the black water. "It's got a motor and everything."

Lucky eased her over the side and set her on her feet, then frowned as he pulled himself into the boat and dug the keys out of his pocket. "They have their uses," he said shortly.

"Yes, they do. Be sure and thank the owner on my behalf for loaning it to you."

"Can't."

"Why not?"

" 'Cause I stole it."

"You what?" Serena clamped her mouth shut and sank down into one of the passenger seats, feeling giddy at the idea that Lucky would commit a felony on her behalf. It had definitely been too long a day. She needed to go to bed and sleep for a year. Unfortunately, there was no time for that.

"How did you know they had me?" she asked, wrapping her arms around herself to ward off the chills that were beginning to rack her body now that she was away from Lucky's warmth.

Lucky didn't answer her until he'd found a blanket stowed in one of the boat's cubbyholes. He draped it around Serena's shoulders and tucked it carefully around her legs. "The distraction they sicced on me had a big mouth and a little brain."

"And could she really suck the brass off a doorknob?" Serena asked, unable to keep the sarcasm from her tone.

"I wasn't interested in finding out." He tipped her chin up and tried to read her face in the dim light of the moon. "Were you jealous?"

"Yes," she answered honestly.

He didn't respond to that, but turned and prepared to start the boat.

"We'll need to tell the sheriff about Burke too," Serena said, finding practical ground safer footing than probing the uncertain territory of their relationship. "I think Burke is the one who paid Willis and Perret to—to—"

"No. He didn't. Skeeter Mouton says Burke was in the roadhouse when Willis and Pou left for their meeting this afternoon." Lucky turned around and sat back against the console of the boat, crossing his arms over his massive chest. The look he leveled at Serena was serious. "I think you'd better face facts, Serena. Shelby did this."

Serena's heart gave a painful jolt. "No."

"You stood in her way, so she arranged to get rid of you."

"No," she said again, shaking her head. She didn't want to believe it. She didn't even want to consider the possibility. It was one thing to know she would never be close with her twin, it was something else to accept that her twin had tried to have her killed. She knew Shelby was emotionally unbalanced; there was no denying that after the scene over the power of attorney, but murder? Serena couldn't bring herself to believe that.

"How would Shelby ever have hired men like Willis and Perret?" she argued. "She wouldn't go near a place like Mouton's."

"She wouldn't have to. All she need do is call up your 'family friend' Perry Davis."

"Perry Davis?" Serena said, bewildered. "But Perry is—"

"Crooked as a dog's hind leg," Lucky finished. "He finances his nasty little gambling addiction by taking payoffs from poachers. He wouldn't have any trouble finding the right men for a dirty job. No trouble a'tall."

Serena leaned over and rubbed her temples. This was all happening too fast. It was overwhelming. In the span of just a few days her entire orderly world had been flipped upside down and inside out. Now Lucky was telling her a man she would have trusted was a criminal.

"What was to stop Burke from using Perry as a middleman?" she asked, lifting her head as the question sorted itself from the chaos in her mind. "He wouldn't want to be linked directly with people like Willis and Perret. It doesn't mean anything that he didn't meet with them himself. He paid them to start the fire and he paid them to kidnap me."

"I don't think so, sugar," Lucky said. "But we'll find out soon enough."

They arrived at Lucky's house sometime later. Serena had no idea of the hour. The night had taken on an endless quality. She sat huddled in the passenger seat of the boat with the blanket wrapped tightly around her while Lucky quietly piloted the boat through the swamp. Neither spoke. When they reached his dock, Lucky tied the boat and carried Serena into the house.

Serena didn't even think of protesting. The aftershock of what had happened, the knowledge of what might have happened, the questions of who had caused it all to happen bombarded her nerves until it was all she could do to keep from falling completely apart. Having Lucky hold her was the best medicine she could have thought to prescribe.

He carried her into the bathroom and undressed her carefully. She kept her eyes on his artist's hands, long and strong and infinitely gentle, as they peeled away her torn, soiled blouse and the whiskey-soaked bra. She thought of the way Willis had touched her and shivered.

"Are you afraid of me, *chère?*" Lucky asked softly.

222

Serena shook her head. "No. It's just that—" She broke off as another shudder of revulsion trembled through her and tears swam up to blur her vision. "He . . . touched me. And I feel . . . so . . . dirty."

Lucky bent his head and kissed the teardrops falling from her eyes. He whispered to her in his low, soothing voice. "It's all right, *chérie*. I'll take it all away."

He filled the small clawfooted tub with warm water scented with a fragrant oil taken from a mysterious brown bottle in the medicine cabinet. When the water was ready, he finished undressing Serena and carefully placed her in the tub.

The water felt like heaven, warm and soft and soothing. The fragrance of the oil drifted up in the steam, filling her head and taking away the remembered smells of sweat and liquor and fear. Serena closed her eyes and leaned back, relaxing for the first time in what seemed like weeks. Lucky leaned over her with one arm around her shoulders and carefully washed away all the dirt. He ran the cloth gently over her face, soothing her with his touch as he washed all the places that had been scratched and bruised. With infinite care he touched the cut at the corner of her mouth, ran the cloth down her throat, stroked it over her breasts. As he pressed soft kisses to her temple, he brought the warm, scented water up in his cupped palm to pour it down over her skin again and again in a cascade of cleansing, healing fluid.

Serena didn't speak for fear of breaking the spell. She allowed Lucky to touch her, to try to take away all evidence and memory of what had happened. She leaned into his strength, absorbed his gentleness, soaked up the love he was giving her, hoarding it away in her heart. Tomorrow loomed on her horizon like a storm gathering at the edge of the swamp, making these moments all the more precious to her. She savored each one and prayed what was left of the night would last forever.

When the water cooled, Lucky lifted her from the tub and dried her, then wrapped her in a towel and sat her down on the commode to carefully comb the tangles from her hair. He tended to the worst of her cuts with more of the mysterious oil from the cabinet, then carried her to his bed.

Serena snuggled into his embrace when he slid in naked beside her, letting her arms find their way around his waist. Her head nestled into his shoulder as if it had been made to fit there.

"Lucky?" she whispered.

"Hush, *chérie,*" he murmured. "You need to sleep."

"No. I need you." She lifted her head and found his eyes in the soft light from the candle beside the bed. "Make love to me, Lucky. I need to feel you. I need to have you love me. I need to have it feel good and right. Please."

Lucky studied her face in the glow of the candle's flame. His heart nearly burst at the earnest plea in her soft, dark eyes. *Dieu,* he loved her so! He hadn't thought it possible for him to feel such emotion again, but now he ached with it in his muscles, in his bones, in his blood; he could taste it bittersweet upon his tongue. He loved her. And while there was precious little he could give her, he could give her this: his touch, his body, a memory of tenderness to take away the pain.

"Please, Lucky," she whispered.

Turning onto his side, he lowered his head and kissed her slowly as he stroked his hand down her side. He made love to her with a patience he hadn't known he possessed, with a tenderness he had long denied. He caressed her and kissed her endlessly, until Serena took the initiative and guided him to the soft heat between her thighs. He slid into her, his breath catching at the exquisite sense of being one with her, and he loved her slowly and gently, until they were both replete.

He didn't withdraw from her afterward, but held her close, stroking her hair, brushing whisper-soft kisses to her temple.

"I love you," she whispered as she finally gave in to sleep.

Lucky gazed down at her as the candle on the stand guttered and died and darkness swept in around them.

"Je t'aime, mon coeur," he whispered into the silence.

Chapter Nineteen

"I must say, I'm a trifle baffled by this sudden change of heart," Lamar Canfield drawled, his dark eyes wandering back and forth between the people who had summoned him to Chanson du Terre at such an unseemly hour of the morning. Young people had no sense of propriety. In the days when manners had still been in vogue, no one would have dreamed of calling on a person before nine o'clock.

He stared at the young woman seated behind Gifford Sheridan's massive cherry desk. She looked cool and composed in a forest-green suit with simple straight lines and a champagne silk blouse. There was a single strand of pearls at her throat. Her honey-blond hair was neatly contained at the back in a French twist. Her mouth lifted at the corners in a placid smile, but she twisted the large topaz ring she wore around and around on her finger, giving away her inner tension.

"It's really quite simple, Mr. Canfield," she said with deliberate calm. "As you know, Gifford has granted me power of attorney. I am to settle this matter as I see fit. Now, I have examined all the options and taken into consideration all factors, and the only logical, *practical* conclusion is to sell the property to Mr. Burke's company."

225

Lamar shifted in his chair, the leather squeaking and sighing as he crossed his thin legs at the knee. He stared up at a water spot on the ceiling for a moment, then returned his gaze to his hostess, looking as if he were about to speak. He opened his mouth, shut it, frowned darkly for a second.

"Is there some problem, Mr. Canfield?" Len Burke demanded to know. He sat in the matching wing chair three feet from the aged attorney, obviously nursing a hangover. The whites of his eyes—what could be seen of them through his squint—had turned bloodred. The color of his complexion matched the green-brown wrapper of his unlit cigar.

Lamar regarded him with the same condescension he usually reserved for common ruffians. "It seems to me, Mr. Burke, to be a rather abrupt change of loyalties. Why, just the other night Miss Sheridan seemed nothing short of appalled by the prospect of Chanson du Terre falling into your hands."

Burke scowled at him. "Yeah, well, she's changed her mind. Woman's prerogative."

"I have changed my mind, Mr. Canfield," she assured him.

"I see," Lamar said gravely. He sat forward in his chair, straightening the lapels of his seersucker jacket. "I must say, I am exceedingly disappointed by this, Shelby."

"Serena," she hastened to correct him.

"Yes, of course. Serena. I know what your grandfather had hoped to accomplish by giving this responsibility to you. He's going to be *very* unhappy," Lamar declared dramatically, shaking his head in disapproval.

Shelby's eyes flashed and the line of her mouth tightened slightly. "Well, it serves him right, if you ask me," she snapped.

Mason stepped in diplomatically, his innocuous smile spreading like sunshine across his face as he strolled behind the desk. "What Serena means to say, Lamar, is if Gifford is willing to give the power of the decision to someone else, then he must be prepared to face the consequences of that decision."

"Amen." Burke hauled a cowhide briefcase the size of a calf onto his lap and popped it open. "Now, can we get on with the paperwork? I have everything drawn up here in the terms we agreed on. All I need is a couple of signatures and we can call it a done deal."

He extracted a thick sheaf of papers, flipped to the final page, and handed the document across the desk to be signed.

"I'm surprised your sister hasn't come in to witness the transaction," Lamar said with just the barest edge of sarcasm in his voice as he watched his hostess take up a pen. "Her moment of triumph, so to speak."

His remark won him a cutting glare, but no comment from the woman behind the desk.

"I'm afraid Shelby is indisposed this morning. She's resting," Mason said. "One of her migraines. Poor dear, she suffers terribly."

"Well, I'm sure she deserves it," Lamar said absently. He regarded the shocked expressions directed at him with bland innocence. "The extra rest," he clarified. "I'm sure she deserves it."

From the breast pocket of his suit he extracted a pair of wire-rimmed spectacles that looked as old as he did. He perched them on his nose and squinted down at the document that was thrust before him. The tension level in the room climbed faster than the temperature on a hot July day as one moment stretched into the next and Lamar showed no sign of picking up a pen. His gaze fixed on the signature; he hummed a bit.

"I'll need to see your signature on the power of attorney." He glanced up and smiled benignly. "A mere formality, of course."

"Of course. I have it right here." She slid the paper across the desk and sat back, forearms on the blotter, the fingers of her left hand twisting her topaz ring around and around.

Lamar examined both signatures with painstaking care, humming. "Yes, they appear to match."

"Of course they match," Shelby snapped.

"Lamar is only looking out for his client's best interests," Mason said placidly.

Canfield nodded. "That's right, Serena."

"Shel—" She clamped her teeth together abruptly and spoke through them. "Shall we get on with it, Mr. Canfield? Mr. Burke is a busy man. I'm sure he'd like to be on his way."

"That's right," Burke growled. "Sign it, I'll present the check and get the hell out of here. I've had enough of Lou'siana to last me."

The venerable old southerner frowned at the Texan. "I can assure you, sir, the feeling is mutual, but I would be entirely remiss in my duties if I did not read the entire document before signing."

Burke's face flushed a shade that clashed horribly with his bloodshot eyes. Shelby made a little squeal of frustration. Mason cleared his throat carefully and made a steeple with his fingers.

227

"If you feel it's necessary, Lamar," he said.

Lamar looked at them all with exaggerated bewilderment. "Well, I'm not entirely certain. Perhaps I should consult with the real Serena."

The faces of the three went simultaneously white as the door to the study swung open and Serena and Lucky stepped into the room. Shelby's eyes riveted on her sister and she gave a gasp of surprise.

"Serena! But you're supposed to be—"

"Dead?" Serena supplied, barely able to speak the word above a whisper. She couldn't bring herself to look at her twin, but fixed her gaze on Burke as if she might be able to compel him to confess just by looking at him. Her heart was pounding with desperate urgency. It had to be Burke. It had to be.

"No," Shelby said. "Gone. Out of the way."

"Is that what Mr. Burke told you? That he'd hired someone to get me out of the way?"

"I don't know what you're talking about," Burke said belligerently, uncomfortably shifting his bulk in the leather wing chair. "I didn't hire anybody to do anything. Whatever went on was all their idea." He motioned to Shelby and Mason with a thrust of his cigar.

"I'm sure I don't know anything about anybody getting killed!" Shelby said indignantly, the fingers of her left hand fussing with the pearls at her throat. Color rose to mottle her face with polka dots.

Serena swung toward her sister, a sick foreboding churning in the pit of her stomach. *Oh, God, please don't let it be . . .* Shelby's glance hit her squarely for one brief, naked second, then darted off.

"I—I don't know anything about that," she insisted breathlessly.

"Don't you, Shelby?"

Serena could feel Lucky's presence behind her. She could feel his heat and his anger. He stepped past her and moved with restrained power toward the desk.

"You don't know anything about how Gene Willis and Pou Perret were gonna take your sister, your own flesh and blood, your *twin,* out into the swamp and rape her and kill her and dump her body where no one would ever find it?" he said, fury strumming through his words. He planted his hands on the desk and leaned across it aggressively. When he spoke again it was in a voice like smoke shot through with strands of steel. "You don't know anything about that, Shelby? Perhaps I can refresh your memory for you."

Shelby's complexion had gone ashen beneath her makeup. The blush that had been applied with delicate skill across her cheekbones

228

stood out like slashes of red paint. Her eyes were wide with fear. She pressed herself back into her grandfather's chair in an attempt to escape the intensity of the man before her.

"I—I don't know what you're talking about," she said, her voice trembling. "You're crazy. Everyone says so."

"*Mais* yeah, *chère,* I'm crazy," Lucky whispered, leaning closer. "There's no tellin' what I might do for revenge."

Tears sprang into Shelby's eyes.

"Lucky, stop it," Serena ordered. She was afraid of what Lucky's prodding would uncover. God help her, she was afraid he was right. She wanted with all her heart for him to be wrong. The idea that her own sister wanted her dead cut like a knife in the deepest part of her soul. She didn't want it to be true. She didn't want to have to face it, not after everything else she had been forced to face in the past week. She didn't think she would be able to stand it.

Lucky turned on her, his face tight with fury. "Stop it?" he shouted. "*Mon Dieu!* She tried to have you murdered!"

"No!" Shelby screamed, slamming her fists down on the desk. "They were supposed to get her out of the way, that's all! Tell them, Mason," she said, swiveling her chair toward her husband. "You said we'd get her out of the way. You never said anything about murder! Tell them!"

Time seemed to stand still for a second as all eyes turned to Mason Talbot. He stood beside his wife, looking resigned. He tucked his hands into the pockets of his rumpled chinos and rocked back on his heels as he looked down at Shelby.

"Now, peach," he said in a weary tone. "As usual, you haven't thought ahead. What did you think would happen once Serena returned? Why, she would have ruined everything, of course. We couldn't have her coming back."

Shelby looked stunned. "But she's my sister!"

"You hate her," Mason pointed out.

Shelby frowned. "Well, yes, but she's my sister. I wouldn't kill her! Mason, how could you think such a thing?" She admonished him as if he were a naughty child.

"You wanted me in the legislature," he said, his voice growing tighter. "You wanted to live in Baton Rouge. We don't have the money for those things, Shelby, not with your spending habits and a new house and an old one that hasn't been sold. But you never think about anything as vulgar as money, do you? All you're interested in is getting what you want and damn the cost.

"What the hell was I supposed to do?" he shouted, the calm façade cracking finally under the strain. He stared down at her with a tortured expression. "What was I supposed to do, Shelby? I had it all laid out in front of me, there for the taking, the opportunity to give us everything we wanted in one shot. And you were standing right behind me, pushing and pushing. What was I supposed to do?"

The full import of what they had done and what all the ramifications might have been hit Shelby in that moment. Serena could see comprehension dawn in her sister's eyes as if suddenly revealed to her in a vision. As Mason had said, Shelby hadn't thought ahead. As she had always done, she had planned only as far as the moment, not even considering the long-term consequences. She sat there now, looking like a little girl who had been given an unpleasant surprise—stunned, hurt, disillusioned.

Serena looked away as an expression of horror twisted Shelby's features, and she turned from her husband, buried her face in her hands, and began to sob. Tears rose in Serena's eyes.

"What about Gifford?" Lucky asked, his attention still focused on Mason.

Mason pushed his glasses up on his nose and tried to compose himself. He answered absently, as if he were explaining nothing more earth-shattering than plans for a picnic. "He would have become despondent over Serena's disappearance and the loss of the plantation. Poor man. He probably would have committed suicide."

Serena listened in stunned silence. She shook her head as a sense of vertigo seized hold of her for an instant. Another facet of her well-ordered life shattered. Mason. Staid, stoical, kind Mason Talbot, a man she had always liked and trusted, had paid to have her killed. He had allowed his greed and his love for Shelby to mutate into an ugly catalyst that had driven him to murder.

"And the fire?" Lucky prodded.

Mason ducked his head. His shoulders sagged. "I believe I've said enough without having my attorney present," he said softly.

"That's all right, Mason," Sheriff Hollings said as he sauntered into the room with a pair of deputies at his heels. "I've heard all I need to hear for now."

Serena watched with a sense of disbelief as the officers each took charge of one perpetrator. Burke protested loudly as handcuffs were slapped on his wrists. Mason said nothing. Shelby fell sobbing across the desk and had to be helped to her feet by the sheriff.

"This is all your fault!" she shouted at Serena as they were being led from the room. Her face was awash in tears and mascara, her mask of beauty melting away to reveal her hate and inner torment. "You never should have come back! None of this would have happened if you hadn't come back!"

There was nothing Serena could think of to say. She stared at her twin and felt a terrible aching hollowness inside. They should have been closer than sisters, but they were poles apart. The only thing left between them now was bitterness and pity and regret.

Lucky came up beside her and put his arm gently around her waist, silently inviting her to lean against his strength. They stood together and watched as the officers herded their prisoners toward the door with the sheriff drawling, "Y'all have the right to remain silent. Anything you say can and will be used against you in a court of law. . . ."

Lamar rose slowly from the leather wing chair, scratching his chest. "I believe I'll go and return this little microphone to Sheriff Hollings. Simply amazing the technology the police have at their disposal these days." He gave Serena an apologetic look and patted her shoulder with a wrinkled hand. "I truly am sorry, my dear, about all that's happened here today. What a terrible shock it must be to you."

"Yes," Serena murmured. "Thank you for your help, Mr. Canfield."

"Don't mention it. I was merely performing my civic duty. If you need any further assistance, don't hesitate to call." He rolled his eyes heavenward and heaved a dramatic sigh. "I may have every appearance of a dotty old codger, but I believe I still have a few tricks up my sleeve."

Serena managed a pale smile as she watched the elderly lawyer stroll gracefully into the hall, Panama hat in hand. She listened as he exchanged a few lines of banter with Odille on his way out. Then the house fell into silence.

She could feel the power of Lucky's gaze on her as she went to the French doors. Trying to block the sound of departing squad cars from her mind, she looked through the panes of glass past the gallery, across the lawn. The bayou was a dark ribbon at the feet of the trees. The sky was a turbulent patchwork of rapidly changing cloud formations and patches of blue; it looked as unsettled as she felt.

She felt as if her life had been thrust into the winds of a hurricane. Everything had blown apart—her family, her image of herself, her sense of control over her own destiny—everything lay in fragments around her and she didn't know where to begin to pick up the pieces. She had come here for a few days of vacation. Instead, her life had been irreparably altered; *she* had been irreparably altered.

"What happens now?" Serena heard herself ask the question, but it felt as if it had come from someone else. She couldn't imagine why it would have come from her; she didn't think she really wanted to hear Lucky's answer.

"There'll be a hearing," he said, deliberately choosing the mundane interpretation of the question. "They'll be charged. Bail will be set—for Burke and Shelby at least."

Serena glanced back at Lucky. He was sitting back against the desk, turning a smooth glass paperweight over in his hands, his gaze steady on her.

"I never would have suspected Mason," she murmured. "Never."

"No one would have." He put the paperweight down and came to stand behind her at the glass doors, his face grave. "No one can guess the kind of things pressure can drive a man to do," he said softly. "I'm sorry about Shelby, Serena. I have my own grievance with her, but I know she's your sister and it must hurt."

Tears stung Serena's eyes as she nodded. "I always wished we would have been as close as twins are supposed to be. We never were. Now we never will be. What's happened will always be between us."

Lucky slid his arms around her and leaned down to kiss her cheek. "I told Hollings I'd take a deputy out to where we left Willis and Perret."

Serena nodded, rubbing her hands over her upper arms as if to warm herself through the fabric of the soft faded chambray shirt she had borrowed from Lucky's wardrobe. It hung to her knees, and she had needed to fold the cuffs back five times to reveal her hands, but it had been a big improvement over her ruined silk blouse and the memories attached to it. She hadn't been able to look at that pile of clothing without shuddering. Lucky had taken the garments outside and burned them, then loaned her his shirt and a pair of old gray sweat pants.

"I suppose I should go and change," she said. "You'll be wanting your shirt back."

"Keep it."

The words seemed innocuous enough, but Serena felt what was coming as surely as if he had just held up a red flag. This was it. This was going to be the moment Lucky chose to end it. He would say good-bye and ride off into the swamp without looking back, and she would be left with a broken heart and an old blue workshirt.

"A souvenir?" she asked dryly, looking up at him over her shoulder. "Something I can pack away in my hope chest and take out whenever I want to remember you fondly?"

Lucky stepped back, frowning. "Serena, don't."

"Don't what?" She arched one golden brow. "Don't remember you fondly? Don't remember you at all? You want me to pretend I never fell in love with you? Is that what you're going to do, Lucky? Pretend you never told me you loved me?"

"I told you from the beginning what we could have."

She held up both hands to ward off his words. Anger rushed into her head and pounded like mallets in her temples. "Don't you try to feed me that line again. I'm ready to gag on it! I don't care what boundaries we set. I don't care that it's been only a matter of days. What we have goes way beyond sex, and you know it."

"I know it can't work," he insisted, glaring at her.

She returned his hard gaze, matching his stubbornness ounce for ounce. "You won't let it work."

Lucky spun away, his hands raised as if to strangle somebody as his temper surged. She was going to make this as difficult as possible for them both. She wouldn't just accept the facts and meekly walk away. No, no, she would tear them all apart and analyze them and try to find a cure.

"Dammit, Serena, you saw what happened out there last night," he said tightly. He stared down at his boots because he was too ashamed to look her in the eye. "Is that the kind of man you want for a husband? Next time I might just slip off that edge."

"I saw what happened," Serena said softly, aching for him. "And I saw you get through it. You saved my life. And I watched you take care of me afterward, and I was there when you made love to me too. What happened with Willis doesn't make me love you less, Lucky. If anything, it makes me love you more."

Lucky shook his head impatiently as he paced before her. "That's not love. That's pity. I know what you see when you look at me, Serena—some poor, crazy bastard who needs someone to take care of him."

"Damn you, Lucky Doucet," Serena snarled. She came around in front of him and grabbed the waistband of his jeans to keep him from walking away. She glared up at him, her face scratched and bruised, fury in her eyes. "I will thank you to stop interpreting my feelings for me. I don't pity you, you pity yourself. You're so damn proud and stubborn, you can't bear the idea that you're not perfect, that you have flaws and frailties like everyone else. You make me mad as hell, but I love you. You're strong and good and tender under all that macho bullshit. And you love me. Look me in the eye and tell me you don't."

He knew he should have done it, but he couldn't. He couldn't look down into that beautiful battered face and tell her he didn't love her, when he loved her more than life. But he couldn't give her what she deserved either.

"I can't give you the kind of life you deserve."

"I deserve to have the man I love."

"I live in the swamp," he said. "I can't tolerate people. I'm lucky if I get through a day without comin' half unglued. What kind of future can I give you? What do I have to offer you, Serena?"

Her answer was simple and devastating. "Your heart."

Lucky closed his eyes like a man in pain.

"Don't try to tell me you don't have one. You're just afraid to give it," Serena said, tears rising again to tighten her throat and sting the backs of her eyes. "I know what it is to be afraid, Lucky," she whispered.

He shook his head, refusing to look at her, the muscles of his jaw working.

"Yes," Serena insisted. She stared up at him earnestly, her heart in her eyes. "I know how it feels. I know what it's like to feel it take hold and let it control you. I also know I could help you conquer it—not because I'm a psychologist, but because I'm the woman who loves you."

"I've got to go," he muttered, looking away, his face a taut, unreadable mask.

Serena felt futility pull down on her like a weight. He wasn't going to give in. He was going to withdraw into himself and close the door on her as he had countless times in the past few days, and none of the tools of her trade would be able to pry it open. Her love was the only key she had, and Lucky was making it clear not even that would unlock the chains that bound him to his past.

"Hiding isn't the answer, Lucky," she said sadly. "You're a good man, a strong man, a man with talents. You've got so much to offer if you'll only stop running from who you really are."

"Let me go, Serena," he said softly. "You'll be better off."

She stepped back from him, lifting her chin defiantly as she tried to sniff back her tears. "You think you're doing this for me? Your nobility is sadly misplaced. I don't want it. I want a future with you. We could have so much more than you're willing to give us, Lucky. You let me know when you're ready to accept that. I'll be here waiting."

Lucky's gaze sharpened on her. "You're not goin' back to Charleston?"

"No." Serena hadn't been certain of an answer until that very second, but it came out strong and sure, the only decision she could have made. "I'll have to go back to settle my affairs, but that's all. Chanson du Terre is my home. I have responsibilities here, and roots. It's time I faced that and accepted myself for who I am inside instead of who I am in Charleston. I'm all through being a coward. You let me know when you are."

She gave him one last long look, then started for the door.

A deputy stuck his head in the open doorway. "Hey, Lucky, the boat's here. You ready to go?"

Serena stopped and stood there, waiting to hear his answer as if it were the answer to the question in her heart. The silence dragged on.

"Yeah," he said at last, his voice soft and heavy. "Let's get outta here."

Chapter Twenty

"Serena? Is that you?" Gifford bellowed from the depths of his study.

Serena paused outside the open door, suitcases in hand. "Yes, Giff, it's me," she called back wearily.

"Hey, Miz 'Rena," Pepper called, grinning at her from his position in a leather wing chair. He lifted his coffee cup to her in salute. "Mighty good to have you back."

"Thanks, Pepper." She wished she could have said it felt good to be back, but all she felt at the moment was exhausted. She thought she could have just laid down on the old Oriental rug between the two blue tick hounds and slept for a week or three. The hounds looked up at her with woeful expressions. One mustered the ambition to woof softly, then fell over on his side, exhausted from his effort.

Gifford abandoned the blueprints on his desk and strode across the room toward her. He looked as vibrant and healthy and cantankerous as ever. There was a flush of color on his high cheekbones. His eyes gleamed with a fierce intelligence. His white hair was in a state of disarray that told of numerous finger combings.

"Where the hell have you been?" he demanded to know. "You were due back two hours ago. Odille waited supper as long as she could."

"I'm sorry. My flight was delayed."

"They don't have telephones up in Charleston?" Gifford said with characteristic sarcasm. He gave her an admonishing glare, took her suitcases away from her, and started down the hall with them.

Serena had all she could do to dredge up the energy to catch up with him. The man was nearly eighty and she thought he could probably work her right into the ground on his worst day. He was amazing.

He stopped at the door to her room and set her luggage down. "You had an old man worried he might have scared you off for good," he said gruffly as he straightened and looked her in the eye. The glare had softened grudgingly with lights of love and unspoken apology.

"No," Serena said with a weary smile. "You can't scare me, you old goat. I'm no coward."

"Damn right you're not." Gifford's shoulders straightened with pride. "You're a Sheridan, by God."

He looked at her for a long moment then, and sighed, all the bluster going out of him. He raised his weathered old hands and cupped her shoulders gently. "I'm glad you're back, Serena. I know I pushed and bullied you into it, but you still could have said no in the end. I'm glad you didn't."

Serena slid her arms around his lean, hard waist and hugged him. What had happened had changed their relationship and complicated it, but when all that was stripped away, the most important fact remained.

"I love you," she whispered, pulling back.

Gifford reddened and looked at his feet, grumbling, uncomfortable with voicing such feelings to a person's face.

"You gonna go after that big Cajun?" he asked suddenly.

The question took Serena by surprise, hitting her too suddenly for her to give a controlled response. She shook her head and looked at the floor, afraid of what her grandfather might pick up from her unguarded expression.

"What's the matter? He's not good enough for you 'cause he doesn't wear silk suits and read *The Wall Street Journal?*"

That brought Serena's chin back up. She glared at Gifford, realizing belatedly that he was once again playing her like a finely tuned fiddle. "That's not it and you know it," she said evenly.

"He's had some rough times, but Lucky's a good man," Gifford said gruffly.

"I know he is. Maybe someday he'll figure that out for himself. I can't push him into believing it."

"Do you love him?"

"Yes."

Gifford frowned, his bushy white brows pulling together in a V of disapproval above his dark eyes. "You want him, but you're not going after him?"

"We're talking about a relationship, not a big-game hunt," Serena said dryly. "I can't go out in the swamp with a dart gun and bring him back to live in captivity. I can't drag him back here and force him to love me. Lucky has a lot of things from his past he needs to work out for himself. When he does—if he does—then maybe he'll see what we could have together."

"Well, I hope so." Gifford's frown softened, and he rubbed his chin. "I sure as hell don't want to think I dumped you on his doorstep just to get your heart broken. I was counting on getting some grandchildren out the deal."

"Gifford!" Serena gasped, her cheeks blooming delicate pink.

The old man showed no signs of remorse. He didn't even have the grace to look guilty.

"You look as peaked and thin as a runt pup," he complained, his gaze raking her head to toe. "I'll have Odille heat you a plate of food."

Serena shook her head in amazement. "Don't bother her," she said absently. "I ate on the plane."

Gifford snorted his disapproval and moved off down the hall in the direction of the kitchen. "Wouldn't feed that trash to my hounds."

Serena watched him go. One of the reasons she had decided to move back home was that she had figured Gifford would need her after everything that had happened. What a joke that was. It was quite clear he could take care of himself. She was going to have to stay on her toes just to keep up with him.

She dragged her suitcases into her bedroom, where she kicked off her shoes, stripped off her travel-wrinkled suit, slipped on her robe, and set about the business of unpacking before she collapsed under the weight of her fatigue.

She went about the task methodically, mechanically. It seemed most of her movements these days were mechanical. She was operating on automatic, taking care of day-to-day matters with an obvious lack of enthusiasm. In her logical, educated mind she knew this lethargy would pass eventually. In the meantime, she simply had to suffer through it, going through each day only to get to the next. It wasn't fun, but it was better than nothing. In her more philosophical moments she reflected it would give her added empathy for her patients in the future—as soon as she had some patients.

She had gone back to Charleston to tie up all the loose ends there, to resettle her patients with new therapists, to sell her condo and say good-bye to friends. All had been accomplished with minimal flap. Tomorrow she would drive up to Lafayette and start looking for office space. She should have been looking forward to the task, but she couldn't come up with any emotion to dent the numbness inside.

Too much had happened in too short a time. Her emotions had gone on overload and shorted out. It was a defense mechanism. It hurt to feel, therefore her mind had shut down the capacity to feel. The only time her emotions turned back on was late at night, when she was too tired and too lonely to keep them at bay. Then they rushed back in a high-voltage surge of pain that left her feeling even more drained and beaten.

A month had passed since the crisis at Chanson du Terre had come to a head. There would still be the trials to get through—Mason, Willis and Perret, Perry Davis, who had in fact been Mason's middleman in hiring the two thugs. Len Burke had gotten off scot-free. There had been no hard evidence connecting him to any crime other than greed. Shelby had already pleaded guilty to a minimal charge of conspiracy and been given a suspended sentence. She and her children had gone to stay with Mason's parents in Lafayette. The Talbots had raised Mason's bail and were reportedly calling in long-due favors to get him the best defense attorneys money could buy. Rumors abounded about deals to avoid the scandal of a trial, but there had been no official word.

Serena found herself oddly incurious about it. She wasn't interested in punishment or restitution. The trust she had lost, the disillusionment she had suffered, couldn't be repaired or replaced. She wanted only to put it all behind her and get on with her life.

Gifford had reinstated himself in the house and was going on as if all that had happened was already little more than a dim memory. He was engrossed in planning the new machine shed as well as in ordinary plantation business. Pepper and James Arnaud had him thinking about crawfish as a new cash crop to rotate with the sugarcane.

239

As it always did, life gradually returned to normal, healing over the wound and leaving only hidden scars behind to remind those who had lived through the trouble.

Serena placed a final stack of lingerie in the dresser and closed the drawer. As she lifted her head her gaze caught on her reflection in the beveled mirror. It was amazing. She looked no different than she had before all this had begun. The cuts and scratches of her harrowing night in the swamp had long since healed, leaving her skin unmarred. It seemed as if there should have been some lasting sign of that whole momentous chapter in her life plain on her face for all the world to see, but the scars were on the inside, on her heart.

Lucky had gone away with the deputy that day and never returned. Serena had been angry, hurt, heartbroken. She had considered going out into the swamp to get him, but had decided against it in the end. It went against her grain to give up on him, but she knew she was right in not pushing him. It had to be Lucky's decision to come back to her. She couldn't force him to love her enough. She couldn't force him to want to have a future. He had to decide his life was empty without her. He had to see that hiding from the world wasn't the answer to his problems.

It had become painfully obvious he was not going to make those decisions.

Maybe she'd been wrong about him. Maybe he didn't love her after all. Maybe what they'd had together had been nothing more than desire magnified and intensified by the circumstances. Maybe she was the only one who had felt something that went beyond passion. Maybe she was the only one left feeling empty.

Even as she opened the dresser drawer and pulled out the faded blue workshirt, Serena chastised herself. This wasn't very healthy behavior. It was certainly no way to get over a broken heart. But her inner critic wasn't very stringent. Some deeper wisdom told her she needed time to heal. None of her practical therapy methods were going to change the fact that she still loved Lucky Doucet or that she missed him or that she hurt because of losing him. No amount of counseling could change the fact that she needed to feel close to him now at the end of a long day, when she was feeling tired and in need of a broad shoulder to lean on. So she didn't stop her hands from lifting the old blue workshirt from the drawer, nor did she try to stop herself from bringing it up to brush the soft chambray against her cheek and breathe in the scent of it.`

Hardly an hour went by that she didn't think of Lucky, wondering what he was doing, if he was all right, if he was still chasing poachers. She couldn't help thinking about him, picturing him standing at the back of his pirogue, poling silently through the swamp, or sitting in his studio staring moodily at a canvas. She couldn't help thinking about him, wondering what he was doing, if he ever missed her.

He had done what he thought was the right thing, the noble thing, in leaving her. Ironic, considering how determined he had been to convince her he was no good. Sometimes it made her angry when she thought of it—how high-handed he'd been in deciding what was best for her—and sometimes it made her ache with sadness that he'd seen himself as so unworthy of her love. Sometimes she told herself he might have known best and she should just give up on him and get on with her life. But she could never manage to tell herself that at night when she lay in her bed, staring into the darkness.

Hugging the shirt to her chest, she closed her eyes and sighed as the pain penetrated the protective wall she'd built around her heart. The scents and sounds of the summer night drifted in through the open French doors. And with them came the memory of the night she and Lucky had made love in this room.

No other man had ever made her feel the way Lucky did. No other man had ever gotten past her barrier of cool control and brought out the true woman in her. It didn't make sense. He was the last man she would have imagined falling in love with, dark, dangerous, rough-edged. And she would never have believed herself capable of falling so hard and so quickly. It defied logic. She could find no pat, analytical answer, but it was true nevertheless. No man had ever made her feel so alive, so filled with passion and yearning to be a part of another soul. She knew with a deep, sad certainty no man ever would.

All dressed up for me, sugar?

The words came to her like smoke, like mist on the bayou. Serena stared into the mirror and imagined she saw him standing behind her, his hot amber gaze roaming over her body, his artist's hands coming up to cup her shoulders and pull her back against him. She closed her eyes as she clutched the shirt to her chest and for just a second imagined his arms around her.

"Serena?"

Her heart jolted in her chest as she swung toward the door.

"Shelby." She couldn't hide the surprise in her voice or any of the

241

other feelings that sprang up at her sister's sudden appearance in the doorway. They had had no direct contact since that fateful day in Gifford's study. Serena hadn't been able to find it in her to be the one to take the initiative, and Shelby had shown no desire to do so either. Serena had wondered how long they would go on in limbo. It appeared her question was about to be answered.

"May I come in?" Shelby asked, sounding as formal as a stranger.

"Yes. Of course," Serena said, folding her arms in front of her, Lucky's shirt caught between them.

"I came by to pick up the last of our things," Shelby explained as she stepped in and closed the door behind her.

Serena made no argument, even though she knew all of Shelby's and Mason's things had long since been packed and sent to the Talbot home in Lafayette. Shelby had taken the crucial first step. What difference did it make if she had felt the need for an excuse?

Serena watched her sister as she moved slowly around the room, Shelby's normal energy level subdued as she straightened a doily here, a lampshade there. As always, she was impeccably dressed in a delicately printed sundress with a full skirt. Every honey-gold hair was in place, smoothed into a chignon at the back of her head. Noticeably absent from her ensemble was the expensive jewelry she so loved. The only ring she wore was her engagement diamond.

Serena watched her with a strangely detached curiosity. The initial rush of confusing emotions had subsided, leaving her feeling blank and empty again, vaguely wary of her sister's motives.

"I suppose you're still angry with me," Shelby said. Her tone of voice was almost annoyed, as if she didn't believe Serena had a right to be angry, but her movements and quick sideways glances said she was nervous about what the answer to her statement would be.

"No," Serena said, turning to watch her in the mirror.

Shelby looked up and frowned at her. "Serena the Good," she said bitterly. "I should have expected as much. Forgive all those who sin against you."

"I didn't say I'd forgiven you. I said I wasn't angry. Anger isn't what I feel when I think about you."

"What do you feel?"

Serena was silent for a long moment as she contemplated her answer. "I don't know if it has a name. It's like grief, I guess, but different, worse in a way."

Their eyes met in the mirror and Shelby suddenly looked genuinely sad.

"We were never very good at being sisters, were we?" she said softly.

Serena shook her head. "No. I'm afraid we never were."

Shelby moved several steps closer, until they stood side by side, close but not touching, alike but not the same. Her gaze riveted on their images in the looking glass. "How can we look so much alike and be so different inside?" she whispered as if she were asking the question of herself.

Serena said nothing. There were no easy answers. As a psychologist, she could have cited any number of theories on the subject, but as a sister none of them meant anything. As a sister all she knew was that she and her twin were standing on opposite sides of a chasm that was too wide and deep to be bridged. There might have been a point in their past when they could have found some common ground and reached across, but that time was gone and they both knew it.

"I wish things hadn't gone so wrong," Shelby said, her dark eyes filling.

That was as much of an apology as she was going to get, Serena thought sadly. There would be no remorse, no expression of regret for what had happened, for what could have happened. Shelby was incapable of taking blame. She was like a thief who was sorry the police had caught her red-handed, but not sorry she'd committed the crime. She was only sorry things had gone wrong.

"Me too," Serena said softly, knowing they had very different ideas about what had gone awry. The blank slate of her emotions filled suddenly with a complex mix of feelings, like a tide rushing in, and, as she had said in answer to Shelby's earlier question, the strongest was something like grief. They may both have been physically alive, but whatever had been between them was dead and she wanted to mourn it like a lost soul.

"My word, Serena," Shelby murmured, still staring at their reflections in the mirror, "you look all done in."

"I'll be all right."

"Yes, I'm sure you will be."

"Will you?"

"We'll manage," Shelby said, lifting her chin a defiant notch.

She moved back a step. The distance between them widened. Her

243

reflection in the mirror grew smaller. When she reached the door and turned the knob, Serena found her voice.

"Shelby?" Their eyes met again in the glass. "Take care."

A single tear rolled down her sister's cheek and a faint smile touched her mouth. "You too."

Serena watched her go, feeling as if she were losing a part of herself she'd never really known. Then, bone-weary and heartsick, she crawled onto the bed, curled up with Lucky's shirt, and did the one thing she did really well these days—she cried herself to sleep.

Gifford slipped into the room quietly. He set the plate he was carrying on the dresser and walked around the end of the bed to look down at his sleeping granddaughter. The tears were still damp on her cheeks, her breathing still shaky. She held an old blue workshirt wadded up in her hands, reminding him of when she'd been no more than a toddler, dragging a ragged yellow security blanket around the house with her everywhere she went.

He remembered the day they'd put her mother in the ground, how he had slipped in that night to check on the girls because Robert had been too lost in his grief to think of it. He had found Serena asleep on top of the covers, still wearing the little black velvet dress and white tights she'd worn to the funeral, one patent leather shoe on and one off. The tears had still been damp on her cheeks, and she had clutched in her hand that ragged old blanket.

He remembered it like it was yesterday even though tonight he felt every one of the years that had passed since then. The love he'd known for Serena that night hadn't lessened a whit. It didn't matter that Serena had grown into a woman or that life had complicated things between them. He still experienced her pain more sharply than if it had been his own. His grief over what Shelby had done was magnified by the grief he knew Serena was feeling. Her pain over Lucky's defection was more than enough to break his own heart.

He knew he had pushed her over the years and bullied and manipulated her, but he hadn't done anything without loving her, and he just about couldn't bear to see her suffering. He couldn't change what had happened between them, and he couldn't mend the rift between her and Shelby, but he could do his best to knock some sense into that big Cajun rogue. In fact, it was the least he could do, all things considered.

Careful not to wake Serena, he leaned across the bed and pulled the coverlet back over her. He looked at her again, turned slowly, and shuffled out of the room, taking the dinner plate with him and shutting the light off on his way out.

Lucky checked the rope attached to the nose of the half-submerged rowboat one last time, then slogged out of the bayou and onto the bank. The day was hotter than summer in Hades. The sun beat down on the bare skin of his back through a haze of humidity, burning him an even darker shade of brown. Sweat rolled off him. He pulled on a pair of worn leather work gloves and took up the end of the rope he had looped around the trunk of an oak tree, paying no attention to his discomfort. He focused his mind on his job.

He'd been hauling junk up out of the bayou for weeks now, working literally from sunup to sundown, cleaning up dozens of sites careless people had chosen for disposing of such things as old refrigerators, iron bedsteads, stoves, mattresses, bicycles, and tires. It was a job that needed doing and one that he could devote himself to and exhaust himself with in the hopes of gaining a few hours of sleep at the end of the day.

When the job called for it, he used a gas-powered winch, but he fell back on it only after he'd spent a good long while trying to pull the object out by himself—no matter what it happened to be. The exertion cleared his mind and made certain the overriding pain he felt was in his muscles.

He took up the rope now and tightened the slack gradually until he was leaning back hard against it, straining to inch the boat up out of the water. He heaved, his every muscle standing out, physical pain blocking all thought from his mind. Beads of sweat slipped past the bandanna he wore around his forehead, stinging his eyes. He leaned back, pulling until his blood was roaring in his ears. He didn't even hear the outboard motor till the bass boat was nearly to the bank.

From the corner of his eye he saw Gifford and groaned inwardly. Why couldn't the world just leave him alone? He adjusted his grip on the rope and heaved backward again, doubling his concentration on his task, dragging the boat up another six inches toward the bank. The sound of the outboard ceased abruptly, but Lucky worked on as if he were completely oblivious of Gifford Sheridan's presence.

"I had me a mule once could pull like that," the old man drawled. "He was a damn sight smarter than you, though, I reckon."

Lucky sucked in a lungful of humid air, adjusted his grip, and hauled back on the rope again, the corded muscles in his neck and shoulders standing out as he pulled. The nose of the old rowboat lunged forward as the back end pulled free of the mud. Within a couple of minutes he had the dilapidated craft halfway ashore. He dropped the rope then and went to tip the water out of the boat. Gifford sat patiently watching him from under the brim of a battered old green John Deere cap.

"What are you doin' here?" Lucky growled, not looking up from his task. He pulled a small anchor from inside the boat and heaved it onto the bank. "I thought you got everything you wanted, old man."

"What would it matter to you if I did or didn't? Everybody knows you don't give a damn about anyone but yourself."

Lucky said nothing as he drained the boat. He didn't need this. His life was miserable enough without having this cantankerous old man chewing his tail. He'd done what he had to do. That was the end of it.

"You broke her heart," Gifford said succinctly.

Lucky flinched inwardly, the words like a whip across tender flesh. He focused on the junk in the boat as he stood there waist-deep in the bayou. "I didn't ask her to fall in love with me."

"No, but she did anyway, didn't she? God knows what she sees in you. I look at you now and all I see is a stubborn, selfish man too caught up in his penance to see he doesn't have anything left to pay for." Gifford shrugged and sighed, his shrewd dark eyes on Lucky the whole time, never wavering. "Hell, I don't know, maybe you like pain. Maybe you like thinking you could have had a decent life with a wonderful woman, but you passed it all up to suffer. Catholics do like their martyrs."

He didn't so much as bat an eye at the murderous glare Lucky sent him. The old man sat leaning forward with his forearms on his thighs and his big hands dangling down between his knees, as calm as if he were sitting over a fishing pole waiting for a bite. Lucky turned abruptly and waded ashore, dragging the old rowboat with him. When the boat lay on its side like the carcass of a whale, he turned back toward Gifford.

"I did what was best."

Gifford snorted. "You did what was easiest."

"The hell I did!" Lucky snapped, taking an aggressive step toward the bow of the bass boat. "You think I wanted to walk away from her?

246

No. But what kind of life could I give her? What kind of husband would I be?"

"Not much of one until you get yourself straightened out. I don't see any sign of that happening any time soon," Gifford said sarcastically. "I guess I can just go on home and tell Serena she's crying herself to sleep at night for no good reason."

The blow was on target, even more so than Gifford could have hoped. Lucky had heard Serena's tears. He had found himself on the gallery of Chanson du Terre late one night, just to catch a glimpse of her, just to ease that one longing a little. He'd seen her curled up on her bed, crying into the shirt he'd left behind. He'd told himself then he'd done the right thing; he didn't deserve her tears. But the sound of them, the idea of them, had been enough to tear his heart in two.

"I can't give her what she needs," he said, staring down at his boots.

"What do you think she needs, Lucky? Money? An executive husband? Serena can make her own money. If she wanted an executive, she could have had one long before now. All she needs is for you to love her. If you can't manage that, then, by God, you are one sorry soul indeed."

"She knows I love her," Lucky admitted grudgingly.

"Then come back."

"I can't."

Gifford swore, his patience wearing thin in big patches. "Goddammit, boy, why not?"

Lucky gave him a long, level look. The corner of his mouth curled up in a faint sardonic smile. "I got my reasons."

The old man's jaw worked and his face flushed, but he held his temper in check. "Well, Lucky," he said at last on a long sigh, "you have a nice life out here all by yourself." He reached around for the starter rope, his fingers closing over the handle. "Don't worry about Serena. She'll buck up. She's a Sheridan."

The engine sputtered, then roared to life, and Gifford calmly rode away, leaving Lucky feeling as unsettled as the bayou in the churning wake of the outboard motor.

The feeling still hadn't subsided by sundown when he abandoned his job for the day and made his way home. It hadn't lessened any by midnight when he sat on the floor of his studio drinking and staring morosely at his paintings in the moonlight. He had managed to keep the worst of his feelings at bay these past few weeks, denying them,

247

dodging them, burying them, but now they rose to the surface like oil on the bayou. They clung to him, refusing to be ignored even as he tried to study the painting on the easel before him.

He hadn't painted in weeks. He had expected to find the same peace in it as he had after returning from Central America, but when he'd taken up the brush and applied it to the canvas he'd felt nothing to compare with the peace he had found so briefly in Serena's arms. That kind of peace he never expected to find again.

That had been an unwelcome revelation. The solace he had once found in this place was lost to him. He had retreated from the love Serena had offered him and found not peace, but misery in the form of a terrible wrenching loneliness that felt as if a vital part of him had been torn out and taken away.

He couldn't go out into the swamp without thinking about the way she had given him her trust there in the place she had been so afraid of. His house was haunted by her memory. He hadn't slept a night in his bed because he couldn't lie there without remembering the feel of her body against his. Every time he turned he thought he caught the scent of her perfume in the air. He could feel her presence but he couldn't touch her, couldn't see her, couldn't take her in his arms and have her chase away the darkness in his soul.

"Damn you, Serena," he muttered, pushing himself to his feet.

The emotions rose higher and hotter inside him, tormenting him. He paced back and forth before the easel with his head in his hands as he realized with a sense of panic there was no escape. He could work till he dropped and the feelings would still be there inside, waiting for a chance to torture him. He could drink himself unconscious and they would still come to him through the haze of oblivion.

Crying out in fury and frustration, he grabbed the unfinished painting from the easel and smashed the edge of it against the floor with all his strength, snapping the stretcher like a toothpick. He let the ruined mess drop from his hands and backed away from it blindly.

"Damn you, Serena!" he shouted to the heavens. He whirled toward his work table and swept an arm across it, knocking bottles and brushes to the floor. And he shouted in anguish above the crash, "Damn you! Damn you!"

He stumbled back across the room, reeling at the inner pain, exhausted from fighting his feelings. Slowly he sank back down to the floor, on his knees on the dropcloth where they had first made love, feeling as bleak and desolate inside as he had ever in his life. He tilted his head back, turning his face up toward the skylights and the cold white light of the moon. Tears trickled from the outer corners of his eyes, across his temples, into his hair.

He hadn't asked to fall in love. All he had wanted was to be left alone. Now he was so alone, he couldn't stand it.

This was hell on earth, and Gifford had the gall to accuse him of taking the easy way out.

Serena had called him a coward. She'd said he pitied himself, that he was afraid to give their love a chance to work.

Of course he was afraid. He had known they would only end up hurt in the end, and he'd had enough pain to last him a lifetime.

But Serena was hurting now, despite his noble sacrifice, and he'd never lived through this kind of agony. It was far worse than anything Ramos and his buddies had dished out because it was relentless and unreachable and nothing relieved it. He ached with missing Serena. He ached with the need to touch her. He ached with guilt and the knowledge that she was right.

He was a coward. He'd been afraid to feel again. He had been afraid to let Serena get close to him for fear of what she would see, but she had seen every part of him, every side of him—good and bad—and she'd still loved him.

What kind of fool was he to let a woman like that get away? What kind of fool was he to go on suffering like this?

A noble fool who had pushed away the woman he loved for her own good. A frightened fool who had been too wary of love. A fool who had nothing to offer her but himself because his life had been stripped down to mere existence.

Where did he go from here?

Lucky stared long and hard at the painting on the floor before him. It lay in a crumpled, twisted heap, ruined, worthless. He could throw it out or he could try to salvage it, restretch the canvas, start over on the painting.

A sense of calm settled inside him as the answers came to him.

If Serena deserved a better man than he was, then he would have to become a better man. If his life offered her nothing, then he would have to change it, because he didn't want to live without her. He didn't want to be a martyr to his past. It had taken so much from him already —his youth, his hope, his family—he couldn't let it take Serena too.

The time had come to leave it behind and try to take that first step forward. He had a long way to go before he would feel whole and

249

healed, but he would never get there if he didn't take that first step, and his life wouldn't be worth living if he stayed where he was.

Slowly he reached for the ruined canvas and pushed himself to his feet.

Chapter Twenty-one

Serena stood on the sidewalk, looking up at the sign above the black lacquered door. RICHARD GALLERY was spelled out in flowing gold script on a black background. The building was three narrow stories of old brick sandwiched between similar buildings that had been lovingly restored more than once in their long histories. There was ornate grill-work over the windows, and flower boxes spilling scarlet geraniums and dark green ivy over their edges. Two doors down, a young man sat on a stoop playing a saxophone for tips. Just beyond him locals and tourists alike had begun to gather for dinner at a sidewalk café. A mule-drawn carriage clomped by on the street, its driver reciting the history of the area for his passengers. Just another hot summer night in New Orleans.

The French Quarter address of the building matched the one on the invitation she held in her hands, but still Serena hesitated. It had been four months since she'd last seen Lucky. He had made no attempt to get in touch with her until now, and this could hardly be construed as personal contact—an engraved invitation sent out by an art gallery. All it meant was that she was on his mailing list. How flattering.

A group of tourists brushed past her, laughing and chattering, parting to go around her like a stream around a boulder. Serena didn't move. She looked at the invitation in her hands, remembering how she felt when she first opened it. There was a mixture of joy and sadness—joy that Lucky had taken this step, that he was making an effort to put his life on track, sadness that she wasn't being included in that life.

She acknowledged the fact that she wasn't getting over him. She was getting on with her life without him, but she doubted she would ever be completely free of him. In fact, she knew she never would be. She was carrying his child.

She nibbled her lip and stared at the door of the gallery. All the way to New Orleans she had told herself she was going for Lucky's sake, to show her support. But the truth was this was an opportunity to see him on somewhat neutral ground, and she needed that. She told herself she would be calm and cool and tell him that while he was going to be a father, she expected nothing from him. She would be the picture of sophistication and poise, and then she would probably pass out.

"So, are we going to go inside or is this all you wanted to see?"

Serena jumped at the sound of the voice. She glanced around at the man who had insisted on accompanying her to New Orleans. Blond and handsome, David Farrell looked down at her with kind eyes and a gentle smile curving his wide mouth.

She had joined David and another psychologist in practice in Lafayette, and they had quickly become good friends. David was easy to talk to, understanding, intuitive. Serena had found herself confiding in him within days of meeting him, something that was very unlike her. There was something about him that seemed so trustworthy, so nonthreatening, everyone wanted to confide in him. It was a trait that made him very successful in his profession and popular with his friends. Serena had it on good authority he was considered prime husband material by every single woman in Lafayette.

He had insisted on driving with her to New Orleans to give her moral support. Now he stood beside her with his hands in his pants pockets, waiting patiently for a response. Serena gave him a look.

"Yes, we're going inside. I just wanted to be certain this is the place, that's all."

David raised his eyebrows. "Mmm."

"Save it for your patients, Dr. Farrell," she said dryly, and led the way inside.

The gallery was cool and light. Stark white walls were used as

252

backdrops for the paintings, lights were strategically spotted toward the works, bleached wood floors were polished to a brilliant sheen. An impressive number of people milled around, admiring Lucky's work, talking, nibbling on dainty canapes and sipping white wine from tulip-shaped glasses. Cajun music floated out of cleverly hidden speakers, too soft to be appreciated.

Serena found herself missing the bayou country, and she smiled a little at the thought. This was the kind of life she had enjoyed in Charleston, but she found herself wishing she were sitting on the gallery at Chanson du Terre, listening to Pepper and Gifford argue with a blaring two-step playing in the background.

She couldn't imagine Lucky in these surroundings. He was too big, too wild, too elemental. She moved through the crowd half expecting to see him in fatigue pants and no shirt.

"He's very talented," David said over her shoulder.

They had stopped beside a study of the bayou cast in the last bronze light of sunset. Serena looked at the painting, remembering the day she had first seen Lucky's work, remembering how it had drawn her in, remembering how they had made love at the foot of his easel.

"Yes," she murmured. "He's very talented. I'm glad he finally realized that."

"It looks like a lot of people are realizing it tonight. I think your Mr. Doucet is going to be a reasonably wealthy man. Have you seen him yet?"

"No."

"Well," David said, snatching a glass of wine from the tray of a passing waiter, "just say the word and I'll melt into the background."

Serena went abruptly still. She felt Lucky's gaze hit her like a spotlight, and she turned slowly, her breath catching in her throat as her eyes met his halfway across the room. He stared at her as if she were the only woman on earth, completely ignoring the two gallery patrons who had been speaking to him. A vague dizziness swirled through Serena's head as he came toward her. He moved with the grace of a big cat, with a sense of leashed power that was out of place in this setting, but even the city folk knew enough to get out of his way.

Serena steeled herself against the wild mix of emotions seeing him set loose inside her. She gave him a wry look and said, "Gee, they even got you to wear a shirt. This *is* a special occasion."

He frowned at her, but smoothed a hand over the tie he had already pulled loose around the collar of his dress shirt. He looked devastatingly handsome in his pleated coffee-colored linen trousers, ivory shirt, and brown silk tie. His hair was still unruly, still long, but the boot lace that normally tied it back had been replaced by something a little more discreet. Serena felt a nervous flutter in her stomach. She wasn't sure she knew this Lucky. She found herself wishing he had indeed come in fatigue pants.

"I wasn't sure you'd come," he said gruffly. His gaze raked over the man standing beside her. His jaw tightened.

"Of course I came. I got my invitation," Serena said, sarcasm edging her voice. She held the envelope up to him as proof. "I brought a friend with me. I hope you don't mind. This is David Farrell. David, Lucky Doucet."

David stuck his hand out. "It's a pleasure."

Lucky said nothing. Tension rolled off him in waves.

Fighting a smile, David stepped back. "Well, I believe I'll have a look around. You two probably have some catching up to do."

Serena watched him move off into the crowd, then turned back toward Lucky. He was watching her, his gaze as disturbing as ever. Even after all this time Serena could feel her body responding to his nearness. Her heart had picked up a beat. She felt hot and too aware of her every nerve ending.

Forcing herself to ignore the sensations, she looked up at him with genuine warmth in her eyes. "Congratulations on the show, Lucky. I know what it means. I'm very happy for you."

Lucky said nothing for a long moment. He was too caught up in looking at Serena. He had lain awake nights aching to see her, but he hadn't allowed himself to go to her, not until he had something to offer her. Now he drank in the sight of her, absorbing everything about her —her honey-colored hair in its smooth twist, the delicate rose of her cheeks and mouth, the liquid brown of her eyes, the stubborn tilt of her chin. She was dressed in one of her neat business suits, a navy blue skirt and boxy double-breasted blazer, and Lucky caught himself picturing her in nothing but the old blue workshirt he'd left with her. He wondered bitterly if he would ever get the chance to see her wear it, wondered if she had worn it for her "friend."

"You look good," he said, trying to decide what it was about her that seemed subtly different.

"So do you," she whispered.

"How's Giff?"

"Fine."

Bon Dieu, he thought, there was so much he wanted to say to her, but he stood like an oaf exchanging bland pleasantries as if she were little more than a stranger to him. Maybe when he had gotten his fill of looking at her—as if that could ever happen—the words would come. But then, he'd never been much for talk. What he wanted to do was kiss her. He wanted to take her in his arms and feel her against him, soft and warm. He wanted to pull the pins from her hair and run his hands through the silk. He wanted to lay her down and join his body with hers and feel that incredible sense of peace he'd known only with her.

But she had come with another man.

A finger poked Lucky's biceps and he turned his head to glare at the gallery owner, Henri Richard, a slender man in his forties who was just a little too cosmopolitan for Lucky's tastes. Lucky had needed to remind himself too many times over the last few weeks that the man was the owner of one of the best galleries in the city and that Danielle, Lucky's sister-in-law, had gone to a great deal of trouble to get the two of them together. Respect for Danielle was about the only thing that had kept him from telling Richard to go hang himself. That and the fact that this was his big chance to show Serena he was ready to turn his life around.

Richard ignored Lucky's glower and motioned to the exotic-looking woman standing beside him. "You really must meet Annis, Lucky," he drawled. "She's the art critic for the *Times.*"

"They don' teach manners where you come from?" Lucky asked in a silky voice. "I was speaking with Miz Sheridan, here."

Richard's high cheekbones reddened. The art critic eyed Lucky with open interest.

Richard took a step closer to Lucky and spoke in a low, stiff whisper. "Annis is a very important person in the art community."

"Then I'm sure you won't mind kissing her ass," Lucky muttered. "Me, I've got better things to do."

Serena cleared her throat delicately. "Lucky, I can see you're busy. We can talk later."

"We can talk now," he said, swinging toward her, a dangerous look in his eyes. He took her by the arm and started for the back door. "Let's get outta here. I can't breathe in this place."

"But your show—"

"Can take care of itself."

"Lucky!" Serena protested through her teeth, trying not to attract too much attention to them. "These people came here to see you."

Lucky kept moving, his brows low over his eyes, jaw set. "If they came for the paintings, fine. If they came for the free booze, I don't care. If they came to gawk at me, they can take a flying leap; I'm not on display."

The guests parted like the Red Sea as he made a beeline for the door with Serena hurrying to keep up with him. They cut through the small kitchen, past the curious stares of the catering people and out into the courtyard that was shared by several buildings on the block.

Cobbled paths radiated out from a central stone fountain that gurgled gently. The warm evening air was fragrant with the scents of the flowers blooming in riotous profusion all around. Strategically placed brass lanterns had just begun to glow as the natural light faded.

"You're fortunate it's considered amusing for artists to be rude and eccentric," Serena commented dryly as Lucky led her toward a bench at the far corner of the garden.

"Yeah, I'll be a real hit, won't I?"

"A sensation. Do you think I might get the feeling back in this arm anytime soon?"

Lucky swore in French and let go of her abruptly as they reached the wrought iron bench that was sheltered by an arbor of bougainvillea. "I get a little tense in a crowd," he said by way of an apology.

Serena gave him a gentle smile. "It looked to me like you were doing just fine."

His big shoulders rose and fell in an uncomfortable shrug. "I'm working at it."

That dangerous need to reach out to him surfaced in Serena. She wanted to offer him her support. She wanted to offer him a hug and tell him how proud of him she was. But she made herself sit down on the bench instead. Lucky had managed just fine these past months without her. It was clear he was making a real effort to work through the problems his past had left him with. Serena told herself she could be glad for him, but she couldn't allow herself to share in his victory. If she was to survive, she would have to keep her distance from him emotionally as well as physically.

"You've been all right?" he demanded abruptly, his amber gaze boring down on her like a searchlight from above.

"Sure," she answered slowly and without conviction. "I've been fine." If *fine* meant heartsick and lonely. She could have told him the truth, but she had promised herself she would hang on to her pride, at least.

The quiet of the garden closed in around them. The fountain babbled to itself. From beyond the building came the faint sounds of the city—a car honking, someone calling across a courtyard, jazz drifting out a window somewhere above them.

Lucky heard none of it. He stood there, uncomfortable in his new shoes, wondering if he'd missed his chance at a future with the only woman he'd ever really loved.

"I've missed you," he said suddenly.

Serena stared at him in amazement. She thought her heart might have stopped. She knew she quit breathing.

"I've missed you like hell, Serena."

"Then why didn't you come to me?" she asked, some of the pain she'd known these last months rising up to tighten her throat on her words.

"I couldn't. I had nothing to offer you. I couldn't come to you in pieces."

"I loved you anyway."

"Do you love me still?" Lucky asked. His gaze captured hers and held it prisoner as he waited for her answer.

"I've spent the last four months trying to get over it."

"And have you?"

Serena said nothing. She stared up at him, hating him for doing this to her, for knocking down all the walls she had spent these last weeks building, for taking away her pretense of calm control. He leaned down over her, bracing one knee against the seat of the bench, his arms effectively corraling her in place.

"Have you gotten over me, Serena?" he asked, his voice soft and smoky.

Serena tried to turn her head away, but he caught her chin with one hand and tilted it up so she had no choice but to look at him.

"No," she whispered, trembling inside. A lone tear teetered on the barrier of her lashes, then spilled over, washing away her last hope of keeping her pride intact. "No."

"Then what the hell are you doin' here with another man?"

The jealousy in his tone was unmistakable. Serena's eyes widened. "David? He's just a friend. We work together."

"You're not lovers?"

257

"No!" she snapped in annoyance. "Not that it's any of your business."

Lucky took a step back from her, jamming his hands at the waist of his trousers. His scowl darkened from black to bottomless. "It damn well *is* my business, *chère.*"

"Oh, is that right?" Serena said sarcastically, one brow rising in mocking inquiry. "And why is that?"

"Because I love you!" Lucky roared.

The night seemed to go perfectly still. Serena stared up at him, unable to speak, unable to move a muscle. Lucky stared back, his chest heaving.

"I love you," he said again softly, without the anger.

Slowly Serena rose from the bench, never taking her eyes off Lucky. "I'd given up hope on you," she murmured. "I waited and waited for you to come back." She shook her head as tears flooded her eyes and blurred her vision. "Say it again," she whispered as she went into his arms. "Please say it again."

"I love you." Each word was a kiss against her temple as Lucky held her close and gloried in the feel of her against him. *"Je t'aime, ma chérie. Je t'aime."*

He crushed her to him, finding her mouth with his and kissing her deeply, roughly, with all the hunger pent up over the long months without her. His tongue rubbed against hers, drinking in the sweet taste of her, then he pulled back a fraction of an inch and kissed the tears from her cheeks and lashes.

"Don' cry, *chère.* Don' cry," he said. "It's all right now."

Serena couldn't help herself. The rush of emotion was too strong, her control too fragile. She pressed her face into Lucky's broad shoulder and cried as the flood of feelings swept through her. She clung to Lucky, welcoming his strength, thanking God for the pleasure of having his arms around her again.

"Marry me, Serena," he said, his voice tight and smoky with emotion. "I need you so. I can turn my life around a hundred eighty degrees and it still won't be worth a damn without you in it. Marry me."

Serena lifted her head from his shoulder and managed a tremulous smile as she looked up at him. He was a hard man, stubborn, proud; life with him would never be easy or dull, but life without him hardly seemed worth the effort. She loved him beyond all reason, but then, reason had nothing to do with love. Her heart had looked beneath the surface and seen a man worth reaching out to. Now he was reaching out to her.

"Marry me, Serena," he said again.

"Yes," she whispered.

"Have my children."

"Yes." Her smile widened as she took his hand and drew it around to the slight swell of her stomach.

She didn't have to say a word. Lucky read the message in her eyes. Warmth flowed through him as he pictured her holding their child, nursing a dark-haired baby at her pretty breast. Suddenly the life he had nearly thrown away seemed worth living. He pulled Serena close and held her for a long moment as the power of the love he felt swept through him like a cleansing wind, blowing away the last traces of darkness from his heart.

When he leaned back from her, Lucky brushed the last of Serena's tears away with his thumbs. His expression was a mask of concern. "I don' know what kind of a husband I'll make for you, *chère,*" he admitted. "I've been alone a long, long time. Longer than you know."

"It's all right," Serena said, lifting a hand to touch the smooth, hard plane of his cheek. "You won't be alone anymore."

"I'll have my lady with me."

"Always."

Author's Note

I hope you enjoyed the setting of *Lucky's Lady* as much as I enjoyed painting a picture of it for you with words. South Louisiana is a unique environment with a unique history and a unique and rich mix of cultural backgrounds. I have tried to portray some of this cultural diversity to the reader through the use of local dialects—in particular, through the use of a number of Cajun French words and phrases.

Cajun French differs from standard French much as Elizabethan English differs from the English we speak today. The language evolved separately from its mother tongue and has retained many antiquated words and phrases as well as incorporating new ones from other languages. There are many subdialects because this language was passed on for generations only orally. About sixty percent of the words in the Cajun vocabulary can be found in a standard French dictionary. The rest are unique to the patois.

Only recently have any attempts been made to preserve the language by writing it down, and those attempts have been embroiled in controversy. Arguments abound over how to go about saving the language, which dialect is the most correct, and whether or not the language should be saved at all. There are those who look upon it with disdain and call it simply "bad French." Personally, I look upon it as a unique part of a unique heritage, something that deserves to be preserved.

My sources for the Cajun words and phrases used in *Lucky's Lady* include *Conversational Cajun French* by Harry Jannise and Randall P. Whatley as well as translations of various Cajun folksongs performed by the group Beausoleil (translations by Sharon Arms Doucet, Barry Ancelet, and Ann Savoy). My thanks to these people for their work in keeping Cajun French alive.

Glossary of Words and Phrases Used in This Book

allée	avenue, path
allons	let's go
américaine	american
baire	mosquito netting
bien, ma chère, casse pas mon coeur	now, my dear, don't break my heart
bon Dieu	good God
bonsoir	good night
bourré	a Cajun card game
c'est assez	that's enough
c'est bien	that's all right
c'est ein affaire à pus finir	it's a thing that has no end
c'est pas de ton affaire	that's none of your business
c'est toi que j'aime	it's you I love
Chanson du Terre	song of the earth
cher/chère/chère catin/chérie	dear/darling/etc.
coonass	a generally derogatory slang term for Cajun
Dieu	God

262

espèsces de tête dure	you hardheaded thing
foute ton quant d'ici	get away from here
grenier	attic
il n'a pas rien il va pas faire	there's nothing he won't do
j'aime te faire l'amour avec toi	I'd love to make love with you
je t'aime	I love you
je te blâme pas	I don't blame you
ma douce amie	my sweet love
mais non	but no
mais yeah	but yes
ma jolie fille	my pretty girl
maman	mama
ma petite	my little one
merci Dieu	thank God
mon ami	my friend
mon ange	my angel
mon coeur	my heart
mon 'tite coeur	my little heart
m'sieu	shortened form of *monsieur*, mister
non	no
oui	yes
pas de bêtises	no joking
pichouette	little girl
rien	nothing
sa c'est de la couyonade	that's foolishness
vien	come
viens ici	come here